MURDER ON THE WATERWAY

THE CASE OF THE KANAIMA DEMON

RYAN HOLDEN

CONTENTS

FIRST MURDER

1

'*What a bloody horrible way to start a new job.*' George mutters between sips of coffee, feeling his stomach bubble and rumble. Part nerves as expected. Part something else. His breathing filled the air with white plumes, bellowing to the front as he walked. His heels clattered quickly across the pavement in sharp, uneven echoes, cutting through the miserable, damp night.

George was in a rush but was walking another route. Instinct pulled him that way. It was a longer way to do it but another escape path for the killer. He had no good reason to think like that, call it intuition. Or some obscene niggle that will not leave him be. It had been some weeks, and George still hadn't shaken the ordeal with his foster brother. The one that woke the beast within.

Hunger writhed through—a feral, unrelenting need that had grown sharper with each new moon, gnawing at his core. It may sound farfetched to most. This feeling, this itch he couldn't scratch, was primal, dark, clawing its way beneath his skin. George could barely keep it caged. And it worried him. Tonight wasn't the night to lose control—not on his first shift back. Not with the city's shadows watching, waiting for him to falter. Maybe even reveal his hidden self. George's true self.

Detective George Reynolds had his first case for the murder task force to work on tonight. Whether his instincts would obey was another matter entirely.

He straddled two worlds, each demanding its pound of flesh or, recently, a pint of blood. The first was the mundane: a grim procession of human crimes driven by greed, passion, and desperation. The other was hidden beneath it, simmering like a cauldron—an underworld of supernatural horrors and truths too monstrous for the waking world. George was born into the second, a reluctant heir to its darkness but stolen away by forces even blacker. With the truth burning through his veins, he had sworn to protect the fragile boundary between the two worlds. The vow had cost him more than he dared to admit, and tonight, the price loomed heavier than ever.

The East London Canal greeted him with open arms and scared him. Its cold embrace is steeped in history and rot.

The smell hooked George first. Metallic and thick, it knifed through the damp air, sharper than the lingering stink of diesel. Blood. The scent unfurled in the darkness like a beckoning hand tugging at the feral thing inside him. George inhaled deeply, his breath hitching as it sank its hooks into his senses. Above, the swollen clouds pressed low, heavy with a storm that refused to break. They choked the faint glow of the city, plunging the canal into a suffocating gloom.

Before him, the water stretched like an unholy vein, black and lifeless, whispering secrets from its hidden depths. The algae-streaked shoreline reeked of decay, mingling with the sharper stench of something that had no place in the natural world. The surface quivered, disturbed by ripples that vanished before his eyes could trace their source. In the distance, a houseboat loomed in the shadows; its silhouette huddled against the dark like a secret waiting to be unearthed.

Waterways had always haunted George, their depths calling up memories best left buried. As a child, he had listened to Conrad's stories—gruesome tales told with a voice full of pride and something far darker. Conrad spoke of fire and ash, bodies consumed by flames, and the boat swallowed by the canal's black maw, never resurfacing. George should have perished with it. Conrad had ensured he never forgot that.

Now, standing under the same suffocating air, George felt the weight of those stories coiling around his chest. The canal didn't just hold memories; it devoured them, whispering fragments of what could have been—and still could be. His eyes traced the jagged, skeletal railings lining the path, their peeling paint reaching skyward like gnarled fingers. Beneath them, the vegetation writhed, bubbles breaking the surface in silent screams that vanished into the abyss.

The path was narrow, hemmed in by the skeletal railings and the canal's silent depths. A single misstep, a careless move, and anyone could tumble into that abyss. The thought was more than plausible—it was inevitable for someone like George, with his heavy limbs and uneasy grace. But this stretch of water wasn't just a hazard. It was a trap, baited and waiting for prey.

The emptiness around him was unnerving. No sound or figure was walking the path ahead or lingering by the railings. Only the occasional rustle of unseen leaves caught in a breeze that seemed colder than it should be. George tightened his grip on the torch in his pocket, its weight comforting even though its light couldn't pierce the oppressive dark.

Then it came again—the smell. Stronger now, more alive. Blood, thick and near. George's breath caught as he realised the truth: it wasn't just a crime; he was walking toward it. It was a feeding ground. And the night was still young.

The nearest streetlamp stood a hundred feet away, its weak glow barely piercing the oppressive darkness. Another lamp flickered farther down the road, threatening to extinguish entirely. In the suffocating void between, paranoia gnawed at George like a feral animal. His sixth sense tingled—an itch that no amount of rationality could scratch. He was being watched. He knew it, though the watcher remained hidden in the black.

The frosty grass crunched beneath his boots as George trudged along the narrow strip bordering the canal, scanning the shadows for answers. Each step felt heavier like the ground sought to pull him under. The image of the woman roped and nailed to the bridge loomed in his mind, her lifeless body suspended ten feet above the inky waters. He couldn't shake the thought—how could such a thing be possible?

Bow was a borough of contradictions. The working class laboured tirelessly, keeping the city's heart beating, while the wealthier residents fussed over trivialities—parking disputes and delayed milk deliveries. Yet none of it seemed to matter anymore. The cloud of murder and the misery of missing persons had plagued the area for decades. DI Thompson's frustration boiled over in every briefing, his words sharper with each grim statistic. But no one had dared confront the menace openly. Not until now.

For George, this was more than just another murder. It was his first case as a detective, and it was heavier, shaping into a nightmare.

George slowed as he neared Gunmakers' Lane Bridge, stepping into the skeletal shadows of overhanging trees. Their bare branches creaked in the faint wind, twisting like gnarled fingers clawing at night. Across the canal, the hulking silhouettes of abandoned warehouses loomed, their jagged rooftops etched against the dim glow of the crescent moon. Something stirred there—a shadow within the shadows, shifting deliberately.

The feeling of being watched intensified, pressing against his chest like a physical weight.

The night air carried an unsettling cocktail of scents. The sweet aroma of fresh dough rolled out from somewhere nearby, a deceptive comfort that clashed violently with the stench of stale beer and urine just a few feet to his left. The smells mingled like a sickly omen, saturating the cold.

The moon's pale light fractured across the rippling canal, guiding George's gaze to a mooring on the bank. The structure was grimy, encrusted with moss and filth. Around it coiled a thick, brown rope, its frayed end glinting with something dark—blood. The sight prickled the back of his neck.

He crouched, brushing a gloved hand along the rope's coarse strands. It was damp with moss and slick residue, but a faint smear of red lay beneath the grime. Fresh. Whoever had used this rope wouldn't have escaped without injury. His mind reeled back to the rope he'd encountered during the incident with Andy—less weathered but equally sinister. Was it a coincidence? He doubted it.

Standing, George scanned the canal's shivering waters, straining for sounds beyond the faint rustling of leaves. Then, the sharp snap of a twig shot through the silence. His hand instinctively hovered near his hip, his breath catching.

A pair of low, yellow-glowing eyes stared back at him from the shadows—a fox. The creature lingered for a heartbeat, its unblinking gaze fixed on George before it turned and darted into the darkness. The encounter brought no comfort—only an eerie reminder of the night's peculiarities.

At last, George reached the cordon, where an officer stood with slouched disinterest, his puffed Hi-Viz vest doing little to mask his boredom. Beyond the barrier, a scattering of onlookers huddled, their curiosity kept at bay by uniformed personnel. Their murmurs carried through the cold like the hiss of an open wound.

"I can see her gross insides," one whispered, their tone somewhere between horror and morbid fascination.

"She's nailed like the fucking Christ," another adds, their voice tinged with disbelief. "Look at her hands and feet."

George shuddered to hear those words, the gruesome image of the victim growing sharper in his mind. He squared his shoulders and stepped forward. The night wasn't done with him yet.

George clenched his jaw as he flashed his warrant card, forcing his way past the murmuring crowd. The path ahead was constricted, hemmed in by the oppressive weight of shadows and the quiet dread of onlookers. The streetlamp hanging over the bridge offered little comfort, its fragmented light casting jagged shapes against the wall—half-formed monsters that flickered with evil intent.

The air thickened as he approached the final checkpoint at the base of the steps. Rain lashed the scene, relentless and cold, but it did nothing to mask the stench of decay that seemed to crawl into George's nostrils, settling there like an unwelcome guest. This was no ordinary death. The scent was ancient and foul in a way that spoke of something unnatural as if the body had absorbed more than the passing hours.

Leaning over the railing, George caught sight of Detective Sergeant Michael Dalton, his hunched form silhouetted against the faint glow of the bridge light. "Does anyone have an ETA on LFB? And where the hell is the bloody camera?" Dalton's voice cracked through the heavy silence, his thick Cockney accent brimming with irritation.

George stepped closer, rain slicking the ground beneath his feet. Each footfall felt like a dare, every creak of gravel a reminder of the abyss below. The body hung above the canal like a grotesque offering, nailed to the underside of the bridge with a deliberate brutality that made George's stomach twist. The sound of cartilage stiffening—a series of sharp clicks and muted pops—punctuated the air, a grotesque symphony of death that made the hairs on the back of his neck stand on end.

"So, you started without me?" George called out, his voice flat, though his unease gnawed at him like a predator circling prey. His question shattered the quiet, drawing Dalton's attention. The older man turned sharply, the mist of his breath forming ghostly tendrils in the air.

"You took your time, didn't you?" Dalton grumbled, his tone frayed. The usual glint in his eye had dimmed, replaced by something darker. The years had weathered Dalton; his stiff movements betrayed a lingering injury, his right arm twitching as though haunted by a phantom ache. Still, something was reassuring in his presence—a human anchor against the encroaching madness.

George nodded at the gruesome scene. "It's not every day you find a body strung up like this." His voice was low, a concession to the weight of what hung above the canal.

Dalton grunted. "First one like this since... well... since everything went to hell." He glanced upward, searching the sky for answers, but none came.

"What's your take on time of death?" George asks, his eyes locked on the bridge's underbelly. The shadows writhed, alive in the flickering light, and a chill seeped into his bones.

"Three, maybe four hours ago," Dalton mutters, his voice dropping. "You'll need to get up close. Check for anything... out of the ordinary." The hesitation in his tone was telling.

Dalton knew George's insight went beyond the usual detective's intuition, though he'd never say it out loud or tell anyone else.

As George stepped closer, gravel shifted beneath his feet, tumbling into the inky waters below. The canal responded with a passive ripple, the surface deceptively calm, like a mirror hiding nightmares beneath its sheen. The mooring ropes nearby twisted in the wind, their movements serpentine, as if mocking the lifeless body above.

The corpse was a grotesque masterpiece of cruelty. Its hands and feet were nailed in perfect symmetry, reminiscent of a macabre crucifixion. Blood had pooled along the edges of the wounds before dripping rhythmically into the canal, the sound merging with the rustle of the current. Rainwater mingled with the blood, carving crimson rivers that streaked the lifeless flesh.

George's grip tightened on the railing as he leaned over, his gaze narrowing. His senses, both human and otherwise, prickled with unease. The body wasn't just a message—it was a warning, a harbinger of something darker lurking in the shadows.

George's breath caught as he leaned closer. The body's bare feet, suspended above the water, dripped steadily, the icy droplets splattering onto his shoes with a cruel rhythm.

"Well? What do you see?" Dalton's voice broke through the heavy silence, laced with unease that matched George's rising dread.

"More blood... but something's not right," George murmurs, his voice tight as he takes the torch Dalton handed him. The beam of light sliced through the oppressive darkness, casting grotesque shadows as it settled on the victim's face.

Bruises bloomed like dark flowers across her once-fair skin, the swollen patches blending into a sickly purple mosaic. Her eyes, wide open, stared blankly into the void, their glassy sheen reflecting the torchlight. George's stomach twisted as he followed the grim trail of congealed blood pooling beneath her and the frozen drool glistening mid-drip at the corner of her mouth.

And then he saw it.

"Her tongue..."George's voice faltered. "It's gone." He swallowed hard, bile clawing at the back of his throat. "There's something in her mouth. A note."

Dalton stiffened."What the hell?" he muttered, his jaw tightening. "This murder's already messed up enough. Now, someone's taking trophies?"

George nodded grimly. The note—tucked where her tongue should have been—sent a shiver racing down his spine. It wasn't random; this was planned, deliberate, and ceremonial. Whoever had done this wasn't just a murderer—they were a puppeteer, pulling unseen strings to orchestrate terror.

Beneath the bridge, three figures cloaked in black wetsuits moved with the precision of practised predators. They huddled aboard a small boat, its engine a faint hum against the night's stillness. The operator's gloved hands moved deftly over the controls, maintaining a steady pace as the vessel glided through the inky waters, leaving a frothy wake.

The other two figures worked together, stretching a large rubber sheet taut across the water's surface. Their movements were unnervingly synchronised, efficient, and devoid of hesitation. The sheet gleamed faintly under the crescent moonlight, its slick surface awaiting the grim burden.

The low arch of the bridge loomed overhead, casting jagged shadows that danced on the water like ghosts. The deceased woman's body swayed gently in the night breeze, a macabre pendulum marking the passage of time. Every subtle shift in her suspension seemed to mock the stillness around them.

Above, London Firere Brigade rescuers descended the bridge with ropes taut; they practised movements slow but methodical. The ropes creaked faintly under their weight as they neared the victim, the harsh light from their helmets illuminating the horror of her battered form.

The rescuers began their grim task, working to pry the nails from the woman's hands and feet. The sound of flesh tearing from wood echoed in the hollow space, a wet-visceral noise that made even the most seasoned responders flinch. Each nail's removal brought a dissonant symphony—the groan of splintering wood, the metallic clang of tools against steel, and the haunting rasp of lifeless flesh peeling away.

Watching from the shadows, Detective George Reynolds clenched his fists, his nails biting into his palms. The gruesome scene played out like a twisted nightmare, each second stretching longer than the last.

Dalton stood a few paces away, his cigarette smouldering between two fingers, a faint ember glowing in the dark. His posture betrayed his agitation, and one foot was tapped against the pavement in an uneven rhythm.

"You were supposed to be cutting back," George quips, the words a weak attempt to pierce suffocating tension.

Dalton chuckled dryly, shaking his head. "I was supposed to take a week off, too. But then I realised the monumental shitstorm I'd be facing if I didn't show up."

The attempt at levity was weak, but even a brittle joke felt like a relief in the suffocating gloom of the bridge and the horror concealed. George allowed himself a faint smile, though Dalton's words hung heavier than he let on. Trouble had a way of clinging to both of them like shadows they couldn't outrun.

"So," George began, his voice lighter but edged with curiosity. Have you heard from our elusive friend yet?"

Dalton took a deliberate drag from his cigarette, the faint ember glowing defiantly against the night. "Not a bloody word," he replies, his tone flat. Smoke curled around his face, momentarily shrouding his expression. "Not that I expected to. Skip's been off the grid since..." He trailed off, his voice hardening. "Since the betrayal. It tore him apart—physically, yeah, but more so the other kind. Needed space. Hell, I don't blame him."

The acrid tang of the cigarette smoke clawed at George's senses, but he stayed silent. Dalton's bitterness was palpable, and George knew better than to press too hard. Moments like this were rare when the hardened exterior of the seasoned detective cracked just enough to reveal something raw and human beneath.

"What about the home front?" George ventured after a pause, cautious but genuinely curious."Last I heard, she'd stepped away for a bit. Is there any chance of patching things up?"

Dalton sighs deeply, the sound heavy with resignation. His hand hovers near his cigarette as if considering another drag before deciding against it. The ember smoulders faintly between his fingers as he shakes his head.

"Nah, mate," he says finally, his voice low. "That ship sailed a while ago. Out of sight is best left out of mind." A faint, bitter smile touched his lips. "She's probably knee-deep in her rubbish way of life by now. I'll get a dog instead. At least they're bloody loyal."

George chuckled softly, the sound almost foreign in the oppressive atmosphere. "A loyal dog for a seasoned detective like you? Bet you'd pick a bulldog. Stubborn and gruff—seems fitting."

Dalton cracked a reluctant grin, the first sign of warmth breaking through his hardened demeanour. "Cheeky bastard," he mutters, shaking his head. But the insult carried an undercurrent of camaraderie, a momentary reprieve from the tension clinging to them both.

The laughter faded as quickly as it had come, overtaken by the grim reality surrounding them. Beneath the bridge, the lifeless woman dangled in the biting wind; her body grotesquely posed like some twisted offering to the night. The rain fell steadily, mixing with the scent of blood and decay, painting the air with an unshakable weight.

HIDDEN SECRETS

2

The first arm dropped free, its descent grotesque, accompanied by a low creak of stiffening joints. Detective George Reynolds' torch danced across the body, its beam slicing through the oppressive darkness. His mind struggled to process the macabre tableau before him.

There was a twisted artistry in this—the positioning, the brutality—a statement in death that defied ordinary explanation.

As the torchlight brushed across her wrist, George hesitated. At first glance, it seemed like a smudge of dirt, but as the light hovered, the unsettling truth emerged.

A stark and sinister upside-down cross was inked into the top ridge of her forearm.

A shiver ran through George's body. This was no random act of violence. It was part of a larger, darker narrative.

"Things are getting stranger," George murmurs, his voice laden with unease. She's got a kind of U.V. stamp on her arm. It might be a clue to where she was last."

Dalton, standing nearby with furrowed brows, leaned in. "What kind of stamp?"

"An upside-down cross," George replies, his tone flat but laced with tension.

Dalton scoffed softly. "Isn't that some devil-worship, Antichrist nonsense?"

"I'm not sure," George admitted. "But when we return to the office, we should check out clubs or late-night places. It could be an entrance stamp or something."

Dalton nodded, pulling out his pocketbook and jotting down the details. "It doesn't sound like a place I'd frequent," he mutters.

The stamp, eerie as it was, offered a peculiar distraction from the horrors of the scene.

It was a puzzle piece for George that momentarily drew his thoughts away from the recurring nightmares that plagued his sleep.

"I suppose you're coming to the farewell gathering on Friday?" Dalton asks, his voice breaking through George's thoughts. "The guv'ssend-off?"

George hesitated, unsure how to respond. "Feels in poor taste, but I can't resist a free drink. Where's it happening? And any idea who's stepping into his shoes?"

Dalton smirked knowingly. "Oh, you won't believe it. Locke.The Acting Detective Inspector. Seems eager to join our merry band."

"Oh, joy," George replies dryly, a hint of irony creeping into his voice. "There's something about Locke that doesn't sit right with me. He helped us eventually, but his attitude was grating. Reminded me of you, to be honest."

Dalton let out a hearty chuckle. "What's that? Suave?" He grinned, shaking his head. "Cheeky bastard. But you're right. He's... off. Or maybe not. There's just something peculiar about him. A strange vibe."

The banter offered a brief reprieve, a flicker of humanity amid the grotesque scene. But as the woman's body descended closer to the ground, the horror returned with unrelenting force.

Her mutilated face came into sharper focus, each bruise and wound a testament to unimaginable pain. The paper inside her mouth—a small beige scroll—was clutched between teeth where her tongue should have been. Blood trickled steadily from the wound; George's torchlight illuminated its path.

The crimson drops hit the water below, rippling outward in haunting concentric rings. The sight mesmerised George, a grotesque beauty in the otherwise horrifying scene.

His heart thudded painfully in his chest as he stared into the reflection on the water's surface. For a moment, he swore he saw her image move.

And then she smiled back at him.

George's breath hitched, and his head snapped from side to side. No one was there. No ghosts. Not yet.

But the upside-down cross on her arm played on his mind. This wasn't just murder—it seemed religious or ceremonial, reminding him of the basement—a grotesque declaration of something far beyond his comprehension.

Nearby, rubber sheeting was spread across the uneven pavement for the body. The graffiti-covered wall provided a stark, jarring backdrop, its obscenities and crude symbols standing in cruel contrast to the victim's silence.

The air was thick with a nauseating blend of smells. Stale beer dregs oozed from discarded gold "Special Brew" cans, mixing with the acrid stench of human and animal urine. The offensive bouquet blurred into a singular, vile odour that George couldn't escape with any breath.

"Poor girl. She didn't deserve this," Dalton murmurs as the makeshift lights flicker to life, casting harsh shadows that highlight the grotesque scene.

"She was quite the attractive woman. At least... she was," one of the LFB rescuers remarked from behind George. Their voice carried a note of melancholy truth, a stark acknowledgement of the brutality that had robbed the victim of her humanity.

The darkness enshrouding the crime scene seemed to press in tighter, amplifying the macabre nature of the crime. The upside-down cross etched into the woman's skin felt less like a clue and more like a calling card—a mark left by something otherworldly.

D alton and George, their gloved hands steady, moved closer for a better look. Dalton focused on meticulous note-taking, his sketches outlining the woman's body and cataloguing visible signs of trauma. Meanwhile, George was drawn to the strange symbols on her skin and the enigmatic scroll protruding from her mouth.

The biting cold cut through the air, but George paid little attention. Establishing a clear timeline for the crime was essential—preferably within the three-to-four-hour window they'd estimated earlier.

"Hey, can you get some photos now?" George called to the officer holding the camera, who seemed transfixed by the bloodied holes and smears on the bridge's underside. Their first task was to preserve as much evidence as possible before SOCO arrived.

"Make sure you get everything: the paper in her mouth, her clothing, all her injuries," George instructed, pointing to the grotesque scene. The bizarre nature of the crime demanded thorough documentation; without it, their reports would strain credibility.

After all, crimes like this weren't encountered every day. Even for investigators seasoned by the extraordinary, this scene felt unearthly.

"I need some tweezers," George mutters, flicking Dalton's arm to break his trance. Dalton's wide-eyed expression betrays unease, his focus on something George can't yet see.

"What's worth trading for a human tongue?" George muses, his voice low and laced with morbid curiosity.

Dalton snapped back to reality; his tone was sharp. "What do you take me for? A walking utility belt?"

Despite the retort, Dalton's hand moved instinctively toward his coat pocket. His gruff exterior often masked his readiness; he'd built a reputation for carrying an arsenal of evidence bags and tools, always prepared for contingencies.

"SOCO will be here soon," Dalton adds, his voice quieter now. Let's not mess with the scene."

"Come on, Dalton. Don't tell me you haven't thought about it," George says, a sly smirk tugging at the corner of his mouth.

Dalton grumbled but didn't argue. Finally, he produced a pair of silver tweezers from his pocket, holding them out with a begrudging sigh. "Yeah, yeah. Just remember who's in charge here."

The body rotated slowly as it hung, and George's sense of smell turned against him. A toxic cocktail of decay filled the air, a familiar stench that clawed at his stomach.

The thought of retrieving the body from the water dredged up memories of Lewis—the bloated corpse wrapped in bin liners from last month. George remembered the gases escaping in a grotesque hiss, the overwhelming stench forcing him to retreat before he lost his balance.

He pushed the memory aside and reached for the paper scroll.

At first, it resisted, the damp parchment clinging stubbornly. Blood trickled from the edges, staining his gloves as he worked. The tension in the air grew thick, and every small sound—the creak of the bridge, the faint rustle of the wind—seemed magnified.

Finally, the scroll came free with a wet, gurgling sound that startled George. He jerked back instinctively, his breath catching as he stared at the bloodied scrap now resting in his hand.

The twisted significance of the note and the unnerving method of concealment solidified one thing in George's mind: this was no ordinary crime. This was a message, and whoever sent it was beginning to speak.

A woman's voice echoed sharply from their left, slicing through the tension like a knife. "You best not be messing with our body."

As quick as always, Dalton fires back, "Given half a chance."

Two figures emerged from the darkness. One of them, a woman with blonde hair tied back neatly, had a complexion as clear as milk. Thin-framed glasses perched on her button-like nose, and she wore tailored suit trousers beneath a warm blue parka. George immediately pegged her as the pathologist, arriving just as he discreetly tucked the scroll into his coat pocket.

The second woman, presumably the SOCO, wore a black overcoat and grey suit trousers. Her brown hair was pulled into a tidy bun, and she carried a holdall in one hand and a camera slung over her shoulder.

"Now, old man, I'm not in the habit of teaching old dogs new tricks," the pathologist quips, her tone light but her eyes sharp.

Dalton, ever eager to banter, replies, "What about wolves? Ah, Georgie, I forgot to mention. Thanks to this new initiative, we've got a dedicated pathology officer and SOCO for the team."

The SOCO offered a small, bemused smile, her demeanour professional but approachable. George couldn't help but note the quiet authority in her presence.

"For how long?" George asks, his tone tinged with scepticism.

"As long as the funding's there and we're getting results," she replies briskly.

"Speaking of which," the pathologist interjected, her tone firm, "if you two don't mind, we need to examine our friend here to get those results."

Dalton gestured between the group. "Georgie, meet Ms Walker and Ms Wainright. And ladies, this miserable sod is Detective George Reynolds. Bit of a shit magnet, but he grows on you—like a rash."

"Charmed, I'm sure," Ms Walker says smoothly, her confidence unwavering. "Besides, I've got three brothers, so I'm used to troublesome men. And I imagine, Mr Dalton, that you've had your share of rashes in all your years on this earth."

George smirked as Dalton chuckled. "Give it a month, and you might regret saying that. Excuse the old git—he forgot his meds today, which means his manners went missing, too."

Turning to Ms Wainright, George gestured toward the body. "Can you swab the inside of two fingers on her right hand? There's a brown residue that looks odd."

Ms Wainright nodded, her movements efficient as she stepped past them. Her sweet perfume lingered in the air, a faint contrast to the metallic tang of blood and the acrid stench of decay. Dalton and George parted instinctively to give her room, observing the quiet determination she worked with.

As George watched, he couldn't help but note the subtle contrasts between the two women. Ms Walker exuded sharp intelligence and a polished edge, while Ms Wainright carried an understated confidence, her quiet demeanour adding an enigmatic allure. Having them on the team might prove invaluable.

"Dalton, have the uniforms scout the surroundings for CCTV," George says, his gaze shifting toward the nearest entrance to the park. "The park closes at 3 p.m. this time of year. In what ways could the perpetrator have come and gone?"

Dalton nodded. "The uniforms are canvassing as we speak. But let's be honest—we're fishing in the dark without witnesses. We've already got a statement from the guy who found her, but it's incoherent. He's a drunk, and his signature looked like a toddler scribbled it." Dalton rubbed his jaw and added with a grin, "What do you say we grab some food and compare notes? There's a nice little Indian place, Bhouraj's Palace, just down the road. I passed it on the way here, and I've been drooling ever since. Chicken Jalfrezi is calling my name."

George glanced at the scroll in his pocket, considering its compelling mystery. But before he could respond, a commotion outside drew their attention.

Excited voices rang out: "We got something! We got something!"

Two uniforms sprinted toward them through the darkness, carrying a medium-sized black handbag. The gold buckle and safety catch gleamed under the temporary lights, adding an incongruous touch of elegance to the scene.

Dalton stepped forward to take custody of the bag, testing its weight in his hands. The faint jingle of keys inside suggested it might hold critical evidence.

The bag's black leather—or perhaps faux leather—looked pristine, offering a chance to capture fingerprints if gloves hadn't been used. But given the meticulous nature of the killer, gloves seemed likely. Then again, the trace of blood on the rope left room for doubt.

Dalton turned the bag in his hands, his expression pensive. "Let's see what secrets you're hiding," he muttered, his voice low as the darkness pressed around them.

While the team examined the handbag for potential evidence, George kept drifting back to the scroll tucked securely in his pocket. The bag might hold vital clues for identification, but the scroll felt like the key to something much darker.

Ms Wainright stepped forward, her voice steady but firm. "Please hand it over. I'll take custody of it as part of the chain of evidence, especially if you want it dusted," she said, her attention to detail as precise as ever further solidifying her librarian-like aura.

The surrounding scene remained grim. Ms Wainright, gloves on, carefully sifted through the bag's contents. The chill in the air made her shudder slightly, but she pressed on with determination. Outside, the wind howled faintly, its echoes amplifying the heavy suspense over the investigation.

One by one, the handbag's contents emerged: keys, makeup, a thin scarf, and a paper driving license. George leaned closer as the license was examined.

"Rachel Darnley," Dalton read aloud. "She would've turned thirty-two on December twelfth." A name badge followed, marking Rachel as a teacher at Roman Primary School.

Dalton tapped the license thoughtfully before jotting down additional notes. "We'll need to visit her home and see if anyone reported her missing. She seems like someone who'd be missed," he remarked.

Their focus was interrupted by a commotion outside. Voices murmured, and shoulders shifted to make way as the potent scent of a sharp, unidentifiable aftershave wafted into the scene. The clack of heavy heels descending the steps cut through the stillness, bringing a familiar air of arrogance.

"We have company," Dalton muttered. His tone dripped with exasperation. "The new acting D.I. is here."

George's stomach sank. Acting D.I. Locke had followed them to the unit, and George could already feel the disruption his presence would bring.

"Just what we need," George mutters under his breath.

"What's the story here?" Locke's low and deliberate voice cut through the scene as he strode forward. His hands stayed buried in the deep pockets of his wool coat, the upturned collar framing a face set in calculated indifference. The faint scent of aftershave followed him, sharp and intrusive. Ms Walker straightened at his arrival; her stance was professional and commanding. In this male-dominated field, her confident body language asserted her expertise.

"I've got this," she declares, stepping forward. "The autopsy will reveal more, but here's what we know so far: the victim is a thirty-one-year-old female. She appears to have been strangled first, likely rendering her unconscious. Rope marks around the neck show she was bound and hoisted to the ceiling."-

- "I've collected rope fibres embedded deeply into the neck wounds. Blood dried around the nail holes, suggesting she was still alive when they were hammered in. This goes far beyond a simple crime—it's a brutal, ritualistic act of violence. A sinister precursor to something far worse."-

"While it might initially suggest a vicious sexual assault, the true nature of what happened will require further examination. Pooling of blood near her chest suggests broken ribs, likely caused by the assailant's relentless assault."-

- "The brutality didn't stop there. She was left to drown in her bodily fluids. The only semblance of decency from the perpetrator—if it can even be called that—was pulling her trousers back up after the attack. It's an unsettling contrast to the savagery inflicted beforehand."

George's breath hitched slightly as Ms Walker continued.

"Her shoes were caked with grass and mud, but there were no signs of dragging. She was likely carried here, down the canal side, before being strung up under the bridge, hidden from view."

- "This is the secondary crime scene. The primary scene, where the true horror began, could be anywhere along this canal. Judging by the clues, it might be two hundred feet closer to Old Ford Road. The details paint a grim picture but are far from complete."

Locke listened intently, nodding as Ms Walker laid out her findings. When he finally spoke, his voice was low, careful not to draw undue attention from the growing crowd of responders outside.

George and Dalton exchanged a glance. They hadn't shared the scroll's presence or contents with Locke. A distrust lingered; they couldn't afford to reveal too much.

As the chilling details of the crime unfolded, George felt the weight of something far worse than a murder pressing down on him. This was calculated. Ritualistic. Malicious.

And it wasn't over.

They had more questions than answers, and every step forward felt like descending deeper into a darkness they weren't sure they could escape.

THE LOOMING FIGURE

3

George's feet remained glued to the ground, his head fixed forward, lost in thought. The chilling atmosphere weighed heavily on him, the biting cold seeping through his coat. Around him, the temperature seemed to drop further, spits of rain glistening under the flickering streetlamp. The cordons, meant to deter the public, did little to stop curious onlookers from gathering along the pathway. Wet shoulders bumped and jostled as figures moved through the darkness, their hushed murmurs blending into the night.

The lamplight flickered weakly, casting warped shadows across the scene. The grotesque picture felt surreal, like a waking nightmare. The crowd's whispers melded with the distant howl of the wind, creating an eerie symphony that gnawed at his composure.

"There's no tongue. They've taken a souvenir," George blurts, his voice cutting through the ghostly noise. He didn't realise he'd spoken aloud until the words hung in the air.

Ms Walker's head snapped toward him, her brows knitting in surprise. "How do you know that?" she demands, her tone sharp.

George remained silent, his gaze fixed on the body. Ms Walker dropped to the rubber sheeting where the victim's handbag rested, her movements swift and methodical. Using a small silver torch and a swab stick, she examined the bloodied cavern of the victim's mouth. Her face tightened with confusion.

"He's right," she finally confirmed, her voice faltering. "No tongue."

Besides George, Dalton stifled a chuckle though his eyes betrayed his unease.

"As in gone? Completely gone?" Locke's voice rose, sharp and incredulous.

"Yes," Ms Walker replies, her tone flat but laced with disbelief. "It's been removed."

The rain fell steadily now, its rhythmic hiss on the pavement mingling with the rustling of nearby trees. The branches groaned and swayed, their movements like mournful gestures over the horrors that had unfolded beneath them.

"Guv," Dalton says with mock formality, "as I'm sure you're aware, Georgie has a unique attention to detail. We were here first." His mischievous tone carried a hint of pride, a subtle jab at Locke's late arrival.

Locke didn't rise to the bait, though his lips twitched in irritation. "Oh, I haven't forgotten," he mutters. "The man with nine lives."

"The man!" George interjected, his voice sharper now.

"Yes, Georgie, the man," Locke replies, exasperated. "You seem to have nine lives."

"No," George says firmly, his voice low. "The man. In the crowd."

The sudden shift in his tone silenced the group. George'seyes darted toward the onlookers. "It has to be a man. Too big not to be—six-two, maybe six-three. Wide build. Dark hoodie, black or navy. Second rowback. His face is shielded. He's still while everyone else is barging and leaning on one another. His hood doesn't move, and he's staring this way."

George's voice trailed off as his instincts sharpened. Something about the man's behaviour didn't fit the chaotic atmosphere. While most of the crowd whispered and jostled, this figure's stillness screamed incongruity.

Locke, visibly unsettled, reached for his radio, concealing the action from the onlookers.

A sudden loud pop shattered the tense moment. The sound echoed sharply, and the entire group instinctively ducked. Dalton raised his arms over his head, his posture betraying the scars of long-buried fears from a life spent in dangerous places.

The panic subsided as quickly as it began. Another lesser pop followed, accompanied by the sputtering rev of a struggling car engine—a backfire. The crowd stirred, the tension breaking like a snapped wire.

George scanned the area, his pulse hammering in his ears. The hooded figure was gone.

Locke spoke into his radio, his voice calm but commanding."Any available units, this is Acting D.I. Locke. I need the area around the crime scene, particularly the route toward Old Ford Road, combed immediately. We're looking for a tall man, possibly in a black or navy hoodie, six-foot-two or three. Left the scene rapidly. Do not engage alone."

Locke turned his gaze to George, his expression a mixture of scepticism and grudging respect. George met his eyes steadily. He wasn't losing his mind. Not anymore.

"Holy shit," Ms Walker mutters, her voice pulling the group's attention back to the body. She leaned closer, shifting blood from the base of the skull. "There's a hole here. At the back of the head."

The words hung in the air, heavy with implication.

"What are you saying?" Locke asks cautiously, his voice low.

Ms Walker straightened, her face pale. "It looks like the tongue was removed... from the back of the head."

The revelation settled in. Ms Wainright turned away, her hand covering her mouth as her stomach churned. Dalton's face tightened, his usual levity evaporating in an instant.

The implications were clear. This wasn't just a murder. It was a calculated, ritualistic act. The perpetrator wasn't just a killer—they were a collector.

As the coroner began preparing the body for transport, Locke left with Ms Walker and Ms Wainright, their voices low as they discussed the next steps.

George and Dalton lingered in the cold, the night pressing around them. The zip of the body bag echoed faintly, a grim punctuation to the macabre scene. The crowd had thinned, the voyeurs departing with their fill of grisly details to gossip about. But for George, the unease remained, clawing at the edges of his thoughts.

The hooded man's image burned in his mind. Could the killer be so bold as to return to the scene?

He glanced toward the darkened street beyond the cordon. Somewhere out there, a monster moved among them.

Shadows seemed to shift and twist, their shapes taking on the haunting outline of the hooded man. His presence felt like a spectre lurking at the edges of George's vision, a reminder that he could hold the key to the gruesome puzzle they were trying to solve.

Why would he return to the scene of the crime?

The question gnawed at George's mind as they retraced to his car. Dalton's earlier craving for Indian food resurfaced as a much-needed escape. After witnessing such a grotesque scene, neither was in the right headspace, and a brief reprieve felt almost essential.

They stopped at the mooring area, about two hundred feet from the crime scene. The soft slap of water against the canal walls filled the silence, and the chilly night pressed against them. George lingered, his eyes scanning the shadows as Dalton strode ahead.

When Dalton realised he was alone, he turned back, his warm breath visible in the freezing air. "What the hell are you doing?" he asked, his voice sharp and impatient.

"This was the spot with the frayed rope," George replies absently, his gaze fixed on the area. "Should I have looked at it differently?"

"If it's as you say, don't worry," Dalton muttered.

"That's good," George says, his voice lowering. "Because it's gone."

Dalton's face darkened. "So, someone's cleaned up?"

"You could say that," George murmurs, his eyes darting. The unsettling sensation of being watched returned, and his hackles rose instinctively.

Dalton sighed and changed the subject, his hunger winning out. "So, what are you having?"

"What?" George blinked, momentarily thrown off.

"Indian," Dalton says, rolling his eyes. "Come on, mate. I'mHank Marvin. I can't function on an empty stomach. Besides, I want to know what you hid from the others on that note."

George's stomach growled, a reminder of his hunger. The scroll in his pocket seemed to weigh heavier after Dalton mentioned it, the mystery tugging at him almost as much as the promise of food.

After an eternity of circling the block for parking, they finally found a spot a hundred feet from *Bhouraj Palace*. The car slid into the narrow gap between an old brown Escort and a red Nissan Sunny. The meters were suspended until 6 a.m., but finding parking after 6 p.m. was still an ordeal.

Dalton remained quiet in the passenger seat, his pencil scratching against his notebook. He sketched the victim's wounds with meticulous precision, marking the nail holes on the wrists and feet. His expression was grim, that of a man who had seen too much death to be easily unfazed but understood the significance of each fresh case.

"This is just the beginning," Dalton mutters to himself, almost inaudibly. George caught the words anyway.

George scanned the area before stepping out of the car. The streets around them seemed to breathe with an unnatural stillness, the shadows elongated and whispering secrets he couldn't quite hear. Or wasn't ready for.

Dalton climbed out of the vehicle, stretching his legs and wincing as he shifted his shoulder. George couldn't help but notice the faint stiffness that still lingered from Dalton's old bullet wound.

For a fleeting moment, George wondered what Dalton would be like if he were *one of them*—a werewolf or some other shifter. With his cockney bravado and fierce loyalty, Dalton would be formidable. Add yellow or blue eyes, claws, and supernatural strength, and he'd be unstoppable.

The idea lingered as they approached the restaurant. Would Dalton ever want the bite? The thought was as intriguing as it was dangerous. George owed him a debt of gratitude for his loyalty and help, but could he ever offer such a gift—or curse—to someone he trusted so deeply?

George shook the thought away as the warm light of the restaurant spilt out onto the pavement. They both needed a moment to decompress, but George couldn't shake the shadow that clung to his thoughts even as they stepped inside. Somewhere out there, the hooded man—or worse—was watching, waiting.

The "palace" was anything but regal. The restaurant was empty, its red carpet blending seamlessly with heavy curtains that framed the dimly lit windows. The warmth inside was a welcome reprieve from the biting chill of the night, and George was craving a drink almost immediately.

An overly friendly host, whose nameplate read *Irfan*, greeted them with an enthusiastic smile. His accent was more London than anything else, his tone cheery yet inconsistent with the restaurant's subdued atmosphere.

"Corner table out of the way, please," George requested, his voice measured but firm.

"Of course. This way, please," Irfan replies, gesturing exaggeratedly.

As they followed him to the table, George glanced over his shoulder, his instincts still sharp from the night's unsettling events. Shadows flickered across the windows as a car passed outside, and the faint echo of distant laughter from the street sent a shiver down his spine.

The corner table offered a clear view of the restaurant, which was sparsely decorated and filled with heavy silence. Dim lights cast uneven shadows that pooled in the corners, making the space unsettling. Irfan's warm service was at odds with the subtle dread that seemed to permeate the air, the occasional creak of the floorboards amplifying the sense of unease.

Settling into their seats, George scanned the room with practised caution. They had learned from past mistakes—not holding onto evidence too long and being mindful of corruption. This was a new unit, a fresh start. But new beginnings didn't erase old patterns. George's thoughts turned briefly to Whitlock. The backdoor deals and bribes cycle could easily surface if he reappeared.

The moon loomed in the window like a framed painting, pale and looming, its light casting shifting shadows that seemed to writhe in the restaurant's corners. The enticing aroma of ground curry spices filled the air, teasing George's senses and stirring his hunger. Yet, beneath the pleasant scent, there was an unsettling undertone, a feeling that something unseen lingered nearby.

Dalton, as relaxed as ever, hadn't even bothered to pick up a menu. He leaned back, his fingers tapping idly on the table.

"Well?" Dalton prompted, his tone casual but edged with curiosity.

George shook off his unease. "What are you having?"

"Rogan Josh, all the way," Dalton says with a grin, his eyes lighting up like a child in a sweet shop.

George played it safe, ordering a medium madras. As the host left to prepare their order, George reached into his pocket, the weight of the evidence scroll pressing against his thoughts. The memory of its bloodstained ribbon and the grim discovery surrounding it churned uneasily in his stomach.

He used the red leather menu folders to create a makeshift barricade on the table, discreetly pulling the small evidence bag into view. The scroll, about two inches long and tied with a thin ribbon stained with dried blood, sat like a malevolent relic between them.

"What are your guesses?" Dalton asks in a hushed whisper, his eyes fixed on the yellowed parchment.

"If the past is anything to go by? A taunt," George replies grimly, his voice barely audible. "At least it's not a tape recorder this time."

The words barely left his mouth before unease rolled over him. Had he just jinxed them?

He opened the bag cautiously. A potent, metallic scent hit him like a gust of wind, the aroma of blood unmistakable even in the warm confines of the restaurant. George's nose wrinkled as he quickly sealed the bag shut, the pungent smell lingering in his nostrils.

"Hello, mate. Can we have a 29 and a 62? A side of poppadoms and two shandies, please," Dalton says smoothly, breaking the moment's tension as a waiter approaches their table.

The waiter gave the makeshift wall of menus an odd glance before nodding and hurrying away, leaving behind a curious silence. Daltonsmirked, but George's focus remained on the scroll.

"Go on, then," Dalton murmured. "Let's see what it says."

George hesitated, his hand hovering over the bag. The anticipation churned in his gut, a mix of dread and determination. Whatever secrets lay within the scroll were bound to pull them deeper into the darkness, already unravelling their world.

"George, what the hell? Your eyes," Dalton remarked, his voice a mix of curiosity and concern.

George could feel it—the familiar rush of heat behind his eyes. The eerie glow crept into his vision, an uninvited reminder of the beast that lingered within. He squeezed his eyelids shut, drawing a deep breath to steady himself.

"Sorry about that," George mumbles, his voice low.

"It's okay," Dalton replies, though his tone betrayed unease. But they're changing—more of a full blood-red. It must be because of the moon soon. Have you decided what you're doing?"

George sighs, the weight of the coming transformation pressing down on him. "The same as always. Skip and I are in that abandoned warehouse in Hackney Wick, where the Sunday market is set up. At least the muddy land is empty."

"Yeah," Dalton nodded, "but this is the big one for you. It's different from what Andy will go through."

"That's why I need you to chain me separately in the boiler room," George replies, his voice tinged with resignation.

Dalton nodded again, eyes scanning the restaurant to ensure they weren't overheard. The coast was clear. Slipping on a glove, he reached for the scroll, carefully removing the bloodstained ribbon. The parchment felt dry and coarse beneath the material, its texture suggesting it wasn't as old as it appeared.

As Dalton unfurled the scroll, the writing came into view. Black ink glistened under the dim light, the fountain pen's italic script both precise and unnerving.

She made the vow to forsake all others, and till death, we part. Now, the world can forsake her like the many seeking new pastures. My judgment will be true.

7 a.m., Tuesday, October 27th.

"Brrr. Brrr. Brrr."

The abrupt ringing of the phone shattered the predawn silence, jolting George awake.

"Erghhh... Oh... okay, I'm coming. I'm coming. What time is it?" he mumbles, groggy and irritated.

The landline phone's harsh rattle reverberated in his ears like a woodpecker hammering on a tree. George groaned, glancing at the clock on his bedside table. The red digits glared back at him—it was painfully early.

Barely awake, he reached for the receiver. The lingering effects of last night's curry churned unpleasantly in his stomach, a grim reminder of his late-night indulgence.

"Hello," he mutters, his voice gravelly.

"George, you up?" a voice on the other end inquired.

"I am now. Who is this?" George replies, his exhaustion showing through.

"There's been another."

The voice belonged to Frank Locke, the new acting D.I. The words sent a chill down George's spine. Another murder. Another gruesome scene. The dread coiled tightly in the pit of his stomach, heavy and unrelenting.

He sighed heavily, the weight of the situation pressing down on him like a vice. It had been less than 24 hours since the last murder, and the previous scene still lingered vividly in his mind.

"You got hold of Dalton?" George asks, his voice resigned.

"Not yet," Locke admitted. "Can't get through to him."

Typical Dalton ignored calls when he felt like it. George couldn't blame him—after the night they'd had, Dalton probably needed the rest as much as he did.

"Okay, I'll swing by his place and see what's up," George says reluctantly.

"Appreciated. And get there as soon as possible," Locke urges, though something is in his voice—something off.

George frowned, sensing there was more Locke wasn't saying. Honesty was essential if they would work together and catch this killer. "What aren't you telling me?" George pressed.

There was a pause on the other end of the line, a hesitation that only deepened George's unease.

"The killer," Locke finally says, his voice low and strained. "I think they're seeking an audience."

George's eyes widened as he sat upright in bed. His pulse quickened, the implications of Locke's words slicing through his grogginess like a blade.

"What the hell does that mean? We've kept most of it from the papers," George replies, his tone sharp with confusion and concern.

"No," Locke says, his voice barely above a whisper. "This is an audience of one... *you*."

The line went silent, Locke's chilling revelation echoing in George's ears.

The realisation hit George like a punch to the gut. The killer wasn't just taking lives—they were studying him. Delving into the gruesome murders George had worked on, using them as inspiration for their macabre artistry. It wasn't a novel tactic, but it was disturbingly effective, stirring fear and panic in a way only a twisted mind could manage.

"Well, let's catch this depraved shit before it gets worse," George declares, his initial shock giving way to grim determination. "I'll grab the old git, some coffee, and get down there."

"Great," Locke replies, his voice laced with something George couldn't quite place—was it resignation or unease? "Pathology and SOCO will meet you there. They'll debrief the findings from the last one. It's worse than we thought. But from what you've been through already..." Locke trailed off before adding softly, "I reckon you'll understand it better."

The line clicked dead, leaving George alone in the quiet of his room.

A sudden gust of wind howled through the cracked window, lifting the curtains in a ghostly dance. The chill it carried wasn't just from the cold air—it was something darker, a presence that seemed to seep into the very walls of the room.

George's eyes scanned the shifting shadows, his instincts prickling with unease. The faint creak of the floorboards and the muted hum of distant traffic only amplified the sense of something watching, waiting just beyond his line of sight.

His chest tightened. The day ahead promised to be long and horrifying, but there was no room for hesitation. Whatever evil they were facing, it was time to confront it head-on.

PAIN KILLER

4

The phone call had ended abruptly, leaving George with a gnawing unease that burrowed deep into his mind. The killer felt like more than just a person—more than flesh and blood. It was as though something ancient, an evil force beyond comprehension, had latched onto his past, drawn like a moth to the flame of his darkest cases.

Of all the grotesque horrors in his history—supernatural and human—why had this savage chosen to mimic *that* case? The one that had left scars too deep to heal? And why had it set its sights on him, a single, insignificant detective in the grand scheme of it all?

George stood in the dimly lit room, his thoughts swirling in the oppressive quiet. The bottle of whiskey on the counter caught his eye, gleaming like a beacon. Its allure was undeniable, a siren's call offering an escape from the storm brewing ahead. The shadows seemed to tighten around him, the weight of unseen eyes pressing in from the darkest corners.

With a reluctant sigh, he poured a small measure into a glass, the amber liquid swirling like liquid courage. The first sip burned his throat, the heat spreading through his chest, offering a fleeting numbness. It wasn't enough to quiet the dread clawing at his insides. It had been weeks since his last drink—a small victory in the fight against his demons—but today was different.

Supernatural evil wasn't suited for a sober mind.

George placed the glass down with a trembling hand, forcing himself to stop. Another sip wouldn't help or change the reality of what lay ahead. His head needed to be clear. The shadows of his past haunted him, but now they were merging with something far darker—something alive, ancient, and infinitely more sinister.

When George arrived at number 8, Tanton Drive, in Stepney Green, it was a little past 8:30 a.m. The house's facade was quaint but unremarkable, with a sleek black door and a neglected front garden, the weeds encroaching like skeletal fingers.

As he approached the doorstep, the faint smell of cigarettes hung in the crisp morning air, mingling with something foul and unnatural. The stench hit him like a wave—an open grave's sickly, earthy rot.

George stopped short. The front door was ajar.

The sight sent a chill crawling up his spine. It wasn't just unusual; it was wrong. A door left open was an invitation, a breach in the fragile boundary between the ordinary world and something far darker.

He nudged the door with his shoulder, its creak echoing unnaturally in the stillness. The hall stretched before him, bathed in the weak light filtering through the grimy windows. The cream-coloured walls, light brown carpet, and scattered furniture all appeared mundane. But the silence was suffocating, heavy with an unnatural weight as if the spirits of the house were holding their breath.

"Hey Dalton, youthere?" George called, his voice breaking the eerie quiet.

"In here, matey," came a trembling reply from the other room.

George followed the voice, his steps slow and deliberate. The weight of the open door and the silence pressed down on him.

He found Daltons sitting on the edge of a black leather sofa, his eyes locked on the unlit television screen. His face was pale, his expression tight with shock. But there was something deeper in his gaze, a fear that went beyond the ordinary horrors of their work.

"What's going on?"George asks, his voice firm but cautious. "The guy's been trying to reach you. There's another body."

Dalton didn't respond immediately. His hands trembled slightly as they rested on his knees, and his breath came in shallow bursts. George stepped closer, his instincts on edge.

"Dalton," he pressed, his tone sharper now. "What's happened?"

Dalton finally tore his gaze from the blank screen, his eyes meeting George's. The fear in them was raw, almost primal.

"You're gonna want to see this," Dalton whispers, his voice barely audible.

The words hung in the air like a curse, pulling George deeper into the nightmare unfolding around them.

Dalton's gaze remained fixed on the shadows flickering across the walls, his voice low and haunted. "I know. About the body, I mean."

George's brows furrowed, unease prickling his spine. "How?"

Wordlessly, Dalton handed him a box, his face taut with anxiety.

Blood smeared the edges of the small container, the crimson streaks stark against its dull surface. But it wasn't just the gore that made George's claws stir within, their dormant tips prickling under his skin—it was the unmistakable aura of malevolence radiating from the object.

George carefully took the box, its weight unnatural in his hands. Slowly, he lifted the lid. Inside lay a severed left ear, pale and mottled with hues of purple and white. The ear rested in a small, dark pool of blood, its presence both grotesque and otherworldly.

It wasn't merely a body part—it was a message.

"Is there anything else?" George asks, his voice steady but his stomach twisting in anticipation.

Dalton's expression darkened. "Of course, there's more."

Beneath the ear, George found a piece of parchment folded and stained at the edges. Unfolding it, he saw a cryptic inscription, not in any recognisable language but an intricate series of runes written in blood. Among them, a chilling quote emerged, scrawled in jagged letters:

Friends, Romans, countrymen, lend me your ears;
I come to bury Caesar, not to praise him.
The evil that men do lives after them;
The good is oft interred with their bones.
If I lend you mine, perhaps you'll listen.
By the time I'm done, my evil will live long after I'm gone.

Dalton leaned closer, his face pale. "Wow," he mutters, his voice trembling. "He wants to make a name for himself in the darkest annals of history. He's trying to get your attention, Georgie." He gestured to the runes. "This doesn't just murder. It's a spectacle, a ritual."

The realisation struck George like a bolt of dark lightning. This wasn't the usual run-of-the-mill killer. This was something far worse. The entity, whatever it was, had latched onto George's past and was now dragging him deeper into a world of supernatural horror.

"What do we do?" Dalton asks, his voice barely above a whisper. He was scared.

George's response was immediate: "Bag it. Bring the box. The forensics team can analyse it at the scene." He paused, considering the implications. "If your address is known, stay elsewhere until this ends. An ear could be the least of our troubles."

Dalton forced a nervous chuckle. "Perhaps Andy's feeling more hospitable now."

Despite the feigned fun, both men knew the truth. What they faced wasn't just flesh and blood—it was evil incarnate, something that thrived in the shadows between worlds.

R egent's Canal, 9:30 a.m

As George and Dalton approached the crime scene, the air was heavy with anticipation. The macabre puzzle pieces were falling into place, each more horrifying than the last. Dalton clutched the evidence bag containing the severed ear as they navigated the narrow path along the canal.

"How bad do you think this one's going to get?" Dalton asks, anxiety lacing his words.

George hesitated, his instincts telling him one thing, his mind another, leaving only one certainty: "I'd bow to your experience, but I fear we're in for a rough ride."

The bridge loomed ahead, its shadow stretching ominously across the pathway. They parked nearby, George's eyes scanning for surveillance cameras or anything that might have captured the perpetrator's movements.

A cordon appeared as they descended the steps, stretching about a hundred feet down the pathway to a mooring. The presence of gawking onlookers was thicker this time, their whispered speculations adding to the pressure to solve the case.

"Well, well, well," George mutters as Ms Walker approaches, clipboard in hand. "Looks like we aren't the only ones being run ragged."

Stepping beneath the arch that led to the crime scene, George froze. The wall to his right bore an inverted cross, eerily similar to the U.V. stamp they had found on the previous victim. Blood splatters surrounded it, forming a crude but unmistakable tableau. Nails pierced the outlines of hands and feet in the wall—a chilling mimicry of crucifixion.

"What the hell is this supposed to mean?" George mutters, more to himself than anyone else.

Ms Wainwright worked diligently nearby, her face a mask of professional detachment as she catalogued evidence. George approached her cautiously. "How far have you gotten?" he inquired, hoping for clarity amid the chaos.

"We're piecing it together," Wainwright replies, her voice steady despite the horror around her. She gestured toward the wall. "The positioning of the blood splatters suggests it wasn't just a postmortem display. They... did this to her while she was still alive."

George's stomach churned, but he forced himself to maintain composure. This killer wasn't just taking lives—they were sending messages, and those messages were becoming increasingly twisted.

Detective George Reynolds felt his breath hitch as the ghostly figures of **Tracey Kent** and **Rachel Darnley** shimmered faintly at the canal's edge, illuminated in the dim, shifting light. Their ethereal presence sent a chill through him, colder than the damp air that clung to the early morning. They stood still, their expressions hauntingly blank, yet their eyes carried an unspeakable sorrow, boring into him with an intensity that made his stomach twist.

He froze, instinctively gripping the edge of the canal wall for balance. The eerie silence around him seemed to deepen, broken only by the faint rustling of leaves and the distant murmur of voices from the others at the scene. The ghosts didn't move, but their whispered plea reverberated in his mind.

"Please... help us."

The words were barely audible, more a feeling than a sound, yet they struck with the force of a scream.

"George?" Dalton's voice broke the trance, sharp and laced with concern.

George blinked and tore his gaze away from the Spectres, his heart racing. He glanced back toward the others to find Dalton watching him with a furrowed brow. George realised he must have looked as pale as the ghosts he'd just seen.

"What's going on? You look like you've seen..." Dalton trailed off, his usual quip faltering.

George shook his head quickly. "Nothing. It's nothing," he mutters, trying to sound convincing, though his voice betrays him.

Dalton wasn't buying it. "Don't give me that, mate. You've got that haunted look again. What is it this time?"

George didn't answer, his eyes flicking back to the canal. Tracey and Rachel's figures were faintly shimmering against the dark water. But now, they seemed closer, their presence heavier, as if the weight of their deaths had settled around him like an oppressive fog.

He swallowed hard, choosing his words carefully. "It's just... this case. It's getting under my skin."

Dalton gave him a wary look but nodded. "Yeah, well, join the club. This one's twisted, even by our standards." He turned back toward the wall, gesturing toward the inverted cross. "Walker thinks these marks were carved with something not of this world. What do you reckon?"

George barely heard him, his mind still fixated on the apparitions. He knew he couldn't say anything—how could he explain seeing ghosts to someone like Dalton without sounding insane? And yet, the feeling was undeniable. The victims were trying to communicate with him, and he couldn't ignore it.

He forced himself to focus, stepping closer to the wall, where the markings glowed faintly under Walker's U.V. light. The inverted cross, surrounded by jagged, chaotic symbols, seemed almost alive as if the wall pulsed with darkness. George ran his gloved fingers along the edges of the marks, feeling a strange heat radiating from the cold stone.

"They're not random," he says, his voice low. "This is a message. But I don't think it's meant for just anyone."

Walker looked up from her magnifying glass, her expression sceptical. "What do you mean?"

George hesitated, then glanced back toward the canal. The ghosts were gone, their fleeting presence now a void that left him unsettled. He exhaled slowly, turning back to Walker and Dalton.

"Someone's orchestrating this," he says, his tone grim. "And they want us to see i t. They're not hiding—they're performing."

Dalton frowned, crossing his arms. "Performing for who?"

George met his partner's gaze, the weight of the truth pressing down on him. "Us."

The word hung in the air like a death knell, and for a moment, no one spoke. Walker's scepticism melted into unease, and even Dalton seemed momentarily shaken.

Finally, Dalton broke the silence, his voice gruff. "Let's ensure they regret inviting us to their twisted little show."

George nodded, though his unease lingered. He couldn't shake the feeling that the killer wasn't just taunting them but drawing them into something far darker—something that went beyond human comprehension. And the ghosts of Tracey and Rachel were only the beginning.

THE MISSING DOT

5

George pushed Andy's troubling thoughts to the back of his mind. The ghosts, the chilling symbols, and the otherworldly sensations had already taken their toll. There was no telling how Andy would handle stepping back into the fold, and George wasn't sure he was ready to take that risk—not yet.

"We'll start with the smaller warehouse," George says, glancing at the notes scattered across his desk. "It's off Roman Road, closer to where Tracey was found. Something about its proximity keeps tugging at me."

Dalton nodded, his hand brushing against the photographs. "Roman Road, eh? Every grim lead this month seems to circulate back to that place. You think it's the primary scene?"

"Could be. Or it's where they're holding their little... performances before moving the bodies," George mutters, the weight of his words sinking in.

He grabbed his coat, pulling it tightly around himself, as the cold seemed to seep into the very bones of the station. The dull hum of the office, punctuated by the ringing phones and murmured conversations, felt like a distant echo as his mind sharpened on the task ahead.

T he drive through East London's grey streets was as dismal as ever. Rain streaked the car windows, blurring the jagged skyline of warehouses and derelict buildings. Dalton sat in the passenger seat, fiddling with the radio until George shot him a look that silenced the tinny sound of a morning talk show.

"Fine, fine. Just trying to lighten the mood, Georgie," Dalton grumbled, crossing his arms.

George ignored him, eyes scanning the map he'd laid on the dashboard. Roman Road loomed closer with every turn, the run-down buildings growing denser. The area had always carried an air of neglect, but now it felt eerie and a little seedy as if the very streets held onto the echoes of the crap that happens in the shadows.

Pulling up the warehouse, George cut the engine and surveyed the surroundings. The building was squat and ominous, its gated metal siding rusted and graffiti-laden. A chain-link fence surrounded the property, its padlock rusted but suspiciously loose.

Dalton followed George's gaze. "Looks like someone's been here recently," he observed.

George nodded, exiting the car and adjusting his coat against the biting wind. "Keep an eye out. If this is where they're staging things, I doubt they've completely cleared out."

The pair approached the gate cautiously. George quickly examined the padlock, noting the faint scrape marks around the lock's edge. Someone had tampered with it, but the signs were recent—maybe within the last day.

"Someone's been busy," Dalton murmurs, his breath visible in the cold.

George pushed the gate open, its creak slicing through the stillness. The warehouse loomed ahead, its broken windows staring at them like hollow eyes. Inside, the faint smell of mildew and decay hung in the air, mingling with a coppery tang that George's instincts recognised immediately.

Blood.

"Stay sharp," George says, his voice low as they enter.

The interior was dim—weak light filtered through the broken windows, casting long shadows across the cluttered space. Stacks of crates and abandoned machinery littered the floor, creating a labyrinthine maze. A cleared area stood out in the centre of the room, the concrete stained dark.

George crouched beside the stain, running a gloved finger along its edge. The liquid was dry, but the pattern was unmistakable—someone had been restrained here. Rope fibres were embedded in the ground-floor grooves, and faint scratch marks told the story of a struggle.

"This isn't just a dumping ground," George says, his voice tight. "This is where they bring them first."

Dalton knelt beside him, his face grim. "The chalky residue you mentioned... it's here, too."He pointed to a nearby crate, its surface dusted with the same pale substance they'd found on the victims.

George's eyes narrowed as he scanned the room. "It's not chalk. It's something else...something deliberate."

His gaze landed on a small, crude altar against the far wall. A makeshift table covered in black fabric bore a collection of objects—candles, vials of an unidentifiable liquid, and a weathered book with an ominous insignia burned into its cover.

"Looks like we've found their stage," Dalton says, his voice barely above a whisper.

George's stomach churned as he approached the altar. The book's cover seemed to pulse faintly, the carved insignia resembling the inverted cross they'd seen on the victims. Reaching out, he opened the book cautiously, its brittle pages filled with a jagged, cryptic script that seemed to writhe under the light.

"This isn't just a killer," George says, his voice steady despite the growing unease. This is a ritual."

Dalton's hand went to his sidearm instinctively, his usual bravado replaced by a quiet tension."Whatever they're summoning, Georgie, I've got a bad feeling it's not done yet."

George nodded, the weight of the discovery settling over him. This was only the beginning. Whatever horror awaited them was still gathering strength—and they ran out of time.

Detective George Reynolds watched Dalton's brow furrow, his gaze darting between the shadows of the warehouse interior and the distant, empty windows overlooking the courtyard. The air carried an unsettling chill that whispered through unseen eyes.

"I don't like how quiet it is," Dalton mutters, his hand instinctively brushing against the holster at his hip. "Too damn quiet. If someone's been using this place, they've either cleared out or hiding."

George nodded, his unease building on every step into the derelict complex. The space was vast, its emptiness amplified by the rhythmic dripping of water from a broken pipe somewhere in the distance. The walls bore faded graffiti, and the floor was a minefield of discarded debris—broken pallets, rusted tools, and shards of glass that crunched beneath their boots.

"Let's split up," George suggests, his voice low but firm. "I'll take the east wing. You cover the main floor. Keep your comms open."

Da.lton raised an eyebrow, and scepticism showed through as always. "You sure about that, Georgie? This place has a bad vibe. Feels like the walls are watching."

"I'm sure," George replied, his tone resolute. "If there's something here, we're more likely to find it if we cover more ground. Stay sharp."

Dalton turned toward the loading bay with a reluctant nod, his flashlight cutting through the gloom. George headed deeper into the warehouse, his footsteps echoing in the cavernous space. The smell of damp concrete and decaying wood permeated the air, mingling with the faint tang of something metallic—blood? Or rust? He couldn't be sure.

The east wing was eerily silent, the kind that pressed against the eardrums and amplified every small sound. George's flashlight swept across the space, illuminating stacks of rotting crates and tarps draped over forgotten machinery. He paused near a row of filing cabinets, their drawers half-open and contents spilling out like entrails.

He rifled through the papers. Most of them are faded invoices and outdated inventory lists. But one document caught his eye—a crumpled sheet with smeared ink that read:

"Salvation lies within the wound. Blood binds the willing to the path. The marked shall guide the way."

George felt his stomach twist. The cryptic message mirrored the dark, ritualistic nature of the murders. Was this place connected to the killer? Or was it a red herring meant to mislead them?

"Dalton, you find anything?" George's voice crackled over the comms.

"Just more trash. It looks like this place has been abandoned for years," Dalton replies, though his tone suggests unease. "You?"

"Found a note.Might be connected. I'm heading deeper into the east wing."

"Copy that. Watch your back," Dalton says, his voice conveying tension.

George pressed on, his flashlight beam cutting through the shadows. The floor sloped downward, leading to what appeared to be a basement level. The air grew colder, and the faint hum of machinery echoed from below—a generator? His instincts screamed at him to turn back, but the need for answers outweighed his fear.

He found a heavy steel door slightly ajar at the base of the stairs. The hum was louder now, accompanied by the faint flicker of fluorescent light. George drew his weapon, his heartbeat pounding in his ears as he pushed the door open.

The room beyond was a stark contrast to the decay above. It was sterile, almost clinical, with rows of tables and shelves lined with tools, vials, and what looked disturbingly like surgical equipment. In the centre of the room stood an an altar-like structure, its surface stained dark with what George could only assume was blood.

On the wall behind it, the same inverted cross symbol he had seen on the victims was painted in vivid red. Beneath it, a message was scrawled in jagged letters:

"The blood moonrises. The offering begins."

George's breath caught in his throat. This wasn't just a murder scene. It was a place of ritual, of summoning. And it wasn't abandoned.

The faint steps behind him made him spin around, his weapon raised. But no one was there—only the oppressive silence and the feeling of being watched.

"Dalton, I found something," George says into his comms, his voice steady despite the rising dread. "Get down to the east wing basement. And hurry."

He didn't dare take his eyes off the room, knowing that whatever answers lay within would come at a cost.

"It's the logistics of it all, mate," Dalton says, his voice barely cutting through the oppressive quiet. "The killer's taking an enormous risk—hauling a lifeless body all that way. Hundreds of feet up the slope, down the steps, and under the bridge? It doesn't add up."

Dalton's words hung in the air like a challenge. George felt their weight pressing against his thoughts, amplifying the creeping unease growing since they arrived. He couldn't argue—how could anyone pull off something so grotesque alone, especially in the dead of night? The uneven pavement, the sheer distance...it was madness. And yet, there was the rope. That damned rope. The frayed section they'd found nearly two hundred feet from the crime scene clawed at George's mind like an unwelcome spectre. He glanced back at the hulking silhouette of the warehouse. Ignoring this lead wasn't an option—not if they wanted answers.

"We should check it out," George says, forcing the words past the knot of dread in his throat. His voice betrayed the conflict in him: the sharp edge of fear tempered only by the need to uncover the truth. "At least to rule it out."

The wind shifted then, colder than before, slicing through the fabric of the night like a blade. George stiffened, his instincts screaming at him to turn back. But it wasn't just the cold—it was the sound. Low, almost imperceptible at first, then louder, whispers drifted on the breeze, broken and desperate.

"Please help us. We're so tired. Help us rest, please."

The words slithered into George's ears, burrowing deep. He froze, his breath catching in his chest as the voices swelled, filling the hollow spaces around him. They weren't real—they couldn't be real—but they pulled at something primal, buried in the marrow of his bones.

His trembling hands fumbled with the padlock. The clinking of the chain as he wrenched it free seemed deafening in the oppressive quiet, the sound reverberating like the toll of a bell. George didn't dare look over his shoulder as the gate creaked open, its rusted hinges groaning like a creature stirring from slumber.

"Do you think anyone's watching?" he asks, his voice barely more than a whisper.

Dalton scanned the broken windows above, his features carved from unease. He wasn't the steady, pragmatic figure George knew—something about this place had shaken him, too. "I don't know, George," he says, his voice tight. "But you might be right. The logistics of this...it doesn't feel possible. None of it does."

Ahead, the warehouse loomed like a forgotten tomb, its cavernous maw swallowing what little light remained. George stared at the void inside, his gut twisting in protest. Every instinct screamed at him to turn back, to leave whatever horrors lurked in the darkness, to rot. But he couldn't—not now.

The air inside was thick, stagnant, clinging to his lungs like tar. Dust hung in a suffocating haze, muting the faint glimmers of light that filtered through the shattered windows. The floor was a wasteland of shattered glass, toppled desks, and scattered debris. George's eyes were drawn to faint tracks in the grime as whispers etched into the dirt. He climbed onto the ledge, his fingers brushing against the gritty surface. That same brown residue again—the same stuff they'd seen smeared on Tracey's jeans and Rachel's fingers. His heart thundered in hischest.

Had they been here? Had they tried to escape this place? Or had this been where the nightmare began?

"What are you thinking?" Dalton asks, his voice cutting through the stillness.

"That they might've been here," George murmurs, though the words felt like an admission of guilt. "Or maybe...it's just a coincidence."

But George didn't believe in coincidences—not in this place.

The room stretched ahead of them, a labyrinth of shadow and decay. Iron pillars rose like skeletal sentinels, their rusted surfaces glinting faintly in the dim light. Abandoned boxes leaned haphazardly against the walls, their contents spilling out the bones of long-dead secrets. The air reeked of damp rot and the acrid stench of pigeon droppings, each breath thick with decay. The silence was deafening, broken only by the occasional drip of water echoing through the vast emptiness.

George's pulse quickened as he took another step forward. Every shadow seemed alive, writhing at the edges of his vision. The room was suffocating, heavy with the weight of having eyes on it yet elusive.

Something about this place felt wrong—not just unsettling but deeply wrong. As George pressed deeper into the darkness, he couldn't shake the feeling that whatever they were looking for was waiting for them.

George and Dalton paused in the doorway, their hesitation palpable. The space ahead loomed like a trap, its shadows yawning wide with quiet menace. Neither dared to take a step without gauging the unseen dangers lurking within. Above, the cacophony of pigeons flapping and cooing echoed off the rafters, masking the silence of whatever else might share the darkness with them. George's steps were cautious, each one deliberate, while Dalton's heels clicked sharply, their sound bouncing off the cold walls like a warning.

They ventured further into the warehouse, the air thickening with every step. A new odour joined the stench of decay—sour and sharp, cutting through the already foul atmosphere. George's stomach churned as the reek clawed its way into his lungs. His eyes fixed on the red double doors ahead, marked as offices, their grimy windows reinforced with chicken wire that obscured any view inside.

"Go straight ahead," George says, his voice tight with unease.

Dalton's eyes narrowed. "What've you found, mate?" he asks, his tone cautious but tinged with dread.

"Blood," George whispered. The single word felt heavier than it should have, weighted with implication and a creeping chill up his spine.

Dalton's expression darkened, the colour draining from his face as the reality of the situation sank in. The oppressive air seemed to grow heavier, each breath a struggle against the suffocating dread pressing down on them. George didn't elaborate further, but the sinister implications gnawed at the edges of his mind, stirring something primal within him—a disturbing hunger that made his mouth water. He swallowed hard, forcing the sensation away.

The red door groaned in protest as George pushed it open. A plume of thick, toxic dust erupted into the air, particles glittering faintly in the dim light like the remnants of a long-buried secret. The space beyond exhaled its confinement, breathing a history of despair into the room. Whatever lay inside had been waiting for them.

"Should we update the boss?" George asked, his voice low as he glanced at Dalton. Though he hated to admit it, deferring to Dalton's experience assured him.

"Not yet," Dalton says, shaking his head. "We can't go back with some story about smelling blood from a mile away. Let's look first. It might be nothing."

Neither of them believed that.

"We can only hope," Dalton mutters, though his words ring hollow.

George studied him. "You don't sound very optimistic. Any reason for that?"

Dalton's eyes flicked at the shadows creeping around the room. "It's the patterns," George answers for him, his voice tight. "The connections. They always fit together, but when they do, it usually means trouble."

The room beyond the doors was cavernous. Two smaller offices merged into one sprawling expanse. Its blacked-out windows loomed along the walls like watchful voids, with small, crudely cut eyeholes allowing only narrow glimpses of the outside world. The air inside was different, thick with a pungent mixture that twisted George'sstomach. Sweat, stale beer, urine, and blood mingled into a noxious stench that overpowered the dust and dampness of the warehouse outside.

George stepped further inside, his boots crunching softly on the grit-covered floor. He could feel the room's weight pressing against him, its secrets coiled tightly in the air, waiting to strike. This place wasn't just abandoned—it had been left behind deliberately, the echoes of its former occupants lingering like ghosts in the stench and grime.

He glanced at Dalton, whose jaw was set, his eyes scanning the room for signs of movement. Neither of them spoke. The silence inside the office was worse than any sound, every creak of the floorboards or rattle of the wind carrying the threat of something unseen—something alive.

And George knew, without question, that this place was steeped in darkness.

The brown grit on George's hands mirrored the residue he'd seen on Tracey's jeans and fingers. The connection gnawed at him, intensifying the unease already coiled tightly in his chest. This place wasn't just a waypoint in their investigation—it felt like the heart of something far more sinister, a grotesque nexus where the answers they sought might finally surface. And yet, every instinct screamed that he wouldn't like what he found.

Carefully navigating the scattered paper boxes littering the floor, George's attention was pulled to the far-right corner of the room. A lone stained mattress lay slumped against the floor, its presence oddly deliberate. But it wasn't the mattress that stole his focus—it was the grotesque pattern on the floor beneath it. Blood stains had seeped into the concrete, forming an unmistakable symbol: an upside-down cross.

The sight chilled George to the marrow. He clenched his fists, forcing himself to breathe steadily, but the air felt heavier, tainted. Whoever had orchestrated this scene wasn't just deranged—they were calculating. Manipulative. They were being led, strung along like puppets on fraying strings. George's jaw tightened. He hated the thought of playing this twisted game, of following a trail of gruesome breadcrumbs designed to toy with them. But for now, they had no choice.

He turned toward Dalton, who was rifling through a line of rusted cupboards along the left wall. As George's gaze swept the room, it caught on a chaotic collage of newspaper clippings tacked to the wall. The articles chronicled the horrifying crimes of Ethan Conrad—the so-called "brother" George refused to acknowledge. The name "Charlie" felt even more alien, a term that didn't belong to the monster depicted here. His stomach twisted further when his eyes locked on the blood-painted symbols at the centre of the display: a distorted smiley face, another mark—the same one tattooed on Dalton's arm.

"Look at this," Dalton called out, his voice tense, pulling George's attention away. Dalton stood near a large whiteboard that George hadn't noticed before.

"He knew we'd come," George whispers, his voice barely audible, as if speaking the words might summon something from the shadows. The revelation hung heavy between them like a noose tightening around their necks.

Scrawled across the whiteboard, written in a bold, taunting hand, was another riddle:

"What is greater than God, eviler than the devil? Rich people need it. You people have it, and if you eat it, you die?"

"Bloody hell, more riddles," Dalton mutters, running a hand through his hair, his frustration breaking the tense silence.

"It's nothing," George replies, though his voice wavered. "We're being taunted again, made to feel like we have nothing."

But as much as George tried to dismiss it, the words seemed to crawl under his skin, burrowing into the spaces where his doubts already lingered. This wasn't random—none of it was. They were being tested, pushed into corners where their only choice was to stumble deeper into the unknown.

George's eyes returned to the board, then to the bloodied symbols, his mind racing to connect the fragments of information that seemed designed to elude them. Every answer felt out of reach, and their vulnerability bore down on him like a vice. The room, the symbols, and the cryptic taunts weren't just clues. They were warnings.

PLACE FAR AWAY

6

"So, what are your thoughts so far?" Dalton asks, breaking the silence. His head rested against the car window, his eyes distant, as if searching for answers beyond the glass. George didn't blame him. The warehouse had been a dead end, and now they were crawling through traffic toward another location, expecting little more than disappointment. The gruesome images of their last discovery—the severed ear delivered like a grotesque calling card—still lingered, casting a shadow over Dalton's thoughts.

Dalton let out a low, restless grumble, his patience thinning as the car idled at the temporary traffic lights. Grove Road was a gridlocked mess, leaving them trapped for ten excruciating minutes. George flipped through the A-Z map in his mind, estimating they were barely five to seven minutes away from their destination—if they walked.

"My thoughts?" George echoed, glancing at Dalton. "I think Locke's going to keep us working all night. It feels like we got called back in earlier than planned."

"Meaning?" Dalton asks, though the resignation in his tone suggests he already knew.

"We're in for a long haul," George replies. "And I need a damn fine cup of coffee to shake off this rust. This killer already had us chasing our tails, and we've got two bodies in less than twenty-four hours."

Dalton's lips tightened. "Yeah, but what's the endgame here?"

"Shits and giggles? Who the hell knows? Maybe they're just starving for attention. A little splash of infamy to spice up their lives."

Dalton shook his head, unconvinced. "If that's the case, why the extras? The pineal gland? Some freaky aphrodisiac? And don't forget—this psycho's got the skill to break into a skull without making a mess."

"Yeah," George mutters, his voice dark. "It's a weird one. Life's supposed to get 'interesting,' but I didn't expect *this* bizarre level."

That was the truth. The chaos surrounding Ethan Conrad—if that was even the perpetrator's real name—was far from over. The cryptic warnings, the calculated brutality... it all felt designed to keep them off-kilter. George could only hope it was all a bluff, but something told him it wasn't.

At last, the traffic crawled forward, the endless line of lights behind them. George took the next left onto Roman Road, his eyes scanning for anything of note—a cafe came into view just beyond the second crime scene. Dalton slumped slightly in his seat; it looked like he was seconds away from calling it a night. George needed him sharp—grounded—in case the night spiralled into something worse than either of them expected.

"What are we doing here?" Dalton asks, the faintest edge of curiosity breaking through his exhaustion.

"A pit stop," George replies. "Before we take an unconventional route. These bastards will only show themselves when they want to. So, we'll take a path they wouldn't expect us to take."

Dalton arched his back, giving George a slow nod of acknowledgement. It was a decent plan as far as improvisations went. George glanced left, noticing the overgrown greenway—a narrow pathway cutting through the trees that led toward the canal and back toward the warehouse. It was a hidden route, less predictable. And besides, he thought grimly, he needed a proper coffee. The cheap, watered-down sludge from the office wasn't cutting it anymore.

They parked and stepped out, the stale city air thick with the stench of diesel fumes from a passing bus. George paused outside the cafe—a yellow-painted shop front with the uninspired name "All Day Breakfast" emblazoned across its window. Originality wasn't on the menu, but it hardly mattered if the seats were filled. He glanced toward the Hi-Viz uniforms of two officers going door to door, barely two hundred feet from the last crime scene. The sight made him scoff under his breath.

"Closing the barn door after the horse has bolted," George mutters, shaking his head.

Dalton didn't respond, his eyes drifting toward the greenway instead. George followed his gaze, the shadowy pathway half-obscured by the overgrowth. It looked inviting in a way that made his skin crawl.

"So, what's the real reason for coming here, mate?" Dalton asks, his tone edged with curiosity. He is studying George as if searching for some hidden motive. The two of them had just taken a table to the left of the entrance, the one closest to the window. George, as always, chooses the seat facing the glass—a habit born from his unsettling coffee meeting with Conrad. His gaze flicked outside every few moments, his guard never lowering.

"I want to get a sense of what's nearby," George says, his voice low and thoughtful. "The first body taunted us, and the second was hidden behind barriers that kept it out of sight. It's got me thinking—the killer must have gone somewhere discreet to find their prey. We need to scope out the routes they might have taken and the places they could've gone where they wouldn't be easily seen. Right now, we're already on the back foot."

Dalton leaned back in his chair, nodding as though impressed. The decision to explore the overgrown greenway was risky—little more than a shot in the dark—but it was a start. George's instincts told him that a route less travelled might hold the answers they needed.

"So, it looks like we're going fishing?" Dalton cracked a grin and reached for a menu from the rack on the table.

"You could say that," George replies, his tone distracted as his eyes scanned the cafe. The place wasn't busy, just a smattering of elderly patrons quietly sipping their tea or picking at toast. But something drew George's attention—a brown noticeboard on the far wall, cluttered with papers. Among the jumble was a bright pink flyer with bold black text advertising a local event.

"A lady's night," George murmurs, his gaze narrowing.

"What about it?"Dalton asks, not looking up from the menu.

"It's advertising lady's night," George repeated, his voice taking on the edge of intrigue.

"Right. Sounds like a good time," Dalton smirked.

"Absolutely.Especially if you're looking to stray, given half a chance."

Dalton chuckled dryly, his expression darkening. "I know that well. Finally, I threw my bed out last week—couldn't shake the stink of betrayal off it."

George's attention snapped back to the poster. Could this be a way the killer was scouting? An event like that, catered to specific demographics, might be the perfect hunting ground. If this poster was here, where else had it been plastered? And more importantly, who was behind the event? It felt too convenient, too neat—like an"all-you-can-kill" buffet" for someone with twisted appetites.

"Ready to order?"The voice broke his train of thought. An olive-skinned waitress had appeared at their table, an older woman in her early fifties with sharp eyes and a faintly weary expression. Her name tag read *Marcia*. She was like someone running the cafe for years, likely part of a husband-and-wife team.

"Coffee. Black," George says curtly, his appetite gone as his mind lingered on the flyer.

"Same for me," Dalton adds, sensing they wouldn't be here long enough for anything more.

As Marcia turned to leave, George leaned forward. "Excuse me—one more thing," he says, sliding his warrant card discreetly from under the table. He kept it low, out of view of the other patrons. "That notice on the board—'lady's night.' How long has it been up? And do you know who put it there?"

Marcia paused, her eyes flicking briefly to the badge before nodding. "Must've been a couple of weeks now. A lovely young lady said she was tired of all the 'old boys' clubs.' She wanted at least one night a week where a group of ladies could let their hair down."

"What did she look like?" George pressed; his voice was tight with urgency.

Marcia tilted her head as though searching her memory. "Slim, tall, maybe mid-thirties? Pretty, unconventionally—had this sharpness to her, like she'd seen a thing or two. Brown hair, shoulder-length, tied back loosely. Wore a leather jacket. Oh, she had a penetrating smile that made you feel like she knew something you didn't."

George exchanged a glance with Dalton. The description was generic enough, but how Marcia described her—the calculated sharpness and confidence—pricked George's nerves.

"Did she leave any contact details?" he asks.

"No," Marcia says, shaking her head. "But she seemed...I don't know, purposeful. Like she wasn't just putting up that flyer for fun."

George nodded, filing away the information. The pieces weren't connecting yet, but he couldn't shake the feeling that they were circling something.

"Ooh, now you're asking," Marcia began, her expression sharpening as she searched her memory. "I think she was a white girl, with long red hair, slim build, and those legs—almost like stilts. She was quite attractive."

George nodded, filing away the description. "Thank you. Out of curiosity, did anyone else show interest? Any men, perhaps? Someone unusual?"

Marcia glanced uneasily toward the man behind the counter—presumably her husband—her expression flickering with discomfort. George leaned forward slightly, sensing her hesitation. Two lives had already been lost, and every second they delayed allowed the killer to slip further into the shadows. He had no patience for ambiguity.

"There was one man," Marcia says after a pause. "Tall. At least six feet, maybe more.

He wore a jumper with a hood that hid most of his face."

George exchanged a glance with Dalton, whose expression mirrored his curiosity.

"Did he say or do anything memorable?" George pressed; his voice was steady but insistent.

Marcia hesitated, her fingers curling slightly over the edge of her apron. "He came in not long after the lady put up her poster. He stood momentarily, looking at what she'd posted, and then left. Didn't order. Didn't say a word."

Dalton leaned forward, his tone soft but deliberate. "Did anything else about him stand out? Anything unusual?"

Marcia's lips parted as though she wanted to dismiss the question, but her expression changed. "The eyes," she says, her voice whispering. They glowed."

George's pulse quickened. "Can you recall the colour?" he asked, his voice low and calm despite the storm brewing in his chest.

"Green," Marcia replies."Bright green. Piercing the darkness under his hood."

The mention of glowing green eyes sent an icy shiver down George's spine. An unexpected detail that didn't fit their tracking pattern: *Alpha Red. Beta: Yellow. Omega: Blue.* But what could green eyes signify? A new player? A deviation in the killer's modus operandi? Or something entirely beyond their understanding?

T he overgrown greenway was oppressively quiet as George and Dalton continued their exploration. The trees lining the path towered above them, their gnarled branches casting long, distorted shadows across the dirt trail. George didn't like the silence; it made him uneasy.

A chill ran down George's spine, prickling his skin and forcing his hackles to rise. He scanned the area, his gaze darting from shadow to shadow, every movement in the corner of his vision feeding the gnawing paranoia that had taken root. The feeling of being watched clung to him like a second skin. Whether it was those glowing green eyes or some other unseen force, he couldn't tell.

A dog walker, bundled in a thick blue parka, sat on a nearby bench, idly flipping through their phone. At first glance, the situation seemed harmless, but George wasn't in the mood to dismiss anyone. Paranoia, he reminded himself, was better than carelessness.

The air grew heavier, carrying with it a strange, unsettling scent. It wasn't quite blood but close—an acrid, faintly sweet odour that made George's stomach churn. His mind flashed back to the time Lewis's body was pulled from the Thames. The memory of decomposing flesh and organs soaked in filthy water clawed its way to the surface of his thoughts. The stench had haunted his dreams for months.

"Dalton," George says, his voice cutting through the oppressive quiet. "Let's look around here."

Dalton stopped, glancing over his shoulder at George. His hand hovered near the edge of his coat, close to where his weapon rested—a small but telling movement. George didn't need to say more. Whatever was out there, they both knew the greenway held more than just shadows.

"What for? Do you smell something?" Dalton asks, his tone light but curious. Then, chuckling, he adds, "Oh, and for Christ's sake, we know more about each other than I'd ever share with my ex-wife. So, when it's just us, call me Michael. All this official crap makes me feel like your bloody schoolteacher."

George allowed a faint smile. Their bond had grown throughout the investigation, camaraderie blooming in the shadows of the gruesome cases they'd faced.

"Alright, Mickeyboy," George teases, a smirk tugging at the corner of his mouth. "And yeah, I smell something. It's the scent of death—not quite the usual, but let's be real. Nothing about this case *is* usual."

Michael grinned, the lines on his weathered face softening. "Watch it, sunshine. Don't go tying a noose for yourself. Who needs a sniffer dog when I've got you, eh?"

"Now, who's the one talking about hangman's nooses?" George shot back, his tone light, though his eyes remained sharp, scanning the path ahead. Despite Michael's humour, George could see the strain in him—the isolation, the cold turkey break from the camaraderie of the outside world. It had taken its toll.

"Well," Michael says, his tone shifting, "I've just seen what you're smelling. Look." He pointed toward the water's edge, where a cluster of dead animals lay half-hidden in the brush. Their placement was deliberate, concealed enough to avoid casual notice but undeniable to those looking closely.

George froze, his stomach knotting as he scanned the gruesome scene. He listened intently, straining his ears for any sound that might betray a lurking presence. His mind raced with questions, but one thought loomed above the rest: *Is this a lure?* The killer had already proven their ability to taunt them—how much more did they know?

"This isn't good," George says, his voice heavy.

"Why's that?"Michael asks, his tone losing its playful edge.

"Look closer at the marks," George replies, his words clipped.

Michael squinted, leaning in. "Is that what I think it is?"

"Yep," George says, his unease deepening. "And I don't know if it's a test or a need."

"Either way, it's bloody alarming," Michael mutters, his gaze lingering on the carcasses.

"Have we received any toxicology results on that clear substance?" George asks, though he already suspected the answer.

"Only preliminaries," Michael admitted, shaking his head. "It's some sort of paralytic, but damned if I can make sense of it."

"In that case, leave everything untouched," George cautions.

They found a fox, three squirrels, a cat, and two pigeons among the gruesome pile. Each animal bore the same clear fluid seeping through its fur or feathers, the faint shimmer catching the light like oil on water. Worse still were the holes—clean, deliberate punctures at precise points in their skulls. George knelt closer, his stomach twisting at the thought. The marks weren't just injuries but evidence of something far darker. The animals' deaths had been purposeful, as though feeding a hunger beyond the natural order.

The realisations settled like lead in George's gut. The killers weren't just murdering—they were *feeding*. Whatever this need was, whether born from some horrific transformation or something far older and primal, it was unnatural. And deeply disturbing.

A familiarsensation crawled up George's spine, a whisper of something he hadn't entirelyovercome—the same unshakable unease that crept in with the blood moon'sapproach. It wasn't justification for murder, but for a fleeting moment, George felt a pang of empathy for the monster behind this. They were fighting something impossible, something ancient and relentless.

"Right," George says, standing and brushing off his hands. I'll radio dispatch and have them clear this mess before the wrong person stumbles across it. The last thing we need is some curious kid touching these carcasses."

"Make sure they're sent to Rachel," Michael suggests. "Check the timelines. If these deaths happened before the bodies, it could be a marker—something to tell us how long the killer's been at this."

George nodded and placed the call, his voice calm and precise despite the churning unease beneath the surface. As they waited for backup, the silence pressed in on him again, heavier this time. The feeling of being watched crept over him like a second skin. His eyes darted to the shadows, his ears straining for any sound that might betray an unseen observer.

Then he saw them.

The ghosts of Tracey Kent and Rachel Darnley stood in the periphery of his vision, more decomposed and tormented than the last time he'd seen them. Their hollow eyes burned with a desperate plea. They were trying to communicate, their spectral forms flickering with anguish. George's breath hitched, his pulse pounding in his ears. They yearned for closure—something he and Michael might never truly give them—but he swore silently to try.

ANOTHER BODY

7

"So, here we are, huh?" Michael says, his voice uncertain as his gaze shifts between the canal and the warehouse. They stand a hundred feet from the water's edge, the murky canal stretching out, kicking up a god-awful stink. With its rusty, corrugated sheeting roof and worn, brown exterior, the warehouse looms in an 'L' shape to the right. A narrow towpath and a low wooden border are the only things separating it from the water.

George nodded, his eyes scanning the surroundings. "Yep, there's not much to it. I heard the shifts between the canal, and previous owners used it as a garage."

Michael tilted his head. "So, any guesses? More of that cryptic nonsense?"

George opened his mouth to respond but stopped as his gaze wandered back to the canal. Three boats caught his attention—a blue, a green, and a red-and-blue vessel with *Rosie Lyn* painted on its side. Something about them gave him pause. Could the killer be using the slow, winding route of the canal to move unseen?

"Hey?" Michael asked, snapping George from his thoughts. "Did you hear me? Come on, share your thoughts."

George hesitated, still focused on the boats. "Michael, I'm not sure my thoughts are worth a penny. They sound far-fetched, even to me."

Michael chuckles dryly. "Yeah, but so does 'seeing ghosts.' Yet here we are."

George sighed, glancing back at the boats. "I was wondering if the killer was travelling by canal. Using the boats, I mean."

Michael raised a sceptical eyebrow but didn't dismiss the idea outright. "I'd say 'bullshit,' but hey, never say never. The problem is, each one's like a floating house. We'd never get warrants to search them without solid evidence. Even then, they could drift off before we got close."

"So," George mutters, "bottom line: my thought gets us nowhere."

"No," Michael says, clapping a hand on George's shoulder. "It just means we must be smart and, most of all, sure."

Shaking off his strange moment of contemplation, George followed Michael to the warehouse entrance. Michael pulled the shutter wide, and a rush of stale air hit them, reeking engine oil and grease. Inside, the space opened into a dimly lit garage with a small office at the back, a mechanic's pit, and a narrow flight of metal steps leading upward.

"You won't like this," Michael mutters, his voice low.

George exhaled sharply. "Oh, for fuck's sake. The shit magnet strikes again?"

Michael smirked but nodded grimly. "Yep. There's blood. It is not like the last warehouse with the cross; this is so much more. And old."

The stale air shifted, carrying a heavier, more putrid scent that George recognised instantly: death. It seeped into his nostrils, turning his stomach. The hits just kept on coming.

The metallic clang of their boots echoed through the empty warehouse as they ascended the narrow staircase. Each step felt heavier than the last, the unknown pressing down on them like a physical weight. George kept his focus sharp, though his instincts screamed caution. He wasn't picking up any heartbeats, but that didn't ease his nerves. It felt too soon—too close to discovering the other bodies—too much happening simultaneously.

It felt mostly too soon for another ghost to appear, pleading for release. Thought lingered as they climbed higher, the stench of death intensifying every step. Pigeons and rat droppings littered the stairs, their present grotesque reminder of the neglect that permeated the space.

Daylight filtered weakly through two holes in the newspaper-covered windows, casting uneven beams of light across the grimy floor. George's eyes adjusted quickly, picking out details in the shadows. Then, he saw a stained mattress eerily similar to the one in the previous warehouse.

He moved closer, his pulse quickening. And then he froze.

"It's…" Michael's voice faltered, his face pale with the weight of realisation. That look again—impending doom.

George's stomach dropped as his gaze locked onto the figure sprawled atop the mattress. "Yep," he murmurs, the bile rising in his throat. "The one with long red hair. And even…"

He didn't need to finish. The woman lay still, her fiery hair fanned out like a cruel mockery of life. Her body bore the telltale signs of the killer's work—clean, deliberate punctures in the skull. The fluid seeped from her wounds, the same clear substance they'd seen before, glistening faintly in the dim light.

George turned away, swallowing hard. The killer's pattern wasn't just continuing—it was escalating.

"Hotel Tango Despatch, this is DS Dalton from the Murder Task Force," Michael says into his radio, his voice steady despite the grim scene before them. "We need help at the warehouse near the train tracks at the bottom of Mile End Park. A non-emergency linked to the crime scenes this morning and last night. Please send a request for ADII Locke, SOCO, and pathology. We'll update you further as we go."

"Received by Hotel Tango," came the crackled response. "Calls being made to ADI Locke now."

The air in his radio the warehouse felt heavier than before, thick with the metallic tang of blood and the overwhelming stench of decay. The body hung upside down, nailed to the wall beneath the window. Her feet were pressed flat, secured by large, rusted nails. Her arms were splayed wide, palms facing upward as though in mock surrender. A scaffold board ran beneath her back, its rough surface biting into her pale, bloated skin, held in place by nails driven through her hands.

It was deliberate. Ritualistic. Another grotesque manifestation of the killer's obsession with the upside-down cross.

The woman's-undress mirrored the grim state of Rachel and Tracey before her—clothing stripped, modesty discarded. Her body, swollen with decomposition, had turned a sickly shade of pale red. Flies circled the polluted air, their buzzing blending into the oppressive silence of the warehouse.

Her left eye was missing—a gaping void that once held what George imagined was a striking emerald-green iris. The right eye fared no better; its decayed remains partially eaten away over the past few days as she lay abandoned here.

The killer's work didn't stop with the eye. George's sharp gaze traced the trajectory of the weapon that had burrowed deep into the empty socket, reaching the recesses of the woman's brain. It wasn't just cruelty but precision—methodical and chillingly detached.

Her larynx was crushed, wide patches of bruised flesh bulging unnaturally around her throat. She'd been taken from behind, George concluded—no defensive wounds, no chance to fight back. At least five foot ten, she was tall, but their killer must have been taller still, at least six foot three, to exert the leverage needed for the attack.

One question rattled in George's mind as he studied her lifeless form: *Was she missed?*

While Michael busied himself with radio calls and organising the scene, George seized the opportunity to look closer, unburdened by prying eyes. His red-tinted vision caught the faint outline of a U.V. cross painted down the woman's upper left arm, glowing faintly under the flickering light. The mark tied her to the others, part of the dreadful pattern the killer had been weaving.

The smell of blood mingled with the pungent odour of death as George leaned closer, scanning Michael busted for more details. Unlike the others, this victim hadn't been sliced open. At least, not obviously. Her wedding ring—gold with a decent-sized white diamond—remained on her finger, ruling out robbery as a motive—a married woman.

George examined her head again, his stomach tightening at the jagged edges of her mutilated pocket. The skin had been torn outward, ragged and brutal, as though the weapon had been inserted and withdrawn in one swift, relentless motion. The optic nerves dangled limply toward the bridge of her delicate nose, torn as though plucked by invisible hands.

He traced his gaze across her slender frame, noting the lack of defensive wounds and the unsettling stillness of her form. His stomach churned, a strange sweetness rolling across his tongue. It wasn't hunger, not in the traditional sense. It was anger—primal, gnawing rage at the monster who had done this. The unfamiliar sensation gripped him tighter, his breath quickening as the urge to tear apart the killer swelled within him.

George tightened his grip on his pen and pad, awkwardly sketching the state of the body and its surroundings, mimicking Michael's methodical approach. He frowned as his extended claws scratched faint lines into the notebook's edge. He hadn't noticed them before, hadn't felt the shift. The realisation jolted him, and he flexed his fingers, willing the sharp tips to retract.

His attention drifted back to the victim's flame-red hair, dulled and dusted from the filthy warehouse floor. A speck of blood matted a section of the strands near her scalp, subtle but distinct. George leaned closer, his sharp eyes narrowing as he studied the tiny detail.

The killer had not left her here randomly. There was a purpose to it all—one George couldn't yet decipher.

At first, George thought the blood could be from the eye's removal, the natural drip-off from the gruesome mutilation. But as he lowered his head, peering through the strands of the victim's flame-red hair, something caught his eye. His stomach churned violently, and before he could stop himself, he gagged, a bitter taste rising in his throat.

"Michael, you need to see this," George called, his voice unsteady.

Michael spun on his heels and strode over quickly. The moment his eyes landed on the victim's head, his face twisted in disbelief. "What the hell?"

"The sick bastard," George mutters, his voice dark with anger. "They've removed the top part of her skull and brushed her hair back over it, like a sick surprise."

"But why?" Michael asks, his voice edged with frustration. "The eye's gone—that's the souvenir, right?"

George shook his head. "I don't know. Maybe they were toying with her. Or...practicing."

Michael exhaled sharply, rubbing the back of his neck. "Well, Ms. Walker's going to have her work cut out with this one."

He wasn't wrong. The scene raised more questions than answers. Where was the missing piece of her skull? What happened to her handbag? Every detail pointed to a methodical, calculated killer, but the motivations remained a chilling mystery.

George and Michael continued to scour the warehouse for clues; their movements deliberate as they combed through the dimly lit space. Outside, the towpath was now cordoned off, with four checkpoints separating the site from the public. Uniformed officers swatched their faces grim under the harsh glow of portable floodlights.

Inside, Ms Walker and Mrs Wainright worked tirelessly, their tension palpable. Walker had already snapped at a uniform for fetching the wrong evidence kits, her patience fraying with every misstep. George and Michael kept their distance, knowing better than to interrupt. Instead, they focused on the logistics: how the killer could have done this without being noticed.

Three dead bodies, each uniquely staged, and a collection of dead animals. The pattern—or lack thereof—gnawed at George. The first two victims had been paraded, their grotesque displays meant to taunt and terrify. But the third body, the oldest of the three, had been hidden, left to rot in a warehouse found purely by chance.

"Why?" George mutters to himself, his mind racing. "Why hide this one?"

It didn't add up. The incongruity made him think the killer might have been practising, refining their craft, and mastering something new. George's thoughts turned darker. Perhaps the killer had been normal once, and some event had warped them into this. A transformation he could almost—*almost*—understand.

"Ah, I'm glad you're still here," Ms Walker called out, her voice cutting through the smothering air. She emerged from the warehouse with an air of bluster, her blonde hair whipped across her sweat-slicked face, her movements sharp and hurried. We've Got two bits of information for you—and one chilling problem."

Michael smirked faintly. "What treats do you have for us this time? Have you finished touching up the body yet?"

Walker shot him a withering look but continued, "Her driver's license and what seems to be her husband's bank card were found in her pocket."

"That's a start," George says, taking a mental note. "Adds another house call to the list. Out of the three, this is the one I want to visit first. My sixth sense is tingling."

Walker raised an eyebrow, her tone sharp. "Leave out the impromptu lobotomy, Sherlock. And for my chilling problem—brace yourselves. She was alive when it happened. Paralysed."

George's stomach dropped, his pulse quickening. "What?" he asked, his voice barely above a whisper.

"The worst part," Walker continues, her voice low, "is the section of her exposed brain. It's the area that controls movement and speech. It's coated in that fluid—the toxin. And here's the kicker: its chemical compound doesn't exist on the periodic table."

The words hit like a hammer, leaving George momentarily speechless. The implications were staggering. The killer hadn't just paralysed the victim—they'd done so with something beyond the realm of known science. A substance that shouldn't exist. And the blood moon loomed ever closer.

"What on earth does that mean for our victims?" Michael asks, his voice tinged with disbelief. He looks visibly shaken and clearly out of his depth.

"It means this toxin is highly dangerous," George replies, his tone grim. "Touch it, and you're numb, completely immobilised within seconds. And we've no idea how long it takes to wear off—if it wears off at all."

He paused, his gaze hardening as he considered the implications. "I hate to say this, but I think this borders on—"

"—a critical incident," Michael finished, cutting him off. His expression darkened as the realisation hit them both. "He could wreak havoc with this, go on an endless killing spree. And I don't think he knows the peak he can hit."

They were on the same wavelength now, a damning conclusion forming between them. If no chemical composition of the toxin could be identified, it could mean one thing: *this wasn't natural.*

"Right," Michael says, shaking himself back to the task at hand. "So where's our beloved ADI?"

"No idea," Ms Walker interjected, her voice betraying a faint tremble. "We've tried raising him, and so has the main channel. All we've gotten back is that he has no scheduled meetings. Wherever he is, it's personal."

George glanced at her. The serial killings had put everyone on edge, and Walker's worry was becoming increasingly visible. Not that he could blame her—there was a growing sense that this case was slipping beyond their control.

"That's settled, then," Michael says, taking charge in Locke's absence. "Me and the 'death knell' here will head to our latest victim's home. Then we'll visit our beloved ADI—*if* he's resurfaced by then." His tone carried a hint of frustration, but his focus was unwavering. Their workload had doubled, with Locke missing, leaving no room for delay.

"What's her name?" George asks.

"Annabelle Kumar," Walker replies. "Dead a little under two weeks."

"As we suspected," Michael mutters, then adds grimly, "The next question is whether Locke's in trouble."

The car stopped, its tyres spinning slightly as they churned through the mud and rubble overflowing from a skip behind them. The street was eerily quiet, broken only by a council worker sweeping leaves and McDonald's wrappers from the curb. A neat row of parked cars lined the road, their windshields fogged from the morning chill.

"This it?" Michael asks, leaning forward in his seat.

"According to the license. Number 87 Wilmot Street," George confirmed, glancing at the unassuming house ahead.

The small front garden was bordered by a three-foot brick wall separating it from the pavement. Roses bloomed in neat clusters, their petals dewy from the cool air. The front door was painted light green, and its six glass panes gave the house a quaint, almost grandmotherly charm. It seemed incongruous with the darkness they carried into the neighbourhood.

"Right, mate," Michael says, straightening his jacket. "You've delivered death messages before, but this one differs slightly. We don't know exactly who the suspect is. So, I'll take the lead. You? Play low-key detective. Listen to the heartbeats and the changes in tone. Even if it's not likely, we have to treat the husband as a suspect. I'll give him the basics, but you quiz him like I'm—"

"—Assuming this is the right place?" George cut in, smirking faintly despite the tension.

"Exactly," Michael replies. "Granny's house or not, we're treating this by the book."

Michael knocked sharply on the door. "Knock knock."

There was no answer. He shifted his weight impatiently, tapping his foot against the concrete. George, however, could hear the faint, fluttering thud of a heartbeat inside—at least eighty feet deep in the house. The rhythm faltered with the knock, startled but steady.

Michael knocked again, harder this time. "Bang, bang."

The heartbeat raced. George felt a flash of worry. *What if they're elderly? What if we just scared them into cardiac arrest?*

"Hello? Who is it?" A man's voice, tight and uncertain, called out from behind the door.George's heightened senses picked up the rapid pace of his heart, his fear spiking like static electricity. Late twenties, early thirties, George guessed. This wasn't the sound of an elderly couple—it was someone who feared something else entirely.

"It's the police, "George called, stepping forward and holding his warrant card to the spyhole. His tone was calm, but his instincts were sharp. The man's fear was palpable, not just because of their presence. Something else was lurking behind his hesitation.

The question was: *What?*

The door creaked open slowly, revealing a frightened man with light brown skin and messy, curly black hair. His unshaven face and wary eyes suggested he was hiding from something or someone. George studied him, his mind racing to connect the dots to Annabelle's murder.

"Mr Kumar?" Michael asks, his tone calm but firm.

"Y... yes," the man stammered, his voice trembling.

"I'm DS Dalton, and this is DC Reynolds. We have something sensitive to discuss. May we come in?"

Mr Kumar's eyes darted nervously. "Have you found it?"

George exchanged a sharp glance with Michael, both equally confused. *Found it?* Mr Kumar wasn't on the same page. His wife wasn't an *it*. What could this man value more than his missing—and now murdered—wife?

Michael broke the silence, his voice steady. "I think we should come in to save the gossip merchants two doors down the trouble of staring through their twitching curtains."

"O... okay," Kumar says, stepping back to let them in. Please, come this way. Excuse the mess—my work follows me home. I'm cleaning delicate artefacts, and the old dirt gets ingrained everywhere."

The house's interior was like stepping into another era. In stark contrast to its modest, dated exterior, the space was filled with glass cabinets displaying ancient artefacts. Dust motes swirled in the air, caught in the weak light streaming through the curtains.

"Please, take a seat," Kumar gestured toward a brown sofa that looked far more comfortable than it should have in such a tense atmosphere. He remained standing, perching awkwardly on a chair by the dining table. His hands shook, and he glanced frequently at the front door.

Michael leaned forward slightly; his tone measured. "What did you think we were looking for, Mr Kumar?"

"Something extremely valuable," Kumar replies, his words tumbling out in a rush. "A relic. I'm an archaeologist at the Natural History Museum. Six months ago, I was part of a dig in Egypt. We uncovered some unique relics, most of which are in the museum. But one, in particular, was requested by our sponsors to be kept off the manifest. In exchange for two million pounds."

George raised an eyebrow. "And what happened to it?"

Kumar swallowed hard, his eyes darting toward the cabinets as though the answer were hiding there. "I brought it home, as I often do, to work on and delicately restore. Two weeks ago, I brought the box here. Arrangements had already been made to transfer it to the buyer. But when I opened the box, it was empty. Someone had already stolen it. And I'd already received the money."

Michael's voice hardened. "What exactly was this bloody relic?"

Kumar hesitated, licking his dry lips before answering. "Not much is known about it. But the information I was given—what the buyer believed—was that it's the relic holding a trapped Kanaima demon."

The words hung in the air like a curse. George felt his pulse quicken, the weight of the revelation pressing down on him.

Kumar continued his voice a mix of fear and disbelief. "I think it's just a story to bump up the sell-on price. But the buyer believed it. I sold it for more than I probably should have, and now... now I'm scared for my life. I've been searching everywhere, so I reported it missing."

George leaned back slightly, his mind racing. A missing artefact. A tale of a trapped demon. A husband is seemingly more concerned about stolen goods than his murdered wife. It wasn't a coincidence. It couldn't be.

Michael's tone grew sharper. "Let me get this straight—you lost the relic *after* receiving two million pounds, and your first instinct was to cover your owners?"

Kumar flinched, his voice rising defensively. "You don't understand! The buyer—he's dangerous. He thinks I betrayed him. If he finds it missing, I'm as good as dead."

George's gaze sharpened. "And what about Annabelle? Do you think any of this could be connected to her death?"

Kumar's face was crumpled, and guilt and fear warred in his expression. "I don't know," he admitted, his voice barely above a whisper. I loved her, but... I think she found out about the relic. She... she warned me not to bring it home."

George glanced at Michael, their unspoken understanding clear. This wasn't just a case of stolen artefacts or murder. Whatever this relic was—whatever it represented—it had unleashed something far darker than any of them were prepared for.

"Speaking of missing," Michael began, his tone soft but firm, "we need to talk about your wife."

Mr Kumarstiffened. "What about her?"

"When was the last time you saw her?"

"Two weeks," Kumar replies, his voice faltering. We... 're in the middle of a temporary separation because of my job. I was always away. Annabelle felt lonely and...strayed."

Michael's gaze didn't waver. "I have to as—wass it all one-sided? Are there any other issues she might've picked up on?"

Kumar shifted uncomfortably, his fingers fidgeting in his lap. "I may not have been present, but I stayed loyal. I was more loyal to my job, I suppose. But... why all these questions?"

Michael leaned forward slightly, his expression grave. "I'm afraid we have some bad news. A short while ago, we found the lifeless body of a woman in her late twenties. Flame red hair. Identification on her listed her as Mrs Annabelle Kumar of this address." He paused. "We're sorry for your loss."

Kumar's face became pale. His legs turned to jelly, and though he was seated, he slumped sideways as if the weight of the words had physically struck him. "H-H...how su... sure are you?"

"As sure as we can be based on ID and preliminary identification," Michael replies evenly.

"She was tall," Kumar whispers, his voice trembling. "With long legs."

"I'm afraid that matches," George says quietly.

Kumar's eyes glistened as he straightened slightly, clutching the table's edge as if it might anchor him. "When can I see her? I need to see my wife. Please."

"As soon the initial investigation at the scene is complete, arrangements will be made for you to travel to the morgue," Michael explains. "We'll arrange for a car to—"

"Scene?" Kumar interrupts, his voice climbing with panic. "What happened? How did she die?"

Michael'sexpression darkened. "I'm afraid she was murdered. There's not much else we can divulge at the moment other than this: she is the third victim we've found in twenty-four hours."

"A serial killer?"Kumar's voice broke, his fear palpable.

"Afraid so," Michael says grimly. "We'd appreciate it if you kept that detail to yourself."

Kumar nodded slowly, his face pale. "Yes, of course."

Michael shifted gears, his tone sharpening. "As for the relic, you'll need to get together all the paperwork you have on it—documents, records, anything. You'll pass it to another department in CID, and we'll need copies as well. Particularly details about—"

"I can give you the name," Kumar blurts, cutting him off. "But if they find out I've talked, they'll kill me."

The room fell silent. George exchanged a tense glance with Michael, the weight of Kumar's Confession settling heavily over them. Another death—especially tied to this case—would stretch their already fragile resources to the breaking point. George also couldn't shake the gnawing fear creeping into his thoughts: What if the demon story wasn't just a story?

"For now, we'll let that slide, Mr Kumar," Michael says finally, his voice measured. But only until our current problems are resolved. Is that clear?"

"Yes," Kumar murmurs, his voice barely audible. "But... what do I do in the meantime? They will be watching."

Michael's response was firm. "File your crime report as proof of the theft and return the money. Your focus now should be on identifying your wife's body."

George's stomach churned as he watched Kumar, a man teetering on the edge of devastation. His position wasn't one George envied, but it was one he understood all too well. The loss wouldn't fully sink in until the dust had settled, until the distractions and chaos faded, and all that remained was the weight of grief—both from the living and, George feared, from something far more unnatural.

LADIES NIGHT

8

"How many so far?"George asks, slumping into his chair with a weary sigh.

"Just this pile? Thirty-seven," Michael replies, gesturing to the stack of paperwork and the growing collection of *Ladies' Night* posters confiscated by the door-to-door officers.

"Thirty-seven posters scattered across the first two crime scenes," George mutters, running a hand through his hair. The sheer volume felt overwhelming, another breadcrumb in a trail that led nowhere definitive. The drive back from Mr Kumar's house had stirred an idea—if the killers were targeting victims through these events, cutting off their supply could force them to change their tactics. The problem was that they didn't know how many posters were still out there or if the strategy would even work. And worse, George was suspicious about who was arranging the events.

They were still steps behind, always playing catch-up. A relic linked to the Kanaima demon myth was missing, and they had no sensible way to explain it to their colleagues. George felt the weight of it all: another brush with the supernatural, another thread spiralling into the inexplicable.

To unravel it, they needed answers. Who had bankrolled the expedition that unearthed the relic? Who was desperate enough to pay two million pounds upfront? That kind of money didn't change hands lightly, especially in the current economic climate. The alarm bells in George's head were deafening.

"Well, let's turn that frown upside down," Michael says, breaking the tension. "I've got this list from Mr Kumar. He's holed up in an interview room for safety. According to DC

Cartwright, who's handling the stolen antiquities angle, if Kumarcooperates, we might nail the person who stole the relic—and the company that paid for it."

Michael handed George a thick stack of over two hundred items, each labelled *priceless.* George frowned as he scanned it. How did the two-million-pound figure come into play? It wasn't a number you threw around blindly. Someone had an inside track, and it wasn't Kumar.

"Two things," George says, glancing up. "Any word on ADI Locke? And can we find out who's liaising with Kumar for the development side of this?"

Michael smirked."Oh, there's smoke coming out of their ears. Could go either way. As for our fearless leader? Still missing in action. I've asked for a car to head over there. Road trip?"

"Exactly what I was thinking," George replies.

"That's good, then," Michael says, pulling two takeaway cups from a carrier. "I didn't fetch these for nothing."

"*Fetched?*"George raised an eyebrow.

"Okay, loose term—bought," Michael admitted with a grin. "I can only tolerate the cheap stuff here for so long, and I've got to keep you firing on all furry cylinders."

Michael had grown on George over the past few weeks. Between the coffees and the shared moments of fun, he'd become an unexpected ally in a case that felt heavier by the hour. George had just sipped his coffee when the office door swung open.

"Just the people I need to see," ADI Locke says, breezing in with his usual air of authority.

"Sir," George says, standing automatically.

"No disrespect, Guv," Michael cut in, his tone direct. "But where the hell have you been? We've been trying to raise you."

"Nice to know you care, Michael," Locke replies, brushing past them with a smirk. "But I've been busy saving you boys some leg work. I went dark for a bit to notify the partners of the first two victims and to take statements. I thought I'd give you some space to manage without me looming over you—trust and all that. I did phone the control room, so don't fret."

George glanced at Michael, both trying to read between the lines of Locke's abrupt explanation. Something about his calm, almost dismissive tone didn't sit right. But for now, there was no time to pry. They had too many unanswered questions, and a killer was still on the loose.

"Right, then," Locke continues. "Catch me up. What's our next move?"

George couldn't shake the feeling that Locke was playing a deeper game. Whether he was sincere remained unclear, but his demeanour carried an air of assessment like he was still sizing them up. The tension lingered, a heavy cloud hanging between them. Still, George had to admit Locke's efforts had saved them some leg work.

"Thanks for that," George says cautiously.

"What's the consensus?" Locke folded his arms, waiting.

"Husbands with busy jobs and unfaithful wives enjoying the freedom it brings. Rachel Darnley's husband had just returned from being away on business and hadn't even realised he was... gone." George shuddered at the thought but pressed on.

"Well, the latest—the earliest—the victim was a tester," George continues. "The killer toyed with her. Removed part of her skull, then used a paralytic agent. That seems to be the theme of all three murders."

Michael mutters a curse as Locke quickly adds his two penneth worth. "Oh, while I remember. I received the memo about a potential critical incident. Right now, I'm tentative about raising the alarm. Panic won't help us. But I've contacted neighbouring boroughs and response team duty officers to keep them in the loop. The DCI's Arranging for community volunteers to help with legwork and reassurance."

"They can start by removing these." Michael pointed to the *Ladies' Night* posters stack. The sweat beading on Locke's forehead betrayed his strain, and George noted it with quiet satisfaction. Locke might have been a smooth operator, but this case pushed him to the edge.

"A ladies' night?"Locke asks, raising an eyebrow. "You think this is how the killer targets victims?"

"It's all we've got so far," George admitted.

"Not quite all," Michael interjected. "We've got a lead. Unfortunately, it's not the kind you can explain easily."

Locke studied them both for a long moment before nodding. "Run with it. I trust you will loop me in when the need arises. I can only have your backs if I know what's happening."

The comment lingered in the air long after Locke left, his footsteps fading into the hallway. George exchanged a look with Michael, wondering *If Locke knew more than he was letting on.*

'*Cromwell Rd, South Kensington, London SW7 5BD.*'

George burned the address into his mind as he glanced out the car window. Halfway through the journey, his focus sharpened. A blacked-out Ford Granada had been trailing them for miles, maintaining a steady distance two cars back. Despite the labyrinthine mess of London traffic, it never strayed.

"Don't look now," George says, his voice low, "but I think we've got company."

Michael didn't turn but adjusted the rearview mirror slightly. "How sure?"

"Sure enough," George replies, his tone clipped. "Two occupants. They've circled the block twice now, keeping their faces hidden."

Michael frowned. "Think they're after the relic?"

"Could be," George admitted. "We can't afford to linger longer than necessary. I'll feel better once we're back on home turf... in case there's another."

"You think there'll be another?" Michael asks, his voice quieter than usual. It wasn't rhetorical—there was a raw edge to the question as if he was seeking reassurance or perhaps bracing himself for the answer.

George's gaze stayed fixed on the side mirror, tracking Ford's movements. "Honestly? My heart hopes there won't be, but my head says otherwise."

The car crawled through traffic, Michael guiding them toward their destination while George kept watch. Every glance over Michael's shoulder confirmed the Ford was still there, doggedly keeping pace. The knot of tension in George's stomach tightened.

"Office over there," Michael says, nodding to the right. His voice is tense. And yeah, our shadows are still with us."

George's pulse quickened as the car eased into a parking spot. They had work to do, but first, they had to figure out what—or who—was waiting for them outside their sightlines.

"I bet they don't know we're police. They probably saw us turn up at Mr Kumar's place, putting two and two together and coming up with twenty, thinking we've done a deal for the relic on the side for more money."

"Michael, I agree. For the life of me, I can't figure out how these pieces fit. Other than the relic is real and dangerous. The demon has possessed or changed whoever has its hands on it."

"For fuck's sake. And they're going around killing women."

"Yep, so we need to piece together a trail—from the expedition to when it vanished—and figure out exactly what this demon is capable of," George said, his voice clipped."Preferably before another murder."

As they approached the museum office, George noticed two middle-aged men standing near the entrance. Both looked flushed, their faces tight with stress, engaged in what appeared to be a heated conversation.

"Excuse me," George interrupted, stepping forward. "We're looking to speak to someone in charge of a recent expedition to Egypt. This museum took possession of nearly two hundred artefacts, correct?"

The men froze mid-conversation, their expressions shifting to startled *rabbits in headlights*. They exchanged uneasy glances, each seemingly hoping the other would take responsibility.

"Who's asking?" one of them ventured.

The speaker was tall and gangly, his grey hair neatly swept back. In his fifties, he wore a sharp black suit and carried himself with an air of authority—until he caught sight of the warrant cards in George and Michael's hands.

"I'm DS Dalton, "George said, holding his badge. This is DC Reynolds. We're with the murder task force."

"M... murder?" the man stammered, his well-spoken tone faltering as his composure cracked.

"Yes," George said bluntly. "First, we need to discuss an excursion involving Mr. Kumar."

"Um... please, come this way," the man said, his name badge reading *Nigel Bentley*. His trembling hand gestured toward the back, his heart hammering audibly in George's enhanced ears. He was perilously close to hyperventilating.

As they followed Bentley, George listened closely, isolating footsteps and breathing patterns beyond the immediate conversation. People were pacing back and forth in nearby rooms, darting between desks and whispering in low voices. The erratic energy was unmistakable—this museum had more to hide than a missing relic.

Bentley led them into a backroom that could generously be described as *organized chaos.* Dusty relics lined shelves, travel crates were stacked precariously, and paperwork spilt across every available surface.

"Mr. Bentley, do you recognize this list?" Michael asked, handing him the inventory provided by Mr. Kumar.

Bentley retrieved a pair of black-framed glasses from his jacket pocket and perched them on the edge of his nose. "Sadly, yes," he said after a pause.

"What's sad about it?" George asked.

"The expedition was chaos from the beginning," Bentley replied, his voice steady but tense. People were chopping and changing who was going, and logistics were falling apart. And then there were the injuries."

"Injuries?" Michael prompted, his brow furrowing.

Bentley nodded grimly. "We don't know why. These were highly skilled people—hundreds of digs between them. But no sooner had the first relics been uncovered than the problems began."

"How bad did it get?" George asked.

"Well... we learned today one died. Louisa Sidwell stayed behind in Egypt to be treated for broken ribs. She died of a sudden heart attack. Mrs. Sidwell was only 28."

George's jaw tightened. "How does that even happen? And you said *Mrs.*—I take it she was married?"

"In a manner of speaking," Bentley said, his tone growing more guarded. "From what I understand, they were like passing ships in the night. She was often away on digs, and her husband worked nights on the trains."

Bentley's demeanour seemed calm, his speaking pace and heartbeat steady as he relayed the troubling details. But the shift came when Michael pressed further.

"The list," Michael said, his tone firmer. "Is anything missing?"

Bentley adjusted his glasses, his fingers trembling slightly. "I... I... don't believe so. No," he stammered, his pitch rising noticeably.

"We urge you to look closely," Michael said, his eyes narrowing. "We have information that says otherwise."

Sweat began to lay on Bentley's forehead, his heart racing as he scanned the list again. "I...I... I am very..." His voice trailed off as he grabbed a blank sheet of paper.

George exchanged a sharp glance with Michael. Bentley's sudden shift was suspicious—panicked, even.

"Mr. Bentley," George said evenly, "we urge you to be sure."

Bentley didn't answer. Instead, his hand shook as he scribbled something quickly on the paper. When he finished, he handed it to Michael with a trembling hand.

Michael glanced at the note, his expression darkening as he turned it so George could see.

"I can't; they're listening."

Bentley's eyes darted around the room, paranoia etched across his face. George didn't need his heightened senses to tell that the man believed he was being watched—or bugged.

"We're here to determine if the story surrounding a particular item could be true," Georges said, watching Mr. Bentley scribbling furiously on a sheet of paper.

After a moment, Bentley slid the note across the table.

"Yes. Two are," it read.

Bentley reached for a dusty book on a nearby shelf, carefully tearing out a page. He handed it over, his hands trembling slightly.

George scanned the text, his eyes narrowing as the story unfolded:

*"Kanaima, the demon of vengeance. For centuries, it has been trapped in a relic designed to mirror its image and hidden, hoping it will never be uncovered again. It can only be released through fragments of its heart encased in a gemstone slotted in the relic's base.

They will attack and kill their victims in retaliation for some injustice. They are a human/lizard-like creature. Some say they are like the werewolf, but instead of seeking a pack, they seek a master. Once the master gains their trust, he can make them kill or harm anyone and anything. Their paralytic toxin, delivered through their claws, can immobilize a victim within seconds.

Kanaima tracks its victims to any location where they may flee or hide. An interesting aspect of the Kanaima is that it seeks the painful suffering of its victims, never killing outright. Instead, the Kanaima ensures a slow and agonizing death three days after its attack. During this process, it slashes its victim's tongue to prevent them from speaking about what is happening.

Besides killing, the Kanaima finds satisfaction in consuming its victims' pineal glands. This act enhances the potency of its toxins, functioning as an aphrodisiac. Kanaima is also prone to collecting souvenirs and mementoes to please its master.

Kanaima possesses supernatural powers, including shape-shifting and the ability to inhabit animal and human bodies. It is believed to drive people insane with a single look.

Weakness: When the Kanaima is not in control, the human half is susceptible to its venom."*

George lowered the page, his brow furrowed. "How real is this?"

Bentley swallowed hard and wrote a single word: *"Very."*

"These relics," George pressed. "Have they been uncovered?"

Bentley nodded, his gaze darting nervously around the room.

"How many staff were involved in this expedition?" Michael asked, breaking the silence.

"Upwards of seventy," Bentley replied quietly.

"Can you provide us with a list of names? Mark who is injured and who is dead."

"Yes," Bentley said, his voice shaking as he retrieved a folder and began leafing through its contents. His hands trembled so badly that papers slipped from his grip.

George leaned forward, his tone softening. "Mr. Bentley, who is threatening you?"

Bentley froze, his sweaty forehead glistening in the dim light. His hand hovered over the paper, his pen quivering as he wrote: *"I can't. They will know. They threaten my family."*

George exchanged a grim glance with Michael. They had the root of Bentley's fear, but it tied their hands. Moving forward without jeopardizing innocent lives was a precarious balancing act.

George slid a business card across the table. "If you find yourself in trouble, call this number," he said, his voice low but firm.

Bentley hesitated before pocketing the card. "Different question," George said, redirecting the conversation. "Have you ever heard of the myths relating to werewolves?"

Bentley blinked, momentarily startled by the shift. "Myth deemed fiction," he began, slightly steadying, "but most definitely a fact. The stories return to the ancient gods who created a relic to make the shift between forms painless. No broken bones."

"Has this relic been found?"

"Yes," Bentley admitted. "We used to have it. But it was stolen ten years ago during a burglary."

"Any idea who might have taken it?"

Bentley shook his head. "Not at the moment, but I can ask around. If it's surfaced on any black markets, someone will know."

As Bentley checked off names on a list, George tuned out the sounds of paper shuffling, focusing instead on the subtle vibrations of the building. Those footsteps—the ones he'd heard earlier—were gone now. The lack of movement was unnerving.

Had the eavesdroppers left? Or were they hiding?

George's instincts prickled. Something wasn't right.

DELIVERY

9

George commandeered the conference room, shutting the door behind him. A jug of cheap coffee sat untouched on the side, its faintly burnt aroma mingling with the tension in the air. On the table, fifteen crime scene photos lay in a grim cluster. Across the room, a whiteboard bore hastily scribbled notes about the ancient relic, the list of names provided by Mr Bentley, and an inventory of the recovered artefacts.

Bentley had been terrified, his fear palpable and genuine. He claimed people were listening and threatening his family if he revealed too much. George believed him. Whoever had been following Bentley's office movements had likely been the same shadowy figures tailing George and Michael to the museum. But by the time they'd left, their pursuers had vanished.

George suspected the culprits believed he and Michael were buyers, assuming Mr Kumar had brokered a secret deal behind their backs. The identity of the financier-buyer remained elusive, but George had a strong suspicion: the Whitlocks. The same name had surfaced more than once, a thread tying itself to the deeper mystery of this case. And then there was the unresolved question of who had George's blood. *Conrad* had boasted about selling it to a collector, but the trial had gone cold.

Seventy-eight names adorned the cursed expedition's list—two dead, fifteen injured. An undeniable connection threaded through it all, one pointing toward a demon. But how could they present that to the public? The words supernatural shapeshifter and *revenge mission* didn't fit neatly into an evidence report.

Michael had gone to collect lab results on the victim's blood. The toxin, already known to be paralytic, was unlike anything on the periodic table—a fact that firmly anchored George's thoughts in the "Kanaima" corner. They needed to know how much toxin was required to paralyse someone who was wielding it and how the murders connected—souvenirs—eyes, tongues, even an ear sent to Michael; pointed to a ritualistic element.

George couldn't ignore the dark possibility: the creature was likely already hunting its next victim, or worse, the next victim might already be in its grasp.

He worked methodically, dividing the names into male and female groups. There were far too many to visit in person. Fortunately, the list included addresses and contact numbers. He played a hunch, marking each location on a map and noting their proximity to bodies of water. It was uncanny—all three victims had been found near canals. "

"Knock, knock,"

"Come in," George called, his attention still on the map.

Michael stepped inside, glancing around at the organised chaos. "Making a bit of a mess there, George."

George smirked faintly. "How are the lab results?"

Michael leaned against the doorframe. "The dribble by the ear hole on victim number two? One hundred times more lethal than standard Lidocaine. Imagine that—a paralytic agent that strong."

George let out a low whistle. "That confirms it. What about you? What's in the box?"

Michael held up a small square package. "This just arrived. 'FAO Murder Task Force.' Do you have any ideas?"

George frowned. "Not a clue Locke's vanished again, so we should open it, right?."

Michael placed the box on a spare chair, and maps and files occupied the tab. "It doesn't look like fan mail," he says dryly, ripping one side open.

"Stop!" George shouts, rising abruptly. His nostrils flare, catching the unmistakable scent of fresh and potent blood. "What's wrong?" Michael freezes, glaring at the box. George's stomach knots as the overwhelming scent grows stronger. "There's blood," he says, his voice tight. "Fresh blood."

Michael grimaced but braced himself, his hand hovering over the box. "You're sure?"

George didn't respond immediately, his body stiffening as the sensation crept over him. His claws threatened to extend, and his vision drifted hazily with a foggy red glaze. He clenched his fists, willing the transformation to subside. The freshness of the blood wasn't just a smell—it was a *pull*.

Michael noticed the shift in George's demeanour, his eyes narrowing. "Georgie, you, okay?"

George gritted his teeth. "Open it carefully. Whatever's inside is bad."

Michael nodded, his face set with grim determination. Slowly, he peeled back the cardboard flap, exposing the contents. George's stomach churned as the scent intensified, and the air around them was thick with dread.

What was in that box wasn't just a message but a warning ".

"Georgie, quick! Control yourself—your face, you're shifting," Michael snaps, his voice cutting through the tension like a blade.

George blinked, the foggy red glaze retreating from his eyes as he forced the claws to retract. His breathing steadied, and the primal pull subsided, but the potent, thick, and overpowering smell of blood lingered in the air. Michael watched him warily for a moment before turning back to the box.

With a gloved hand, Michael gripped the polystyrene lid. Adam's apple bobbed as he swallowed, a flicker of apprehension crossing his face. The blood-smeared words on the lid—Stay Away—were stark and deliberate, their warning impossible to ignore.

The lid slid off with a squeak, releasing a trapped rush of iron-saturated air. George instinctively stepped back, but the smell hit him like a freight train. They both gasped in unison.

Inside was the severed head of Mr Bentley.

Michael recoiled, George's stomach twisted, caught in a grotesque tug-of-war between bile and an unnatural, gnawing hunger. Bentley's wide, terrified eyes stared upward, his mouth frozen mid-scream. His nose, ears, tongue, and teeth were still intact, each feature painstakingly preserved as though to send a message: that wasn't the work of the Kanaima or its master. This was a warning.

The words on the box burned George's mind. *Stay Away.* Whoever was behind this wasn't just watching—they were ready to silence anyone who dared to help.

6 :00 PM

"So, let me get this straight—you think this all started in Egypt?" ADI Locke leaned back in his chair, one foot propped on the corner of his desk. His gaze flicked between George and Michael to the whiteboard behind them, covered in crime scene photos and notes connecting the victims.

"That's the working theory, Guv," Michael replies cautiously. Locke's sharp eyes turned to George. "You've been quiet, Georgie. What's on your mind?" George's thoughts churned as he pieced through the chaos involving Bentley's head, which had been sent to forensics, hoping that something could be gleaned from the savagery. But George had already noticed a faint fingerprint smeared along the blood on the lid. A mistake? No. This wasn't amateur hour. Whoever did this wanted them to see it, to chase ghost ".

"Shir," George began, choosing his words carefully. "Bentley spoke to us just hours before he was killed. He told us they uncovered a relic in Egypt that they believed could alter human behaviour. He said the story involved demons and that they used a paralytic substance to render their victims helpless. It might sound far-fetched, but every victim we've seen was immobilised before being slowly killed."

Michael kicked George's foot under the table, a subtle warning to rein it in. But George continued, bending the truth just enough to make Locke think without pushing him over the edge.

"The toxicology report confirmed a substance with an incredibly high paralytic concentration," George adds. "Nothing on the periodic table. And I've got someone mapping addresses for you. So far, we've identified twenty-five locations near or in neighbouring boroughs, but seven are near canals."

"Seven," Locke mutters, rubbing his chin. "Better than twenty-five, but still too many. What about the 'Ladies' Night' angle?"

Michael stepped in. "Forty-eight more posters were collected. The last event was near the first crime scene at The Palm Tree. People call a number on the poster and are told where to meet."

"Whose number?" Locke asks sharply.

"A payphone," Michael replies. George's mind raced. A payphone? That wasn't random. It was deliberate—a controlled point of contact. The hamster wheel in his brain spun wildly, and a chilling thought surfaced. The pay phone wasn't just for setting up meetings—it was a trap—a place for the Kanaima to hunt.

"Is that the only location?" Locke asks, tracing the canal system on a smaller map.

"That we know of," George says. "But we're waiting on more legwork to confirm."

"Okay. For now, please get some rest. It's been a quick turnaround, and we're still paddling in the calm before the storm. Unless another victim drops, the others can carry the load for a bit tomorrow night. I need you two sharp."

Rest. George almost scoffs at the word. How could he rest with Bentley's mutilated head and the stark warning playing on a loop in his mind? They had a serial killer out there. There were too many moving parts and obstacles, and they were no closer to closing in.

GUNMAKER WAREHOUSE

10

The dark swirls of clouds chopped and bounced with the wind, rippling the full moon's light. George's blood simmered as he walked along the canal, the pathway stretching between the crime scenes. He knew he should head home and take the rest Locke had recommended, but who was he kidding? What good would sleeping do? With Halloween mere days away and the blood moon creeping closer, everything felt too fragile, too dangerous. If what the late Mr Bentley had revealed was true, George might be one of the few capable of confronting it.

Fireworks cracked and boomed in the distance, painting the night sky in bursts of therapeutic colour. They were coming from the estates behind the Gunmaker warehouse. The sounds and fleeting lights made George pause and stare, the fleeting beauty a momentary distraction. Louder bangs followed from a smaller group, likely those who had snuck into the park after hours. George exhaled, his warm breath clouding the chilly air as the acrid scent of burning filled his nostrils. It was nostalgic, almost comforting—a reminder of winter's approach. For once, he was grateful the smell wasn't burnt flesh.

Continuing his path along the canal, George couldn't help but wonder if Michael was as restless as he was. Michael's sanctuary had been invaded; he'd received a gruesome "present" in a box. George could relate to the violation, and the thought lingered as he reached the first bridge.

Even in the dark, George could make out the holes in the stone roof. He crouched by the water, studying the area, replaying the events in his mind like a worn VHS tape. Every detail from the previous night seemed burned into his memory. He pictured the scene—the poor girl suspended there—and tried to determine if one person could have hoisted her alone. His thoughts drifted to ADI Locke. If the timelines had been accurate, Locke and the man in the hoodie would have been nearby, and they matched the suspect's description.

George frowned. The man in the hoodie had initially seemed like the suspect, but now he wasn't sure. Would the master be involved in the hunt, or was this all part of a well-planned game? Marcia had mentioned green eyes—a detail that stuck with him. Could the master exhibit that trait, too, signalling some bond with the Kanaima? There was too much they didn't know, too many fragments scattered across the case like pieces from a cursed puzzle.

George's hackles rippled against the burnt breeze as a creeping sensation of being watched settled over him. The world seemed to grow quieter, unnaturally so. The edginess of the full moon wasn't helping, amplifying every sound and sensation. He flexed his hands instinctively, wincing as claws slid forward, sharp and unbidden. Blood dripped from his fingertips onto the canal's edge, the metallic tang wafting upward.

Fangs followed, and a red haze tinged his vision. George gritted his teeth. He had never fully "cut loose," never let the other part of him take control. He wasn't ready—not yet. But in three days, under the blood moon, he might not have a choice. According to Conrad's twisted stories, Halloween could mark his full transformation—a *demon wolf*.

The thought brought him back to the present. The red glow in his vision sharpened, highlighting small patches on the ground—streaks and drops standing out in faint contrast. George crouched lower, studying the area. The marks formed a staggered pattern close to the wall, leading toward the steps. Across the water, more faint traces mirrored the same path, clinging to the ledge near the canal's edge. Footsteps. The lines were faint, but the rain had held off today, and last night's drizzle hadn't been enough to wash them away.

George's hackles ruffled like a belly dancer's shimmy, his instincts on high alert. Someone's eyes were on him. He felt the heat prickling at the back of his neck, his claws refusing to retract. He scanned the area, listening for the rhythm of heartbeats. Excited, erratic pulses filled the air, masking the possibility of someone nearby. Laughter soon broke the silence, echoing from the group inside the park as they played with fireworks.

He exhaled sharply, the tension loosening but not disappearing. *Kids with fireworks*, he thought grimly. He still didn't understand the appeal.

George edged closer to the wall, keeping his guard up. Whoever or whatever had taken an interest in him wouldn't reveal itself tonight—not yet. But he didn't have time to dwell. He needed to find the missing pieces of this puzzle, to connect the dots before Halloween came and everything unravelled.

George shook his head at the distant pops and bursts of fireworks, the fascination utterly lost on him. *Fireworks,* he thought, *were the ultimate waste of money.* Once a rarity, they'd become an all-year-round nuisance. Kids sneaked into parks with boxes of the stuff, trading a quick bang and a few seconds of fleeting fun for twenty quid up in smoke. The futility of it all grated on him, though perhaps the futility of everything lately was grating.

He crouched near the first pattern, embedded in the rough ground. The impression was faint but deliberate—lines that could match the tread of a shoe. Dust clung stubbornly to the pressed dirt, not quite sawdust but something close, heavy enough to resist the breeze, fine enough to go unnoticed. George leaned closer, inhaling deeply to push past the acrid smell of spent fireworks and the metallic bite of frost in the air. The scent struck him as familiar—aged, ancient even—but the why eluded him. The memory teased the edges of his mind, an itch just out of reach. *Why do I know this smell?*

Curiosity tugged at him as he slipped an evidence bag from his pocket. The habit was new—borrowed from Michael's playbook—but effective. He scooped a small amount of the dust into the bag using a claw, sealing it tight. Maybe Mrs Wainright could determine its composition. Maybe it would come back as nothing of note. But George was certain he'd encountered it recently. The thought lingered like a nagging whisper as he jammed the bag into his pocket.

The rustling came next, faint but distinct, near the bushes weaving in and out of the park fence line. George instinctively turned, scanning for the telltale glint of fox eyes. None. His ears pricked slightly as he focused, picking up the steady thrum of a heartbeat amidst the faint sounds of the night. He was on edge, his claws extended as he stepped under the bridge and onto the other side, heading toward the second crime scene.

A twig snapped behind him, sharp against the frost-hardened ground. His body tensed, hackles rippling as he turned his head, his senses on high alert. The sound sent his thoughts spinning—whether predator or prey. There was something nearby. The claws stayed out as he continued forward, every step measured. The water beside him, dark and slow-moving, was the least of his concerns.

Then he noticed—a moored boat near the bank. His vision caught the faint shimmer of green and red paint, muted in the low amber glow of a small light inside, visible through the middle of three windows. The boat sat still, its reflection barely rippling in the icy water. The temperature had plunged, and the cold was through his coat. Part of him was tempted to knock on the boat's door to meet whoever had braved such a life. But curiosity warred with caution; he didn't have time to indulge in idle chats.

The snapping of twigs behind him continued, and we were closer now. The frost-crusted grass crunched with every deliberate and unhurried step. George stilled, his focus splitting between the steady heartbeat and the noise. His common sense screamed at him to *keep walking,* to let it go, to move. But the swirling questions in his mind demanded otherwise. They urged him forward, pushing him to take advantage of the opportunity to gather information, no matter the risk.

He stepped closer to the boat, his left foot brushing dangerously close to the water's edge. A small cascade of loose stone and shingle tumbled into the canal, disappearing with faint splashes. He reached out instinctively, balancing himself, his hand hovering in the icy air.

"What ya doing, Georgie?"

The voice cut through the night, freezing him in place. His hand hung midair as the crunch of grass signalled the speaker's approach.

"Michael?" George's voice was tight, equal parts relief and exasperation.

Michael emerged from the shadows, his breath clouding the frosty air. "Couldn't give in either, I see?"

George let out a breath, lowering his hand. "Guess not."

Michael smirked faintly, glancing toward the boat. "You've got that look again. What'd you find?"

George straightened, and the tension in his shoulders was eased slightly. "Not sure yet. But whatever it is... it's close."

"No," George replies, his tone thoughtful. "I needed a second look. A chance to work things out in my head. That information from the museum—it's stuck with me."

"In what way?" Michael asks, his cigarette glowing faintly in the darkness.

"If it's true, and the killer has a master... which one did I see last night?" George's voice dropped, laced with uncertainty.

"Beats me." Michael exhaled a cloud of smoke, his eyes narrowing. "I wanted to revisit everything for inspiration. We've got Mr Kumar, the archaeologist who uncovers a relic linked to a Kanaima demon. He agrees to sell it on the side but finds the box empty. Convenient, huh?"

The light on the boat flickered out, pulling George's attention momentarily. Michael's appearance had distracted him earlier, but they both needed to work through the facts. They continued walking, the rhythmic clipping of their shoes the only sound as the night settled around them. George's claws were retracted, though his hackles were still uneasy.

"That's just it, Michael. I'm not sure I believe Kumar's story," George admitted. "Someone pays two million pounds upfront, and you just 'lose' the relic? No chance. Not unless you've got other plans for it."

Michael smirked, dragging deeply on his cigarette. "Georgie, are you suggesting money is the root of all evil?" He chuckles, exhaling spirals of smoke into the black air.

"Not quite, but it's suspect," George says, his tone firm. "He cared more about the relic than about his wife's death. Barely registered when we told him she was gone. At the very least, he's screwed someone over. Probably badly."

The air grew heavier as Michael fell silent, his thoughts churning audibly in the quiet. The fireworks had fizzled out, leaving the streets eerily calm. The only sounds were their shoes clipping against the pavement. George glanced back at the darkened boat, a nagging sensation gnawing at him. *Did I miss something?*

Michael finally broke the silence. "Matey, if I had a quid for every time someone got screwed over, I'd be a millionaire, too. But you're asking the right questions. Where is it now? And how does it fit?"

"What if it's still with Kumar?" George asks, pulling the evidence bag from his pocket and handing it to Michael. "Oh, and I found this."

Michael raised an eyebrow, his expression caught somewhere between confusion and amusement. "What've you been doing, Georgie? Late-night walks to collect random crap off the streets?" His grin faded as George's serious expression told him otherwise.

"It's the little things," George replies, his tone steady. "The things we overlook make the biggest difference. We've learned that the hard way."

Michael opened the bag and sniffed its contents cautiously. He recoiled slightly, his face contorted with recognition but with no clarity. "What is that smell?" he asks, exhaling sharply. "It's familiar, but I can't place it."

"Exactly how I felt," George says. "I found it by the bridge—amongst the grass, close to the wall. There's a similar pattern on the opposite side. It's not mud, not regular dust, and it's not naturally occurring."

Michael looked back toward the bridge and then down the canal in the direction they'd come from. The gears in his mind turned visibly, and the realisation dawned in his eyes.

"You think someone was watching the crime scene?" he asks.

"That's my guess," George replies. "The pattern follows a trail—places where someone might have stood or crouched. They were careful, though. Whatever this stuff is, it was left by accident."

Michael's gaze darkened as he glanced toward the shadowed bridge. "So, whoever it was, they've been watching. Either us, the scenes, or both."

"And they're leaving more than footprints behind," George muttered. His voice carried an edge now, the realisation sharpening his focus. *Someone was there, and they wanted to be noticed—just enough.*

"Not just the scene?" Michael asks, his voice low.

"Us," George replies. "And the Kanaima."

Michael raised an eyebrow, his scepticism clear. "Oh, you're jumping feet first into the supernatural angle now?"

George flicked his wrist, his claws sliding out with ease. "If I have these," he says, gesturing to the sharp tips, "and everything else that's coming... anything is possible. Trouble is proving it."

Michael flinched slightly, leaning back momentarily as he adjusted to the sight. George didn't blame him; he wasn't entirely used to it.

"So, what more do you want to find?" Michael asks, recovering quickly.

"More of the same," George says, eyes scanning the ground. "If we can find more of this stuff—here and near today's body—we might have a connection."

Michael shook his head, exhaling a long breath as he reached for another cigarette. The previous one still smouldered on the ground. "Hey, still not giving up?" George quips.

"Matey, I did a week," Michael says defensively, lighting the cigarette with a flick of his lighter. "If I'm willing to walk around in the dark with you when I'd rather be asleep, you can forgive my vices."

George rolled his eyes as the pungent smoke wafted into the cold air. Every exhale felt like a hundred, thick and smothering. He turned his focus back to the holes in the wall, each marked by trickles of dried blood. With his enhanced vision, the outline of the second body stood out starkly, inverted like a grotesque stigma.

"If the victims were paralysed," George muses, his voice quieter now, "I wonder how long it took them to die."

Then it came—the whisper, cold and sharp, cutting through the night like a blade. *Please help us.*

A sharp breeze curled along the canal. George turned, his eyes scanning the black water, and froze. He saw them—four ghostly figures lined up in eerie silence—Tracey, Rachel, Annabelle, and now Mr Bentley, holding his severed head.

The water rippled through their translucent forms, distorting them momentarily before they reappeared, their gazes locked on George. The weight of their silent plea pressed against his chest. They didn't deserve this, any of it. Trapped in the cruel aftermath of their deaths, they begged for help. Could he even grant them that? Help them find peace after their bodies have already been dissected. For evidence?

"Georgie?" Michael's voice broke through the trance. "You okay, matey? Seeing them again?"

George blinked, his throat tightening. "Mr Bentley's there too now," he says quietly. "Holding his head. We still need to find out who did that... who sent it to us."

Michael's expression softened, pity flashing across his face. It struck George as ironic. *He feels sorry for me because I see them, but at least I'm still alive.*

George shifted his focus, his eyes catching movement beyond the ghosts. "There's more," he snaps.

"More what? Ghosts?" Michael asks, his voice tense.

"No," George says, stepping closer to the canal's edge. "That stuff. There's a path tucked beside the bridge support."

Michael followed George's line of sight, cigarette in one hand, the other buried in his coat pocket. His trust in George was far beyond George's experience but shone through as his gaze followed the direction George pointed. George moved further along the wall, his sharp eyes scanning every inch. Something caught his attention near the steps, just inside the park perimeter.

"There's more over there," George mutters, his voice tightening with curiosity. The faint traces of the strange substance linger along the fence line, barely visible in the weak light. Whoever left it had been careful, but not enough.

"We need to get this analysed," George says, his jaw set. "See if it holds any secrets."

Michael smirked, though his expression held a faint edge of fatigue. "Matey, we can't rule out that it's just a pile of shit. Not being on the *period table* doesn't make it supernatural."

"*Periodic table,* Michael," George corrected, shaking his head.

"Yeah, that's the one." Michael stubbed his cigarette on the wall, brushing ash from his fingers. "Right. Is your curiosity satisfied now?"

"A little," George admitted. "One more place for the full set. Then we're done for the night."

Michael groans, letting his head fall back dramatically. "Great," he mutters. "Let me guess—back to the warehouse?"

George nodded. "If we find it there too, that connects all three scenes."

Michael sighs heavily, the lines on his face deepening as he resigns to another long walk. "Fine. But you're buying the coffee next time."

COINCIDENCES

11

The roads lay barren, bathed in the eerie glow of streetlights reflecting off the glistening pavement. The temperature had plunged sharply, and George sought the solace of his car just in time. The journey back from the warehouse was silent, punctuated only by the occasional hum of the tyres against the wet asphalt. He'd carefully avoided the outskirts of the lake, steering clear of where the lifeless animals lay. The distance wasn't just for comfort; it was deliberate. George wasn't chasing shadows—this time, the pieces seemed to fall into place, a blind shot in the dark yielding the first real chance to gain ground.

A part of him had longed for home, a fleeting comfort in the chaos. The abrupt turn of events, the gruesome discovery of two bodies for the price of one, had been far from pleasant. But the night's shocker wasn't among the unearthed secrets—it was Michael's unexpected presence. It had made George question whether he was being trailed, and the thought lingered even now.

Safely behind the wheel, the unease didn't fade. It followed him, a looming shadow that felt almost tangible. His claws tapped rhythmically against the steering wheel, the moonlight glinting off their sharp edges. His foot pressed harder on the accelerator as if he could outrun the unseen—or perhaps his paranoia.

The car raced down Bow Road, past the train station, before George turned left onto Mornington Grove. It wasn't home—just a temporary move closer to work. He'd sold the flat; too much baggage there, too many reminders of Helen. Her memory lingered like a ghost, haunting the walls where she and the baby had met their end. *Conrad* had left his mark, too, bugging every inch of George's life, listening in on every whispered conversation. The flat was a scar he couldn't bear to keep.

Now, he rented a modest three-bedroom house from a colleague. It wasn't much, but it was enough. End of a terrace, sturdy and quiet neighbours who left him in peace. A semi-fresh start. As he pulled up outside, exhaustion washed over him, and the thought of collapsing into bed was the only comfort he could cling to. At least here, he thought, it would be difficult for anyone to sneak up on him.

Yet the nagging feeling of being watched refused to leave. George glanced over his shoulder, his sharp senses on high alert, but the street lay still. A set of headlights appeared in the distance, the brightness carving through the shadows, and his grip on the wheel tightened. This case had him tightly coiled; his nerves frayed, haunted not just by ghosts but by the expectation that they might someday materialise on his doorstep.

The distant melody of blue lights reached his ears, faint over the muted buzz of London traffic. George stepped out of the car, the bitter wind stinging his face. Now, the car carried only the acrid scent of petrol—at least there was no blood. The thought wasn't comforting.

He approached the gate leading to his front door, his instincts prickling with unease. A glance left and right revealed nothing out of place, yet the feeling persisted. As he reached the wall near the side road, something caught his eye—a box neatly placed on the brown mat in front of his door.

An A4-sized, thin package adorned with a red ribbon.

George froze; his breath caught in his chest. Every sound around him seemed amplified—the rustle of leaves, the faint shuffle of a cat darting under a parked car. His senses screamed caution, every nerve on edge. The box didn't belong there. No one should know this address, not even Skip. Only Michael. And George hadn't ordered.

Caught between instincts, George hesitated. *Report it or open it?* The thought circled in his mind, but neither option felt safe. The ribbon fluttered slightly in the breeze, its crimson hue stark against the darkness.

George's claws flexed involuntarily, his mind racing. Whatever this was, it wasn't innocent.

The memory of the severed ears Michael received echoes in George's mind, refusing to be silenced. *Is this going to be one of those situations?* The thought gripped him tightly as his eyes scanned the street, his instincts on high alert.

In the distance, two hundred feet away, something caught his eye—a faint amber spark in the shadows. It glowed behind a white Fiesta, the unmistakable ember of a cigarette, its brightness intensifying with every drag. A thin plume of smoke drifted past the car's roof, curling in the crisp night air. The sharp and acrid scent reached George's heightened senses, making his hackles rise. His sixth sense screamed at him, a silent alarm going haywire.

Have they delivered the parcel and stayed behind to gauge my reaction?

Unconsciously, George's claws extended, his fangs creeping out as his body responded to the unseen threat. He crouched low, his instincts pulling him forward. Curiosity, coupled with a growing unease, pushed him to investigate. He moved slowly, retreating from the parcel and sneaking toward the shadowy figure. Staying low, he used the cover of parked cars and the nearside pillar line, keeping himself out of sight.

As he closed the distance, he counted three car lengths between himself and the Fiesta. Then, with a sudden roar, an engine sprang to life. A dark Audi sat just beyond the Fiesta, its windows too tinted to discern the occupants even with the glow of the cigarette. George's grip tightened around his warrant card, though he knew it would be useless now. He darted forward, heart pounding, but the Audi screeched into action.

The wheels spun furiously, churning rubber against the asphalt before the car sped off. George's sharp eyes caught a glaring omission: *no license plates.* His claws dug into his palms as the engine's roar faded into the distance, swallowed by the night. Whoever was in that car, their presence here was no coincidence.

George stood motionless for a moment, scanning the street for anything else out of place. Nothing stood out. The air was still, save for the lingering smell of burnt rubber and cigarette smoke. Frustration simmered beneath his skin as he turned back toward the parcel on his doorstep.

The package was light—far too light to contain anything metallic, like the makings of a bomb. No stamps, no postage, no address. It had been placed deliberately, with purpose. George's claws twitched as he debated whether to open it. The idea gnawed at him, but he pushed it aside. *Please don't give them the satisfaction.*

No. He wouldn't let whoever had left it see his anxiety. This was their game, but he wouldn't play it on their terms. He would wait. The box would be checked thoroughly at work, where Locke's watchful eye could provide some protection. For now, George resolved to leave the parcel untouched, its secrets locked away for another day.

As he stepped inside, the lingering scent of smoke clung to him, a reminder that someone had been watching—and might still be.

OFF LIMITS

12

'2 pm 28th October.'

T he door groaned open, its creak cutting through the chaotic din inside. It strained as much as George felt he was, the sound crawling up his spine like an unwelcome wake-up call. Radios blared, overlapping voices created a cacophony of disjointed conversation, and cigarettes' faint but pervasive scent clung to the air. The office felt like a carnival gone wrong—frenetic yet slow, its chaos blending everything and nothing into a dizzying haze. George wasn't ready for another day like the ones before.

His shoulder slipped off the doorframe as he dragged himself inside, balancing two flat whites in one hand and a mysterious box in the other. He cradled the package as it might shatter, its red ribbon tied tightly around secrets he wasn't sure he wanted to uncover. He loved surprises in another life, but not now. Not this.

Sleep had been elusive the night before. The box sat on his table like a lurking ghost, daring him to open it. He had resisted for hours, fighting the growing itch to untie the ribbon. The temptation felt like Michael's smoking habit—one George had mocked but now understood. When the tension became unbearable, he gave in—not to the box, but to a bottle. Dinner was forgotten, and he drowned his anxiety with a drink, staring at the box as if it might blink back. Oddly, The ribbon looked familiar, and George's mind raced with possibilities. Was it connected to the scroll? Or was that a coincidence?

By 4 a.m., George had slumped in his chair, a glass still in hand. The hangover clung to him like the stale fog lingering near the office ceiling, matching the dreary British weather outside. Aspirin had done little to touch it. The grey gloom mirrored the mood inside. Looking thunderous, Michael alternated between glaring at George and studying a sprawling map across the desk. ADI Locke wasn't faring any better, pacing in tight circles with a phone glued to his ear, his movements sharp and restless—a harbinger of bad news.

George's stomach churned as he stepped into the room, sensing the storm. He read their faces through the haze of smoke and tension. Another body, he thought grimly. That's what had them in knots. For a moment, George considered turning around, retreating to deal with his problems in solitude. But something kept him rooted, the box in his hand weighing heavier with each step.

"Perfect timing, matey. Ooh, coffee—you're a lifesaver," Michael says, swiping a cup with a smirk. He didn't even glance at the box in George's other hand before dashing back to the table, his whirlwind energy leaving George awkwardly in the doorway.

"Well, erm, yes," George says, clearing his throat. "What the heck is going on?"

Michael's grin faded. "Only if the party's in the morgue."

"Another?" George asks, though he already knows the answer.

"Afraid so, sunshine. Aww, you got me a present, though? You shouldn't have." Michael's gaze landed on the box in George's hand, his tone laced with forced levity.

"I didn't," George replies, holding it out as if it might explain itself. "This was kindly left on my doorstep. I caught a black Audi leaving—no plates."

Michael's eyebrows shot up. "And you haven't opened it? Why not?"

George hesitated, the words catching in his throat. *Because I was scared,* he wanted to admit. *Because it reminded me of the past, and I didn't want to face it alone.*

"Well," he says instead, "after your experience with the ear, I figured it was best to get everyone on the same page."

Michael snorted, his grin returning. "Ah, so, you crapped yourself, then?"

"Glad the shoe's on the other foot, eh?" George replies dryly, though his tone betrays his unease.

Michael laughed, the sound breaking some of the tension in the room. But the box remained a stark reminder that their problems weren't just out there—they were on George's doorstep now, waiting to be confronted.

"George, don't get too comfortable," Locke says curtly. "You and the cockney prince have a drive to take. 'Wick Lane Bridge.' Now, which one of you geniuses decided it was okay for Mr Kumar to use that place as a drop-in centre?"

"He was being kept safe there while they investigated the artefact," Michael replies defensively. "It's a lot of money."

"That's fine," Locke says, though his furrowed brow suggests otherwise. "Except he keeps coming and going, muttering about work and pets to manage. Claims he feels like he's being followed. He's turning into a complication we can't afford right now."

Michael looked at George, but neither had the time or bandwidth to untangle Kumar's mess. Another body had turned up—the fourth in three days. Chasing the relic had to wait.

"As long as he's safe, we can clean that up later," George says, placing the box on the table. "Right now, we need to see what's in this."

Locke eyed the box with suspicion, his expression tight. He looked more constipated than composed, his discomfort palpable. George ignored him, focusing on the box. He pinched the bow ends of the red ribbon and tugged, the knot slipping free like a dressing gown rope. Glancing up, he caught Michael's darkening expression, the cigarette in his hand casting faint spirals of smoke around his head. The tension in the room was thick, almost suffocating.

The lid came free with troubling ease. Michael's breath, thick with cigarette smoke, brushed George's collar as he leaned in too close. George suppressed the urge to step away, his mind praying against the inevitable. Whatever was inside, he knew it wouldn't be good. The only question was *how bad*.

At first, the contents seemed underwhelming, even anticlimactic. But then George noticed the significance.

Inside was a card, its glossy front depicting the night sky painted in dark blues and blacks, with a blood-red moon glowing ominously. The words *"Hope you have a howling good time"* were scrawled across the cover, too, on the nose. Whoever sent it knew.

T he calm before the storm.

The card opened, revealing a handwritten message that sent a chill down George's spine:

Dear Detective Reynolds,

I wanted to take this moment to wish you a happy, bloody birthday. After all, you'll be far too busy, I'm sure. As the message says, I hope you have a howling good time.

I apologise if you're all a little overworked. Unfortunately, it's the nature of the beast. Eager to please, places to go, people to kill. Call it...making up for lost time and punishing the wrong. I'm sure we'll see each other again soon. Especially if you have an ounce of the intelligence I think you have. We could be two peas in a pod.

Bleed you later.

The room was silent. George didn't know how long the silence stretched—maybe a minute, maybe longer. Locke paced back and forth, his polished shoes slicing across the carpet as he mumbled into his phone, his eyes flicking to the card every few seconds. No one spoke, but the tension in the room was deafening.

George's stomach twisted into a tight knot, his body betraying him. The card wasn't just a taunt—it was a message from the one controlling the Kanaima. They knew about him. The blood moon on the cover wasn't a coincidence. It was a symbol, a declaration that they understood what George was. Worse, the words carried a chilling familiarity, as if they weren't just threats but an olive branch, a grotesque invitation.

His legs felt weak, and the room swayed slightly. The coffee in his hand trembled, and cold clamminess spread over his face. George fought to hold himself steady, aware of the eyes in the room. He could feel their stares burning into him.

Michael's whisper cut through the haze. "You okay, matey?" he asks, low enough to avoid drawing Locke's attention.

George nodded faintly, though it was a lie. His body was betraying him—weakening under the stress, the weight of the realisation crashing over him. Whoever had sent this card wasn't just watching. They *knew*. And they weren't done.

George nodded, though his response felt hollow. "Yes." The moment was fleeting, but its weight lingered. It was as if an invisible target had been painted on their backs, inviting potshots from the bad guys, who were enjoying the game far too much.

"You eaten?" Michael asks, his tone tinged with concern.

"Not since... that curry," George admitted, his voice trailing.

"Bloody hell, mate," Michael says, shaking his head. "You've got to look after yourself. There's too much going on as it is. The last thing we need is you losing control of your urges—or the blood," he adds in a low whisper, resting a hand on George's shoulder in a gesture reminiscent of Skip.

"Yeah, well, between the lack of sleep, unexpected presents, and a pile of dead bodies, that's a little low on the 'to-do' list," George replies dryly.

"Here, take this," Locke interjected, holding a breakfast bar. George blinked, startled. He hadn't noticed Locke move, much less catch the exchange.

"Erm, thanks, but—"

"Sound travels in these offices," Locke says, cutting him off. "When you whisper, it's not exactly quiet. Besides, I have eyes, too, and you've turned a shade of Casper."

George managed a faint smile, off guard by Locke's unexpected gesture. The chaos around them was relentless—phones ringing, people darting back and forth. Yet Locke's sharpness cut through the noise effortlessly. George noticed the number of bodies in the room for the first time.

"Where'd all the extra hands come from?" he asks, watching the blur of movement around them.

"Volunteers," Locke replies, handing a piece of paper to Michael. "They're manning phones, gathering information. Neighbourhood watches, community groups—they've banded together to help. Everyone's eager to know more."

Michael scanned the paper briefly before folding it neatly into quarters and slipping it into his pocket. "Looks like we're off to Wick Lane, Middle Lock Number Two," he says.

3 PM - Wick Lane, Body No. 4

The scene was already bustling when they arrived. Two locks stood one hundred feet apart and twenty feet from the bridge, which was large enough to accommodate an ambulance, the coroner's van, and the requisite sea of blue lights without blocking the road. A sizable crowd had gathered along the sweeping pathway to the left, separated from the scene by a low fence bordering an industrial estate and a sprawling car park. To the right were the rear gardens of a row of houses, their construction betraying an age of at least twenty years.

It was broad daylight. Someone had to have seen something. They couldn't keep relying on whispers and speculation.

While the body demanded their attention, George's thoughts kept straying elsewhere. He scanned the gravel and grass banks secretly, searching for traces of that strange dust. He moved cautiously, only when he was sure no one was watching.

"Detectives, nice of you to show up," a voice called, sharp and sweet, snapping George's attention back to the bridge.

Ms Walker stood there, clipboard in hand, her piercing gaze locking onto him like a laser.

"Well, aren't you a sight for sore eyes," Michael says, his cockney charm in full effect.

"If I were you, I'd save those lecherous eyes for the other body," Ms Walker quips, her sharp smile softened by a cheeky wink in George's direction.

Cordon tape stretched across the ramp to their left, further up the incline. The crowd had already pressed close before the Hi-Viz uniforms put it in place. Michael, sensing trouble brewing, gestured to a nearby officer. "Run another line of tape between the trees," he instructed. "Let's give ourselves a little breathing room from the peanut gallery."

George approached the curved arch reluctantly, the heavy air beneath the bridge pressing against him. Most ground here was rough stone, cracked and weathered, with weeds forcing their way up the walls and through every crevice. The newly erected piped fencing along the canal edge narrowed the tight walkway. He couldn't shake the feeling that this "masterpiece" would be different, somehow worse than the others.

"This one is worse," came Mrs Wainright's voice, echoing from under the bridge.

George ducked his head and strode into the shadows. His stomach churned as he saw what she meant. This time, the victim had been arranged in an upright cross. The psychology had shifted—rougher, more frantic, more aggressive. The killer's methods were escalating. The woman, likely in her early thirties, bore light brown hair and was bruised. Her neck had been broken, and her heart removed.

Her body told a story of cruelty. Black underwear exposed, her jeans barely pulled up to her thighs, and her ripped bra missing its clasp. George's gaze flicked to Mrs Wainright, moving between paperwork scattered on the floor and the body, examining each bruise with clinical precision. Her movements were methodical but more hurried than usual.

"What's that you're doing?" George asks, his voice tight.

"Body mapping," she replies without looking up. "It makes the autopsy easier and provides a clear record of injuries. ADI Locke and I discussed it earlier. We're struggling to keep up with this many bodies piling up."

She paused just long enough to glance at George, her sharp, focused eyes blazing like headlights. "Horrible, isn't it?"

"It's awful," Ms Walker's voice chimed in, returning to the scene with her usual piercing presence. "The pineal gland's gone again, extracted through the back of her head. We also found her tongue stuffed into her right jeans pocket. The heart was the focus here."

Ms Walker slithered closer to the body, shining her torch along the waistband of the woman's jeans.

"Any sign of the toxins?" George asks, trying to steady his voice.

"Left rear of her neck," she replies.

"Any messages?" George asks quickly, feeling the pressure of the moment.

"What?" Ms Walker turned to him, her brows furrowing in confusion.

"What Georgie means," Michael interjected, stepping into the scene with the scrape of his shoes against the concrete, "is if there are any taunts or cryptic words?"

"Like that?" Ms Walker asks, raising her torch to the opposite curve of the bridge.

The beam revealed a crude message painted in blood. A crimson moon, smeared into the shape of a wolf, loomed on the stone surface. The taunt felt personal—first, the card, now this. George's stomach twisted. Fearing the inevitable questions from the others. Michael, at least, wouldn't probe. But the rest? He wasn't so sure.

"Ah, erm, do you know what it could mean?" George asks, attempting to steer the conversation before anyone can direct their suspicions at him.

"Read one too many horror books, maybe?" Ms Walker smirked, her voice light with mockery.

George forced a strained smile, but Mrs Wainright opened her mouth before he could respond. The interruption hung heavy, leaving George dreading what might come next.

If George didn't know better, he'd swear Ms Walker knew about him. Her gaze lingered a second too long, her words laced with a sharpness that felt deliberate. *Perhaps she's just really observant,* he thought. *Michael wouldn't be careless enough to let anything slip without my say.*

"Michael, you got a minute?" George asks, motioning toward the canal edge. He needed a moment of cover, someone to block him from view while he searched for more traces.

"Sure," Michael says, striding toward him, the click of his heels muffled by the damp ground.

George leaned in close, his voice low. "I need you to keep a lookout. Block their view while I look."

Michael nodded and turned his back to the water, crossing his arms casually, pretending to survey the scene. "Sure thing. You hoping for more of that stuff?" he asks, his tone light but his expression sharp with curiosity.

"If it's here," George murmurs, keeping his eyes fixed ahead, "then we've got a solid lead to work from. Did you notice the body's older than the first one yesterday?"

"Yeah," Michael replies, his voice thoughtful. "But not as old as the girl in the warehouse."

The timeline made no sense. The killer had to be keeping some victims somewhere, torturing them for longer, drawing out their suffering. George's stomach churned as he crouched lower, scanning the areas where the bridge met the ground. His gaze moved deliberately, his heightened senses working overtime. There—are small traces along the edge. Subtle, almost invisible, but unmistakable to him.

"Well?" Michael prompted, his voice pulling George back to the moment.

"Yep," George says, straightening. "Enough to be the link. The question is, master or beast?"

"I'm leaning toward the master," Michael replies, glancing at the others to ensure no one is watching. "We'll need more samples for continuity. If we're going to catch this bastard, we need to piece it all together. This stuff is the common denominator."

"Ooh, big words," George says with a faint smirk, though his focus didn't waver. "We need the lab to tell us what it is."

"Eww, really? Could it get any sicker?" Ms Walker's voice broke the moment, her tone high-pitched with disgust. George and Michael turned sharply to find her holding a pair of tweezers in her gloved hand. Pinched between them was another blood-soaked scroll wrapped in the same crimson ribbon as the one on George's card.

"Great," Michael mutters, the heaviness in his voice matching the weight of the discovery. "Any guesses on the time of death? Or an ID?"

"At least a day," Ms Walker replies, her sharp tone returning. "I found an ID in her back pocket. Mrs Michelle Walters—"

"Archaeologist," George interrupts, snapping his head toward her. "Part of the National History Museum."

Ms Walker arched a brow at him, surprised by his quick identification. "A connection?"

she asks, shining her torch on the victim's side.

George's stomach tightened as he nodded. Michelle Walters was on the list Bentley had provided. "She was one of two with that surname," George adds, his voice low, "and she lived near the water."

"That's another from the expedition," Michael says grimly. "Chalked off."

George's thoughts churned as the weight of the revelation settled over him. Another name crossed off Bentley's list. Another victim connected to the money Kumar had received for the missing relic. The web was tightening, but the bodies were raising more questions than answering.

MILE END

13

'4 pm 28th October,'

They arrived at 35 Eastfield Street, Mile End, a little after 4 p.m. The house was tucked away on Jamuna Close, a side street that led straight to Regents Canal. The area wore a veneer of respectability, but George saw through it—the quiet practically invited trouble with its lack of foot traffic and prying eyes. Mile End Underground was at least a fifteen-minute walk, and bus stops were scarce. The nearest car park was empty, an oddity in a city like London.

"This part of Mile End caught my eye when I ditched South London," George murmured as they stepped out of the car. He took a moment to scan the area, taking in its isolated charm. Most people here seemed employed elsewhere or indifferent to car ownership, though the latter felt like a stretch given the public transit desert.

Perfect for someone looking to disappear—or for someone hiding secrets.

As George strolled along the pathway, his gaze lingered on the black bollards guarding the entrance to a canal-side walkway. Remove them, and you'll have an uninterrupted route straight into the water. Chain railings bordered the canal's edge, with a removable section leading to a few steps descending to a small dock. Boat parking was eerily empty. Across the canal, a patch of green space offered only a few black metal benches and scattered trees.

"Nice digs," Michael says, lighting a cigarette and surveying the scene. He sounded impressed, though George couldn't tell if it was genuine or just Michael being Michael.

"A nice view," George replies, a smirk tugging at his lips. "Picture this: you get one of those squat, short-legged dogs. You live here, and the little guy shuffles to the edge, takes a tumble, and you're diving in right after. Might as well move to the countryside; the fresh air'll do you good in your golden years."

"You cheeky bastard," Michael shot back, grinning as he took a long drag. "How old do you think I am? I look this haggard from being around you, bloody idiot."

George chuckled, but his smile faded as he returned to the house. "Think he's in?" he asks.

Michael exhaled a cloud of smoke, his brow furrowing. "Do you think he's still alive?"

The question hung heavy between them, and George felt a sinking sensation clawing at his gut. It wasn't just pessimism—that gnawing sixth sense that had been with him for days, whispering that the remaining names on Bentley's list were in grave danger.

The drive here had been a whirlwind of thoughts. Michael had taken the wheel, leaving George free to sift through the evidence. The list of names had consumed his mind, grouping victims by proximity to water and separating the deceased to uncover connections. Rachel Darnley, Tracey Kent, Annabelle Kumar, and Michelle Walters—all victims tied to the canals and, somehow, the Egyptian expedition.

Annabelle's husband had been part of that ill-fated expedition, agreeing to smuggle relics that had since vanished. Michelle Walters and her husband, Ross, were among the seven listed dig members. That left five other names still unaccounted for: Donna Armitage, Jack Sexton, Emily Fulton, Brian Thistle, and Melanie Blake. All of them lived near the water.

"Hey, Michael," George says, his voice cutting through the quiet tension. "Annabelle Kumar's place is 87 Bancroft Road, right?"

"Yeah," Michael replies, flicking ash from his cigarette. "Why's that?"

George hesitated, piecing his thoughts together. "That address isn't far from water, but here's the thing—it wasn't on the list. Neither was Annabelle's name. But... a few details overlap. Did you notice Mr Kumar has a blank space beside his name?"

Michael paused, narrowing his eyes at George. "What are you getting at?"

George shrugged though his mind churned with possibilities. "I don't know yet. But blank spaces don't sit right with me. Especially not with everything else going on."

Michael's gaze sharpened, and George felt the weight of his scrutiny. He wasn't sure if Michael thought he was onto something—or just losing the plot. Either way, the question lingered unanswered as the shadows lengthened around them.

"No, I didn't," Michael admitted, rifling through his notes as they approached the front door.

"Locke," George says, his tone sharp with curiosity. "Did he spill anything about the other locations?"

"Just mentioned Hackney," Michael replies, glancing up briefly. "Near the market area, not a canal."

The comment nagged at George as they walked. A driving instructor turned informant making "calls" to report sightings seemed too convenient. His mind, already in overdrive, latched onto a theory that sounded far-fetched, even to him.

"What if we've got three massive cogs in this puzzle?" he began, the words tumbling out quickly. "First, the Lady's Night murders are for kicks, maybe a vendetta. But what if they're a diversion?"

Michael burst into laughter, the sound echoing off the narrow street. George's face reddened as if he'd just admitted to a crime.

"What the hell are they hiding?" Michael says, reigning in his laughter enough to form the words.

"The relic," George says plainly. "The agreed theft and sale, the cash split a few ways."

Michael's expression shifted, his laughter replaced with intrigue. "Alright, I'm listening. Your brain's in overdrive today."

"At its core, it's greed," George continues, the pieces falling into place in his mind. "One of the expedition members gets greedy and steals the relic but accidentally unleashes a demon."

Michael tilted his head, considering. "So, they figure, 'kill two birds with one stone'—eliminate the others, keep their share of the profit, and cover their tracks?"

"Exactly," George says, relieved that Michael wasn't dismissing him outright. "The murders make sense if we look at them that way. But how do we prove it?"

"That," Michael says, "is the real question. Still, it's a starting point."

George nodded, using Michael as a sounding board to weave the pieces into something actionable. "And the third part of the theory?" Michael prompted.

"Ah, yes. The demon itself. A revenge demon in search of a master. If it's loose, it won't stop unless we stop it. Makes the situation... unpredictable."

Michael exhaled a long breath, flicking ash from his cigarette. "Got it. And let's not forget the tiny issue of the blood moon."

The blood moon, though ominous, wasn't at the forefront of George's mind just then. The low, blue wooden gate creaked as it opened, revealing a cement path flanked by towering sunflowers that led to a red door.

The stench hit them before they reached the door. Spoiled meat, sour milk, and rotten fish had a distinct reek, but old blood was worse. Left to rot, it carried the unmistakable essence of death. George signalled Michael to keep quiet, his stomach turning as the smell thickened.

They stood on the raised stone doorstep. The front door was ajar, a crack wide enough to let the smell seep out. No heartbeat reached George's ears, just the lively cacophony of birds outside enjoying the autumn sun. Inside, there was nothing but silence.

"No signs of life," George whispers, keeping his voice low. His eyes flicked over Michael's shoulder, scanning for any signs of movement—or threat.

"Excuse me, dear, can I help you?"

The unexpected voice made them both jump. They turned quickly to find an elderly woman partially concealed behind the sunflowers next door. She was barely five feet tall, her grey, curly hair framing a face lined with age but friendly in demeanour. Her voice was warm, even as she adjusted her glasses on the bridge of her small nose to inspect them.

Michael and George instinctively whipped out their warrant cards, eliciting a quizzical look from the woman. She tilted slightly, her curiosity piqued but tempered with grand-motherly calm.

"Officers?" she asks, her voice lilting with genuine interest. "Is something the matter?"

"Hello, madam. I'm DS Dalton, and this is Detective Reynolds," Michael says, step-ping forward with a polite nod. His broad frame subtly shielded George from the sun-flowers swaying in the breeze. "Do you know the people who live here?"

The elderly woman leaned against the gate, her glasses catching the light as she adjusted them. "Oh yes, husband and wife," she replied her voice light and with a hint of amuse-ment. They used to be such nice people. Not so much lately—lots of shouting."

"How long has that been going on?" George asks, peering over Michael's shoulder. He kept his tone casual, careful not to alarm her or draw attention to the unmistakable smell wafting from the open door.

"Oh, let me think," she says, her brow furrowing as she searches her memory. "Must've started before the summer. And they've had people coming and going, too. Not always the same ones."

George's ears perked up. "Did you notice anyone unusual? Someone who stood out?"

The woman hesitated as if considering how much to share. Then, with an abrupt turn, she hobbled back toward her house. Her uneven steps thudded faintly against the stone path, likely from arthritis. George and Michael exchanged puzzled glances, unsure if they'd lost her cooperation.

Moments later, the sound of banging and shuffling drifted from inside. "Oh, there it is!" she exclaims, her voice muffled. She reappeared holding a photograph, her fingers gripping it carefully.

"My Harold snapped this a few days ago," she explains, handing the picture to Michael. "We're part of the neighbourhood watch. Harold got a bit worried and bought one of those fancy Polaroids. Thought it might come in handy."

Michael held up the photo for George to see. It showed Mr Kumar standing near the house, accompanied by two others. One was a tall man in a black hoodie with his face obscured. The second figure, between tall and short, wore a distinctive outfit: a khaki coat, blue jeans, and a wide-brimmed brown hat—often worn on expeditions. Only a sliver of a black beard and the edge of a pale ear were visible beneath the brim.

"Do you recall seeing their faces? Or anything specific about them?" George asks, studying the photograph. The image deepened his suspicion that Mr Kumar was far more involved than he had let on.

"Not, dear," she replies, shaking her head. "But if you leave me a card, I'll call you if anyone returns. It's been a few days since I saw the husband. The wife's been gone even longer. Harold thinks she was tired of arguing and left to cool off."

Michael handed her a card and offered a polite smile. "Thank you. We'd appreciate it."

George gestured toward the ajar door. "Have they ever left their door open like this before?"

"Oh, never!" she says, her tone firm with pride. "We take security seriously here. You'd never see a neighbourhood watch member leaving a door open."

"Right," Michael says, gripping his radio. "We're going in, yeah?"

George nodded. "Best to be sure." He pressed the door gently, the creak echoing into the stillness.

"Oh, one more thing," the woman adds, halting their movement. "I saw some of them before—getting on one of those canal ships."

"A barge?" Michael asks, his head tilting with interest.

"Yes, one of those," she confirmed. "It was late, too. Maybe a few nights ago."

The mention of the barge reignited George's fixation on the waterways. The question burned in his mind: *Who was on the barge? And why?*

"Thank you for your help," George says, his tone softer now. "You should head inside while we check things out. If you see anyone unusual, call us."

The woman nodded and shuffled back toward her home. George turned his attention back to the door, the ominous smell seeping out stronger than before. He and Michael exchanged a grim look, the unspoken question hanging between them: *What are we about to find?*

A flight of narrow steps to the left revealed a faded floral carpet in blue and black. The pattern was worn, as unremarkable as the rest of the house's decor seemed to promise. The front doors swung inward, revealing a twelve-foot hallway lined with cream walls. At the end stood a twelve-pane glass door, likely a cupboard. Two open doorways branched off to the right, leading to the kitchen and the lounge.

The stench hit harder inside, clinging to the air like a fog. It was everywhere and nowhere, diffused through the space with no obvious source. George's senses flared, his instincts gnawing at him, but there was nothing to ground the unease. The uncertainty clawed at his patience, driving him to distraction.

Behind him, Michael trailed close, his radio crackling softly as he reported their findings. "House is insecure," Michael mutters into the receiver. "No sign of the resident, but there's a smell. Could be a dead person inside. Proceeding with caution." He paused, glancing back toward the open door. "In case the occupant returns—or anyone else."

George moved cautiously into the lounge. The carpet was a dingy brown floral, matching the blandness of the cream walls. An ornamental mahogany fireplace dominated the far wall, flanked by alcoves. One housed a shuttered bureau, and the other an overflowing bookcase stuffed with old and new titles. Dust coated every surface—thick on the coffee table, the TV, and the mantelpiece. The room bore all the signs of neglect, as if its occupants were rarely present or didn't care.

His gaze swept the alcoves before landing on the bookcase. A single spine stood out from the jumble: *The Art of War* by Sun Tzu. Not exactly light reading. George's fingers brushed across the worn cover but found nothing unusual.

"Michael," George called, wandering to the TV. "Check this out."

On top of the dusty set sat a stack of letters and documents, but a photograph drew George's attention. He picked it up carefully, the faint chemical tang of recent development still clinging to it. He handed it to Michael, who squinted before pulling a pair of black-framed glasses from his pocket.

"It looks like their travel party," Michael mutters, scrutinising the faces. The photo wasn't a Polaroid-like the one provided by the neighbour, but its crispness hinted at a more deliberate preservation.

"Yeah," George agrees, "but look here—two of them have red crosses smeared across their faces."

"Ticking them off?" Michael muses, adjusting his glasses and studying the image further. "Hard to tell. But that's a woman, and I'd bet it's Michelle Walters."

George flipped the photograph over, his pulse quickening when he saw the scrawled writing on the back. "'Two peas in a pod,'" he read aloud, the words sending a chill down his spine. The phrase matched the message on the card he'd received, cementing the connection between himself and whoever orchestrated this nightmare.

Michael grunted, his tone dry but edged with concern. "Looks like you've got a fan."

George ignored the comment, his attention drawn back to the room. The cryptic note explained nothing about the pervasive stench that filled the house. His gut told him Ross Walters was dead, but there were no immediate signs to confirm it. He scanned the room again, his gaze combing the dust-coated surfaces for disturbances, but nothing stood out.

The stench remained thick and suffocating, an invisible spectre that deepened the house's ominous silence. Something was here, something unseen, and George knew they were running out of time to find it.

"Hey, check out this fancy desk," Michael says, his voice edged with concern. He stood by a bureau in the corner, his expression tightening as he gestured toward the surface.

"What's up?" George asks, moving closer, the acrid stench of decay intensifying with every step.

Michael pointed. "Look—two blood dots. Two peas."

George slipped on gloves with a sharp *ping*, apprehension coiling in his stomach. He gripped the desk's front panel, sliding it open with a juddering rattle.

"Ugh. Oh, my God. The sick bastard," Michael choked, staggering back a step as the contents came into view.

Inside was a severed head, stripped of flesh and oozing decay. The empty eye sockets stared into nothingness; the contours of the face grotesquely warped.

"That's probably Ross's head," George says, his voice strained as he wrestles with the smell. "Although it's hard to tell. The face skin is gone."

Michael turned away, his hand covering his mouth, but something on the floor caught his eye. "Hey, look what else I found," he says, crouching to pick up a crumpled pink paper.

George leaned closer, squinting to make out the text before Michael thrust it toward him. "'Lady's Night,'" George read aloud, his brow furrowing. "Had Mrs Walters attended one of these?"

Before George could process the implications, Michael bolted outside to update the despatch on their gruesome discovery. George lingered, a dizzy sense of urgency compelling him to search for more connections—and the rest of Ross Walters's body.

The walls were lined with photographs, capturing snapshots of family life and professional achievements. Group shots from archaeology digs and happy family moments mingled in dusty frames. One A4 landscape photo, dated a month ago, leaned haphazardly in a broken frame. The image featured Mr Kumar, grinning sheepishly, flanked by Mr and Mrs Walters and others, likely their expedition team.

George fished a bag from his pocket, carefully securing the two photographs and the crumpled poster for later analysis. The kitchen drew him next. It was worn and outdated, a relic of the 1970s, with avocado-green cabinets and yellowing countertops. The smell of decay grew thick and clinging to the air, though no blood was visible.

He moved cautiously, each step tentative, bracing for another gruesome find. His gaze landed on a dusty khaki-coloured canvas bag resting on the bar. The bag had a weathered look, as though it had travelled the world and back, its stories etched in every scuff and stain. The flap hung open, revealing a battered brown jacket half-tucked inside.

George hesitated. The scent of stale air and old fabric filled his lungs as he pondered the ethics of his next move. Invading someone's privacy by rifling through personal items felt different from cataloguing evidence like the desk and the severed head. Everyone was entitled to their secrets. What if the bag held something intimate—a journal, a book of private thoughts?

His hand hovered, fingers brushing against the jacket. A faint, familiar scent mingled with the musk, tugging at the edge of his memory. Was it related to the strange dust they'd been collecting? Or was it something else?

Pulling back, the flap revealed a black cord looped around the edge of what appeared to be an old leather-bound book. The smooth cover had a tactile quality, worn from years of use. George flipped it open, dust wafting from the pages and triggering a rough cough.

Michael's voice drifted through the doorway as he delivered the grim news to the waiting officers. George's thoughts lingered on the diary; its title scrawled across the inside cover: *Egypt.* He halted at the last entry, his pulse quickening as he realised its potential importance.

George opened the leather-bound diary carefully, the old pages brittle under his fingers. Dust motes danced in the air as he flipped through, stopping at an entry dated "Day 86." The handwriting was hurried, almost frantic, as if the writer had scrawled their thoughts in frustration. He began reading, his stomach twisting with every line.

D *ay Eighty-Six. The thrill is long gone. We've recovered hundreds of artefacts. People have been hurt, and two have died. There's an agreement that it's time we get our share. The museum makes us do all the dirty work to preserve history. We get told this after each one: "It's a shame there's no way to do the same for our bank balances."*

'Yusef' has lined up a buyer. Twenty-five bloody million, split seven ways. That's a lot of money for years of toil. Since we agreed, the group has an edge. We're looking over our shoulders, wondering if the injuries aren't accidents but purposeful mistakes casting doubt over the project; if someone dies, it's a curse. As for Yusef, something is happening to him. He's becoming more volatile. He wanted to control the relics; I couldn't let him do that. I won't.

Being group lead, I've held the relic for the longest. I feel its pull and heart. A few times, I swear it's called my name. I can't give it up. I feel stronger around it. Michelle thinks I'm losing the plot. I'm not. She would say that, covering the fact I found out she's been cheating on me.

'Cheaters never prosper,' I say to myself. Who am I kidding? The bitch fucks anyone with a pulse. It seems to be a man or woman.

George snapped the diary shut, the words leaving an acrid taste in his mouth. The jarring mix of greed, paranoia, and fury vividly depicted a fractured expedition group teetering on the edge of collapse. His mind churned with questions.

Had Mr Kumar's ambition gotten the better of him? Did greed consume him, or was something else driving him—the relics "pull" he described? The diary hinted at dark forces, a sinister influence bleeding through the group, but it also revealed a man unravelling under the weight of betrayal and distrust.

George's eyes lingered on the worn leather cover, his fingers brushing the raised edges of the title: Egypt. The smell of decay still hung in the air, mingling with his rising sense of unease. The diary had answered some questions, but it raised far more.

From the doorway, Michael's voice pulled him back to reality. "You alright, matey? Found anything useful?"

George hesitated; the weight of the diary was heavy in his hands. "I don't know," he admitted, his voice low. "But something tells me Mr Kumar wasn't just a victim of all this."

Michael raised an eyebrow, stepping closer to inspect the book. "Greedy bastard, wasn't he?"

"Maybe," George says, staring at the leather-bound pages. "But if what's in here is true, greed's just the tip of the iceberg."

ROSS WALTERS

14

Ross Walters. Or at least, that was the name they had to go with. The voter's register claimed he and his wife, Michelle, had kept their names on the books for a decade. Whether they'd lived there the whole time was another question entirely.

"Michelle Walters, the latest victim, right?" A.D.I. Locke's voice cut through the still, suffocating air.

The scene was supposed to be sealed off, waiting for reinforcements. Locke was in deep conversation with P.O.L.S.A., pushing for a systematic search—possibly even digging up the garden.

"Yeah, boss. We're assuming it's Ross Walters," George murmurs, his voice brittle against the quiet weight of the house.

"Ah, yes, the missing body," Locke replies, almost too casually.

Michael, standing off to the side, let out a sharp breath. "Guv, it could be in the shed for all we know. But you said stop."

His irritation was palpable. George didn't blame him. No one liked their work interrupted—especially not for bureaucracy. The idea of stopping, of letting the case stall, was maddening.

"I had my reasons," Locke says with a small shrug. "A mate's already on P.O.L.S.A. duty and is itching to help. Plus, it frees you two up for what's next. And anyway, I need you to gather the exhibits and evidence—I'd rather you weren't buried alive in paperwork."

George watched Locke closely, his words hanging like damp fog. This wasn't just a procedure. There was calculation in the way he spoke, something deeper at play.

"Why?" George asks abruptly. The question escaped before he could rein it in.

Locke turned his sharp gaze on him. "There's something about you, Georgie. I felt it when we met, and it's still bugging me. You've got a detective's instinct that even twenty years in this job hasn't given me. I'm sure your partner can vouch for that. You two make a good team, and if that gets me a permanent promotion, so be it."

There it was. Locke's self-interest was laid bare beneath a veneer of mentorship. He was playing the long game—catch the bastard behind all this- and ride the wave of success straight into a full-time promotion. That could have been chalked up to George's inexperience if they failed—a win-win for Locke.

George listened as the man spoke, the rhythm of his voice underscored by the faint, erratic drumbeat of his pulse. Every time he mentioned instinct, George noted the subtle uptick in Locke's heart rate. Something about him was... off. Different.

Michael chimed in with a smirk, tapping the lid of his near-empty cigarette box. "I agree with the Guv. George is still green around the gills, but he'll get there."

George's hand drifted to his pocket, the diary and Polaroid weighing heavier than they should have. He hadn't shown Michael yet—not with the chaos of the scene and the local duty officer breathing down their necks—but now seemed as good a time as any.

"Guv, there's this," George says, holding the book.

"What is it?" Locke's brow furrowed as he took it, the corners of his mouth tightening with suspicion.

"Go to the last entry," George instructed, pointing to the frayed ribbon marker.

Locke's eyes skimmed the pages, his face shifting as he read. The silence stretched thin. Then came the grinding of teeth, the slow clench of his jaw, like a dog gnawing on a bone.

"What the hell is this?" Locke finally growled. "How big is this thing? I know Donna Armitage, Jack Sexton, Emily Fulton, Brian Thistle, and Melanie Blake are by the water from this list. Any idea if they're involved in this... relic business? Or how does it tie into 'Lady's Night'? This reads like Walters was a paranoid bastard, riddled with greed."

George's stomach tightened. Pandora's box had been opened, and whatever was inside was clawing its way out.

"Go to the last entry," George repeated, his voice steady but carrying an undercurrent of unease. He pointed to the frayed ribbon marker resting in the diary. "You'll understand what I want to do next."

Michael, pacing slowly as his eyes roamed the room, said, "I think we should track down Mr Kumar and ask him some questions."

George's mind drifted, pulled like a string to the severed head crammed inside the bureau. His gaze darted between the gruesome sight and the photograph clutched in his hand, comparing the jawline. It was difficult to tell from such a small, faded image, but the shapes didn't quite match. Something about it gnawed at the edges of his thoughts.

Outside, the low rumble of approaching vehicles fractured the heavy silence. A trail of units pulled up, their metal doors slamming open with a clang reverberating through the air. A flood of uniforms spilt out, accompanied by the rising static of radio chatter.

Michael glanced toward the window. "Someone stocking up for Christmas?" he mutters dryly.

"Sorry, what?" George says, startled by his thoughts.

Michael smirked, his attention shifting to the plate in front of George. "You've piled enough food to feed both of us. Weird combination, though."

George glanced down, self-conscious. "Yeah, I couldn't decide, and my stomach seems to crave everything," he admitted, heat creeping up his neck.

Michael chuckled, shaking his head. "Fish, steak pie, and sausage? All in one sitting?"

George shrugged, stabbing at the remnants of cod with his fork. They'd snatched a rare moment to grab food before plunging back into the chaos, but the ravenous hunger George often felt was sharper now. He swallowed, the taste of salt lingering on his tongue, but the nagging guilt over Michael's comment soured the meal.

"So, what're your thoughts?" Michael asks, gulping his coffee.

"About what?" George replies absently, pushing his empty plate aside and curling his fingers around his coffee mug. The warmth seeps into his palms as he stares out the window. For a moment, his mind goes blank.

That wasn't entirely true. His thoughts were racing, tangled and fragmented as if he were trying to unravel a knot in the dark. The murders, the trail of bodies, and the ever-watchful eyes of whoever had followed them to the museum weighed heavily on him. Everything seemed connected, but the connections were blurred, obscured by chaos and dread.

"You know what I mean," Michael pressed.

George exhaled, his breath fogging the mug's rim. "I think the route he's taken each time—'checking on pets,' as he calls it—might be his line of sight for stalking his victims. Did you notice any pets? Because I didn't."

Michael shook his head. "Honestly, mate, I wasn't paying much attention to the details. Too much going on."

"That's fair," George says. "But how he carried himself—so detached, no emotional reaction to what we showed him—felt off. And not just in the obvious way."

Michael leaned back, checking his watch. "What time did the station officer say?"

"Six o'clock," George answers, glancing at his watch.

"Well, look at that," Michael mutters, tilting his head toward the window. "Right on cue. Beige bomber jacket, blue jeans, brown driving cap. Nine o'clock."

George's pulse quickened as he tracked the figure outside. "Is he driving, then walking the rest of the way?" he murmurs, piecing the logistics together.

Bethnal Green or Bow Station—either could've been his starting point. The routes didn't line up perfectly, but there was enough ambiguity to make it plausible. George's mind raced, every possibility turning into another dark thread in an already tangled web.

"Correct me if I'm wrong, but there's a river route between the station and where his home is supposed to be," Michael says, downing the last of his coffee in a single gulp.

George nodded, his voice low. "Yes. The main road cuts through the heart of it all. We estimated his time—whether by car or on foot—and got lucky. Now I've got his scent and heartbeat. Let's move." He finished the last bite of his meal and stood, his focus narrowing on the task ahead.

They had been holed up in the Ocean Fish Bar, five doors down from Stepney Green Station. From there, it was a short walk: left to Globe Road, ten minutes straight, then a right onto Bancroft. George glanced outside. The mild evening breeze was gnawing at the edges of daylight.

"Come on, matey," Michael mutters, stepping outside. The streetlights flicker weakly as darkness creeps in. George inhales deeply, concentrating.

"How far ahead?" Michael asks, his tone sharpening.

"Two minutes," George replies, his senses honed. "But we need to pick up the pace. He's already on Globe, moving fast. His steps are quick, his heart racing—too fast for someone who doesn't know he's being followed. He's spooked."

George scanned their surroundings, his mind pinpointing others nearby who might be tied to their target. The chase felt precarious, as though the night was conspiring against them.

When the man veered right into Alderney, George frowned. It didn't add up. Instead of heading straight toward home, the route now twisted into uncertainty.

"You think he's made us?" Michael asks, glancing at George with unease.

George shook his head. "I don't know. But he's running scared—from something."

George's unease deepened as they neared Carlton Square, a small park flanked by rows of shadowy houses on either side. The road ahead would lead toward the canal, yet it forced a crossing onto the other side of Bancroft, nowhere near the target's supposed destination.

"This route isn't making," George murmurs. "Should we call it in? This could be a trap."

Michael hesitated, wheezing. "Give it another minute. We're nearly at the corner. Look—no one's in the park. He's not meeting anyone there."

George's eyes swept over the park's empty expanse, his ears catching the faint shuffle of their target's hurried steps. The night seemed to hold its breath, but then a low growl of an engine shattered the stillness. A dark saloon car barrelled in from Bancroft, its sleek body cutting through the shadows like a predator.

The target froze mid-step, his body stiffening as if he'd turned to stone. George's pulse quickened as he watched the man backtrack slowly, then pivot sharply on his heels. The target was running straight toward them now, his heart pounding wildly—a frantic, uneven rhythm that seemed like it would burst.

"Shit. Things are going sideways," Michael hisses. "I'll stop him. You get the details, then call it in."

George barely had time to nod before Michael sprang into action. Their startled rabbit bolted, his movements erratic and panicked.

"Mr Kumar! Police—stop right there!" Michael shouts, his voice cutting through the night like a blade. "We're here to help!"

Mr Kumar was one of the many loose ends they'd picked up after leaving Mr and Mrs Walters's house. He was supposed to be just another interview—a cog in the larger machine they were trying to assemble. But now, how he ran and the sheer terror in his eyes suggested he was much more than that.

Behind them, the saloon halted, its tyres screaming against gravel and asphalt. George turned just in time to see the faint outline of a figure in the driver's seat before the car roared away, vanishing into the encroaching darkness.

Michael had caught up to Kumar, grabbing his arm to stop his desperate flight. But Kumar struggled like a wild animal, thrashing and twisting, his limbs flailing in every direction. His eyes, wide and bulging, gleamed stark white in the dim light. The fear etched into his face wasn't for them—it was for whoever had been in that car.

"Calm down, mate!" Michael barks, tightening his grip. "We're not here to hurt you!"

But Kumar wasn't listening. His breath came in ragged, shallow gasps as his gaze darted wildly as if the shadows themselves were closing in. Whoever was chasing him, George realized grimly, had already done far more damage than they could ever do.

The engine's roar grew louder, a visceral growl tearing through the stillness. The car—shaped like an Audi but moving far too fast for the narrow streets—hurtled toward them. All its windows were blacked out, concealing the occupants and turning the vehicle into a faceless predator. George's heart pounded as his gaze darted left and right, scanning for signs of life—children playing near parked cars, an unlucky pedestrian stepping into the path of death.

Then he heard it: the metallic click of a gun being cocked. The sound sliced through the air, colder than the evening breeze, sending ice down his spine.

He searched for cover. The options were sparse and pitiful: a line of parked cars with a glaring gap on his left, a park bench, and a concrete bin bolted to the ground—not enough to shield them from what was coming.

"Michael! Get to cover!" George shouts, his voice raw with urgency.

Michael's face twisted in alarm as he yanked Mr Kumar forward by the handcuffs. Kumar stumbled, his feet tangling beneath him, as they scrambled toward the overgrown grass edging the park. They dived headlong, crashing into the weeds as time seemed to slow, every second stretching into an eternity.

George turned back to the car. The driver's window lowered with an agonizing grind, the glass dragging against the rubber seal. His breath hitched as the gun barrel emerged, glinting coldly under the fading light.

Then it came—the hammer dropped, triggering a loud clap that seemed to tear the world in half.

He heard the bullets before he felt the fear. He fully registered the distinct whine as they spun through the barrel, carving grooves unique to the weapon. Instinct surged to the forefront, the dormant beast inside him snapping awake. It took everything George had to unleash it—a forbidden transformation he had resisted for as long as he could. But this was survival—life or death.

In a blur of raw power, George launched himself twenty feet to the right, landing heavily behind the body of a battered red Ford Sierra. The impact rattled through him, but he didn't stop to process it. His breathing came fast and shallow, and his senses sharpened to a knife's edge. The beast within him whispered, eager to take control, but he shoved it back into submission.

'Clap. Clap.'

Two more shots cracked through the night, each one louder and angrier than the last. The car swerved violently, its tyres shrieking as it skidded sideways, nearly spinning out. George risked a glance just in time to see the navy blue Capri slam into a parked van with a sickening crunch, bouncing off two other cars before regaining control.

The driver didn't stop. The vehicle whipped left, disappearing into the shadows with a final, ear-splitting screech of tyres.

Silence reclaimed the street for a moment, broken only by the faint echo of the gunshots. George lay sprawled behind the Ford, his chest heaving, his ears ringing. He saw them through the gaps in the park bench—Michael and Mr Kumar, crumpled in the grass, motionless.

The world around him blurred, narrowing to that single image. Were they alive? The thought clawed at his mind, but he couldn't move. Exhaustion rooted him to the spot, the surge of adrenaline leaving him weak. He stared at their still forms, his vision flickering. Somewhere deep inside, the beast growled, restless and hungry.

The streetlights buzzed faintly overhead, their weak glow casting long, jagged shadows across the carnage. George stayed where he was, his heart hammering against his ribs, the silence as deafening as the shots had been.

SHOTS FIRED

15

The cold, unforgiving stone pressed against George's head as he pushed himself up, the sting of cuts and bruises grounding him in the fallout. His elbow throbbed, his lower back ached, and the side of his knees and right palm burned where the skin had split. But already, the wounds were knitting themselves together. A dozen angry scratches faded before his eyes, leaving only faint streaks of drying blood behind.

He jammed his finger against the emergency button, the action sharp and decisive. It was only the second time he'd ever had to use it.

"This is Detective Reynolds. Urgent help is needed on Alderney Road, opposite the park and number thirteen," George barks into the radio, his voice steady but laced with urgency. "Shots fired by the occupants of a navy Capri, unknown number plate, sustained damage to the near-side front. They made off toward Argyle Road. Detective Dalton and a public member are down—condition unknown."

The metallic voice of the controller responded quickly, repeating the alert and issuing the call to nearby units. Within moments, the hum of sirens grew, a distant storm of noise rushing to meet the scene.

George didn't wait. He dashed to Michael and Mr Kumar, his heart pounding. Michael was slumped sideways against the metal bench, his head resting awkwardly, while Mr Kumar lay face-down in the grass, his hands cuffed behind him. The faint metallic tang of blood hung in the air, but it wasn't overwhelming.

"Mr Kumar, are you okay?" George asks, gripping the man's shoulder and giving him a firm shake. Kumar let out a low mumble, his head twitching slightly in response. No blood—at least, none that George could see or smell.

"Shit, magnet strikes again," came Michael's voice, faint but tinged with the dark humour George expected from him. It was a minor comfort—Michael's sarcasm meant he was still alive.

"Fuck off," George shot back, crouching to tilt Michael's head. "Any pain anywhere?"

"Yeah, just my head," Michael groans, gasping as he shifts. "That was bloody close, though."

He gritted his teeth and pulled himself upright, using the bench for leverage. His movements were slow and deliberate.

"I'm okay too, thanks for asking," Mr Kumar piped up, his voice sharp with irritation as he spits a glob of mud-streaked saliva onto the grass.

George narrowed his eyes but uncuffed him. "I know you are. There's no blood. Besides, you're in no position to be flippant." He trusted Kumar wouldn't run—not after what had just happened. Fear clung to the man like a second skin, sharp and palpable, his wide eyes darting to every corner of the street.

"So, matey, care to bloody fill us in on what the hell you're mixed up with?" Michael asks, brushing off his coat and taking a cautious look around.

Kumar's face, smeared with dirt and sweat, twisted with raw fear. This wasn't a fear of guilt or getting caught—it was deeper, more primal. His hands raked repeatedly over his chest and arms as if searching for invisible wounds.

"I... I can't. Not here," Kumar stammers, bolting his head to the side as the rising wail of sirens filled the street.

George's eyes followed his, scanning the scene. The air was tense, the silence between the sirens almost deafening. He looked for signs of the bullets and their trajectory, but the grass betrayed nothing. A small dent in the "No Ball Games" sign caught his eye, but it was impossible to tell if it was from the gunfire or some kid throwing rocks.

The sirens grew louder, closing in, but George focused on Kumar. The man was trembling now, his fear so raw it felt like a contagion. Whatever Kumar was involved in, whatever he was running from, George had the sinking feeling that the bullets and the car were only the beginning.

"Do you know how lucky you are?" George growls, his voice low but seething with barely restrained anger. His eyes bore into Mr Kumar, who flinched under the intensity. "You could be dead—and you nearly took us along for the ride. For your sake, you'd better tell us the truth."

The rage surged through George like wildfire, blood boiling beneath his skin. His hands trembled, his vision narrowing. The world around him seemed to dim, eclipsed by the pulse of fury pounding in his head.

"Georgie, you got a second?" Michael's voice cut through the haze. He darted over and threw an arm around George's shoulder, yanking him away from Kumar with a firm grip.

"What?" George snaps the word, a snarl that feels foreign even to his ears.

Michael's eyes were sharp, his tone low but urgent. "Get a bloody good hold of yourself. You're changing."

The words hit like a slap. George froze, his anger evaporating as he glanced down at his hands. The claws were out, sharp and unmistakable, curving like talons. They glinted faintly in the muted light, a terrible reminder of the beast lurking beneath his skin.

He turned toward the reflection in the car window. His stomach dropped. His ears had sharpened to pointed tips, his fangs fuller, his facial hair thick and untamed along raised cheekbones. But his eyes struck him the hardest—deep crimson, glowing faintly like embers.

"I didn't even notice," George mutters, his voice hollow. He watched the reflection intently as his features slowly softened, the claws retracting, the red draining from his eyes. Whatever normal was, he was inching back toward it.

"But it happened," Michael says, his voice sharp with a reprimand. "We're lucky his head's elsewhere right now." Michael's tone was steady, but the underlying tension was clear. He rarely wasn't rattled, but he knew how close they'd come to catastrophe.

George exhaled shakily, forcing himself to focus. He blamed the adrenaline, the aftermath of being shot at. His body's heightened response, the beast clawing to the surface. Whatever the reason, it had to stay under control.

The flashing blue lights of patrol cars surrounded them, painting the scene in cold, flickering hues. George scanned the chaos, his mind racing. Was this the Whitlock family showing their hand? It didn't feel right—too chaotic, too reckless for broad daylight. Warren Whitlock didn't strike him as the type to let things get this messy.

"You guys okay?" Locke's voice broke through, his tone laced with concern. He was signing off on forms, and an officer in uniform badgered him for a signature.

"Bruised, but we'll cope," Michael replies, gingerly touching the butterfly stitches on his head.

Locke sighed, tucking the paperwork under his arm. "Has he said anything? Does he know anything?" he asks, gesturing toward Kumar.

"Not on the way here," George says. "He just kept twitching, staring out the window like something would leap out at him." He accepted a folder Locke handed over, his eyes flicking to the report inside. "Pathology on the head?"

"Yep," Locke replies, flipping through his notepad for reference. "And you won't believe it."

"It's not Ross Walters," George says, catching the name on the page.

"No. Arthur Conroy. Born in '56. Chronic drunk, been in and out of prison most of his life," Locke says, rubbing the bridge of his nose. "The body hasn't been recovered —P.O.L.S.A. came up empty. We only got the ID from dental records."

George frowned, his mind drifting back to the head left in the bureau. The missing eyes, the way the mouth was shut. He shuddered inwardly at the memory. "Why take the eyes?" he mutters aloud.

"It feels sloppy," Michael says, echoing George's thoughts as if reading his mind. The shooting, the burnt head—it all felt amateurish, rushed.

"If I were to guess," Locke says, tapping his pen against his notepad, "they were buying time. And we got lucky no one got hit. But Mr Kumar knows something." He leaned forward slightly, his voice lowering. "Make it clear he'll be arrested for all the murders unless he cooperates."

George observed Locke. A steady heartbeat matched his calm, measured tone. If the pressure was getting to him, it didn't show. But the way Locke's eyes narrowed, the subtle shift in his stance, told George he was thinking—planning the next move, weighing the angles.

"Does he know what's coming? Has he asked for a brief or anything?" Michael asks, pulling his notebook from his pocket and flipping it open with a practised motion.

"He's got an idea," Locke replies, focusing on the map spread before him. "We're his safest bet right now, even if he hasn't admitted it. He hasn't asked yet, so strike while the iron's hot. I'll shout if anything pops up." Locke's tone was calm, but his eyes were sharp, scanning the map like he was trying to predict the next move—not a matter of if, but when.

George watched them both, a knot tightening in his chest. This was his first time sitting at this side of the table for an interview. The uncertainty gnawed at him, but he buried it deep. Whatever doubts lingered, they had no place here.

Michael's hand shot up in the interview room, halting Mr Kumar's mid-protest. "Why am I in here?" Kumar had started, but Michael cut him off with a gesture toward the gash on his head. His bruised ego paired perfectly with the physical injury, making his annoyance resonate.

"That's all, Officer Mathews. Thank you," George says, dismissing the constable stationed at the door with a nod.

He turned back to Mr Kumar, his voice steady but edged with steel. "You're in here because you're going to stop messing around and tell us what's happening. People are dying, Mr Kumar and we think you know more than you're letting on."

Kumar sat hunched forward, his muddy, grass-stained bomber jacket making him look even more dishevelled than when they'd found him. He fidgeted with his hands, grubby fingers picking at the invisible dirt, avoiding their eyes. His heart raced, audible to George's keen senses, its frantic rhythm betraying the secrets Kumar was trying to keep buried.

"Mr Kumar, you're not under arrest," Michael adds, his tone deliberately calm. "You're what we call a witness. Do you understand?"

Kumar gave a hesitant nod, his fidgeting slowing. The reassurance seemed to dull his immediate fear, but the tension in his shoulders remained.

Michael leaned forward. "Let's assume you've heard about the murders over the last few days. One victim was your wife. Another was on that excursion with you. So, what's going on?"

"I don't know," Kumar stammers, his voice cracking. "Not exactly."

George laid a series of crime scene photos on the table, each a grim snapshot of horror. He withheld the image of Annabelle at the warehouse, keeping it for later. Kumar's eyes darted to the photos but didn't linger.

"You see these?" George says, his voice low and deliberate. "All these people were murdered. Paralysed by a substance, we still can't identify. We've been asking questions at the museum you're tied to, Mr Kumar. One relic you handled contained a demon of vengeance. A demon that paralyses its victims before it kills them."

"I didn't do it," Kumar yells, his voice rising in panic. "I didn't—"

"Who has the relics?" George pressed; his tone was sharp, getting pissed off.

"I'm not sure anymore," Kumar mumbles, his words barely audible.

George reached into the file and pulled a photocopy of Ross Walters's diary. "We've seen Ross Walters's diary," he says, his voice cold. "We know more money was involved than you've admitted. Here, listen to this..."

He flipped to the marked page and read aloud:

"Day eighty-six. The thrill is long since gone. We've recovered hundreds of artefacts. People

have been hurt, and two have died. There's an agreement between a few of us. It's about time we get our share. The museum makes us do all the dirty work to preserve history. We get told this after each one: It's a shame there's no way to preserve our bank balances. Yusef has lined up a buyer. Twenty-five bloody million. Split seven ways."

George set the diary down and leaned back, watching Kumar intently. "How does that sound so far?"

Kumar's face was drained of colour, and his jaw was slack. His eyes flicked between the photos and the diary, panic swirling in their depths. He opened his mouth to speak, but no words came out. The weight of the evidence and the unspoken accusations pressed down on him, suffocating.

George didn't break eye contact, his steady gaze pinning Kumar like a butterfly to a board. "Start talking," he says, his voice deadly quiet.

"We figured a few wouldn't be missed," Kumar admitted, his voice hollow, defeated. "We'd all make some money, and maybe we could start our venture together. Private buyers, you know, for what we find."

George leaned forward, his gaze narrowing. "How does that fit into your plans now? Was Annabelle involved in any of this?"

Kumar hesitated, his shoulders slumping further. "Not with the relics, no. But... she'd been having an affair with Michelle Walters."

Michael straightened in his chair, his eyes sharpening. "Hang on a minute. Let me get this straight, matey. Your wife was having an affair with someone in the group. Now they're both dead, and you've got nothing to do with it?"

"Honestly, it wasn't me," Kumar says, his words rushing out. "I arranged the buyer, that's it."

George kept his expression neutral but pressed on. "What about this part?" He tapped the open diary before him; his voice edged with suspicion. "'That's a lot of money for years of toil,'" he read aloud. "'The trouble is, since we agreed, the group's had an edge. We're looking over our shoulders, questioning if the ones getting hurt aren't accidents. Instead, purposeful mistakes cast doubt over the project. If someone dies, it's a curse. As for Yusef, something is happening; he's becoming more volatile about the smallest things.'"

Kumar's face twitched, his hands restless on the table. "Yusef wanted control," he mutters. "He wanted to be the one in charge of the relics. I couldn't let him do that. I won't."

"And why not?" George pressed.

"Because I'm the group lead," Kumar says, his voice rising. "I've held the relic the longest. I feel its pull, its... heart. A few times, I swear it's called my name. I can't give it up. I feel stronger around it. Michelle thought I was losing the plot, but I'm not. She would say that, though—after all, it covers up her affair."

George's jaw tightened, the weight of Kumar's words sinking in. "Cheaters never prosper," he thought bitterly. But his focus remained sharp. "So, you're sticking with your story?"

Kumar nodded, his eyes darting nervously. George caught the tell—the man's heart was racing, erratic. There was more he wasn't saying.

Michael slid a photo across the table. "That why you're giving them a look that could kill in this picture?" he asks, gesturing to the group photo from the Walters' home.

Kumar stared at the photo, his expression unreadable. "It's just a look. I wouldn't do anything like that. I wouldn't even know how."

"But you could use a demon from a relic, couldn't you?" George asks, his voice calm but piercing. When he mentioned the relic, Kumar's heart skipped a beat, the spike unmistakable.

Kumar swallowed hard. "I got left with an empty box. I didn't get the relic."

George's eyes narrowed. "Was it true about the two million? How did you set this up?"

Kumar exhaled shakily, his fingers fidgeting again. "Subcontractors. People who've come on a few digs with us. They knew others had connections. I was given a number and a voicemail with instructions. All the communication happened through a 'help wanted' ad in the newspaper."

Michael scoffs, leaning back in his chair. "You seriously expect us to believe all this cloak-and-dagger stuff?"

"It was supposed to be a dead drop by the lake in Victoria Park," Kumar says, his voice growing more desperate. "The others involved spoke to me. The relic was in a small travel crate, no bigger than a woman's handbag. I didn't dare open it, and I didn't need to. When it reached the museum, everything seemed fine."

George folded his arms, his mind racing. The threads of Kumar's story dangled, frayed and tangled, but there was something there—something darker lurking beneath the surface. He leaned forward again, his gaze locking on to Kumar.

"Fine, isn't how I'd describe any of this," George says, his voice a low growl. "Let's cut the crap. What aren't you telling us?"

Kumar's lip quivered, his hands trembling. The room seemed to close in, the silence pressing down like a weight. George could feel the lies hovering in the air, waiting to be drawn out.

And he wasn't leaving until they were.

"Right?" Michael prompted, his patience thinning.

Kumar shifted uncomfortably in his seat, rubbing his hands together. "A dark saloon followed me when I left the museum grounds a few weeks ago," he began hesitantly. "I was told about a specific bench and bin. They taped an envelope under the bench, and I had to leave the box in the bin."

Michael leaned forward, sceptical. "What was in the envelope?"

"Seven cheques," Kumar says, his voice barely above a whisper. "Each just under 3.6 million. No details about who paid, other than the company name — 'Pinnacle Holdings.' But that company's shut down now. Gone."

Michael's eyebrows shot up. "Have you cashed the cheque? Given the others out?"

Kumar nodded. "Yes, and yes. But I haven't spent a single penny. Too scared to. Not long after the drop, I got a call at my house. Threats. They used a voice changer and told me to bring the relics, or I'd die."

George's eyes narrowed, his gaze piercing. "How the hell does this tie in with the murders?"

Kumar shook his head helplessly. "I know... but I don't know who has it now."

"What about Annabelle?" George pressed.

"We split after I found out about the cheating," Kumar admitted, his voice trembling. "She said she'd stay with her mum in Limehouse. That's where I thought she was." His heartbeat stayed steady, his eyes fixed on George and Michael, though he avoided the crime scene photos entirely.

George slid Annabelle's photo across the table, his eyes locked on Kumar's reaction. "This happened to her. Is there anything else you need to tell us?"

Kumar's face twisted as he stared at the photo, his breaths coming in short bursts. "Oh, my God. Oh my God, how could you?" His voice cracked, and tears welled in his eyes. "I... I would never do that. I loved her. She betrayed me, not the other way around. I would never..." His words dissolved into wrenching sobs, raw emotion spilling out of him.

Michael's expression was dead cold, but George could feel the weight of the moment getting to him and feared the impact on the wolf he was barely keeping at bay within.

"Donna Armitage, Jack Sexton, Emily Fulton, Brian Thistle, and Melanie Blake," George continues, his tone measured. "Do you know them? What about Tracey Kent and Rachel Darnley?"

"Yeah, of course I know them," Kumar says, his voice shaky. "They're the others."

Michael frowned. "Come on, sunshine. I'm not in the mood to fill in the blanks. Others, what?"

"Part of the expedition," Kumar says. "Jack and Brian were two of the seven. Emily's seeing Jack, but I think he's married to someone else."

Michael scoffs, leaning back. "Right. One big cesspool of iniquity. And I thought the police were bad. What about Tracey and Rachel?"

"I don't know," Kumar admitted. "I think Annabelle mentioned something about going out with someone named Tracey, but I didn't take notice. If I'd known about the affair... maybe I'd have asked more. Taken more interest. Maybe... maybe whatever she was up to wouldn't have ended like that."

Kumar's voice broke, and he dropped his head, tears streaming down his face as he stared at the photo of Annabelle.

George leaned closer. "Did you recognise who was in that car today?"

"No," Kumar says quickly, shaking his head. "I avoid taking straight routes home, always trying not to be followed. But I've seen that car before—that's why I ran. I assumed they were connected to the relic."

George exchanged a glance with Michael. "Right," he says. "Well, you can't go home. Is there anywhere else you can stay?"

Kumar hesitated, his voice trembling. "I don't know. I don't want to get anyone else involved. I'm too scared."

George nodded, thinking quickly. "Then you'll stay in an office until we can arrange somewhere safe. In the meantime, you'd better tell us if you remember anything else. No more secrets."

Kumar nodded, wiping his face with a trembling hand. George and Michael turned to leave, their minds swirling with more questions than answers.

Just as they reached the door, Kumar called out. "Wait."

George turned, his eyes narrowing. "What is it?"

"If you find the relic—or its heart—don't hold it," Kumar says, his voice low and trembling. "If there's any darkness in you, even the smallest bit, the relic pulls on it. It draws you in. And if the heart is joined... whatever's inside goes free."

George stared at him, the weight of the words settling over him like a shroud. The way Kumar spoke, the haunted look in his eyes—he believed every word.

As they stepped out of the room, George's thoughts churned. *This is how it started. The question is... who finished it?*

HOME

16

'28th night-time - Home.'

When George finally arrived home, it was past 10 p.m—the day had been more than enough—more than anyone should have to deal with. Mr Kumar was tucked away in a dingy, ground-floor hotel room, with a marked unit stationed outside like a fragile thread of protection. But even with precautions, the interview with Kumar refused to leave George's mind. The tangled threads looped endlessly, a cha-cha of half-truths and uneasy suspicions.

He'd asked someone to dig up history books from the archives, hoping to uncover anything about the "Kanaima" relic. So far, the texts had offered nothing but disappointment. Bentley's dismissive scrawl labelled it a spooky story, a crafted legend to scare off trespassers.

Maybe someone's stepping into that role, George thought grimly. *Using the legend to justify murder.* The idea had a grim elegance to it but no answers. He shook his head. He hadn't thought about werewolves much either, not until his own life had gone out the window—doing the cha-cha on its way down.

At his front door, George paused, his eyes darting down the dimly lit street. The shadows stretched long and crooked, each one a potential hiding spot. His gaze lingered on the parked cars, scanning for any sign of the black Audi or the battered navy Capri. His nerves still felt raw, stretched too thin to be anything but cautious.

Satisfied no surprises were lurking in the shadows, he stepped up to the door and let out a breath he didn't realise he'd been holding.

Inside, the flat felt colder than usual. The air carried a heavy stillness, the kind that crawled under your skin and refused to leave. George blamed the lack of memories in the space—this wasn't home yet. But the feeling gnawed at him, regardless.

His eyes drifted to the coffee table. Skip's card sat there, exactly where he'd left it. The words scrawled on the front stared back at him: *"Head down, gob shut, and you'll be OK. And don't screw up."* The advice felt hollow now. What they needed wasn't luck or good intentions. What they needed was a miracle.

The phone rang, slicing through the oppressive quiet.

Brrr, Brrr, Brrr.

George's stomach knotted instantly. He dreaded the sound. Another call, another problem. Another body? He snatched the receiver off the hook. "Hello?"

"Georgie?" Michael's familiar voice greeted him, but the tension in George's chest didn't ease.

"Michael, what's wrong? Another?"

A dry chuckle came through the line. "Ha ha, steady on. I know you're getting used to being yanked back in like you're on a bungee cord. Can't blame you for expecting the worst at this point."

George exhaled shakily, running a hand through his hair. "Yeah, I'm a little jittery. Hard to leave unfinished business sitting on my desk and feel useful at home."

"Georgie, you're still green," Michael says, his tone steady but edged with understanding. "This is the nature of the beast. The world doesn't get fixed in a day. These cases drag on—it's how they work."

"That doesn't make it feel any less wrong," George mutters, his voice low, frustration creeping into his tone.

"That's why I called," Michael says. "I saw your face when we left. There are too many loose ends and gaps with Kumar—and everything else. I've got a bad feeling about this one. Call it intuition."

George pinched the bridge of his nose, the tension coiling tighter. "Yeah, it feels off. I'm not buying the whole 'company' angle. Why would someone so anonymous and cloak-and-dagger spray bullets so wildly? It doesn't add up."

"No, it doesn't," Michael admitted. "None of it does. That's why tomorrow, we strip it all back. No theories, no guesses. Just the facts are simple. Something in all this noise has to lead somewhere."

George nodded, even though Michael couldn't see it. The day's chaos lingered, but Michael's words planted a small seed of clarity in his mind. Kumar's story and the world he'd painted didn't fit. But answers had to be buried beneath the lies, the legends, and the blood.

"Yeah," George murmured. "Tomorrow."

The call ended, but its weight stayed with him. The flat was still too cold, too quiet. George leaned back against the wall, staring blankly at the ceiling.

Somewhere in the distance, a car engine rumbled. His body tensed instinctively, but the sound faded, leaving only the hum of silence. George tried to let it go, but a familiar dread crawled up his spine, settling like a heavy stone in his chest.

He poured himself a stronger drink than usual—and took it to bed. The whiskey burned going down, but it did little to soften the sharp edges of his thoughts.

The day's shadows stretched into his dreams, twisting into something darker.

"Exactly," Michael agrees, his voice thoughtful but edged with unease. "Why meet in a public park with a random box? Anywhere else would've done the job. Newspaper ad columns? It's all too messy—like there are too many moving parts. How about tomorrow? We strip it all back? Just the facts. Nothing else. We'll layer in what Kumar gave us after."

George nodded slowly, Michael's reasoning cutting through chaotic theories. The case was a tangled mess of assumptions, scattered details, and unanswered questions. A fresh, simplified approach might be the only way forward.

"I think Kumar's still holding something back," George admitted, his voice low. "He knows more than he's letting on. Maybe after a night to think about it, he'll remember—or decide it's safer to share."

"Maybe," Michael replies. His tone softened. "Speaking of rest, switch off and get some. You never know when Locke will wake us."

The advice was sound but easier said than done. George hung up the phone, letting his hand linger on the receiver as his gaze drifted across the dimly lit room. The shadows stretched long against the walls, crawling like a living thing into every corner. The air felt heavier than usual, the silence oppressive.

With a weary sigh, George relented. He poured himself a generous glass of whiskey and carried it to bed, hoping the warm buzz would ease his thoughts' relentless churn.

But even as he sipped, the ghosts of the day circled him. Kumar's cryptic words, the relic's cursed pull—they lingered like predators in the dark, pacing just out of reach.

29th - 5 a.m.

B *rrr, Brrr, Brrr.*

The phone's shrill buzz cut through the stillness, a jagged sound that pulled George from a restless sleep. He groaned, fumbling for the handset, his movements sluggish, weighed down by exhaustion. The near-empty whiskey bottle on the nightstand wobbled precariously, its contents a bitter reminder of the night before.

A glance at the clock—5:00 a.m. The harsh red digits stared back at him, an ominous warning.

"Hey," he mutters groggily, his voice rough. He wasn't even sure if the handset was the right way up.

"You need to get to the hotel."

Michael's voice was sharp, clipped, cutting straight to the point.

"Michael?"

"Yeah," Michael says, his tone grim. "We jinxed ourselves last night, didn't we?"

George felt his stomach twist. "Why? What happened?" The question came out hesitant, dread settling over him like a heavy fog.

"He's missing."

"Kumar?"

"No, the pope. Of course, it's Kumar," Michael snaps, the irritation in his voice barely masking the underlying tension.

"Shit," George cursed, sitting up now, his brain sluggishly forcing itself into gear. "How?"

"No clue," Michael says, his voice tight. "The unit outside didn't see a thing. But the guest in the adjoining room called the front desk. Said there was banging—loud, violent."

George swung his legs over the edge of the bed, his pulse quickening. "What's the inside look like?"

"Like a proper fight went down," Michael replies. "The room's a disaster, and the back window's wide open."

"Think he escaped?"

"Maybe," Michael says, his hesitation palpable. "But the officers found blood."

The word hung in the air, heavy and cold. George felt his mind spiral, clawing at fragments of possibilities that refused to connect.

"Great," George muttered. "So, officially missing for now?"

"Looks like it," Michael confirmed. "You'll have to see for yourself. How long until you can pick me up?"

George rubbed his temple, the weight of exhaustion pressing down on him. But there was no room for it now—not with this. "Haven't even had my coffee yet."

"Then hurry. I'll bring the coffee," Michael says, his humour dry but strained. "How's that for a deal, you grumpy git?"

George hung up without answering, his mind racing ahead to the scene waiting for him. He stared at the clock again, the glowing numbers burning into his retinas. 5:02.

The air in the room felt colder now, the shadows longer.

George stood, his movements stiff, and caught sight of himself in the mirror. Dark circles rimmed his eyes, his skin pale under the dim light. He looked more like a ghost than a man. And somewhere in the pit of his stomach, a gnawing fear stirred.

This isn't just a case, he thought. *It's something else entirely.*

He threw on his clothes and grabbed his coat. The cold dawn awaited him, but its bite couldn't match the chill settling deep in his chest.

"Better of two evils," George mutters, dragging himself to his feet. "And less of the 'grumpy.' Not used to waking up like this."

Michael let out a short laugh, but it lacked warmth. "Fair enough. Just get here."

"Fine."

George hung up, but the unease stayed thick and clinging like a damp fog. His thoughts circled back to Kumar—the cryptic interview, the relic, the chaos of the scene. The possibility that Kumar had staged the whole thing to cover an escape wasn't far-fetched. On paper, it made sense. But something deeper here gnawed at the edges of George's mind, just out of reach.

He reached for his clothes, then stopped cold.

Mud streaked his arms and legs, and thin, jagged scratches crisscrossed his skin. His fingertips were filthy, dirt caked beneath his nails.

George stared at himself, a chill spreading through his chest. *I'd swear I fully changed in my sleep... if I didn't know any better.*

The thought twisted like a knife in his gut. The beast he fought so hard to control—he couldn't have slipped. Not without knowing. Could he?

His breath quickened, the rising panic clawing at him, but he shoved it down. *Not now. Not here.*

All he could do was desperately hope that no one had been hurt.

The Travel Inn - Bethnal Green - 6:30 a.m.

The morning light was cold and stark, leeching all warmth from the muted blues and greys of the street. The Travel Inn sat in grim silence, cordoned off with fluttering police tape. Uniformed officers stood stiffly outside, their postures tense and watchful.

George pulled up, killed the engine, and sat momentarily staring at the building. A faint sense of unease crawled under his skin, like static before a storm.

Michael waited by the entrance, holding two cups of coffee. His face was drawn, his usual sarcasm dulled by something heavier. Without a word, he handed a cup to George.

"You're going to need this," Michael says, his voice subdued.

George took the cup, but its warmth did little to steady him. "What are we looking at?"

Michael sighs, motioning toward the building. "Come inside. It's bad."

Inside, the chaos hit like a wave. Furniture was overturned, glass shards scattered across the carpet, and a broken lamp lay lifeless on its side. The metallic tang of blood lingered faintly in the air—subtle but enough to curdle George's stomach.

The back window gaped open, its shattered frame jagged and raw. Curtains billowed lazily in the cold morning breeze like silent witnesses to whatever had unfolded here.

George's jaw tightened as he scanned the room, his tension coiling tighter with every detail.

"Blood here," Michael says, pointing to a dark smear near the window. "Not much, though. Not enough for anything serious. Looks staged."

"Or hurried," George murmurs, his gaze locked on the faint trail. "He didn't go willingly, did he?"

Michael shrugged, his expression grim. "If he went at all."

The unspoken words hung in the air, heavy and cold. George felt their weight settle over him as he turned to the open window. The breeze bit at his skin, sharp and indifferent.

The morning light did nothing to lift the shadows that clung to the room.

Alleyway Near Number Six

T he blue light from a patrol car strobed up the peeling walls, casting fleeting, distorted shadows that stretched and twisted. Two uniformed officers stood before the scuffed blue door of number six, their radios crackling softly in the otherwise muted street.

George parked nearby, watching SOCO Wainwright, clad in protective coveralls, step briskly inside.

Michael glanced at the door and smirked faintly, though the humour didn't reach his eyes. "Does this ever get old for you?"

George shook his head, the weight of the situation settling heavily on his chest.

"I could say yes," Michael continues, "but what else would I be doing? Handling mundane domestics? Nah, matey. Death and murder ruin lives long term, so if I can help even a little, it's worth it. It doesn't get old. Not like that. What about you?"

"Me? What about me?" George says, catching the edge in his voice. He regretted it instantly, but Michael's teasing smirk didn't waver.

"I mean, how's the whole 'howl-at-the-moon' shit?" Michael asks, his tone light but with an undertone that makes George bristle. It was a joke, sure—but not entirely.

Never a truer word said in jest, George thought grimly.

His lips tightened, and he didn't answer right away. Instead, he let Michael's words sit between them like a stone, heavy and unmovable.

The truth was, the beast was always there. Lurking. Waiting. And lately, George wasn't sure he was keeping it at bay.

He exhaled, staring at the pavement as the words tumbled out. "Woke up covered in muddy scratches. Blood under my nails. It's getting worse."

Michael's smirk faltered. For a moment, the humour left his face entirely. "I was joking... but could it be far off? Did you go out?"

"I don't know," George mutters, his voice hollow. "I hope not."

Michael hesitated, then forced a casual tone that didn't quite land. "Well, tomorrow could get interesting."

George didn't respond. The thought burrowed into his mind like a thorn—small but impossible to ignore. He'd pushed it aside before and kept it at bay with distractions, but it was always there. If this kept escalating, how long before he lost control completely? The lure of carnage, the primal hunger for blood—it would destroy him. And worse, it might destroy people like Michael.

T he room was chaos.

The double bed near the left wall had been flipped upright; its headboard smashed against the plaster. The angle wasn't right. The rest of the furniture had suffered a similar fate—the TV, kettle, and a tray of condiments had been swept violently to the right, their remains scattered like debris from an explosion.

George's nose caught a faint whiff of blood near the broken window. He inhaled deeply, letting his sharper senses do the work. Something was wrong. There was no scent of fear. No adrenaline. No sweat or stress lingering in the air, no telltale markers of a struggle.

Michael was speaking to Wainwright, his tone lighter than the scene warranted. George caught the faint glint in his partner's eye—Michael was hovering too close, his Cockney charm in full effect. George let it slide. Michael could flirt all he wanted; it wasn't the priority.

Circling back to the bed, George frowned. The foot end had been flipped with enough force to splinter the headboard against the wall nearly. It wasn't right. His gaze travelled to the front door, where a wooden chair sat askew, its legs scuffed as though it had been jammed under the handle. It was a barricade, hastily and ineffectively made.

Then there was the window.

The jagged shards of glass scattered outward onto the ground told a simple story—this was an escape, not a break-in. George's stomach twisted, the implications sinking in like lead. *Set up.*

The words echoed in his head like a bell. They'd been played. But why?

Wainwright moved methodically, dusting the table for prints. Her calm precision felt out of place amid the wreckage. Michael hovered nearby, notepad in hand, sketching the scene with surprising detail. George watched them both, feeling a gnawing sense of inadequacy. He should have thought of that first. But no—he was too busy chasing the impossible, trying to extract meaning from chaos.

The faint scent of Kumar still lingered in the air. George focused on it, trying to unravel the puzzle. *Calm.* That's what stuck out. No stress. If Kumar had been attacked, George would've caught the tang of distress pheromones, the unmistakable spike of fear.

But there was none of that here.

"What are you hiding, Kumar?" George murmurs under his breath.

His gaze returned to the broken window. The force it took to punch outward wasn't normal for someone like Kumar. It didn't fit. Nothing about this did.

The weight of the room settled heavily on George's shoulders. He scanned the jagged glass edges again, trying to force the pieces into place. But the silence around him only deepened the wrongness of it all.

The faint scrape of glass under Wainwright's boot punctuated the stillness.

Everything about this was wrong. And the longer George stood there, the darker the possibilities became.

"Michael, you got anything?" George asks, his voice low and steady as he crouches to the floor, keeping his gaze downward.

The red haze crept in—a visceral distortion that sharpened every detail and edge. It was different this time, stronger, more vivid. George could feel it more than see it, the heat signatures and glowing remnants of everyone who had passed through the room recently burning in his vision. Two symmetrical prints caught his attention on the wall below the window, leading to further steps halfway up. Glass shards littered the ground on either side of the prints, and faint palm stains smudged the ledge where sweat had marked an escape.

"No," Michael says with a scowl. "And I don't like it."

"Then you won't like what I have to say," George mutters, rising onto his tiptoes to peer through the jagged windowpane. Something about the scene clawed at his thoughts, stirring a twisted sense of familiarity—like a terrible memory lurking just out of reach.

He took a slow, deliberate breath, catching the crisp, dew-laden grass mingling with the greasy allure of breakfast wafting from nearby vents. For a fleeting moment, the contrast made his stomach churn.

"Well, it's no fun when life's plain sailing," Michael quips, dragging a battered pack of cigarettes from his jacket. He lit one with practised ease, and his movements were mechanical. Resigned. He didn't look surprised. Should George have been?

"The only plain sailing in this room," George replies, his tone sharp, "is that it's a set-up."

Michael raised an eyebrow, the cigarette dangling from his lips. He didn't say a word but scanned the room as though seeing it for the first time. Across the way, Miss Wainwright paused, her attention drawn to George.

"Explain," Michael says, exhaling a slow stream of smoke that coiled in the dim light.

George pointed toward the door. "The chair there—it's jammed under the handle. A staged resistance. The bed? Flipped from the base, not toppled like you'd expect in a fight. And the window? He didn't just dive through it. Look at the glass; it tells a different story. The blood? It's just enough to sell it. He forced this scene, but the real question is, why?"

Wainwright began pacing the room, her movements precise and deliberate as she mimicked the actions George described. Her face was unreadable, her gaze narrowing as she reconstructed the scene. She didn't respond immediately, only stopped beneath the window, her head tilted as she stared into the stillness.

"That's not all," George says, breaking the silence. "Just outside the window, there's more of that toxin."

The words struck like a hammer. Michael and Wainwright spun to face him in near unison. Michael's eyes widened, the whites bulging as if to say, *This better make sense, mate.*

"How do you know?" Wainwright asks, her tone calm but her brow furrowing behind thick-rimmed glasses.

"I'm taller than both of you. Maybe even taller standing on shoulders," George says, forcing a wry smirk, though it didn't quite reach his eyes.

"Okay, wise guy. Where?"

George gestured toward the window. "It's dripped down the wall," he says, his voice flattening as he traces the faint trail leading to a small patch on the concrete just outside. "And there's a spot on that fragile ledge beyond the frame. Subtle, but it's there."

"Boo!"

The sudden voice jolted the group, making them spin toward the window. Miss Walker stood just outside, her figure half-shrouded in shadow. George hadn't sensed her approach, which unsettled him almost as much as her unceremonious arrival.

"What the hell, woman?" Michael barks, clutching his chest in mock anger, though the edge in his voice betrayed genuine surprise.

"Oh, calm down, old man. Nothing a good pacemaker wouldn't fix," Walker quips, brushing past the shattered glass as though it were an afterthought. Her expression was sharp, her eyes scanning the room with clinical precision as she retrieved a set of sample tubes from her case.

George remained still, his gaze fixed on her. Something was unnerving about how she moved, how her presence had slipped past his senses unnoticed. His instincts itched, a warning he couldn't quite articulate.

"Why are you here, Walker?" Michael asks his tone sharper now. "Thought you only turned up when someone was officially dead."

"Not yet," Walker replies, her focus shifting to the faint toxin residue on the wall. "But I've been analysing the head from Walters' place. Something about Kumar doesn't sit right."

"Still playing with the dead, I see," Michael mutters, taking a long drag from his cigarette.

Walker didn't look up. "It's called forensic science, caveman. When the weird makes little sense, you dig deeper. How else are we going to make you two look good?" she says, her tone biting but laced with dry humour.

George watched her work, his unease deepening. Walker's presence felt like a disruption—not of the scene, but of something deeper. If she pushed too far and asked the wrong questions... she might uncover things George couldn't let her see.

As Walker swabbed the toxins with practised efficiency, George's thoughts churned. The room was a stage, an illusion crafted to mislead. But for what purpose? And who was pulling the strings?

He glanced back at the broken window. The weight of the unanswered questions pressed down on him, the air in the room heavy.

Something about this felt darker than anything he'd encountered before.

"What the hell, woman?" Michael barks, clutching his chest dramatically, though the crooked smile on his lips betrayed his amusement.

"Oh, calm down, old man," Walker replies with a grin, her tone sharp and teasing as she retrieves a set of sample tubes from her case. "Nothing a good pacemaker won't fix."

George's unease deepened as he watched her work. Something about Walker—sharp, fearless, and unwavering—commanded attention: it was impressive, sure, but it was also dangerous. Her presence felt deliberate, not coincidental, and it set George on edge.

"Why are you here?" Michael asks, leaning back with a cigarette between his fingers, his usual casual bravado masking a trace of suspicion. "Thought you only turned up when someone was officially dead."

"Not yet," Walker quips, her focus unwavering as she examines the scene. "But I've been analysing the head from the Walters' case. Something about Kumar doesn't sit right."

"You're still playing with the dead," Michael mutters, drawing out the words in a low, deliberate tone. "You know, valid point."

Walker rolled her eyes, her expression flickering briefly to Michael before returning to her work. "Science, caveman. It's called science. When the weirdness doesn't explain itself, I dig deeper. Weird is my job. And let's face it," she adds with a faint smirk, "making you two look competent is a full-time gig."

George's stomach tightened at her words. They weren't just a barb—they carried weight, a sharpness that unnerved him. Walker's curiosity was dangerous. She wasn't one to let things go. And if she pushed too far, too hard, she might uncover truths no one was ready for. Truths George desperately needed to keep buried.

Walker moved briskly, swabbing the toxin stains on the wall as though the scene whispered instructions to her. Her confidence in the inexplicable was both admirable and unsettling.

George stood silent, letting her movements blur into the background as his mind repeated the scene. The chair jammed under the door, the flipped bed, the faint blood smears near the window. It all felt hollow—like an echo of something that never truly happened.

The room was a performance. A carefully crafted illusion meant to mislead, to distract. But for what purpose?

Walker's voice snapped him out of his thoughts. "This residue matches what I found in Walters' house," she says, holding a swab with a glint of dark fluid. "Consistent composition. Whatever it is, it's not organic."

Michael blew out a slow stream of smoke, his gaze narrowing. "Not organic? You're saying... what? It's synthetic?"

"I'm saying it doesn't belong here," Walker replies. Her tone carried an edge of finality that brooked no argument. "You need to rethink your theories."

George glanced at her, the weight of her words settling over him. She was too close to something. He could feel it, like the first prick of a needle, just before it sank deeper.

The room felt heavier, the shadows darker. George's chest tightened as the possibilities turned over in his mind. How far would the truth go before it pulled them all under?

And more importantly, how much longer could he keep the beast within him from rising to the surface?

LIME HOUSE CUT

17

"**B**rian Thistle," George says, the name rolling off his tongue like a grim prophecy. "That's who's next. 12 George's Square, Limehouse."

They had pursued leads from the list, but each address had been a dead end so far. Ross Walters' diary proved as cryptic as frustrating, offering misdirection after misdirection. George couldn't shake the thought: was Walters alive and working with Kumar? Or had the demon already taken hold, dragging them both into its web of vengeance?

"What's the chance that either of them is here?" Michael asks, his tone edged with scepticism.

George glanced at his notes. "The diary mentioned it, but checks show the owner as Mildred Thistle, seventy-six. She bought the place after her husband passed."

The estate was tucked near Limehouse Link, the Thames and the Regent's Canal. It was a small, gated community for the elderly, difficult to access and well-maintained—at least on the surface. Number 12 stood among the front houses; its red-brick exterior weathered but respectable.

George scanned the map. "It's near the water. There's a small beach nearby. Probably a selling point for the retirees here."

Michael leaned back in his seat, his brow furrowed. "I don't like this, Georgie. It doesn't feel right. I don't know if we're wasting time or about to step into something worse."

George nodded, his unease mirroring Michael's. "I know what you mean. It feels strange." He paused, glancing at the house again. "But strange enough to make it plausible."

They parked across the road, Number 12 looming ahead with its small, overgrown garden. To George's left, the sharp, salty smell of the Thames hung in the air, mixing with the faint scent of diesel from passing boats.

The house was nearly identical to others they'd seen during the case—red brick, semi-detached, with two bay windows. An unmarked unit sat quietly nearby, the officers inside watching from the shadows.

Both parking spaces in front of the house were empty. The gates into the courtyard were set back about forty feet from the road, adding an air of isolation.

Michael sighed, stepping out of the car. "I don't like this, Georgie," he repeated, his unease clear. "It doesn't feel right."

George followed, the feeling settling deeper into his gut. "Yeah," he says quietly. "But it's strange enough to be worth checking."

As they crossed the street, George felt the weight of someone's gaze on him. He didn't need to look to know who it was.

Outside a small supermarket, a man sat in a battered wooden chair, his posture lazy but his eyes sharp. He watched them intently, a smouldering cigar clenched between his teeth. The thick, acrid smoke wafted toward George, cutting through the salty air.

"We've got a fan," George mutters, his voice low. He kept his gaze forward, resisting the urge to glance back.

Michael's lip curled in a smirk. "Aww, have we? That's a nice change from being called 'pig scum.'"

The sarcasm drew a faint chuckle from George, easing the tension momentarily. "I thought that was a term of endearment," he says as they approached the gate.

Michael swung the black gate open, its hinges creaking. George hung back, his eyes scanning the house. Something felt wrong, a faint but growing itch at the edge of his senses.

"What's up, Georgie?" Michael asks, noticing his hesitation.

George gestured toward the neighbouring house. "Look at Number 14," he says, his tone measured.

Michael frowned, his gaze shifting. Number 14's garden was pristine—neatly arranged potted flowers, trimmed hedges, and clean stone paths. It was picture-perfect.

George gestured toward Number 12. "Now, compare it to this. It's almost mirrored, but everything here is dead. The flowers are wilted, the garden's overgrown, and weeds are pushing through the cracks."

Michael's frown deepened. "You're right. That's not just neglect—it's deliberate."

George nodded, stepping closer to the front door. "There's more. Look at the newspapers stacked by the door—at least a week's worth. And the milk bottles. They've been there long enough to turn."

The sour smell was faint but unmistakable. It mingled with the stale air, adding another layer of wrongness to the scene.

Michael sighed, rubbing the back of his neck. "This place doesn't feel abandoned. It feels... empty."

The yellow door loomed, thick and imposing, its scuffed surface betraying years of neglect. The letterbox sat awkwardly high—chest height for George, above Michael's head. George almost smirked at the thought of suggesting Michael use it.

Michael, as usual, was compensating. George caught him a few times, trying to make himself appear bigger—puffing out his chest, standing taller. It wasn't new. He'd seen this bravado before. Michael had a knack for it, making up for his lack of physical presence with bullish determination. On the streets, he tiptoed to find common ground with scroats; in confrontation, he took the curb to loom over anyone in the road.

Michael's efforts didn't annoy George this time. They made him laugh. Watching him practically bouncing on his toes to pee through the window was almost endearing. George shook his head and stepped closer. Even at his height, seeing through the frosted glass was a task.

The flies were the first thing he noticed.

Not the skinny, lazy houseflies—they were thick blue bottles buzzing loudly against the glass. Their frenzy created an unsettling hum, amplified by their sheer number. The window, divided into four semi-circles of frosted glass, trembled faintly under their weight.

George's stomach twisted. Flies like this meant one of two things, and neither was good. One was tolerable, but the other prayed it wasn't the second. If it was, poor Mildred wasn't just dead; she'd been dead a while.

"No point playing jack-in-the-box," George says, grabbing Michael's shoulder as he wound up for another jump.

Michael turned, his face scrunched in mild annoyance. "Why's that?" he asks, his tone almost petulant like a child denied a toy.

"Listen," George says, slowing him down with a firm but calm tone.

Michael sighed and stepped back, crossing his arms. George turned his attention back to the house. It wasn't just the flies or the smell that unnerved him. The details mattered—every detail.

George slowly grew to respect Michael despite their rough start. Where George relied on instinct and observation, Michael had a knack for getting people to talk, for breaking down walls with charm or sheer persistence. It was a skill George couldn't deny. But in return, George wanted Michael to learn from him, to see the dots that connected everything—the ones most people missed.

"Flies? So what?" Michael mutters, breaking the silence.

George didn't look away from the door. "That's rotten meat, or something's dead," he says flatly, pressing his shoulder against the lock to test its strength. Not that it mattered. Werewolf him could rip it off its hinges without effort, but the man across the street was still watching. Everything needed to look clean and procedural.

"Right, this fucking case is pissing on my last nerve," Michael says, raking his hands through his silver hair. His heart was beating faster now, the nerves creeping in.

"Just bloody watch out and keep quiet a minute," George replies, closing his eyes to focus.

The world sharpened, his senses narrowing to the house before him. He could hear the faint hum of the flies and smell the sharp tang of decay mixing with the stale air. But there was no life inside. No heartbeats. No shuffling feet. Whatever was behind the door was long gone—except for the stench—rotten flesh, at least three weeks old. The heating was on, amplifying the odour.

"It's going to stink," George says, opening his eyes. He considered not warning Michael for a moment to see his reaction.

"Well?" Michael asks, pacing now, his anxiety obvious. "That guy across the road's getting twitchy."

"At least one dead," George says finally. He glanced at Michael, waiting for the nod.

Michael sighed. "For Christ's sake, go on, then. The granny, you reckon?"

"That's my thinking," George says, gripping the silver letterbox handle and bracing the other against the doorframe. With a sharp palm strike, the lock splintered, the door swinging open with a groan.

"Nice move," Michael mutters, stepping beside George. He glanced over his shoulder, giving the man across the street one final look. The old man hadn't moved, still watching with sharp, calculating eyes.

George exchanged a nervous half-smile with Michael, but unease churned in his stomach. Something about this house was worse than the others. It wasn't just the smell. It wasn't just the flies. It was waiting.

He pushed the door wider, and a wall of putrid air hit him like a physical force. He staggered back as the buzzing intensified, the flies surging toward them in a fierce cloud.

George instinctively kept his mouth shut, but Michael wasn't so lucky. He stumbled, choking as a bluebottle attempted to explore his throat.

By the look on Michael's face, the fly was winning. George had to fight not to laugh. It wasn't the time for it—not here, not now—but the image of Michael battling a fly was almost too much.

"Slap, slap."

George clapped Michael hard on the back, maybe harder than necessary. Michael stumbled forward, coughing violently until the fly buzzed out, victorious.

"Cheers for that," Michael gasped, rubbing his shoulder.

George smirked. "No problem. Try not to eat anything else."

The hallway stretched ahead, dim and oppressive, as the stench settled around them like a living thing. And deeper inside, the silence grew heavier, suffocating, as though the house was holding its breath.

"Slap, slap."

George struck Michael's back too firmly, judging by how Michael crashed into the wall, coughing and gasping as the fly dislodged.

"Cheers for that," Michael gasped, rubbing his shoulder as he straightened.

"Cuh, cuh. No problem," George replies, suppressing a smirk. "Try not to eat anything else."

The narrow hallway stretched ahead, dimly lit and suffocating under the weight of the stench that clung to every surface. Beneath the acrid rot was something familiar—a faint trace of stale floral perfume and the sickly sweet scent of decay.

The house felt like it belonged to another time. The old floral wallpaper sagged and curled at the edges, and the dark brown carpet was worn thin in the middle. Straight ahead was a steep and shadowed staircase leading to the darkness above. To the left were two open doorways, the first leading into a sitting room and the second into what seemed like a lounge connected to the kitchen.

The oppressive heat suffused everything, amplifying the foul odour. George's skin prickled under his collar. It wasn't just the stench. The air felt alive, pressing against him like an unwelcome touch.

"Why is it," Michael mutters, his voice low and edged with frustration, "that everywhere we go, there's death?"

George peered into the first room. Dust covered a worn but comfy-looking sofa, and an old TV sat on a crooked stand, untouched. The space felt frozen in time, as though whoever had lived here had stepped out and never returned.

"It has to be this 'Kanaima demon,' spreading its vengeance," George says, his voice steady, though he wasn't sure he believed his own words. "We stop the demon, and maybe—just maybe—death leaves us alone for a while."

The second room was unfamiliar.

She was there.

Slumped in an armchair, Mildred Thistle's frail body was swallowed by the floral upholstery. At first glance, it looked as though she'd passed peacefully, her head tilted slightly to one side as if she'd fallen asleep.

But then George saw the wire.

His breath caught, and he closed his eyes, inhaling deeply before opening them again and stepping closer.

Mildred's sagging, discoloured skin was marbled with bulging blue veins. Her facial features were sunken, her skin stretched tight over the bones. Dark, glistening fluid leaked from her eyes, nose, and ears, trailing down her cheeks and soaking into the chair's fabric.

A fly zipped lazily from her gaping mouth, sudden enough to make George flinch.

The nebuliser cord was pulled taut around her throat, cutting deep into the loose skin. The air tanks beside her chair were full—unused. Whoever had killed her had silenced her deliberately, with cruel precision.

George's gaze drifted to the windows, single-pane and poorly fitted. They wouldn't have done much to keep the smell inside, but the heating—too high—had ensured the rot seeped into every corner of the house.

He turned to Michael, who stood by a glass cabinet near the wall, his expression a mix of confusion and unease. In his hands was a framed photo, one of many inside the cabinet.

George's eyes shifted back to Mildred, her lifeless form etched into his memory. His thoughts raced, circling the same questions: *Who killed her?* Kumar? Walters? Jack Sexton? Emily Fulton? Or maybe Brian Thistle, her son? Any of them could have done it. All of them were tied to the expedition. But why her? Why now?

Michael broke the silence, holding up the photo. It looked newer than most, its colours vibrant compared to the faded family portraits surrounding it. He compared it to the group picture they'd seen earlier, his brow furrowing.

"These don't match," Michael mutters, more to himself than George.

George's jaw tightened as his gaze returned to Mildred. Killing anyone was a line that should never be crossed. But this—a defenceless old woman, silenced and left to rot—felt like a deeper betrayal.

Money. Inheritance. It was the simplest motive, but something about this felt worse.

He snapped on gloves, stepping closer to sift through the small leather notebook on the side table beside her chair. His fingers brushed against something on her dress as he reached for it.

Glass shards.

They glittered faintly in the dim light and thick, scattered across her lap and the swirling-patterned cushion beneath her. George frowned. The shards were too specific, too deliberate.

"Picture frame glass," George murmurs, scanning the room for any sign of a broken frame. But the walls were intact, the cabinet undisturbed.

Michael glanced over, his attention drawn by George's focus. "What's that from?"

George didn't answer immediately, his mind racing. The glass wasn't random. It was deliberate, part of the story left behind. He flipped through the notebook carefully, noting its mundane contents—grocery lists, phone numbers, medication reminders.

But one entry stood out, scribbled in haste.

"Jack is pressuring me again. The relic will bring death to us all, and I can't get rid of it. I won't let him have it. God help me."

George's stomach churned as he read the words aloud. Michael turned toward him, his expression darkening.

"This isn't just about money," George says quietly.

Michael set the photo back in the cabinet, his jaw tightening. "No. It's not."

George's gaze returns to Mildred, the shards of glass, and the notebook's ominous warning. Whatever they were chasing, it was far worse than greed.

It was vengeance.

Mindful that they had stumbled upon yet another crime scene, George snapped on a pair of gloves, his focus drawn to the small leather notebook sitting on the side table to Mildred's left. As he reached for it, his attention shifted to something glittering faintly on her lap—broken glass.

Small shards, barely a centimetre thick, lay scattered across Mildred's dress, the jagged edges catching the dim light. They varied in size, some embedded in the swirling-patterned cushion beneath her. The pieces had no obvious point of origin—until George followed the trail.

The south-facing window caught his attention. Its sill was bathed in weak sunlight, and at first glance, it appeared unremarkable. But then George noticed a faint discolouration near the right edge of the ledge. A rectangular outline—ten centimetres long by two centimetres wide—stood out, a patch of wood lighter than the surrounding surface.

It was missing a picture frame.

"Michael, come see this," George says, his voice low but firm.

Michael heaved a weary sigh as he waddled over, retrieving his glasses from his jacket pocket with exaggerated care. "What now? Not another bloody note, please," he says, his sarcastic grimace masking the unease in his voice.

George ignored the jab, pointing between the window ledge and Mildred's lap. "We're missing a picture," he says, his tone steady but laced with tension.

Michael leaned in, squinting at the faint rectangular outline before shifting his gaze to the broken glass scattered across Mildred's lap. "Shit, you're right... wait a minute. Catch a butcher's at her right fist," he says, his voice lowering as realisation struck.

Mildred's right hand was clenched tightly, her palm facing down as if guarding whatever was inside. The positioning wasn't natural—it was deliberate, defiant. Whatever she held, she had fought to keep it hidden.

George's eyes burned faintly as the shift took over, sharpening his vision. The world around him dulled, colours muting into lifeless hues. Mildred's skin, drained of all warmth, became a pale haze. At first, her hand seemed empty, lifeless. But then he caught a flicker of colour—something faint, barely visible, peeking between her stiff fingers.

"Got something," George says, a flicker of excitement breaking through his grim tone.

Michael leaned closer, his face scrunching as he tried to make out the details. "Yeah, I see it too. Part of a photo, maybe," he murmurs, his voice quieter now. His usual sarcasm was gone, replaced by something heavier. His gaze flicked back to Mildred, and for a moment, he looked... sad.

"Yes, you've got me a little scared," Michael mutters, glancing at George's glowing eyes.

"Them fucking eyes, mate—they're a bit much up close." He forced a small, nervous smile, but George could hear the subtle uptick in his heartbeat.

"Sorry, Michael," George says, pulling back slightly, trying to sound reassuring. "Hopefully, they'll settle a little more soon."

But the truth gnawed at him. The blood moon was looming, its pull growing stronger each day. What if he couldn't hold it back? What if he shifted completely, becoming the beast in its rawest form? People wouldn't just fear him—they'd hunt him. He couldn't afford to lose control. He couldn't do this without Michael.

"It's okay, matey," Michael says, his voice softening. He tilted his head toward Mildred's hand, his brow furrowing. "We'll figure it out. Yeah, I see paper, too. A part of something—a photo, maybe."

George nodded, his jaw tightening. The pieces were scattered across the room like fragments of a shattered mirror. Another lead, another thread to chase. But they were no closer to understanding the picture.

"It looks like we'll need our dynamic duo," George says, his tone lighter, though it didn't mask the weight of the situation.

Michael nodded again, reaching for his radio with practised ease. "Control, we need SOCO and the pathologist here ASAP. Possible evidence in the victim's hand. Over."

As Michael relayed the details, George stared at Mildred's clenched fist, his thoughts circling the same dark questions. The fragment of a photo—felt like another missing piece of a puzzle that refused to come together.

Mildred had fought to keep it hidden, even in death. Whatever secrets she held, they would uncover them.

Another lead, another unanswered question.

George only hoped Mildred could help them now.

TENTERHOOKS

18

The tension in the room tightened like a noose. George and Michael held their breaths as if the sound of oxygen passing through their lungs could disrupt the moment. Mildred Thistle's fingers creaked open; the slow, deliberate movement accompanied the unsettling sound of cracking bones. The noise fizzed coldly up George's spine.

Michael, never one to shy away from adding to the discomfort, absently cracked his knuckles, the sound merging with the macabre symphony. George's shoulders twisted involuntarily with every pop, the sensation making his skin crawl.

Miss Wainwright worked meticulously, her steady hands betraying no sign of unease despite the morbid nature of her task. Her intense concentration was visible even in the faint reflection of her glasses. George's gaze lingered there, watching the tiny reflected world as her furrowed eyebrows held the spectacles firmly in place.

The absurd image of caterpillars dancing on her forehead crossed his mind, but he quickly shoved the thought aside. If Wainwright knew what he was thinking, she'd likely kill him.

Miss Walker hovered nearby, clipboard in hand, sketching with remarkable precision. Her focused expression brought life to her work, and her drawings reanimated the frailty of Mildred's frame and highlighted the angry ligature bruises around her neck.

"This one is different," Walker remarked, shading a dark mark on Mildred's forearm.

"Looks it," George replies, his arms folded, his chin resting in one palm. Mildred's death didn't sit right with him. Something about her clung to his thoughts, clawing at the edges of his mind. "But it's connected. It has to be."

"Why her?" Michael asks, his voice tinged with frustration as he studies Walker's drawing.

Before George could respond, a sharp tug from Wainwright sent a grotesque gurgle from the body. The sound made everyone jump, a visceral reminder of what they were dealing with. A sudden rush of gas escaped from Mildred's bowels, and the room filled with a sickening stench that had George clamping his teeth together to keep his stomach from revolting.

Then he saw it.

A thin trickle of dead blood oozed from the corner of Mildred's mouth, vivid against her pale, lifeless skin.

"Shit," Michael mutters as he grabs George's arm, yanking him to the side. "Eyes down, mate. Don't look."

But it was already too late. George's stomach rumbled with feral intensity, making Michael glance at him sharply.

George's claws shot free without warning, making the room hazy red. He felt his jaw ache and shift, his fangs growing unbidden as the metallic tang of blood filled the air.

"Get a fucking hold of yourself," Michael hisses, his voice low and tight. He reached for his notepad, flipping it open and pretending to jot something down, creating a veneer of normalcy for the others.

"It's getting harder," George whispers back, his voice rough, guttural. "The blood... it's driving me mad."

Michael's eyes darted to George's face, his voice tense but steady. "Your face, mate—it's changing. Everything's sharper. Is it easing?"

George inhaled deeply, reaching inward, clawing for control. He felt the beast resist, fighting him, but with a strained exhale, he forced it back. The claws retracted, the sharp ache in his jaw easing as his fangs receded. His vision cleared, the red haze dissipating.

"It's okay," George says quietly, his voice firmer now. "It's stopped."

Michael nodded, his lips pressed into a thin line. "Good. Let's keep it that way."

They both turned their attention back to Wainwright just as she straightened, delicately holding a pair of tweezers between her gloved fingers.

"I got it," she announced, her voice steady despite the grim scene.

Pinched in the tweezers was a torn, creased fragment of a photograph.

The image revealed a tall woman with long black hair and a smile that didn't quite reach her eyes. Her expression told a story of fear, secrets, and something far darker than the surface could reveal.

"Who is she?" Walker asks, her curiosity laced with unease.

George's gaze narrowed on the fragment. "That's the question."

Mildred had clung to the picture even as she lay dying, her hand locked around it in death. Whoever had killed her had been meticulous, tearing the woman from the rest of the group, removing the evidence piece by piece.

It wasn't chaos. It was control.

George's stomach churned as he stared at the fragment. The woman in the photograph wasn't just a face. She was the next thread in this twisted tapestry of death.

And George knew they were running out of time to unravel it.

George froze mid-step, his gaze locking onto something unseen by anyone else. The whisper slithered into his ears like smoke, chilling his spine. **"Help us, please help us."** The words were faint and distorted, but their weight bore down on him. His breath hitched, and he turned toward Michael, trying not to draw attention to the two forensics girls checking over Mildred.

"Michael," George says, his voice low, trembling. "They're here."

Michael straightened, his expression slipping into one of confusion. "What? Where?" His face paled, a ghostly white that George hadn't seen since their first crime scene together.

"Just behind you," George murmurs, his eyes darting toward the gathered figures. They were all there—every victim they had failed to save, joined now by Med. The Spectres were broken, their appearances reflecting the violence they'd endured. Blood, bruises, twisted limbs—all of it hung heavy in the air.

Michael remained oblivious, but George felt the room shrink, the eerie weight pressing against his chest. Phonic-like whispers filled the space, their despair clawing at his sanity. A part of him wished Michael could see them and share this haunting experience if only to reassure him he wasn't losing his mind.

Guilt gnawed at George's insides. The echoes of their voices, the desperation in their hollowed eyes, dug deep into his psyche. **How many more will gather before we catch the killer?** The question repeated like a mantra in his mind, a cruel reminder of their failings.

Back at Atk, George toyed with the latest evidence bag—a crumpled photograph of a dark-haired woman. The image added to their growing pile of fragments, each one as maddeningly incomplete as the last. He leaned back, staring at the torn edges of the photo and narrowing his focus. Two names came to mind: **Emily Fulton** and **Melanie Blake.**

If the case had taught him anything, it was taboo. It followed logic or reason.

"You okay?" Michael asks, his voice breaking through George's spiralling thoughts. He leaned over George's shoulder, holding the other photos.

"No..." George mutters, his tone edged with frustration. "What the hell is going on? There wasn't even a hint of a demon back there."

Michael handed him the intact photo. "Yeah, but of all the people in this shot, why rip her out? A bit... sus, don't you think?"

George studied the image. The woman in the torn photo stood beside a tall, broad-shouldered man, easily six feet one. Another woman—someone they hadn't encountered yet—was on her right.

"With Kumar and Walters missing, we've got no one to ID them," George says, his voice heavy with resignation. "Think it's worth putting out a press conference? Maybe appeal for witnesses to help identify the people in this photo?"

Michael shook his head slightly. "Guv's with Stenton and the others, hashing out strategy. Heard some shouting earlier—he's not taking any shit. But yeah, it might be worth pitching it. We're running low on leads, mate."

Michael flipped through Ross Walters' diary again, his frustration mounting. It was like trying to navigate a maze blindfolded. The victims' ghosts loomed in George's mind, their phantasmal presence refusing to let him rest.

"Do we still have the list from Bentley?" George asks, racking his brain for any addresses that might still answer.

The sound of heels clicking against the floor made George flinch. His pulse spiked, and his claws slid forward unbidden as adrenaline surged. He quickly curled his hand under the desk, willing the beast back into its cage.

"Ah, there you are," came a voice from the doorway.

George glanced up, his chest still tight. It was only Miss Walker, though her sharp presence carried its bran unease.

"If it isn't our little ray of sunshine," Michael quips, smirking as he adjusts his glasses. "Let me guess, bad news?"

Walker rolled her eyes. "Wow, that's what you think of me? Like I'm the Grim Reaper or something?" she shot back, her sass cutting through the tension.

"What's up?" George asks, noticing the paperwork she holds.

Walker raised a brow. "Well, I'm sure you two geniuses noticed Mildred wasn't like the others. We checked her clothing. Jess is looking over some of the glass shards for prints."

"And?" George prompted, leaning forward.

"Well, whoever killed her... it wasn't just random. The killer got close. Really cClose-means..." Walker paused for effect. "A woman. Or at least someone with smaller hands."

Michael handed over his tie with a theatrical sigh. "Knock yourself out, love."

Walker snorted. "Don't flatter yourself, Sergeant. Not into old dogs and new tricks."

As Walker continued briefing them, George's mind drifted back to the torn photo. The woman's face haunted him now as much as the victims did. Whoever she was, Mildred had died clutching her image, holding it tight even as death took her.

Whoever she was, George thought grimly, **she was the key.**

"Right, sit down and lean forward slightly," Miss Walker instructed, her tone commanding yet light, a curious mix of playful and authoritative. She was no fool. Her sharp mind and quick wit were at the fore in every word. Something about her intrigued George—quiet confidence, the way she effortlessly made men do as she asked. It was a quality he hadn't noticed in anyone since Helen.

Ever the joker, Michael leaned forward with a creak of his chair, a cheeky grin spreading across his face. Walker pulled a chair close, lowering herself beside him with a purposeful motion.

"If you wanted to get closer, love, you only had to ask," Michael quips, his voice thick with mock charm.

George watched the exchange with a smirk, knowing Walker couldn't let the comments slide without a clever retort. Even amid the darkness of their case, moments like these were necessary, a reprieve from the weight they all carried.

"You won't be saying that in a minute," Walker replies smoothly, a sly smile tugging at the corners of her mouth.

In a fluid motion, she whipped Michael's tie around his throat, crossing it on the left side and pulling it taut. Michael's grin vanished as his face gradually reddened, his right arm flailing in protest. George couldn't help but picture Mildred in her final moments—the cord tight around her neck, her attacker oblivious to the picture being torn free as she reached desperately for the ledge.

"See?" Walker explains, demonstrating the manoeuvre. "Her cord was like this, the killer pulling to the right, bringing their head close. Maybe to taunt her, maybe to ask a question. Long-haired girls lose strands all the time—it's inevitable. The hair transfers, especially with close contact. Maybe she even flicked it back out of her face mid-struggle."

George could see the brutal act playing vividly in his mind. The image in Mildred's hand wasn't random. It was a message, a clue. She had died identifying her attacker. But who? Emily? Melanie? Donna Armitage? Kumar's earlier mention of Emily seeing Jack Sexton, a married man, added another layer to the puzzle.

"We need to figure out which one of them has long, dark hair," George says, his voice firm. He watched as Walker finally released Michael, letting him collapse back into his chair.

Michael gasped for air, his face flushed beetroot red as the tie slid limply to his shoulders. Walker looked pleased with her work, a smug satisfaction on her face.

"Well," Michael croaked, laughing despite himself, "that was an experience. I liked what you were doing there."

"You sick bastard," Walker shot back with a grin. "I'll do it for real next time."

"What's next?" Michael asks, straightening his tie and regaining his composure.

"If she's not in the system, the DNA won't give us a name," Walker says, standing and brushing off her hands. "But it'll help us break down her characteristics—maybe even her movements. Spores or particles could still be present if she spent time in a dusty warehouse. A busy girl like this? Washing her hair probably isn't high on her list."

George nodded, appreciating Walker's practicality. Michael had been right the other day—Walker and Wainwright were invaluable, especially if the science could link one of the suspects to the crime scenes. For the first time, it felt like they were building something tangible.

Michael moved to the kitchenette, busying himself with the coffee machine while George sifted through the papers and exhibits on the desk. He was searching for the address list tied to the last expedition when his hand knocked over Ross Walters' diary. It hit the floor with a dull thud and spilled open. A small, crumpled scrap of paper fluttered out, landing just under the desk.

"Found something?" Michael asks, placing a steaming cup beside George.

"I don't know." George picked up the scrap, squinting at the scrawled handwriting. It was barely legible, the letters uneven and rushed. "It fell out of the diary."

Michael leaned closer, peering at the paper. "What's it say?"

"'Berth 72,'" George read aloud, his brow furrowing. The word *berth* was spelt incorrectly, adding an odd layer of urgency to the scribble. It felt significant, though he couldn't yet place why.

A loud crash shattered the quiet.

The door flew open, slamming against the wall as a uniformed officer burst in, panting and visibly flustered. "Detectives! There's another. Corbridge Crescent, under the railway bridge at Cambridge Heath."

George's gaze flicked toward the empty corner of the room, his chest tightening. He braced for the ghosts to reappear, their ranks growing thicker with every failure.

The room fell silent, save for the officer's laboured breathing. The air was heavy with anticipation, the unspoken dread that whatever waited at Corbridge Crescent would only deepen the darkness.

COCKNEY SWAGGER

19

'*29th 5.30 pm.*'

The iron railway bridge towered above George like the spine of some ancient, slumbering beast, its rusted beams casting jagged shadows over the black, restless waters below. Faded graffiti snarled along the walls, garish streaks of colour mocking the grim spectacle. George's gaze fixed on the rope swaying in the cold wind, its frayed end tied to an inverted cross dangling precariously above the water. The metallic tang of blood mingled with the acrid stench of scorched flesh. The scent carried on the icy breeze alongside the faint crackle of charred wood.

Michael exhaled a plume of smoke, the ember of his cigarette glowing dimly as the strobing blue lights reflected off the bridge's decaying surface. "At least we've got answers," he mutters, though the hollow edge to his voice suggests otherwise.

George's eyes narrowed, tracing the macabre scene above. The figure suspended from the cross was burned beyond recognition, save for the tattered remnants of Kumar's clothing clinging to the blackened flesh. The sight was grotesque—a deliberate message carved into the night.

"We know what happened," George says, his voice tight, "but not how. Look at that height." His gaze climbed the rusted beams, imagining the Herculean effort required to hoist a cross and corpse into such a precarious position. "And those tracks aren't exactly accessible. The Fire Brigade will have a hell of a time with this unless they shut down the entire railway."

Michael took another slow drag, the cigarette trembling faintly between his fingers. "Whoever did this isn't just killing—they're making a bloody show of it. Making us work for every scrap."

"Or making a point," George murmurs, shifting focus to the approaching trio: Wainwright, Walker, and Locke. Their grim expressions mirrored the unease curling like smoke in his chest.

Michael stubbed out his cigarette, the sharp hiss drowned by the din of reporters clamouring behind the police tape. He lit another with practised ease. "Just when I thought Kumar might be at the centre of all this, he goes and ends up like that." He gestured to the grotesque effigy with a flick of ash.

"Maybe someone's cleaning house," George offered, his eyes following Locke's silhouette as the man barked orders at the encroaching press. Camera flashes lit the dark like intermittent lightning, but George turned his back to avoid their gaze.

Michael leaned in closer, his voice a low rasp. "What if the money's real?" He hesitated, his cigarette hovering in mid-air. "Hear me out before you laugh."

George tilted his head, the tension in his shoulders belying his calm tone. "I'm listening. But make it quick—Locke's won't wait for us to spin theories."

Michael's words came fast, his cockney drawl sharpened by urgency. "Say the demon's real. I know it sounds mad, but think about it. It's possessed someone—maybe someone tied to the seven who split the cash. Kumar had the relic. What if he got cold feet or greedy and decided not to hand it over?
Meanwhile, the demon's whispering in someone's ear pushes them to clean up loose ends. The killings aren't just warnings but part of some bigger game. Add a dash of misdirection, and we're left chasing phantoms while the real threat closes in."

George's stomach churned as he processed Michael's theory. The cold air felt heavier now, as if the bridge groaned under the weight of some unseen presence. He glanced back at the crime scene, the charred cross swaying like a pendulum, marking time for a reckoning they couldn't yet see.

George tilted his head, weighing the implications of Michael's theory. The cockney bravado was easy to dismiss, but his insights had a way of cutting to the bone. "What about Annabelle?" George asks, his voice low, the name dragging up uncomfortable connections. "She could've known one of them. Loose lips on a night out?"

Michael nodded, his brow furrowing deeper. "That's it, mate. Connections. People who know too much. The killer's tying off loose ends."

The weight of the words pressed into George's chest like a leaden hand. If this killer was covering tracks, more bodies weren't just likely—they were inevitable. The thought slithered through his mind, leaving a shiver in its wake.

Locke's gravelly voice shattered their uneasy moment. "Well, this is a clusterfuck, isn't it?" he growls, his hands jammed deep into the pockets of his coat. His gaze lingered on the grotesque display above before shifting to George and Michael. "Tell me you've got something."

The fading light cloaked the bridge in shades of grey and deep blue, the damp air clinging to everything like a second skin. Kumar's lifeless form hung high above them, a grim marionette swaying in the biting wind. The acidic stench of the Kanaima's toxin-filled the air, its sharp, searing tang blending with the smoky residue of charred flesh. George suppressed a gag, the sickly odour clinging to the back of his throat.

Steeling himself, he stepped closer to the edge of the pathway, his eyes fixed on the burned remains. The red-black fissures snaking across Kumar's skin looked like frozen veins of molten lava, grotesquely vivid against the charred surface. His shredded T-shirt flapped in the wind, revealing the hollow cavity in his chest where his heart should have been. The realisation struck George like a hammer blow. Someone had taken it.

The dreadful thought rooted in his mind, spiralling into a vortex of morbid fascination. He couldn't look away from the dreadful scene, his thoughts churning until something worse—uncoiled in the depths of his awareness.

It began as a faint itch at the base of his neck, a prickle of unease that quickly evolved into a visceral certainty. George's sixth sense ignited, a predator's instinct whispering of danger. This wasn't just a feeling of being watched; it was deeper, more personal. The air around him seemed to hum with malice, a primal force that made the fine hairs on his arms stand rigid.

He spun around, his eyes sweeping the gathered crowd. Reporters jostled behind the police line, cameras flashing with mechanical precision. A few onlookers lingered at the periphery, their curiosity barely masking unease. None of them stood out, yet George knew that someone was there. Their gaze locked on him with piercing intensity.

I know you can hear me.

The voice slithered into his mind like a shadow creeping across a wall. Female, calm and calculating, but laced with a venomous malice. It wasn't audible, not to anyone else. This was something other, something meant solely for him.

George's blood turned to ice. His body stiffened, but his eyes darted through the scene, careful not to betray his rising panic. The voice lingered, curling at the edges of his mind like a smoke he couldn't escape.

Michael, sensing his tension, sidled closer. He kept his movements casual, his body language calm, but his sharp gaze flicked over George's face. "Eww, the heart's missing," Michael says loudly, his voice carrying over the crowd's murmurs. Then, quieter, he leaned in. "What is it really, Georgie?"

"One's here," George whispers, his lips barely moving. "Watching."

Michael stiffened beside him, his casual demeanour cracking for a split second. "Are you sure?" he asks under his breath, his paranoia flaring like a match in the dark.

George didn't answer. His eyes drifted back to the shadows pooling under the bridge, the weight of the unseen presence pressing down on him like a tide, ready to swallow him whole.

George nodded slowly, trying to focus on the voice, its presence relentless, dripping with confidence.

'We know all about you, Detective Reynolds. From the first scene, I sensed you were different. A friend of mine always used to say, Know thy enemy. So, we learnt everything about you. I must say, the newspaper coverage doesn't do you justice.'

The words slithered through his mind like a venomous snake. He whispers back, barely able to steady his breath, "Who are you?"

'Plenty of time for that,' she replies, her voice almost playful, taunting. *'Oh, and in case you're wondering, I'm not the one. You could say I'm the brains, and he's my eyes and ears. It's fucking surreal, the perks of our bond.'*

George's pulse quickened, each word a blade digging deeper into his thoughts. "With whom?" His voice was barely audible now, barely more than a whisper, the air around him thickening.

'I won't spoil your fun,' she teases. *'The running around, the dead ends—it's far more entertaining this way.'*

Frustration flared in his chest, the tension rising as he pressed for more. "Why are you doing this?" The question slipped out with an edge of desperation, raw and trembling.

'Because it's far more satisfying than I imagined. Revenge is... bittersweet for those who cheat.'

Her words echoed in his mind, swirling like poison. "All of them?" he asks, struggling to piece together the cryptic puzzle she was constructing.

'Revenge is bittersweet for cheaters, Detective,' she replies, a quiet, unsettling amusement in her tone. *'Why do men always think cheating in love is the only kind that matters?'*

The remark struck him like a hammer to the skull. The meaning twisted in his mind but didn't come clear, and its weight sank deep into his gut. He pushed forward, desperate for something concrete. "Surely, you have us at such a disadvantage. You could give us something."

'I may have been born at night, Detective, but it wasn't last night,' she sneers, her tone cutting. *'No chance. I hope the fruits of our labour meet your approval.'*

And with that, she was gone.

The oppressive weight in the air suddenly lifted, and George realised he'd been holding his breath, his chest tight. He exhaled sharply, his shoulders sagging as the tension drained from him, leaving behind a hollow, gnawing unease.

Michael was staring at him, brow furrowed in confusion. "What the hell was that?"

"A first," George mutters, his voice distant, the fog of the encounter still clinging to him. "She's not the one doing the killing, but she's the mastermind."

Michael's face darkened, the usual mockery replaced with grim determination. "She's not done, is she?"

"No," George replies, his jaw tightening, the weight of the truth settling in. "And if she's as convicted as she sounds, I don't think she'll stop until every one of her targets is dead."

The scene under the railway bridge felt like a cruel stage, the cold wind howling like an audience to a twisted play. Kumar's body hung above them like the centrepiece of a grotesque performance. The upside-down cross wasn't just a display method—it was a statement. It gnawed at George, a feeling deep in his gut that the positioning was no accident. It felt deliberate—a rebellion against faith or a twisted parody. Kumar's body swayed in the darkness as the wind howled through the rusted beams, spinning slowly like a puppet on unseen strings.

Behind him, painted in fresh blood, was the symbol—the smirking, taunting smiley face. It stared back at them, mocking, daring them to uncover its meaning—the killer's signature, perverse. It wasn't the first time it had appeared, and every time it did, it felt like a challenge—a taunt.

Michael stood a few steps away, his notebook open, his hand moving with eerie precision as he sketched the symbol. His pen danced across the page, capturing every detail with unsettling calm: the fluidity of the strokes, the texture of the blood, the way the lines smudged and dripped in the cold night air. The wind tugged at his hair, ruffling the pages of his notebook, but he didn't flinch. His concentration was unnerving as if the scene was a puzzle he was determined to solve—no matter the cost.

"They used the heart," George says, the realisation settling in his stomach like a lead weight.

Michael didn't look up from his notebook, his voice flat. "Yeah, we know it's gone."

"No." George swallowed hard, fighting the bile rising in his throat. "They used it as a sponge. To paint *that*."

Michael's pen paused mid-stroke. His jaw tightened as his gaze lifted, locking on the crimson smiley face smeared across the wall. A second passed before he closed the notebook with a snap, shoving it into his coat pocket with a jerk. He fumbled for a cigarette, his hands shaking as he lit it, the flame briefly illuminating his grim expression.

"So," he mutters, exhaling a plume of smoke into the icy air, "any enlightening words from those bastards?"

"Yes. Stop smoking," George says, the dry jab slipping out despite the oppressive weight of the moment.

"Fuck off," Michael replies, dragging deeply on the cigarette.

"They said the usual taunting bollocks," George continues, his voice hardening. "'Bittersweet for those who cheat.' That's what she said."

Michael raised an eyebrow, the cigarette dangling precariously from his lips. "She? So, it's a woman then? What, she got cheated on or something?"

"That's what I asked," George replies, the frustration bubbling beneath the surface. "And she mocked me for it. Men always assume cheating has to do with love."

Michael shook his head, muttering curses under his breath. "Anything else?"

"They know about me." The words came out heavier than George expected, the weight of them dragging the air between them down. "They know I'm... different. They've done their homework. She said she could sense it at the first scene."

Michael froze, his eyes narrowing, the cigarette briefly between his fingers. "Shit."

"And there's more." George hesitated, then pushed the words out, the revelation pressing his chest like an iron weight. "She said she's the master. She can see and hear everything the demon does. That's how she was talking to me—through him."

Michael's face darkened, anger flashing as his jaw clenched around the cigarette. "So, he was here," he says, his voice low and sharp. The thought of the killer lurking nearby, mocking them from the shadows, sent a fresh wave of fury coursing through him.

"Who was here?" Locke's voice cut through the tension like a sledgehammer. He strode toward them, his broad frame silhouetted against the harsh floodlights. His tone was demanding, but his eyes betrayed a flicker of concern as they darted between George and Michael.

George didn't answer immediately. His gaze drifted upward, drawn to the full moon dominating the night sky. Something primal stirred within him, clawing at the edges of his control. Sweat trickled down his back despite the biting cold, and his blood felt boiling. For a brief, terrifying moment, he felt the shift—the flash of feral gold in his vision, threatening to overtake him.

He clenched his fists, grounding himself, forcing the beast back into its cage. Steeling his nerves, he turned his attention back to Kumar's swaying body. Something caught his eye—the underside of the shoes, faintly coated in dust. That damned dust again. The same as in the other scenes. The same is true of what clung to the other victims—a breadcrumb, perhaps, but one that had already led them to too many dead ends.

Locke's gaze bore into him, heavy and expectant. George shook off the pull of the moon, steadying his voice. "The demon was here," he says at last, the words sharp and cutting. "And so was she."

"Sir, Kumar's dead, and so is his wife. He broke out of the hotel for a reason. Maybe that reason is at his house—and the murderer wants it."

Locke's gaze sharpened. "What, money or missing relics?"

"Could be," George says, his voice steady but heavy with implication. "We need to get back to his house. We can't let it slip through our fingers if they're after crucial evidence."

ADI Locke nodded, picking up on George's line of thought. "Fine. You two head over. I'll smooth over any grey areas for the entry. If there's something in that house, we need it before they do."

George appreciated Locke's decisiveness, though he doubted they'd find anything tangible. Still, the house might hold clues—threads to pull together the chaotic web they were caught in. More than that, he needed an escape from the lingering stench of blood and the moon's ceaseless taunts.

Michael stood by the railings, staring down at the swirling waters below. His eyes followed a few ducks gliding mindlessly across the surface, their indifference a stark contrast to the weight of the night. Around them were nothing but black metal, a desolate car park, and the faint buzz of a street lamp—a place where someone slapped up a barrier and charged peak prices for proximity to a train station.

"Come on, Michael. Road trip," George says, his tone dry. He knew Michael was looking forward to it about as much as he was. Michael turned, rolling his eyes, the cigarette in his hand flaring like a brake light before dimming. He tossed it to the ground in disdain and crushed it underfoot with unnecessary force as if trying to bury the case itself in the dust.

If only it were that simple.

87 Bancroft.

"Hotel Tango despatch," came the radio crackle, "showing DS Dalton and DC Reynolds at 87 Bancroft. Linked to the crime scene under Cambridge Heath Railway Bridge."

"Received."

The déjà vu was immediate as George stepped out of the car, the small, neglected front garden as unremarkable as before. The moon hung high above, a pale, relentless watcher in the night sky. Its pull gnawed at the edges of his control, the beast inside clawing for release. George clenched his jaw, resisting the insidious urge to give in. Michael's obliviousness had been their saving grace, but someone like Locke wouldn't stay blind forever.

The air smelt different. As George inhaled, his lungs caught a scent that didn't belong—sharp, acrid, and wrong. Someone, or something, had been here. Sending his senses flaring. He flung an arm out, stopping Michael mid-stride, and the sudden movement took the wind out of Michael's step.

"Don't touch the pillar," George says sharply.

Michael paused, his hand inches from the low gate's post. He gave George a wary look but stepped back as directed. "What now?" he mutters.

"Toxin," George replies, his voice low. His sharp gaze scanned the immediate area, catching faint trails of something shimmering faintly in the dark. The edges of the gate, the dying flowers clinging to the cracked soil, even the door handle—all tainted with the demon's unmistakable mark. It clung like an evil shadow, the faint luminosity shimmering in fractals, even under the weak streetlights.

Michael exhaled heavily, the white fog of his breath curling into the cold air. "That was close," he mutters, glancing to the right where the distant glow of shopfronts illuminated the street. To the left, a line of darkened houses and parked cars stretched into infinity.

"Too close," George murmurs, crouching for a better look. His enhanced senses sharpened in the stillness, amplifying every detail around him. He spotted trails smeared along the low wall, tangled in the brittle petals of dying flowers and dripping faintly from the door handle.

Even in the dark, the toxin glimmered unnaturally, its hues shifting between colours that shouldn't exist. George's heightened awareness caught every nuance—the subtle crackle of dust disintegrating on the wind, the faint buzzing of a fly near an overflowing bin. The sound of its wings was deafening in his ears, a staccato that cut through the oppressive quiet.

It was exhilarating and overwhelming in equal measure. Every detail was sharper, clearer, and more intense. The moon seemed to pulse with energy, and George felt it thrumming through his veins, amplifying the beast that lurked beneath his skin.

He forced himself to focus. The toxin wasn't just a trace; it was a warning. The demon had been here. George knew it as surely as he felt the blood moon's pull. And as his mind churned with questions, one thought loomed above the rest: the price of keeping Michael in the dark was becoming heavier by the moment. Could he keep this secret or perhaps offer Michael the same cursed gift that had once saved his life?

"Be careful, Michael," George warned, his tone low and firm. His eyes lingered on the faint, shimmering toxin across the door handle. "If I touch it, the paralysis will wear off quickly. But you? Who knows?"

Michael snorted, his gravelly laugh roughened by the cigarettes he'd been chain-smoking recently. "That's all I need," he says, shaking his head. "Flipping around like I'm having a stroke."

George's lips twitched with the ghost of a smile, though his thoughts were elsewhere. "Random thought," he says, his tone shifting as he tests the waters. "Don't shoot the messenger, but what are your thoughts on savouring moonlit walks?"

Michael turned to him, raising an eyebrow. "With you? Thanks, but I'll pass, matey."

"No, you idiot," George replies, the faint humour in his voice tempered by the weight in his chest. "I mean... I fear what's coming. Here. The next. It will be nothing like you've been used to in this job."

Michael paused, the smirk fading as a flicker of understanding crossed his face. Then, with a dry chuckle, he says, "Oh, I understand. You're looking for a howling buddy."

"Something like that," George mutters, his hand pressing firmly against the front door. The faint shimmer of the toxin seemed to pulse under the dim light, almost daring him to breach the threshold.

Michael's laughter faded, replaced by a rare seriousness. "Let's put a pin in that, yeah?" he says, his voice dropping. "We don't know what it'll do to you with the blood moon coming. Your body could get torn apart."

George glanced at him, surprised by the weight of his words. There was no sarcasm in Michael's tone now, no bravado. His face was solemn, his brow furrowed in unspoken concern. George tilted his head slightly, listening—not just to Michael's words but to his steady and steadfast heartbeat.

It wasn't mockery; Michael was serious. Dead serious.

George swallowed hard, the gravity of the moment sinking in. He knew the truth—if the blood moon intensified what already simmered beneath his skin, he'd need an anchor. Someone who understood what was coming. Someone who could handle it.

And if this case were a preview of horrors to come, the world they knew would change forever.

MR KUMAR

20

'7.30 pm 29th,'

The house felt different from their last visit. An unsettling chaos hung in the air as though the walls bore witness to a troubled soul. Though the place was deserted, the oppressive atmosphere clung to them, thick and suffocating.

Michael wandered to a massive glass cabinet tucked into the far-left corner, its deep mahogany frame coated in dust. Inside were trinkets from old expeditions, faded ornaments, and worn books that seemed forgotten by time. Across the room, the cherry-red wooden fireplace displayed photographs of Mr and Mrs Kumar during better days, framed by ancient artefacts hinting at Kumar's shadowy, enigmatic dealings.

The musky scent of old wood and paper filled the air, mingling with the faint smell of something darker—something alive in the silence—towering piles of books sprawled across the room, creeping like ivy into the kitchen. A dirt-streaked door stood out against the clutter, its grime-streaked surface whispering secrets best left hidden. The mismatched furniture, a toppled coffee table in muted beach tones, and a crumpled multi-coloured rug—possibly Egyptian or Arabian—added a peculiar unease to the space.

"Georgie, you taking all this in?" Michael called, holding up an old leather-bound book plucked from one of the precarious book towers.

"What is it?" George asks, his gaze locking onto the book. Under the dim light, the dull brown leather seemed to shift, swirling with dark, blood-red hues. The raised symbols on its cover sent a chill down his spine; they matched the mark on his wrist.

"Not sure," Michael replies, turning the book over. "It's locked."

George frowned but tore his gaze away. The book's presence lingered in his mind, but there was more to uncover here that demanded their attention.

As George shifted his weight, a creak from the floorboards beneath the rug caught their attention. He glanced at Michael, whose raised eyebrow mirrored his unease. "Check that side," George instructed, gesturing to the far corner of the rug.

Michael hesitated, clutching the mysterious book but eventually setting it aside. "Sure, yeah. We should take this, though," he mutters, nodding toward the book before crouching to examine the cream-tasselled edge of the rug. Beneath the dust, the floorboards appeared lighter, as if recently disturbed.

"What do you think he's hiding?" Michael asks.

"Your guess is as good as mine," George replies. He dropped to his knees, fingers brushing over the wood. Even without the heightened senses granted by his affliction, he could tell this part of the floor was different. Small, about fifteen centimetres by five or six, the hidden panel was easy to overlook. With a sharp flick of his wrist, George's claws extended, glinting briefly before sinking into the smallest cracks. He pried the panel loose, the faint squeak of wood on wood breaking the oppressive silence.

The cavity beneath was dark but shallow enough to inspect without blindly reaching inside. George spotted three keys tied together with a small blue tag through the dim haze. The number *72* was scrawled on it in white ink.

"That it?" Michael asks, his hand outstretched to take the keys.

"I guess so," George mutters, frowning at the number. "This is the second time I've seen 72 recently. It was in Walter's diary too—'berth 72.' Connected?"

Michael's brow furrowed. "Berth? You mean like birth?"

"No," George says, his eyes darting to an ornamental boat on the nearby shelf. "A berth is for boats. Boat parking. Everything about this case keeps circling back to the water."

Michael nodded but gestured to the shorter key among the set. "That door," he says, pointing to the dirt-streaked door at the edge of the room. "It's got a weird keyhole. Might fit."

Before George could reply, his gaze landed on an open cardboard folder lying half-hidden under a stack of papers. Its title read: *Police Officers in the House of Horrors.* His stomach churned as he reached for it.

Michael snatched the folder first, his expression darkening as he scanned the clippings.

The headlines dredged up old wounds—accounts of George's foster brother, speculation about the events of last month, and images of the two of them splashed across the pages. Kumar had known who they were that day. He'd played them.

Michael's face turned red angrily as he shoved the papers back into the folder. "This doesn't seem right," he growls. "They know who we are."

"Why? For what purpose?" George murmurs, his thoughts spiralling.

Michael's voice cut through. "I've got a bad feeling about this. You need to stay on guard."

George nodded, forcing himself to focus. "Let's try this door. The sooner we're done here, the better."

His hand trembled as he inserted the shortest key into the lock. The cold metal slid smoothly into the grooves, the faint click of tumblers echoing in the silent house. The resistance was minimal, almost inviting, but both men felt the unspoken tension between them. Kumar had hidden these keys for a reason. The question hung in the air like a storm cloud: *What else would they unlock?*

Michael's heart raced, his breath quickening as George turned the key. George's own heartbeat thundered in his ears, anticipation and dread battling for dominance. Whatever lay behind the door was part of a much larger game—one they were just beginning to understand.

As the lock clicked, a gust of stale, putrid air hissed through the cracks. George twisted the silver handle and pulled the door toward them. The stench, raw and overpowering, hit him like a sledgehammer, triggering a visceral reaction. He quickly slammed the door shut, sealing it again.

"What the hell?" Michael exclaims, stepping back, his face twisting in surprise and disgust.

"It isn't good," George mutters, trying to steady himself. His gut churned, not just from the smell but from the familiar, haunting dread that clawed its way to the surface. There might not be a heartbeat behind that door, but that didn't mean there wasn't a body.

"Another?" Michael asks, his voice tight.

"Smells that way," George grumbled. He ran a hand over his face, the shadows of old memories surfacing unbidden. "And I think it's another fucking basement." His voice dropped, edged with bitterness. Basements had brought him nothing but pain—memories of burnt bodies and the suffocating heat of flames seared into his mind.

Michael placed a firm hand on George's shoulder. "I get it," he says softly. "What will be, will be."

George shrugged off the gesture, forcing himself to push past his spiralling thoughts. *What would Andy say to shake me out of this?* He wondered. He flicked the handle again with a steadying breath, bracing himself for what lay below. The door creaked open, revealing wooden steps descending into darkness. Partial light from the lounge barely illuminated the top few steps, leaving the rest shrouded in shadow.

George stepped inside, holding his breath as long as his lungs allowed before the stench forced its way in. The fetid air burned his throat, thick with decay. There was no turning back now. He took a cautious step forward, the hairs on his neck prickling with the suffocating sensation of being watched. His eyes darted behind him, but there was nothing—no flames, no shadowy figure lurking. Yet the oppressive air weighed heavily as if the darkness itself had intent.

The further they descended, the more vivid the red hue in George's vision became. The beast stirred within him, its primal instincts heightening his senses to a razor's edge. His pulse quickened as the shadows gave way to a dreadful scene.

The basement was a shrine—an altar to shapeshifters, their images rendered in grotesque detail. Statues of jackals, wolves, Kanaima, and other figures lined the walls, but the centrepiece was a towering idol of Wepawet, the Egyptian god of war and the opener of ways. Its presence loomed over them, oppressive and foreboding.

And then George saw him.

Mr Walters was strapped to a massive chair in the centre of the room, his body butchered beyond recognition. Blood pooled beneath him in a dense, black-red halo. George's stomach turned, but he fought the rising bile. Michael fumbled for a light switch, and when the dim bulb flickered on, the room was bathed in harsh light.

Michael froze at the sight, his breath hitching as he staggered back toward the steps. Walters had been tortured, his body bearing the unmistakable marks of cruelty and precision. Yet there were no signs of the Kanaima's toxin. Whatever had happened here, it was different—colder, more calculated.

"This is different," Michael says, his voice hoarse. He wiped a trail of drool from the corner of his mouth, his hands trembling.

George forced himself to speak, swallowing the nausea and clawing at his throat. "My guess? Walters knew something. Kumar was obsessed with shapeshifters and the Kanaima relic. He tortured Walters for answers but came up short."

"Money?" Michael suggests weakly.

"Could be," George replies, scanning the room. Torn pictures and scattered pages from ancient books littered the floor, their faded ink whispering secrets that eluded him. "Until we find proof, we can't say either way."

"This case just keeps getting weirder," Michael mutters, slipping on his glasses to get a closer look at Walters' mangled body.

George nodded, his gaze lingering on the grotesque details. "We need to clear this place—relics, books, anything upstairs that connects. There's got to be something here to clue us into their endgame."

Michael scoffs, shaking his head. "What? Greed isn't a good enough answer for you?"

"I'd settle for that right now," George admitted, though the unease in his voice betrayed him. The weight of the beast within him and the horrors around him painted a darker picture—one he didn't want to face.

Michael glanced toward the mangled body, twisting his head to examine it from different angles. "What do your werewolf instincts say about this?" he asks, his tone tinged with reluctant curiosity.

"The proof of the pudding is in the eating," George says cryptically, crouching by the blood pool. His voice lowered. "And 43."

Michael's brow furrowed. "43 what?"

"Cuts," George replies, his tone grim. "That's how many wounds Walters has. The last one hit the brachial artery." He gestured to the congealing pool beneath the chair.

Michael shuddered, his face pale as he catalogued the mutilation. "The sick bastard removed his eyelids, fingernails, and toenails," he mutters. His voice cracked with revulsion.

George observed Michael's reaction, surprised by the depth of his disgust. He'd assumed Michael had seen it all by now, but the uncharted horrors this case offered were proving otherwise.

The basement grew quieter, the oppressive atmosphere pressing down on them both. George stared at the flickering light, his mind racing. Whatever game Kumar had been playing, they were still steps behind, and the stakes were only growing higher.

Whatever had been holding Michael's attention now drew George's as well. His disbelief at the supernatural still held a tight grip, though he couldn't deny what he was seeing. Moving closer to the statue and the scattered stones—raw jewels, perhaps—it was hard to tell in the dim light. As he reached out, the symbol on his arm flared to life, faint but unmistakable. It had been silent for some time, and the sudden reappearance sent a cold jolt through him. He cursed himself for even thinking its absence might last.

"Look at this wall," Michael says, breaking George's focus. He pointed to the far-right corner of the basement, an area they had overlooked entirely thanks to the dominating shrine and the grim spectacle of Walter's corpse.

"What is it?" George asks, frowning as he steps closer. Geography had never been his strong suit, and the wall looked like a chaotic mishmash of maps and scribbles.

"Well, indulge an old fool for a moment," Michael began, his excitement glowing through the grim atmosphere. "These look like ancient maps—different regions, burial sites marked. The paper isn't like anything we use today. Feels like we need an expert for this."

George tilted his head, studying the faded markings and strange symbols across the maps. "How do you know? Finding an expert isn't exactly straightforward."

Michael grinned, his enthusiasm cutting through the tension. "When I was younger, I was into this kind of stuff—ancient civilisations, forgotten lore. Still, know a bit, and so do you."

George raised an eyebrow. "Who?"

Michael chuckles, a knowing glint in his eyes. "The lovely Miss Walker. She knows her way around things like this. It was one of her... bragging points when she joined. Got a few strings to her bow, that one."

George nodded slowly. Walker *had* been impressive in her short time with the team. "I've noticed."

"I bet you have. So has she, FYI," Michael adds, his grin widening.

George glanced at him warily. "What do you mean?"

"Don't play dumb," Michael teases. "Few can resist my cockney charm, but it's not me she's interested in. I've seen how she looks at you. You fascinate her."

George scoffs, his discomfort growing. "I doubt that. Probably just a shared interest in doing our jobs well."

Michael rolled his eyes. "Stop talking bollocks. You're just being a chicken. Talk to her at the leaving tomorrow, and you'll see I'm right."

George froze, his mind immediately jumping to the implications. "What? The night of the blood moon?" he asks, trying to mask the panic rising in his chest.

"Ah, right, bad timing," Michael admitted, rubbing his neck. "The way this case goes, we'll probably still be working. But I stand by my point about Miss Walker."

George didn't respond immediately, turning his attention back to the shrine. The melted candles, the aged relics, and the chaos of papers littering the floor told him Kumar had been tending to this twisted obsession for some time. But Michael's words lingered, pressing against his thoughts.

Fear gripped George, though he refused to show it. Five years had passed in a blur of violence, grief, and isolation. What he once thought was an accident had turned out to be cold-blooded murder, and the scars left behind hadn't fully healed. Moving on—letting someone in again—terrified him. The idea of getting close to someone, only for them to be hurt or disappointed, was almost unbearable.

Miss Walker seemed great—kind, sharp, and genuine. But what if she didn't like what she saw when she learned the truth about him? His world wasn't safe. It was dangerous, unpredictable, and now irrevocably tied to the wolf inside him. Worse, what if he lost control and shifted in front of her? The thought of exposing that part of himself, the beast he barely contained, made him shudder.

"You're forgetting the wolf thing," George says, breaking the silence. "How does anyone see past that?"

Michael tilted his head thoughtfully. "You'd be surprised," he says after a moment. "She might be more receptive than you think."

George ignored him, pushing the conversation aside as he sifted through more scattered papers. His focus drifted to the melted candles and the symbols etched into the floor. Kumar had been at this for years—an obsession that had consumed him. But the connection between "berth 72" on Walter's scrap paper and the "72" engraved on the key tag still eluded him.

"We need to figure this out," George murmurs, his eyes narrowing as he pieced through the cryptic notes. Whatever Kumar's endgame was, it felt closer than ever, and every second they wasted felt like another step closer to disaster.

FOLKLORE

21

'*Midnight,*'

The lore of werewolves, deeply entrenched in the ancient folklore of Europe, had evolved over centuries, shaped by the shifting sands of belief and fear. As Christianity spread its influence, the tales of these creatures intertwined with religious interpretations, turning pagan myths into cautionary parables. Over time, these beliefs sailed across the Atlantic with colonialism, the concept of the werewolf shadowing the witch trials, and their shared hysteria, leaving a trail of fear and blood through the ages.

In the early 15th century, whispers of werewolf trials surfaced in regions like Valais and Vaud in Switzerland. By the 16th century, the phenomenon had spread like wildfire across Europe, peaking in the 17th century before gradually ebbing by the 18th. Werewolves and witches became enmeshed in the same web of persecution, even though accusations of lycanthropy comprised only a fraction of the trials. These accusations revolved around tales of wolf-riding or wolf-charming—symptoms of a society consumed by superstition.

One of the most infamous cases, Peter Stumpp's in 1589, ignited fear and executions, particularly in French-speaking and German-speaking Europe. The fear lingered stubbornly in regions like Bavaria and Austria, where records of wolf-charmers and their supposed sorcery extended well beyond 1650. This culminated in sporadic persecutions into the early 18th century in Carinthia and Styria.

As the flames of the witch trials waned, the werewolf shifted from an object of terror to one of curiosity, becoming a fascination for folklore scholars and Gothic horror writers. Stories of lycanthropy traced their roots to medieval romances like *Bisclavret* and *Guillaume de Palerme* before morphing into semi-fictional chapbook traditions of the 18th century.

In regions where wolves were scarce, the werewolf's form adapted to the fears of the land, taking on the shapes of bears, tigers, or even hyenas. In French folklore, the werewolf—or *loup-garou*—dominated the 16th century, with many reports and high-profile executions of alleged shapeshifters. An intriguing variation of the lore suggested that a werewolf could return as a vampire upon death, blurring the line between two of humanity's oldest nightmares.

European folklore painted werewolves with unsettling physical traits, even in their human guise. Eyebrows that met at the bridge of the nose, curved fingernails, low-set ears, and a peculiar, swinging stride marked them as different. When transformed, they often appeared as larger-than-normal wolves, their human eyes and voices betraying their monstrous nature. Indistinguishable from ordinary wolves, others were said to lack tails—a trait shared with witches who took on animal forms.

The methods of identifying werewolves in their human form were crude and brutal. Cutting into their flesh was believed to reveal fur hidden beneath the skin. After reverting to human form, werewolves were described as sickly, plagued by nervous depression and debilitating pain—a grim reminder of the toll their transformation took.

George was lost in the tangled threads of history, immersed in the strange, chilling world of werewolf lore. The weight of centuries of fear and myth pressed on him, each piece fitting uneasily into the mosaic of his fractured reality. But his thoughts were interrupted by a voice from the doorway.

Miss Walker stood there, her silhouette framed by the dim hallway light, a stack of papers balanced in her hands. Her presence was a sharp contrast to the oppressive atmosphere of the room. As she approached, her fruity perfume cut through the air like a subtle challenge, breaking the spell of George's dark reverie.

"You're up late," she remarked, casual but curious.

George straightened, the tension in his shoulders relaxing slightly. "Could say the same for you."

Walker smirked, setting the papers down on a nearby table. "Research doesn't keep office hours."

Her arrival adds an unexpected layer to the moment, a reminder that the line between the mundane and the supernatural is thinner than it seems. George glances at the ancient symbols etched into his arm, now faintly glowing, and then at Walker. For a fleeting second, he wonders if she, too, is drawn to the shadows. They both seem destined to navigate.

"What on earth are you reading?" Miss Walker asks, her voice light but her eyes sparkling with curiosity.

George started, surprised. He scrambled to respond, his words coming out uneven. "Oh, hey. It's, uh, part of Kumar's papers. Crazy to think about the stuff he believed in."

Miss Walker tilted her head, undeterred. "You never know," she says with a casual shrug. "Could be real. I mean, I believe in ghosts—so why not beasts?"

There was something about her tone, something warm and disarming that George hadn't noticed before. His mind, so often tangled in the intricacies of the investigation and his own darker struggles, now drifted to her quirks. She perched herself on the edge of the desk beside him, her legs swinging gently back and forth, catching his peripheral vision with their rhythmic motion.

Yet beneath this innocent charm, the relentless werewolf within George stirred. The primal heat coursing through his veins rose, his blood simmering as his instincts clawed for dominance. He clenched his fists, grounding himself, willing his focus to stay on the case rather than the maddening closeness of his colleague.

"Aren't all people beasts of some kind?" he ventured, strained but attempting levity. "Derived from apes, aren't we?"

Miss Walker smirked, her eyes glinting with mischief. "Oooh, the inhibited primal urges of years gone by," she teases, her words dripping with innuendo. "Raw power and lust. They knew how to handle business back then."

She leaned in closer, her blouse unbuttoned lower than usual, and George's resolve wavered. Her words, her movements—it all intensified the internal struggle raging within him. He noticed the curve of her cleavage, framed perfectly by the loose fabric, a sight that nearly robbed him of speech.

The werewolf stirred sharper this time, its instincts battling against his fragile control. George strained to focus on anything else—the case, the papers, the room's silence. But even as he tried, his heightened senses betrayed him. He could hear the steady rhythm of her heartbeat, the soft rasp of her breath, and the intoxicating scent of her coconut-laced shampoo mingling with her natural perfume. It drowned his rational thoughts, leaving him with conflicting urges.

Desperate to change the subject, George forced a weak smile. "What about the scratch-es?" he asks, flipping through the book's pages in his lap as if the answer might leap out and save him.

Miss Walker's grin widened, still laced with playful mischief. "What's a scratch or two between friends? All good fun," she quips.

George stammered, tripping over his words. "Ah, erm, yeah. Rough with the smooth, I guess," he mutters, his fingers flipping aimlessly through the book. The text blurred in front of him, and his concentration fractured.

Then Miss Walker leaned in even closer. Her playful demeanour faded, replaced with a sudden seriousness that drew his full attention. Her arm muscles tensed as she braced herself on the desk, and George noticed the faint pulse of a vein at her temple. Her breath, warm against his cheek, carried the subtle notes of her perfume, drawing him deeper into the moment despite himself. Inches separated their faces now, and George was hanging on her every word, every movement.

"Look at that," she says suddenly, her tone sharp with discovery. She thrust her hand between the pages he absently turned, stopping him on a particular section.

George blinked, his focus snapping back to the book. The heading read, *Kanaima*.

For a moment, the tension between them dissolved as they remembered the case. Whatever they had just stumbled upon demanded their attention—perhaps a reprieve from the dangerous, unspoken emotions simmering beneath the surface.

"Believable or not?" Miss Walker asks, her voice soft yet probing, drawing George's attention back to the moment.

He blinked, focusing away from the intoxicating pull of her nearness and back to the text before him. The passage detailed the *Kanaima*—vengeful spirits driven by an unrelenting thirst for revenge. They were said to possess animals or people, twisting their hosts into instruments of violent rage. The *Kanaima's* wrath extended far beyond their primary victims, seeking the utter ruin of their enemies by targeting their loved ones, friends, and family. Death was not swift—it was cruel, calculated. Victims were mutilated, their tongues slashed to silence their suffering, ensuring they would perish painfully three days after the attack.

The description sent a chill through George, gripping his professional curiosity as much as it gnawed at his nerves. However, the struggle between his focus on the case and the primal pull of Miss Walker's presence refused to relent.

"Berth 72," he mutters, his gaze flicking between the key he held and the note he'd found in Mr Walters' diary. The words felt like a taunt, dangling just beyond his understanding.

Miss Walker leaned in even closer, her scent mingling with the faint aroma of aged paper and dust, an intoxicating contrast. Her eyes darted between the key and the note, her genuine intrigue breaking through his inner turmoil.

"What's that you got there?" she asks, her tone laced with curiosity.

George exhaled slowly, grounding himself. "This note was in Mr Walters' diary. The keys were in the floorboards of Kumar's lounge," he explains, his words deliberate as he tried to stay on track.

Miss Walker's brow furrowed slightly in thought before her expression cleared. "A 'berth' is a boat parking space at a dock or marina. My dad used to borrow his friend's boat to go fishing."

The revelation clicked into place, illuminating a new possibility. George's mind raced as he pieced it together. A berth could mean a storage site, perhaps for a boat concealing artefacts, evidence, or something more significant, hidden away from prying eyes.

"Maybe they're storing artefacts?" Miss Walker adds, her voice carrying the same spark of realisation that had lit in George's mind.

George nodded slowly, the pieces beginning to align. The note, key, and buried secrets were connected to something larger, far more profound than they realised. Whatever lay at berth 72 wasn't just a coincidence. It was deliberate, hidden, and important.

"Oh," Miss Walker says suddenly, breaking his thought. "I almost forgot—I came to drop off these papers. One of them is the lab report on that dust you found near the bodies."

She held out a stack of neatly clipped papers, and George took them, curiosity knitting his brow. "What is it?" he asks, flipping to the relevant page.

Miss Walker leaned against the desk, her explanation precise. "Old sand, dirt, and compressed clay dust. My friend said you'd find it buried in the desert, especially during excavation or restoration projects."

The revelation deepened the mystery. George stared at the report, his mind turning over the implications. Ancient dust unearthed from the desert, a mysterious boat berth, a vengeful spirit, and a trail of cryptic clues—all threads tangled in a web they were only beginning to unravel.

Miss Walker's gaze lingered on him as he read, her presence steady and warm amidst the dark and spiralling chaos of the investigation. For a moment, George felt the weight of it all press down on him: the unsolved puzzle, the unrelenting wolf within, and whether he could afford to let anyone else into the dangerous world he now inhabited.

But the puzzle demanded his focus. George was determined to uncover whatever secrets Kumar and Walters had taken to their graves—before the shadows claimed another victim.

"Buried in the desert, you say? That's interesting," George muses aloud, his gaze lingering on the papers Miss Walker had handed him. "Kumar mentioned working on artefacts at home."

Miss Walker nodded thoughtfully, her fingers lightly drumming against the desk. The weight of their discoveries loomed large, casting a shadow over the small room. Despite the profound mysteries unravelling before them, George struggled to balance his focus. The pull of Miss Walker's presence, her warm curiosity, and the magnetic charm she carried were maddeningly difficult to ignore.

"Any luck with the maps Michael gave you?" she asks, her voice cutting through the haze of George's thoughts.

He snapped back to the moment. "My friend Fionna had a look," he says, leaning against the desk. "She's a history teacher, and her uni thesis was on the old gods. She's got a sharp eye for this kind of thing."

Miss Walker raised an eyebrow, intrigued. "Old gods, huh? Sounds like your kind of crowd," she teases lightly.

Before George could respond, she handed him a small slip of paper. "Here," she says. "A phone number. If Fionna's as good as you say, I'm sure she'll have some insights worth chasing down."

Her gesture was casual, but George could sense the underlying connection forming between them—a shared fascination with the inexplicable, the allure of mysteries that refused to yield easy answers. As she turned to leave, her perfume lingered in the air, a subtle reminder of her presence.

Left alone, George's thoughts churned. The investigation was becoming more complex with each revelation, each fragment of the past that clawed its way into their present. *Berth 72,* Kumar's hidden artefacts, the ancient dust, hinted at a larger truth that eluded him but pressed relentlessly against the edges of his mind.

And yet, amidst the chaos, the looming blood moon stirred an equally relentless turmoil within him. Its pull grew stronger with every passing hour, awakening the beast inside and eroding the fragile control he clung to. The primal desires threatened to consume him, and the thought of Miss Walker, so close and trusting, only heightened the struggle.

He shook his head, forcing himself back to the task at hand. There was too much at stake to let his instincts distract him. The mysteries surrounding Kumar, Mr Walters, and the cryptic *berth 72* demanded clarity and resolve. The horrors lurking in the shadows would not wait for him to indulge his doubts or desires.

The night was far from over, and George knew their search for answers would lead them deeper into the unknown—a place where the lines between the rational and the supernatural blurred and where the cost of failure was too great to bear.

TRIGGERS

22

It wasn't even bonfire night, and Christmas was already creeping in. The radio had dared to play *Last Christmas,* a grating reminder of a holiday George wasn't ready to face. He was still replaying his near-miss in front of Miss Walker, nearly doing the splits like a clumsy fool. She was getting under his skin in ways that spelt trouble.

What if she flirted, and he couldn't keep the beast in check? The thought gnawed at him. He couldn't tell flirting from casual conversation—a blind spot as frustrating as a toddler learning to ride a bike. He needed to figure it out before something slipped.

"Can I take your order, sir?"

The voice snapped George out of his thoughts. He glanced at the glowing menu board. "Big chicken sandwich meal with a root beer, please," he says, his stomach growling in agreement. Starving and frazzled, he'd taken an aimless drive instead of heading home, hoping the road would help clear the cobwebs from his mind.

The cashier, a young lad with a cheerful naivety, smiled. "Cool eyes. Testing for Halloween scares?"

George blinked, confused, until he caught his reflection in the rearview mirror. His eyes were blood-red, rimmed with an unsettling darkness that crept outward like shadows pooling in the corners of his sockets. His pulse spiked, but he forced himself to smile. "Ah, yeah. Just a Halloween dare," he says, relieved the season provided a convenient excuse. "See how far I can go before someone notices?."

The boy chuckled. "Nice one. They look so real."

"Yeah, in the light, they're normal," George adds, leaning into the lie. "But at night, they glow."

The boy nodded, buying the story without hesitation. "Oh, we're out of chicken burgers. How about beef?"

George's stomach churned. He hesitated, then sighed. "Fine. Big Mac meal, then."

The cashier's grin widened a little too wide, and the pleasant air twisted into something else. "You sure you don't want it raw, detective?"

George froze. His jaw slackened, and his heart leapt into his throat. The words hit him like a blow, and his mind raced to process them. He stared at the boy, whose tone now dripped with something sinister.

"What did you say?" George managed, his voice tight.

The boy leaned closer, his youthful features shifting into something monstrous. His eyes turned pitch-black, two endless voids and pale skin stretched over his face like parchment. Black veins crept beneath the surface, snaking like vines. His voice deepened, gravelly and cold. "Don't be coy now. We both know what's inside you, fighting to come out."

George's head spun as he instinctively scanned the drive-thru window for another witness. The streetlights cast a faint glow on the empty beyond. No one else was there. No one else seemed to see what he was seeing.

"What the hell is happening? Who are you?" George demands, his voice barely above a growl.

The boy's twisted grin didn't falter. "Is it so hard to imagine, detective? While you're out there looking for us, we're finding you. Anywhere. Anyone."

George's blood chilled. "Which one of you am I talking to?"

"Both," the boy hissed. "Over time, we've become like one. At the canal, she whispered to you. This—this is different. Giving you chills. Goosebumps. Hair standing on end."

"You don't sound the same as before," George counters, his pulse racing.

"Soon, you won't be the same as before, either. Nor will the others."

George's voice sharpened. "What do you know of the blood moon?"

The boy tilted his head, his black eyes glinting with cruel amusement. But before he could answer, his features shifted again. His pale skin and dark veins receded, his eyes snapping back to normal human brown. The boy blinked, confused, his East Londonesque accent returning. "Sorry, sir? We're out of chicken burgers. What's the blood moon? Oh, a Halloween wind-up. Nice one!"

George stared, his heart pounding. The sinister presence had vanished as quickly as it came, leaving behind nothing but the young man's innocent grin. George didn't respond for a moment, his mind reeling from the encounter. Then he forced a laugh, nodding mechanically as he reached for the food bag.

"Yeah," George mutters, his voice distant. "Nice one."

As he drove away, the night pressed in around him. The beast within stirred uneasily, and the sinister words echoed in his mind. *We're finding you. Anywhere. Anyone.*

The blood moon was coming, and whatever hunted him wasn't just waiting—it was already here.

A trick he hadn't expected and hoped would be a one-off to keep him on edge. But deep down, George doubted it. Most of all, he was freaked out, left with no illusion that they knew about the other part of him—the wolf.

"Just checking, you're on the ball," George mutters, forcing a casual tone to mask the turmoil boiling beneath the surface. He glanced at the boy one last time, relieved to see his eyes back to normal and the veins gone. But the strange look he received as he collected his food told him enough: the boy had no memory of what happened.

George drove off, leaving his appetite and sense of security behind. The strange, swirling world he found himself in pressed heavily on his thoughts. Fatigue began creeping in, his eyelids growing heavier with each passing streetlight, their glow stretching into blurry yellow streaks on the windscreen. He cranked up the radio, jolting awake as *Genesis* roared through the speakers.

He tried to push the encounter away, letting his thoughts drift to Miss Walker instead. Her phone number sat on the folded slip of paper above the gear stick, taunting him. Had she given it to him as a friend, or was it something more? The question circled his mind, foolish yet persistent. The more he thought about her, the more trouble it spelt. He couldn't entertain whatever feelings lingered—not with the blood moon looming so close.

Her scent was the problem, though. Since the start of the case, it had grown stronger, intoxicating in ways he didn't want to admit. His heightened senses had taken the bait, and now her presence lingered in his thoughts like a forbidden temptation.

But there was no time for distractions. The investigation still had loose threads: the expedition party, the ten-mile stretch where the bodies had surfaced, the elusive berth 72. And who owned it? These questions churned in his mind as the moonlight spilt over the dashboard and steering wheel, casting his hands in an eerie glow. He tapped his fingers impatiently, occasionally digging them into the black leather until his claws flexed out.

They came painlessly, like flick knives, and the sight brought a grim realisation.

He needed to call Michael. If a demon could possess a McDonald's drive-thru worker at the drop of a hat, it could be anyone, anywhere. And that was terrifying. Worse still, they seemed to know his every move. *How?* The thought sent a shiver through him as he pulled to the side of the road, the weight of it too much to ignore.

T he phone rang three times before Michael answered. "Brrr... brrr... brrr." A groggy, grouchy voice barked on the other end. "Hey, what the hell? I just got to sleep."

George grimaced. "Sorry, Michael," he exclaims. He could hear the irritation in his friend's voice and didn't blame him. Locke waking them at ungodly hours was bad enough, but this—this needed to be said.

"Georgie? Thank fuck it's not Locke. Don't need the Grim Reaper dragging me back into the office. Unless... wait. Another body?" Michael's voice sharpened, waking up quickly.

"No, nothing like that. Just had the mindless urge to warn you," George says, his hand trembling slightly as he swirls the whiskey in his glass. Two ice cubes clinked together, the cold condensation smearing across his fingertips. He was doing everything possible to keep his claws from extending again.

"Right," Michael says, his tone cautious. "I'm all ears."

"I was at McDonald's," George began, his voice tight with lingering unease. "One minute, I'm talking to some spotty young lad. Then his voice drops a hundred octaves, and... he wasn't the lad anymore."

Michael didn't reply immediately, and George almost heard him suppressing a smirk. "This late? You must be desperate. The wolf playing up?"

"No, arsehole. Hungry. But the fucking demon jumped bodies just to taunt me."

The wind outside howled against the single-pane windows of George's lounge, rattling them enough to make him jump. He peeled back the curtain to check, knowing what he'd see but unable to resist. The moonlight bathed the empty street in silver, yet the shadows seemed darker than they should have been.

Michael's tone shifted; the humour was gone. "What the hell?"

"They said something. Part of what they said." George paused, recalling the voice and the words still echoing. "'Is it that hard for you to imagine outside the books? While you look for us, we can find and get to you anywhere, anyone.'"

Michael exhaled sharply. "That's what they said?"

George nodded, though Michael couldn't see him. "And they said they're becoming one—like their bond is growing stronger."

Michael was silent for a long moment. Finally, he mutters, "Bloody hell, Georgie. That's not just demons fucking around anymore. That's escalation."

George stared out at the moonlit street, the weight of the night pressing down on him. "I know," he says quietly. "And it's only going to get worse."

"Well, you mentioned the demon being eyes and ears," Michael says over the phone. "Maybe that's progressed?"

Even through the line, George could tell Michael was thinking. His voice dropped slower and more deliberate—a sign he was working something out. When he had an answer, his tone was sharper, higher, as though someone had kicked him in the balls.

"I was worried," George admitted. "If they got to me, could they get to you? To anyone else?"

Michael let out a long sigh. "Ah, I get you. Look, stop worrying about what we can't control."

"Helpful," George muttered. Then, changing the subject to shake the unease clawing at him, he says, "Oh, and thanks for screwing with my head about Miss Walker. I think she's flirting. Not that I'd know—she gave me her home number."

"Told you, mate. She looks at you every time."

George ran a hand through his hair, frustration bubbling beneath the surface. "I nearly lost control tonight. She thought she saw my red eyes."

"That's a problem," Michael replies, his tone growing serious. "But it's just 24 hours. The worst is almost over, yeah?"

"I guess," George says, though he didn't feel convinced. "We still have the case to deal with."

"Any word from Skip?" Michael asks.

"Not a peep. Wouldn't be surprised if he's holed up on some desert island."

Michael chuckles. "Nah, he's too much of a home bird. Too shit-scared to leave his comfort zone."

"Aren't we all?" George shot back. "And you're one to talk. Especially with this Miss Wainwright coffee thing."

"Hey, don't knock it. That coffee was unsolicited. You don't know how monumental that is."

George smirked. "Ah yes, the universal sign of love: caffeine."

"Fuck off," Michael says with a laugh. Then his tone shifted, more serious. "Put the glass down and get some rest, will you?"

George froze mid-sip, startled. "How the hell did you—"

"I can hear the ice rattling in the glass, you muppet."

"Fine," George says, setting the glass down. "Guilty as charged. But remember, Michael, be careful. Black eyes and spider-web veins across the face—that's how you spot possession."

Michael's reply was dry. "Yeah, well, Halloween's around the corner. Good luck spotting the real thing with all the wannabes running around."

George hung up, his mind still racing. Michael had a point—they'd need to play smarter. The upcoming chaos would make distinguishing the real threat from harmless costumes harder.

The darkness crept into his dreams.

'Two peas in a pod, you and I,' a voice whispered, cold and nasty. 'Nowhere is safe. These girls are merely the beginning. You know that, don't you? What are you going to do about it?'

An icy chill rippled across George's skin. The wind rushed past his face, carrying the phantom applause of trees swaying in the darkness. He felt a presence, looming and oppressive, though no one was there. Shadows danced around him, alternating in shape and shade, barely enough to guide his path.

The stench of algae and mud, thick and sickly, pierced his nostrils. He realised he was hopping as a sharp pain bit into his skin. He looked down—a shard of glass glittered in the faint light, nestled among the leaves like a forgotten trap. But there was no blood.

He was on a public footpath. Cold pavement pressed against his feet, starkly contrasting the crunch of glass and autumn leaves. Another gust of wind whipped around him, and he shivered as the chill burrowed into his bones. His senses flared—heightened, almost unbearable. His claws shot out, thicker and sharper than before, glowing faintly in the darkness.

'Tut tut tut,' came a gravelly hiss. 'Don't want to talk to us now? How can you ignore your fate? It's been a long time coming.'

George's breath came in short bursts, white clouds forming in the cold air. The voice carried weight, each word pressing against his chest like an unseen hand. The semi-shift felt wrong and unnatural, and it scared the hell out of him. His eyes wouldn't change, no matter how hard he tried to force them.

"Who are you?" he growls, his voice a mix of fear and defiance.

The voice mocked him, curling around his mind like smoke. 'Who am I? More importantly, who are you?'

"Tell me who you are," George demands, hobbling forward despite the growing stench of burnt blood that filled the air.

The voice chuckled, low and cruel. 'A family that didn't look for you. A foster mother who fears you. Friends who know better than to cross you. And a brother who tried to kill you. Did I leave anything out? Oh yes, an identity crisis. Nobody knows or likes the real you.'

"Fuck off. You know nothing about me!" George snarls, his claws ripping through the air as he stalks forward. His heightened senses picked up faint sounds: the swirl of water, the soft lap of waves against a canal's edge. He realised he was near the park, the distant hum of city life fading into the stillness.

But there was only one heartbeat.

It echoed in the silence, steady and unhurried. His heartbeat quickened as he crept closer, driven by the need for answers he couldn't explain.

'Come now,' the voice sneers. 'Is that all you've got? After all, I've given you? Pathetic.'

George's jaw clenched as he moved closer to the water's edge. He wasn't sure what terrified him more—the voice or the fact that part of him agreed deep down.

"More than you know. Now, will you stop running?" the voice taunted, its tone dark and knowing.

"I'm not running," George mutters, though the words felt hollow. He moved forward, the oppressive darkness ahead pulling him closer. The outline of the canal bridge loomed before him—where it all began. The scene of Rachel Darnley's death. Why here?

Each step felt heavier than the last. His body ached, his muscles stretching and tightening, his bones clicking into place. But this time, there was no pain. Instead, there was a strange, almost welcome familiarity to the sensation. He felt drawn to the darkness as though it was waiting for him—a place where he belonged.

"You've been running since you saw the newspaper clippings," the voice says, cutting through his thoughts like a blade. "Ever since you were told you were the charted boy saved from the burning basement."

The words sank deep, shaking him. Was it true? Had he been running all this time—fleeing from himself, from the truth? Fear prickled at the edges of his mind as he glanced toward the darkness beneath the bridge. He was terrified of straying from the path, afraid of what the shadows might do to him if they pulled him in.

"How do you know that?" George's voice trembled, echoing against the cold stone walls. The air shifted, carrying a wild, untamed scent. It was raw and sharp, tinged with the smoky musk of burnt wood and the crisp bite of the oncoming winter.

"Isn't it obvious by now?" the voice growled, growing louder, more visceral. "I'm you."

The words screeched out in a sharp echo, and George's eyes snapped to the bridge's roof. His breath caught in his throat. There, nailed to the stone where Rachel Darnley had once been, was himself.

Or something like him.

The figure's face twisted with a mix of fear and ferocity. Its jaw was sharp and pronounced, large fangs glinting in the faint light. Its dark red eyes glowed, encircled by a black, flickering aura that seemed alive. The claws extending from its hands were identical to his own, gleaming with sharp precision.

"What is this?" George whispers, his voice barely audible.

"How?" he asks, his words trembling with disbelief.

"I'm what you'll become," the figure says, voice low and resonant. "What you must become to succeed. A demon fused with a wolf bloodline that stretches back centuries. All you have to do is give in. Stop fighting your destiny. You are a pure born, and they didn't know it. And they made you unstoppable if you only embraced what you would be."

The words rocked George to his core. He stared into the figure's glowing red eyes, unable to look away. The pull was magnetic, primal, and impossible to resist. He stepped forward, his instincts screaming to turn back, yet his feet carried him closer. The gritty edge of the stone path crumbled beneath his boots, tiny shards of dust and debris showering into the black waters below.

This time, he felt less sure of himself, less aware of his surroundings. The figure's presence consumed him, its gaze pulling him in like a vortex. He was tiptoeing now, within claw's reach of the monstrous reflection. His hand stretched out, trembling, drawn to help—or perhaps to join it.

"Don't fight it," the figure urges. "You know what you must do."

George's foot slipped, the loose gravel giving way beneath him. His balance faltered, and he felt himself lurch forward, helpless against the pull of gravity. The icy black waters rushed up to meet him.

Splash.

Embrace It

23

'7 am 30th.'

The room lay in darkness, and the faint glow of the clock hinted at an early hour—not crack-of-dawn early, but close enough. The dream lingered, vivid and unsettling: *Werewolf me facing off against Demon me in Rachel's spot by the canal.*

George rubbed his temples and stretched, scanning the room to reassure himself he was awake. Dampness clung to his skin, and a gritty crust between his fingers set off alarm bells. He blinked rapidly, shaking off the morning fog, only to find his arms coated in dried blood and mud. Not the usual aftermath. His body protested with every move, especially his hands and feet, which felt raw and strained.

Red rivulets streaked his forearms, clinging to the wispy black hairs like grotesque decorations. A scratch at the back of his throat erupted into a coughing fit, forcing up thick, hair-like strands. He stared in horror as clumps of coarse, light brown fur emerged from his mouth, as dry and rough as straw. Panic swelled in his chest. He needed a mirror, but he'd removed them all from his bedroom weeks ago.

Fear churned in his gut. *What if I've fully shifted?* Nightmares had left him rattled before, but this—waking up in such a state—was another level of terrifying. Jumping out of bed, he hurried to the bathroom, his bare feet pounding against the floor. He avoided the mirror as long as he could, bracing himself before opening his eyes.

Not blood. Fur.

Dark streaks of brown and black clung to his face and between his teeth. His heart thundered, and he fought to suppress his rising panic. *Worst-case scenario: a cat,* he thought, though he couldn't be sure. Cleaning up was his only option. He scrubbed vigorously, avoiding his reflection. Every glance felt like the mirror was smirking back, taunting him with something darker lurking beneath the surface.

Almost done, feeling human again, a loud thumping at the front door jolted him. His mind raced: *A neighbour? Missing cat? The Kanaima?* The thought sent a shiver down his spine. He wasn't dressed—an excuse to stall. Michael knew better than to show up unannounced without calling. Drying off, George headed for the bedroom to grab clothes.

The sight in the doorway froze him mid-step. Miss Walker and Michael stood there, both looking equally surprised. George, stark naked and towel-less, met their stunned stares with flushed cheeks. Miss Walker's gaze lingered, a devilish smile playing at her lips.

Michael breezed past him, coffee and a box in hand, heading straight for the kitchen like he owned the place. "Morning," he called over his shoulder, far too pleased with himself.

George, still frozen, locked eyes with Miss Walker. Her fitted mauve skirt hugged her hips, and the crisp white blouse emphasised her burgeoning curves. Gone were her usual suit trousers, and George couldn't help but admire the view.

Don't react. Don't react. Don't react.

Neither of them spoke. They traded glances instead—admiring, curious, and entirely too aware of the charged silence stretching between them. Since becoming more wolf than man, George had been in the best shape of his life, but the intensity of her gaze on him made it hard to concentrate. She wasn't subtle, either. Her eyes wandered, and George could hear the rhythmic pounding of her heart, her breaths becoming shallower with every passing second. She bit her bottom lip, sending his senses spiralling.

"This," Michael hollers froyellsitchen, breaking the moment, "is why you should answer the door properly. Did you forget your birthday?"

George snaps out of it. "I, erm, best get some clothes on," he stammers, trying to retreat before things get worse.

"I'd offer to help," Miss Walker says, her voice a playful purr, "but I don't like an audience."

The smirk on her face was lethal, and George's heart raced. "Three's a crowd," he mutters weakly, managing a half-smile.

"Maybe one day it'll just be two," she quips, her sultry eyes locking on his. "And far more fun.”

Heat flushed through him, his blood boiling as bones cracked faintly in his fingers. His claws threatened to extend. He had to move—fast.

“I won’t be long,” he managed, voice tinged with worry.

“Oh, I don’t believe that for a second,” she teases, a glint in her eye that tells him who had her hand. Spoiler: it wasn’t him.

Minutes later, dressed and forcing calm, George rejoined the others in the kitchen. Michael sipped his coffee; his grin was as smug as ever.

“I bet you forgot I had a spare key for emergencies,” Michael says, lowering the mug just enough to talk.

George glared at him. “And this is an emergency?”

Michael shrugged. “You tell me. You’re the one who didn’t answer the door.”

Miss Walker leaned against the counter, a knowing smile still playing on. George avoided her gaze, focusing instead on the clattering of plates as Michael rifled through cupboards.

George nodded and smiled, the warmth of his flushed cheeks still lingering as he caught another sneaky glance at Miss Walker. To his surprise, she was doing the same. The three were around his coffee table, a chocolate-coated fudge birthday cake taking centre stage. It had been decorated with a wolf—just toeing the line of coincidence, considering Walker didn’t know. The gesture felt surreal, especially since it was the first time anyone else had been inside his place.

“Why the wolf?” Walker asks, her tone casual but laced with curiosity, making George’s stomach tighten. For a brief, irrational moment, he wondered if she could read his mind.

“You saw him unshaven?” Michael quips before George can respond, his grin un-apologetically smug.

“Thanks, Michael,” George mutters, attempting to steer the moment away from suspicion. "It's an inside joke. Within a day, I can go from clean-shaven to a full beard. Michael jokes I'm descended from wolves."

Walker giggles as she cuts into her slice of cake. "Ooh, really? Maybe you are. I mean, remember, I thought you had red eyes. Human DNA is a curious thing—watered down over centuries. Who knows?"

Her playful tone made the joke feel harmless, but George's pulse quickened. He focused on his slice of cake, picking at it politely before giving in. It looked too good to resist.

The light-hearted moment was a rare reprieve, a slice of normality before reality inevitably crashed back in. George could almost feel the shift in the air as Michael pulled out his notebook, his fingers flicking through its pages. The peaceful interlude was over.

"Thanks for this, you two," George says, gesturing toward the cake before leaning back in his chair. "Now, Michael, care to share?"

Michael glanced up, a smirk tugging at the corner of his mouth. George felt the weight of Walker's presence pressing against his thoughts. Her scent lingered—intoxicating, overwhelming. He tried to block it out, covering his nose discreetly, but all that earned him was a raised eyebrow from Michael.

George's heightened senses were working against him. Every detail about Walker seemed amplified. A faint swoosh of her hair, and he could identify the three primary ingredients in her shampoo: coconut, chamomile, and honey. Michael was talking, but his words blurred into white noise until a sharp tap on the table snapped George back.

"Erhum," Michael says, raising an eyebrow knowingly. "I have an address for Jack Sexton. One of the places listed near the water is empty, but I tracked down his parents' address. He gave it during custody after a drink-driving charge three years ago."

George nodded, trying to focus. "Is that it?" he asks, feeling underwhelmed.

"Drum roll, please..." Michael began drumming on the table, his gaze darting toward Walker.

She smiled, clearly enjoying the theatrics. "Well, we figured you'd like a birthday present," she says, leaning forward slightly. "Josephine's help got a print off the photo in Mildred Thistle's hand."

George's curiosity piqued. He swallowed a bite of cake, trying not to choke on his eagerness. "Come on, the suspense is killing me."

Michael grinned, letting Walker take the lead. She handed him a folded paper, a hint of pride flickering in her eyes. "Emily Fulton," Walker says. "Caught shoplifting when she was eighteen."

"That's great," George says, excitement sparking. "Do we think she and Jack are the greedy duo, and it's gone wrong?"

"It would make sense," Michael says, reaching for another piece of cake. His appetite seemed insatiable, and George briefly won, but Michael had skipped dinner entirely.

George tapped his fingers against the table, his mind working through the possibilities. "If Emily's the one in control, driving the greed, then whatever's moored at berth 72 carries more weight than we realise."

"Exactly," Walker says, her tone steady, though George could hear her heart beating just a fraction faster. She was as intrigued as he was.

"So," George says, sitting up straighter, "where's the mother's place?"

"Whitechapel," Michael replies, popping another bite of cake into his mouth.

"Hopefully not another 'dead' end," George quips, the corners of his mouth twitching into a grin.

Michael snorted, cottoning on. "Ooh, check out the funny guy," he says, gesturing with his fork. "Next thing you know, he'll be doing stand-up."

George let out a soft laugh, shaking his head. Moments like this felt grounding for all the tension and chaos surrounding them. But the weight of the investigation—and the darker truths lurking beneath it—was never far away.

George sat quietly, his gaze unfocused as he tried to clear his mind. But his heightened senses betrayed him, narrowing in on Miss Walker. Her scent lingered—coconut, chamomile, honey—a maddening combination that tugged at his attention no matter how hard he tried to push it aside.

His thoughts drifted to Kanaima. The encounter at the McDonald's drive-thru haunted him, the way the like had possessed the staff. It had felt wrong—less controlled, less human. What would they find at Jack Sexton's mother's house? If anything? The question gnawed at him, and a faint tension coiled in his chest.

They allowed themselves a rare reprieve for the next twenty minutes. Normality. Calm. The chocolate-coated wolf cake sat between them, an odd reminder of George's dual life. The bitter taste of unease lingered in his mouth, refusing to be washed away by the coffee cooling in his hand.

He glanced around the room, taking in the two people sharing his space. Michael, a friend now but once a tormentor, was now devouring cake with a carefree grin. Miss Walker, seated nearby, exuded a quiet warmth that made George feel, for the first time in years, that he could let someone in again.

For a fleeting moment, George allowed himself to believe his birthday wouldn't be entirely about murder and demons. But the thought was fleeting, and the bitter taste in his mouth remained. A crazy night loomed ahead, waiting to unravel everything.

MORE DEMONS

24

'89 *Cartwright Street,'*

"There's someone home," George says, his eyes locked on the grey-bricked end terrace. The road looped in a lazy 'U,' a narrow alley between the next row of houses.

Michael glanced at him, raising an eyebrow. "How do you know? Can you hear their heartbeats?" His tone dripped with scepticism, though his curiosity surprised him. As it always does. Despite all they'd been through, Michael still wasn't fully accustomed to George's abilities.

"No, you idiot," George smirked. "I saw someone move by the upstairs window."

Michael's expression froze, and George bit back a laugh, relishing the brief levity. "Priceless," he mutters, shaking his head. For all his heightened senses, George was no sideshow. He had to remind Michael of that now and then.

Miss Walker stood nearby. Her presence steadily became a grounding force of nature in his chaotic mind. Her steady, confident body language calmed him, though George wasn't sure how long it would last. The quaint and unassuming house had captured their attention for ten minutes. No one had come or gone save for the shadowed figure upstairs. The hunched posture hinted at someone elderly, conjuring thoughts of Mildred Thistle. At least this one seemed alive.

Still, George's unease lingered. His abilities had been erratic since waking from his dream, a constant reminder of the wolf within. His claws extended and retracted unpredictably, and his fangs threatened to follow suit. The thought of meeting frail Mrs Sexton and accidentally "wolfing out" made his stomach churn. He pictured her startled gasp, her chair giving way, and her knitting needle lodged in her eye. The morbid image popped into his head unbidden, and he quickly dismissed it. *Enough dead bodies already.*

The Kanaima demon's ability to jump bodies weighed heavily on his mind. Was it still with Jack Sexton? Or had it found another host? The thought of it possessing someone he knew chilled him. How would he face it when the time came? The toxins it carried were lethal, and avoiding them seemed impossible.

George's mind circled back to the museum's notes: the Kanaima was weakest when caught between human and demon. If Jack was still its host, they could exploit his human side. Emily Fulton might be the key to that, but they'd have to be careful. If she saw them coming, the demon would too.

"Him or her?" Michael asks, squinting at the house before slipping on his glasses.

"If I had to guess, a 'her,'" George replies, his tone distracted. He tilted his head slightly, trying to tune into the faint sounds of the house, but it was like trying to catch a fading radio signal.

Michael's curious gaze lingered. "What's going on, matey? You seem... different today."

George hesitated, rolling his neck to ease the knot at its base. The ache in his muscles had persisted since he woke, a tangible reminder of the nightmare that clung to his mind like a shadow. "Maybe it has something to do with my senses and abilities going wonky," he admitted, glancing up at the sky as though seeking clarity.

He hadn't yet told Michael about the dream. The confrontation with his demon self had been too vivid, too real. And the morning's aftermath—the blood, the fur—only deepened the mystery of what he was becoming. The lack of evidence outside his home was both a relief and a concern. He could only hope the calls wouldn't start flooding in if he'd gone further afield without realising it. One unbelievable beast on the loose was bad enough. The whispers of another would be catastrophic.

Michael tilted his head, waiting for George to continue. George sighed. He knew he couldn't keep this to himself much longer. Whatever the night had in store, it wouldn't be forgiving. The rabid energy coursing through him grew, and George wasn't sure how long he could hold it at bay.

"I need to loop you in," George finally says, his voice quiet but firm. "No telling how tonight will play out, but you need to know everything."

Michael raised an eyebrow, his usual humour subdued. "Alright," he says. "Lay it on me."

George exhaled, preparing himself for the truth he was about to share—and the chaos it would undoubtedly unleash.

"Eh? What does that mean? You can't control it?" Michael asks, his expression betraying a flicker of fear George wasn't used to seeing. He should've expected it eventually, but it still caught him off guard. He'd always been a nobody, a loner, content to stay under the radar. Now, he wasn't so sure.

"Last night, I had another nightmare," George began with a heavy sigh. "It was mostly a replay of the first crime scene, but this time, I was pinned to the roof. The other me." His voice faltered as he recalled the vivid imagery. "I had a conflict with myself. Only the one on the ceiling... seemed different. Changed. Then I woke up covered in blood, coughing up fur."

Michael listened, his brows furrowing deeper with each word. "Well, I figured something would start kicking off today. That's why I came early—for more than one reason. After your call, I thought I'd keep an eye out. How's your head? Any changes? Temper or anything?"

"My head's fine," George replies, though he wasn't entirely sure that was true. "It's the dreams. Not knowing when changes will happen. And..." He hesitated, feeling the words catch in his throat. "It's Miss Walker. She's... under my skin."

Admitting it aloud sent his pulse pounding in his ears. The surreal weight of acknowledging to someone else that Miss Walker had gotten to him left George feeling exposed. His eyes dropped to his hands, and his stomach sank. His claws had extended, sharp and gleaming. All because they were talking about her.

"See?" George says, holding up his hands to Michael. "We mention her and look." He waved his claws in Michael's face.

Michael smirked, though there was a hint of concern in his eyes. "Told you. Besides, I saw the way she wanted to jump your bones. You don't need super-hearing or laser eyes to pick that up. Look, give yourself a break. If anything good's gonna come out of our recent clusterfuck, it may as well be you getting your leg over."

George shot him a look but couldn't entirely dismiss the idea. "I'm not a dirty dog like you," he mutters. "Or, as Miss Walker put it, an old dog. I've got to get these demon bollocks under control, see where I stand after the blood moon. What if I'm not the same person afterwards?" His voice grew quieter as he leaned against the window, staring at the

Sexton house. It looked peaceful, almost too normal, making it hard to believe the mother of a potential serial killer lived there.

Michael glanced at him, his expression softening. "Right, you got your game face on?"

George turned, baring his teeth as his face shifted slightly into its wolfish form. "What, this one?"

Michael snorted. "Oh, fuck off. See, you've got this. You're just being a little shit now."

The brief banter eased some of the tension, though the weight of the situation lingered. George hoped sharing his stress would prevent him from shifting at the wrong moment.

"Right," Michael says, switching the ignition off. "Let me do the talking. You stay on guard with your shit-magnet radar."

George chuckles, shaking his head as he steps out of the car. "Sure thing, boss."

The Sexton house was neat, bordered by low, white-panelled fencing and trimmed hedges. A flagstone path led to an open porch with four white pillars and a glossy black door. The place was pristine, almost too perfect for their investigating chaos.

Michael knocked firmly, his knuckles rapping against the door. George focused, his heightened senses picking up faint heartbeats inside. Only one. A woman's muffled grumbling reached his ears: *Who the bloody hell is it this time?*

When the door swung open, the smell hit him instantly. Beyond the simmering beef stew was something far more sinister: the faint tang of toxins and the unmistakable scent of dust—the kind they'd encountered at other crime scenes. The Kanaima had been here. The question was whether Mrs Sexton knew.

The woman in the doorway was in her mid-sixties, with short, curled grey hair and thin-rimmed brown glasses shielding her sharp brown eyes. Her face was drawn and cold, her gaze darting between them. She tensed as Michael flashed his badge, her heart skipping a beat.

Michael introduced them, but George barely heard him. The small hairs on his neck bristled, his hackles rising. Someone was watching. He couldn't pinpoint who, what, or how far away, but the sensation was undeniable.

He spun on the spot, his sudden movement catching Michael's attention. "What now?" Michael mutters, his brow furrowing.

The older woman's voice snapped him back to the moment. "What now?" she demands, her tone impatient and sharp.

"Mrs Sexton?" Michael asks, his East London twang softened into something almost polite.

"Yeah. Look, I've already said all I need to say. I'm going to…" Her words trailed off, leaving both men exchanging a bemused glance. Their warrant cards were plain as day, yet she seemed determined to deflect.

George's instincts screamed at him. The toxins, the dust, and the strange behaviour all pointed to something deeper. Whatever was happening here, Mrs Sexton wasn't just an innocent bystander.

And whoever—or whatever—was watching them from the shadows wasn't far away.

"Sorry, but who do you think we are?" George asks, his voice calm as he listens intently to Mrs Sexton's heartbeat, waiting for the telltale pause of hesitation.

"I'm getting old, but I'm not blind. You're police detectives," she replies, her tone steady and deliberate, though the situation only grew stranger.

"Has somebody else been here?" George pressed.

"Yeah, a few of you lot in flashy suits."

"When? And what did they say?"

"Yesterday." Mrs Sexton folded her arms, her thin frame tightening as she spoke. "They were after my Jack. I told them what I'll tell you—he's not here. Hasn't been for a few days."

Her heartbeat remained even, her voice unwavering. Her response seemed truthful, but George wasn't ready to trust it. He'd been fooled before—Mr Kumar's deceptions had taught him that even his heightened senses weren't foolproof.

"They identified as police?" George asks, the memory of the chaotic shootout at Kumar's house flashing through his mind. The thought of another rogue faction made his gut tighten.

"They flashed something," she says, her brow furrowing as she tries to recall. "I was busy and thought nothing of it. Now that I think back, though… it was an odd pair. One of them looked Egyptian, and the other… Well, that scarf didn't go with the suit."

George's radar spiked. His instincts told him there was more to this than met the eye. The mention of an "Egyptian" angle made his thoughts race to the recent relics. Could they be connected?

"Did they ask anything else?" George interrupts as Michael opens his mouth to speak. Michael's sharp glance conveyed his irritation, but George only offered an apologetic smirk.

"They asked if he brought any boxes home. Said they were stolen property," Mrs Sexton says. Her voice softened defensively. "My Jack's no thief. Especially not with that sort of thing. He's a teacher for crying out loud."

Michael and George exchanged a look, their unspoken surprise mirrored in their raised eyebrows. This time, George let Michael take the lead.

"A teacher?" Michael asks. "Where?"

"Some secondary school," she replies, waving a hand vaguely. "Teaches history to the younger ones. Only part-time, though—needs must. His wife left him high and dry, cleared out, took everything."

George watched as her eyes darted to the left. She tried hard to recall details, but George's attention was elsewhere. He caught the faint sound of another heartbeat—then another. Two, distinct, joining the feeling of being watched that had gnawed at him since they'd arrived.

The breeze shifted, carrying a scent that made George's hackles rise. It was the same one he'd picked up earlier—death and sulphur, poorly masked by a pungent deodorant. His stomach twisted as he tried to piece it together. This wasn't the Kanaima; that much was certain. But whoever it was, their intentions weren't good.

Catching George's subtle shift in posture, Michael focused on Mrs Sexton, attempting to wrap up the conversation. "Erm, thank you for your time, Mrs Sexton," he says, his tone professional but tinged with urgency. "If they come back, please call the police. I fear they're impostors. And if your son contacts you, tell him to go to any police station and have them call DS Dalton and DC Reynolds. We must speak to him regarding his colleague, Mr Kumar."

Mrs Sexton's lips thinned, and the worry lines on her brow deepened. "Are they dangerous?" she asks, her voice trembling slightly.

Michael hesitated before replying, his words measured. "Not that we know, but I don't believe they have good intentions."

Her heartbeat quickened, and George's focus returned to the sulphuric scent lingering in the distance. It had to be at least two hundred feet away, but that was close enough. He glanced at Michael, who caught the look and nodded slightly, the unspoken agreement clear between them: they had to figure out who—or what—was watching them.

"Let's move," George mutters as they step back from the door, the glossy black surface closing with an audible click. A sense of foreboding follows them, a tangible weight hanging in the air.

Whoever had been at the house before them wasn't just a coincidence. And the scent of sulphur never ended well.

George tugged on Michael's thick coat, shuffling them away from Mrs Sexton's doorstep. His eyes darted around, scanning for the source of the sulfuric stench that had clung to the air moments ago. Michael shot him a withering glare, clearly irritated by the abrupt exit.

"What's the rush?" Michael asks, his gaze mimicking George's as they scan their surroundings. Across the street, George's sharp eyes picked up on an alleyway tucked between two rows of houses. It was easy to miss, set back from the main road, marked by a rusting metal fence and mismatched lampposts.

"While you were talking, I picked up a scent," George says, his tone grim. "And you won't like it."

Michael's face dropped, his mood darkening. "Not more fucking blood," he mutters, fishing for a cigarette box only to find it empty. His scowl deepened.

"No, not this time. But it's just as strange—sulphur and death," George says.

Michael stopped dead in his tracks, his exasperation palpable. "Sulphur? What, gunfire and a dead body?"

"I don't think so," George says, sniffing the air again, trying to place the lingering scent. "I felt we were being watched. The smell appeared right as I picked up two heartbeats."

Michael's jaw tightened, the wheels turning in his mind. "What're the bets it's the two who visited Sexton before? Watching in case he comes back?"

George nodded. "That's exactly what I'm thinking. Michael, grab the car. We might need you to cut them off if they run."

"Sure thing." Michael jogged toward the car while George turned toward the alley, adrenaline coursing through his veins. The beast within him stirred eagerly, urging him to give chase. Near a flaked silver lamppost, he spotted them—two men. One matched Mrs Sexton's description: Egyptian features, a navy tasselled scarf, and black heavy-duty boots that gave off a military vibe. The other was a white male in his late thirties with a black goatee, a black jacket, and white Converse sneakers.

George withdrew his warrant card. "Police! You two got a minute?" he called out, his voice firm.

The two men froze, their heads turning in unison. Their grins were anything but friendly, radiating a dangerous confidence that sent a shiver down George's spine. The wind shifted, carrying their scent—strong, sickly, and wrong. George's stomach twisted as the realisation hit him: *These weren't human.*

Without a word, the men spun on their heels and bolted.

"DC Reynolds in pursuit of two suspects off Cartwright Street," George barks into his radio. "IC4 male, 6-foot, black jacket, blue jeans, black boots, navy scarf. IC1 male, black jacket, blue jeans, white Converse, black goatee. Heading toward Turnbull Avenue."

Michael's voice crackled through the line. "DS Dalton, unmarked unit HT 17, already heading that way."

George took off after them, every fibre in his body surging with energy. His claws extended, his vision tinted red. He felt unstoppable; the hunt was consuming him. The primal thrill flooded his senses, and for a terrifying moment, he relished it. The urge to catch them, to tear them apart, burned in his blood.

No. Focus. He forced the thoughts back, horrified at the dark lust lingering in his mind. He couldn't afford to lose control. Not now.

The men were fast, but so was George. He matched them stride for stride, resisting the urge to drop to all fours and give in to his instincts. A glance over their shoulders told him everything—their expressions shifted, their grins replaced by unease. One muttered, "We have to go. He's not normal either."

George pushed harder, his senses alive and electrified. "We're near an iron bridge heading over the railway," he relayed, trying to steady his breath.

But the men vanished as they reached the steps leading to the bridge. Black smoke billowed around them, dissipating into the wind. George stumbled, his momentum sending him crashing into the green railings. He landed in a heap, narrowly avoiding a puddle of piss and discarded beer cans.

"Hotel Tango suspects lost," George says into his radio, frustration thick in his voice. "Last seen heading over the tracks. Contact TfL for train movement near Turnbull Avenue."

He stayed on the ground, his fists clenching against the dirt. The beast within him growled, unsatisfied. He'd been so close. The bitter taste of failure stung more than the bruise on his face.

Michael screeched to a stop nearby, rushing out of the car. His breath puffed in white clouds as he crouched beside George. "What happened?"

"They vanished," George mutters, his voice flat.

Michael's face darkened. "What manner of case are we dealing with, matey?"

George hesitated, the words catching in his throat before he forced them out. "I think... I think they're demons."

The dread in his voice silenced Michael, whose fear mirrored George's own.

Whatever they were chasing was no longer bound by the rules of their world.

THINKING OF THE BLACK SMOKE

25

"Shoe wear?" Walker asks, not looking up from the papers she was sorting through.

"What?" George blinked, her question catching him off guard.

"Did you catch what shoes they were wearing?"

George ran a hand through his hair, his mind still tangled in the events of the chase. "Uh, one had black all-purpose boots—maybe military. The other? White Converse."

"Size?"

"No idea. Didn't exactly have time to size them up. If I had to guess, ten or eleven."

Walker nodded thoughtfully, jotting something down. "Could be a match."

George slumped in his chair, his gaze fixed on the ceiling. The foot chase replayed in his head: the flicker of green eyes, the way they disappeared in a cloud of black smoke. It wasn't just strange—it was impossible. When they'd returned to the car afterwards, Michael had sat motionless, his forehead pressed against the steering wheel, staring out the window in stunned silence.

George felt like he'd crossed a line and shared one strange detail too many. Then again, everything about this case has spiralled into madness. *I'm a werewolf. So is the skipper. We're hunting a Kanaima demon. I've seen ghosts. And now, I'm chasing what might be demons.*

He glanced at the photos pinned to the whiteboard—murder scenes, stolen relics, Egyptian artefacts. The familiar chaos of London's streets felt like a distant memory—no more routine calls about domestic disputes or petty theft. Instead, George felt himself unravelling, the weight of what he'd become pressing against his sanity.

Every person around him seemed to carry an unspoken threat. Flashing images clawed at the edges of his mind—blood-drenched figures, their lifeless bodies sprawled across his memories. And then there was Miss Walker. She stood beside him, her voice cutting through the haze of his thoughts, but his mind betrayed him. For a fleeting moment, he pictured her naked, covered in blood, her throat torn out.

George clenched his fists, forcing the image away. The beast within him stirred, feeding on his unease. He needed a distraction, something to keep his thoughts from spiralling further. Maybe a dash of the governor's whiskey in his coffee. Anything to take the edge off.

Michael, meanwhile, was hunched over the whiteboard, scrutinising the crime scene photos. George's attention drifted back to Walker as she spoke again. "Shoe wear for the two that ran. You mentioned they might've been at Mrs Sexton's house, and you could smell sulphur."

"Right, yeah," George says, shaking himself from his thoughts. "Sulphur and something else. One had black all-purpose boots, maybe military. The other white Converse. Size ten or eleven."

Walker raised an eyebrow. "Interesting."

"Why's that?" George asks, his curiosity piqued.

Walker leaned forward, her expression sharpening with a hint of satisfaction. "You know how much we like to go the extra mile? We rigged an infrared lens onto our crime scene camera to photograph areas where that dust was found."

George's eyes narrowed, his interest deepening. "And?"

"We found more of the same around the footpath you mentioned. The one you chased those blokes on," Walker explains, her voice calm but laced with intrigue.

Michael perked up, tearing his gaze from the photos. "Clear enough to gauge size, then?"

Walker smirked. "Clear enough to confirm two sets of prints for each pair of feet. They doubled back in tandem."

George's mind raced. "Are you saying... there were four suspects?"

"That's exactly what I'm saying," Walker replies, her tone measured but confident. "This isn't just two people. There's a group behind these murders."

The room fell silent as her words settled over them. Four suspects. George's chest tightened as he thought back to the chase, the sulphur, the unsettling eyes of the men. He couldn't shake the growing certainty that whoever—or whatever—they were up against wasn't entirely human.

"Look at this," Elena says, sliding a bird's-eye sketch of the crime scene across the table. Her tone carried a note of excitement, though her focus remained sharp.

George leaned in, studying the intricate diagram. The footprints—varied in size—were meticulously marked, each one overlaid with the areas where the strange dust had been found. A pattern was emerging, and as Elena connected it, the pieces fell into place for George, too.

"A small set of footprints on the outskirts, a woman's," Elena explains, pointing to the periphery of the sketch. "Size four. Then here, the largest—size twelve—committing the deed. The other two, sizes ten and eleven, loitering nearby."

George frowned, his mind spinning. "Wait. What sizes are you estimating?"

"That's the interesting part," she says, her excitement tempered with curiosity. "The size four belongs to a woman, watching from the edge. The size twelve? The killer. The other two—ten and eleven—were lingering. Maybe observing, helping."

"How sure are you these weren't ours?" George asks, his voice low, cautious.

"The dust residue," she replies, tapping the diagram. "Three sets carried it. Most wouldn't have been noticed without the infrared lens."

George sat back, digesting the revelation. Elena's work had blown the case wide open, giving him a new perspective. His thoughts churned, building connections between the prints, the demons, and the victims. "The two on the outskirts," he asks slowly, "do you think they were watching the murder?"

Elena hesitated, then shook her head. "No. The prints are fresher. I'd say they were at the scene *after* the murder. The 'how'—that's the part I don't know yet."

George's mind raced, assembling the puzzle. Emily Fulton—likely the mastermind. Jack Sexton—the possible Kanaima or its next target. The two demons with green eyes lurking at crime scenes, seeking something. But what?

"Three left to be called. Hopefully, Mrs Sexton was telling the truth," Elena says, breaking the silence.

"She was," George replies firmly, though he couldn't tell her why. Reading heartbeats wasn't exactly something you shared over coffee and case files. That'd be too far, even in their line of work.

2 PM, *Hamdenbrook Secondary School*

T he imposing red-brick building loomed, encircled by a five-foot-high stone wall
    topped with red fencing. George couldn't suppress a shiver as they approached.
Schools always gave him the creeps. The echoes of screaming children, laughter, and the
relentless scrape of chair legs on tile made his skin crawl. It felt like a prison—just one for
smaller inmates.

"We're cutting it close," Michael says, flicking his cigarette. "School closes at 3:15.
Darkness will be here a little after four. And we both know what happens by six."

The thought hung heavy in the air: the blood moon. George's pulse quickened, though
he tried to ignore it. Instead, he focused on the gate ahead. Two main entrances broke the
wall's expanse, wide enough for cars but just as uninviting as the rest of the place.

Michael took another drag from his cigarette, his hand trembling slightly as he exhaled
smoke. George glanced at him, raising an eyebrow.

"Any vibes?" Michael asks, his voice taut.

"Not yet. Just a lot of noise," George replies, his ears catching every laugh, every squeak
of trainers on the playground. Then he adds, smirking, "What's got you so jittery? Your
hand's shaking like a crackhead looking for a fix."

Michael shot him a withering glare, stubbing his cigarette on the metal gate. "Funny.
I don't like schools. Never did. Places like this? Too many bloody memories."

George chuckles softly, though his nerves aren't much steadier. The oppressive atmosphere of the school mingled with the tension of the case, tightening the knot in his gut.
He tried to shake it off, focusing instead on the task ahead.

Inside these walls was a potential lead—maybe even Jack Sexton himself. But the closer
they got to answers, the more the shadows seemed to lengthen, creeping ever closer.

And with the blood moon looming, time was running out.

"It's these places," Michael mutters, flicking the remnants of his cigarette to the pavement and stamping it out. "It's the kids. Bad memories, that's all."

George smirked, sensing an opening. "Don't tell me you were bullied?"

Michael's expression darkened, his voice low. "No, it's the mess with Andy's kid. That bloody haunts me. I hate these places."

The smirk vanished from George's face. Life had a way of dragging everyone back to their past. He didn't press further; mentioning Andy's kid was enough to stir a lingering ache. He could see now why Skip hadn't shown his face recently. Too many demons to confront.

The intercom buzzed loudly as Michael pressed the button, the shrill sound grating on George's sensitive ears. Wincing, he shielded them with the collar of his coat.

"You okay?" Michael asks, concern creeping into his voice.

"Yeah," George replies, though his voice is tight. "Just fighting against my body. I don't know what'll happen from one minute to the next."

As he spoke, a shiver ran down George's neck, the sense of an invisible presence prickling his skin. His senses flared, picking up something beyond the mundane noise of the schoolyard.

"Okay," Michael says, glancing around. "Now we're being watched."

"Again?" George asks, his voice edged with irritation.

"Yep," Michael replies, his eyes scanning the perimeter. "And it's too chaotic to tell where."

"It feels like we're puppets on strings, doing the dirty work," he adds after a beat.

George sighed. "Speaking of which, have you seen Locke lately? He keeps disappearing."

Michael shrugged. "Nope. Chalked it up to the handover. Remember the leaving do tonight?"

"Ah, yes," George says, the thought of adding to his already growing unease. "For the first time, I'll be happy to be late. Don't think it's wise, do you?"

Michael smirked. "Part of me says yes. Then again, we don't need the bloodshed, do we?"

The intercom crackled to life. *"Hello, Hamdenbrook."*

Michael stepped closer. "Ah, yes. DS Dalton and DC Reynolds. We need a chat."

"Okay, come in. Head to the main door to the left. Reception is just inside," a woman's voice replies over the speaker, followed by the distinct buzz of the gate magnet releasing.

They crossed the pavement, heading toward the entrance. George felt the weight of eyes on them as they walked past rows of windows filled with baying children. Their laughter and shouting reverberated like a symphony of chaos, the energy of the school's jungle wrapping around them like a suffocating blanket.

Inside, the reception area was dimly lit, a polished floor reflecting the sterile glow of fluorescent lights. A woman behind the desk glanced up as they entered, her expression bright but professional.

"Hi," George began, flashing his badge. "DS Dalton and DC Reynolds. We're looking for Mr Jack Sexton. We were told earlier he's in today."

The receptionist's smile faltered slightly as her eyes flicked between them. "One moment, please," she says, reaching for her phone.

George's gut tightened. He caught Michael's glance out of the corner of his eye.

Being inside the school narrowed the sounds and smells, focusing on George's senses. He knew Jack was here—he could feel it. But was Emily nearby, too? If Jack was in his human form, was this his weak point?

"Okay, yes, he's teaching Year Seven history," the receptionist, Sally Fig, says, adjusting her name badge. She was a white woman in her late forties, with neatly bobbed brown hair, dressed smartly in a navy skirt suit and a sky-blue blouse. "I can show you to his room if you like."

George leaned closer to Michael, whispering, "He's here."

Michael gave a brief nod, his expression tight. He understood the weight of George's certainty.

"Tea or coffee?" another voice piped up, belonging to a cheerful woman behind the reception desk.

"Pardon?" George asks, surprised.

"Would you like tea or coffee? You boys are always so busy," she says with a smile.

"Oh, we're fine, thank you," George replies, shaking his head. Running into trouble on a full stomach didn't appeal to him.

Sally led them down the hallowed corridors, the varnished wooden floors creaking underfoot. The faint scent of school dinners hung in the air—mashed potatoes and gravy. It mingled uncomfortably with the growing unease in George's gut. Jack was close. Too close.

They stopped outside Room Ten. George peered through the wire-embedded glass panel in the door. A tall white man in his late twenties stood at the front of the room. Jack Sexton had black curly hair and glasses and was at least six feet three inches tall. He didn't look like a killer. His wide grin as he spoke to the students made him seem warm and approachable—almost fatherly. To an outsider, he was the epitome of a dedicated teacher.

George stepped back; his senses heightened. He strained to listen, to pick up the telltale signs of his master. Emily. It wouldn't be easy to hide if she were here, especially not in a school. Then, a faint draft from a side door opened by a teacher preparing for the afternoon exit rush came.

The breeze carried the sickly stench of sulphur mixed with old dust and the acrid tang of toxins. It was unmistakable. The Kanaima and the others were here. George's stomach turned as the realisation struck. Things could turn ugly fast.

He glanced around, counting the potential collateral damage. Three hundred students. Dozens of teachers. All oblivious, going about their day. His body tensed, the wolf inside him clawing at the edges of his restraint. His senses were sharpening—hearing, sight, and smell levelling up in ways he couldn't control. He felt edgy and aggressive. Different. Whatever "it" was, it was changing and terrified him.

"This is bad," George mutters, his voice barely audible.

"What?" Michael asks, taking his turn to peer through the glass.

"We're not alone," George replies, his gaze scanning the hallway.

His sharp eyes caught a glint of something in the light. Inside the classroom, Jack was handing out exercise books to the students, each one streaked with a clear, viscous fluid. It shimmered unnaturally, catching George's attention like a beacon.

"They're expecting us," George says, his voice low and tense.

Michael turned sharply. "What do you mean?"

George didn't answer immediately, his mind racing. The children weren't just by-standers. They were being used—woven into the trap. The Kanaima, Jack, and whoever else was here had planned for this moment. The students were their safety net. If George or Michael made a move, the consequences would be catastrophic.

"We're walking into a trap," George finally says, his voice like a growl. His claws flexed involuntarily, scraping against the wooden railing. He could feel the shift happening, little by little. The demon wolf inside him was awakening, and he didn't know if he could stop it.

Michael's face hardened. "What do we do?"

George's jaw tightened, his mind calculating their next move. "We tread carefully. And pray we're not too late."

JACK SEXTON

26

Whether Jack acted on instinct or intent, every blue exercise book in the classroom carried the poison. Fortunately, for now, the children had only seen the books on their desks. The danger hadn't yet touched them—but it was only a matter of time.

George could feel the invisible threat pressing in, a suffocating presence all around yet maddeningly elusive. He was caught between two impossible choices: let the children touch the books and risk paralysis while Jack walked away clean, or evacuate the students and risk Jack vanishing into the ether, free to strike again. It wasn't like Jack was trying to hide.

The texts they'd recovered had hinted at hunting. What if Jack's next victim was here, in the school? The thought sent a chill through George, sharpening the urgency in his mind. Next to him, Michael kept talking, his words a stream of chatter that faded into the background. George's heightened senses filtered out the noise, focusing instead on the symphony of heartbeats around them. Maybe charm was their only way out of this mess. Or maybe it wasn't enough.

They stood three doors down from the classroom in a corridor that felt like a labyrinth. Three doors ahead to the right, three more on the left. The stairway loomed to the right, an exit nearby. Behind them stretched another hallway with at least five more doors. If the demons wanted chaos, this was the perfect setting for it. Releasing the students all at once could create pandemonium—enough to distract the kids from the books but also enough to let the demons slip away.

George saw the sun dipping lower on the horizon through the wire-meshed window.

The looming blood moon filled him with dread. The chance to unravel Jack's human side pained him, but the school wasn't the place to cuff him—not with so many lives at stake. Besides, no one had ever faced a Kanaima and lived to tell the tale. George's instincts screamed caution.

Heartbeats surrounded them, a maddening circus of sound. Yet, among them, George couldn't pinpoint the master—the puppet master controlling this grim play. His head darted around as he half-expected something to lunge at him from the shadows. Sally, the receptionist, eyed him curiously, her brow furrowing as if she could sense his unease.

Jack had clocked them twice in the classroom. His glances were quick, calculated, and entirely unfazed. The subtle confidence unnerved George. It was as if Jack knew exactly how much power he held in this situation.

"Michael," George murmurs, stepping aside. "Can I bend your ear for a second?"

Michael tilted his head, following George a few steps away from Sally. "Sure. What's eating at you?"

"We can't push this," George says, his voice low, glancing over Michael's shoulder toward the playground door.

Michael's brow furrowed. "Why not?"

"I can smell the two I chased," George replies. His voice carried a grim weight. "They're here. They've been dabbing toxins on those books."

Michael's face darkened. "Shit. So they knew we were coming."

George nodded. "I think they were tipped off."

Michael hesitated. "You think the old lady warned him? She knew about the school."

"If she did, then my faith in her truthfulness is shot," George says, a bitter smirk betraying his disbelief. If Mrs Sexton had lied about knowing the school, what else had she lied about?

George glanced back at Jack, his nostrils flaring as he caught the sulfuric stink mixed with the faint innocence of the children. His chest tightened. He knew they couldn't act impulsively. Not here, not now. But his eyes snagged on the fire alarm mounted near the stairwell, its red handle gleaming under the dim hallway lights.

It was risky, but it could work. An evacuation would leave the books—and the demons—behind, giving them a chance to regain control of the situation.

"Michael," George says, his voice steady with resolve. "Distract Sally. I'm pulling the alarm."

Michael arched a brow, then smirked. "See, I knew we kept you around for a reason.

Not your charming personality or coffee-making skills—both need work. But this? Genius."

George gave a faint smile, though the weight of what they were about to do pressed heavily on his chest. If this didn't work, the cost could be unimaginable.

"The moment it goes, chaos ensues," George murmurs, his eyes locked on the fire alarm.

"When it does," Michael replies, a hint of wry humour in his tone, "we go straight into the room, herd the kids out, and gather the books while keeping Mr Sexton occupied."

"It's a plan," George agrees, though the weight of what could go wrong hung heavy between them. "But a lot can go south if the Kanaima suspects anything."

Michael shifted gears, laying on the charm as he led Sally off to one side. Meanwhile, George slithered toward the alarm, every step a quiet calculation. Even in shoes on the solid varnished wood floors, he moved as silently as a predator stalking prey.

Once in position, George took a deep breath, steadying himself. He could feel the sting in the air, a warning from his heightened senses. His hackles rose as though they, too, knew what was coming.

*C*lick.

The fire alarm exploded into a chorus of metallic thumps and shrill sirens, a cacophony that sent the school into instant chaos. To George, the sound cut deeper than most—like a dog whistle at a frequency designed to pierce his mind. He fought the overwhelming urge to bury his head and block it all out, but the stampede had begun.

Children poured into the hallway in a disorganised rush. George darted across the floor, his werewolf agility carrying him swiftly past the oncoming tide. His eyes locked on Michael, who motioned for the kids to leave the classroom. Amid the chaos, George focused on the steady thrum of one distinct heartbeat, louder and more deliberate than the rest—Jack's.

Reaching the doorway, George felt it—the Kanaima's presence stirring within Jack. It triggered a response, and he felt his claws extending involuntarily. He clenched his fists, hiding his hands as his eyes scanned the children rushing past. He counted them automatically: seven blondes, five brunettes, four with black hair, two with afros, and two redheads. His gaze flicked to their hands, searching for anyone who might disobey instructions and carry their belongings. But they left the books behind, as he'd hoped.

When the last child crossed the threshold, George turned his focus inside the classroom. Jack Sexton stood with his back to them, facing the window. The lowering sun cast a golden glow through the glass, painting his broad frame in silhouette. There was an uncanny stillness to him. Jack's size alone made him an intimidating figure, but George felt something deeper—a shift in the air, a thickening tension that made his heart race.

Michael was sweating. George could hear each bead of sweat tracing over the stubble on his jaw, the sound amplified by his heightened senses. It matched the rising tempo of George's heartbeat. Every instinct screamed at him to grab Michael and leave, to run from the evil energy pulsing from Jack's silent form.

"Mr Sexton, I'm DS Dalton," Michael says, stepping beside George, his voice calm despite the tension. "This is DC Reynolds."

Jack remained still, his shadow unmoving.

George took the momentary distraction to scan the room, his werewolf vision sharpening. He searched for anything unusual—thermal signatures, footprints, traces of toxins. The outlines of Jack's footprints glowed faintly on the floor, their heat fading but unmistakable. Moving methodically, George turned his attention to the desks. The blue exercise books sat untouched, their surfaces glistening faintly in the dim light.

The toxins, he realised grimly, were there. Their clear residue shimmered like oil on water, barely perceptible to anyone without enhanced senses. George's jaw tightened. They'd been walking into a trap all along.

Still, Jack made no move. The eerie calm of the man before them only deepened George's unease. He exchanged a glance with Michael, who gave the faintest nod of acknowledgement. The two officers were alone now in the lion's den, with Jack Sexton at its centre. Whatever was about to happen, they both knew it wouldn't be easy—or safe.

"Mr Sexton, are you okay?" Michael asks, his voice steady despite the tension crackling in the room.

"What took you so long?" came the reply, but it wasn't Jack's voice.

The words were low and guttural and seemed to echo unnaturally, surrounding them in a way that made every hair on George's body stand on end. The voice sounded like death incarnate, the embodiment of the Grim Reaper itself. George froze his instincts at war. He was a detective sworn to protect and a werewolf capable of immense power. But fear coursed through him, a stark reminder of his humanity.

"Is Jack there with you?" George asks, his voice tight, betraying the unease creeping over him. He fought to keep his feet planted, every instinct screaming at him to run—or attack.

The figure in front of them shifted, its presence growing darker. "I am Jack, and Jack is me," the voice says, laced with sinister confidence. "Yin and Yang, I think you call it. We are one."

George swallowed hard, stepping slightly to the right to get a better view of Jack's face. "What about when you were teaching?" he asks, his voice low and cautious.

The figure chuckled, a sound that seemed to reverberate through the walls. "We're not stupid. If we are to coexist, we have to work together."

Hearing the demon speak, George realised something he hadn't considered before: the demons weren't as dependent on their master as he had thought. They were autonomous in ways that made them even more dangerous.

"What about your master?" George pressed, his tone calculated, and every syllable was a careful prod for answers. "Where do they stand in your partnership?"

The demon tilted its head, considering. "We aim to please," it replies with a menacing calmness. "We like to hunt. We like to play games. And this game," it says, its voice dropping even lower, "is only better. The master will be pleased."

"The game is over," Michael interrupts, stepping forward with a calculated shrug, feigning nonchalance. "You're in a busy school. You don't want to risk exposure, do you? Would that please your master?"

The demon's lips curled into something resembling a grin, though it was too wide and unnatural to belong to Jack alone. "Really? What's the time?"

Michael and George exchanged wary glances. "Just turned three," Michael replies, his voice edged with suspicion. "Why?"

"Wait for it," the demon says, its voice filled with menacing certainty.

George's stomach dropped. They'd been played. They weren't leading this game—they were pawns in it. Rage built inside him, the wolf clawing at his chest, demanding release. But he forced it down, knowing that exposure would only worsen things. He glanced at Michael, whose furrowed brow mirrored his confusion.

"For what?" Michael asks, his voice sharp. "Look, why don't you come with us? Stop doing what everyone tells you to do, and nobody gets hurt."

"Too late," the demon replies, raising its hand and turning to face George fully.

The fluorescent lights above glinted off its eyes—bright, piercing green, inhuman and reptilian. As they watched, crocodile-like scales rippled over Jack's skin, spreading in waves that shimmered unnaturally. The raised hand was changing, elongating grotesquely. Where there were once fingers, there were now talons—thick, black, and razor-sharp, glistening with a clear fluid that dripped ominously to the floor—the toxin.

George and Michael instinctively stepped back; their movements synchronised in an unspoken understanding of the threat before them.

The wolf inside him snarled for release. But this wasn't the time. Not in a school filled with children and teachers. Not with this monster standing between them and the chaos it had orchestrated.

They were outmatched, and they both knew it.

It wasn't just what Jack had become; it was what he did with those monstrous hands that captured George's focus. His taloned fingers counted down slowly, deliberately. Five... four... three... two... one.

Jack's broad smile widened as he dropped the last finger, the room sinking into an eerie silence. George's ears strained, catching only the rhythmic thud of heartbeats and the distant stampede of children evacuating the school. And then — *"DS Dalton and DC Reynolds from the murder task force receiving?"*

George stiffened, his hand instinctively moving toward his radio. He hesitated before replying, his voice cracking under the weight of dread. "Go ahead."

"There's a call that requires your attendance," came the dispatcher's voice. "A deceased female at the location under the bridge, upper North Street, the Limehouse Cut."

Michael's jaw tightened, his face a mask of barely restrained horror. "Received," he says tersely. "Show us assigned."

His eyes met George's, and the unspoken fear between them crystallised. Michael turned to Jack, his voice trembling with fury. "You bastard."

Jack's grin deepened. "Now, now. All in good sport. Besides," he gestured with mock innocence, "I've been here all day. I have witnesses to prove it."

"Is this really a game to you?" George growls, his voice thick with disdain. He feels his claws extend again, his hands growing larger and heavier. Killing these people—it's just fun for you?"

"Don't tell me you don't want to do it yourself," Jack sneers. "Embrace those animal-istic urges. They're clawing at you, aren't they?"

"I'm nothing like you," George spat, though the beast within him roars in defiance, challenging the claim.

Jack's eyes glinted, his voice dripping with smug certainty. "Don't deny it. Not to me, and not to yourself. We're very much alike—I can smell it on you." He inhaled deeply, exaggerating the motion as though savouring George's scent. "Don't worry," he adds with a chilling grin. "You know where to find me. There's more to come yet. We're building to a big finish."

George's breath caught. "Finish?" he asks, his voice edgy with unease.

Jack's tone grew gleeful, mocking. "A game ends when only one player is left standing. It'll all be over soon. But right now, you've got a mess to clean up."

Michael stepped forward, his face flushed with anger. "We'll be the ones dancing on your cold, dead body, you sick bastard," he snarls.

Jack's smile didn't waver. "We'll see," he says, his voice smooth, as though they were discussing the weather. He glanced toward the window, the lowering sun casting shadows across the room. "You best run along. After all," he smirks, "it's getting darker."

As if on cue, the transformation slowly faded. The crocodile-like scales rippling across Jack's skin receded, his talons shrinking into human fingers. By the time the door swung open, revealing a flustered Sally, Jack appeared as harmless as any schoolteacher.

"Mr Sexton," she says, her voice sharp with irritation. "Your class needs you."

"Of course, Mrs Fig," Jack replies smoothly, his tone pleasant and professional. "I just realised I had the wrong books out. These gentlemen were just ng." He scooped up the toxin-smeared exercise books as though they were nothing more than a minor inconvenience.

George and Michael exchanged glances, a collective *'what the hell just happened?'* hanging between them. Silently, they turned and left, their footsteps echoing hollowly in the corridor.

Outside, Michael fumbled for his cigarettes, the pack trembling. He lit one with shaking fingers, exhaling smoke in a long, unsteady breath. George stared at the pavement, wishing for a hip flask he didn't carry.

They were chasing a killer who not only taunted them but now had an alibi for another dead body. And as the sun dipped lower, the blood moon looming, the game they'd been thrust into felt less like an investigation and more like a trap tightening around them.

THE KANAIMA VS JACK

27

Amber bled into purple as the sky deepened, the colours smearing together like bruises across the horizon. George's skin buzzed—not alive in any conventional sense, but thrumming with heightened awareness as if every cell had its pulse. He sat motionless in the passenger seat, transfixed by the strange euphoria coursing through him. His senses sharpened to a razor's edge, almost unbearable in their intensity. He could see the fine hairs on his arms, each swaying like black corn stalks under an invisible breeze. Moisture clung to them like dew, though it was just the cold air from the vents brushing his skin. His heart pounded, each beat reverberating like the thunder of a distant freight train. For a fleeting moment, the sensation was intoxicating—euphoric, even.

Then he caught sight of the blood moon.

It loomed through the windshield, glaring down at him with its crimson glow, burrowing into his mind and taunting him with its unrelenting pull. George gripped the armrest, willing himself to keep it together. Beside him, Michael's jaw was set, his knuckles white as he clutched the wheel. They hurtled toward Limehouse in tense silence.

Upper North Street was alive with chaos when they arrived, the night flashing with blue lights and bustling with high-visibility jackets. George's stomach twisted with déjà vu. Another scene. Another body they'd been too late to save. The weight of inevitability bore down on him like a leaden hand. Neither man said it aloud, but the truth lingered between them like a ghost.

The Kanaima demon—Jack—and his master, Emily Fulton, had them locked in their relentless grip. Dragging them deeper into this sick game, they'd turned George and

Michael into unwilling players in their theatre of horrors. Hundreds of children had been at risk today, yet they'd been powerless to stop a creature that could shift between man and monster at will. Jack's mastery was chilling. The way he half-transformed, just enough to taunt them, showed control—not the helpless possession of a victim.

George thought that if Jack had been a victim, there would have been fear or confusion when he reverted. A flicker of terror, perhaps, as he returned to his human form just in time for the receptionist, Sally, to walk in. But there was nothing. Jack had worn the demon like a mask, slipping it off as easily as someone might shrug off a coat.

Michael slammed the brakes hard, the car skidding to a stop near the faded grey stone bollards lining the waterway. The metal bridge ahead loomed starkly against the encroaching gloom, its peeling blue paint catching the dim light. Frustration boiled over as Michael slapped his hands against the steering wheel. His cheeks flushed red, his breath shallow and uneven. George could feel his partner's tension in the confined space, the palpable thrum of his anger.

Neither man wanted to get out.

George's gaze drifted upward, drawn again to the blood moon climbing higher into the night sky. The glow seemed alive, pulsing with an evil energy that pulled at something deep inside him. His thoughts turned to Skip. Was he somewhere off the grid, safely embracing his nature? And what about George's family? Were they out there now, revelling in the moon's power, running wild and free beneath its crimson light? The thought carried a strange allure, one that George quickly pushed aside. Maybe one day he'd find them. But tonight, there was another body waiting for him under the bridge.

"God," Michael muttered, unclipping his seatbelt but remaining slumped in his seat momentarily. "This is a steaming pile of shit we've landed ourselves in."

"Yep," George said, forcing his voice to stay steady. "We need to neutralize the Kanaima and keep Jack alive long enough to get answers. Maybe even make him answer for these murders." The optimism in his words felt hollow, and he knew Michael could hear it, too.

"Putting him down might be the best way to neutralize this," Michael replied, his voice heavy with resignation. "A Trojan unit or you get up close and rip his throat out. You're the one built for it."

"How would I even justify that?" George shot back, though his voice lacked conviction. "Eye for an eye might sound good in theory, but the consequences—"

"—don't matter when the killings stop," Michael interrupted, his tone grim. He leaned back in his seat, his eyes scanning the waterway ahead. "Let's be honest, mate. Do we even care how it ends, so long as it ends?"

George didn't answer. Deep down, he knew Michael was right. The blood moon's pull wasn't just physical; it was emotional and primal. Every instinct in him craved the fight, the kill. He wanted the slaughter to end—no matter what it took.

"I have a feeling our ADI Locke might be more receptive than we realize," Michael said after a long pause, his voice quieter now.

George turned to him, surprised. "You've noticed it too? Something's... different about him. Not like when we first met."

Michael nodded. "Yeah. Disappears a lot, doesn't he? I can't put my finger on it, but I'd bet he knows more than he lets on."

A faint spark of hope ignited in George's chest for the first time in what felt like hours. Maybe they weren't as alone in this fight as they thought. Or maybe Locke was just another layer in the ever-deepening nightmare they'd found themselves in.

"Yeah, there are only so many meetings one man can stomach in a day," George muttered, pulling himself out of the car.

The smells hit him before his boots touched the cobblestones. Blood, toxins, old dust—all mingling with the tang of a brewery four hundred feet away over the bridge. The cacophony of scents was overwhelming, flooding his heightened senses. Even the mundane details stood out: cheap aftershaves and floral perfumes lingering in the damp air, the faint tang of rust on the railings, the salmon-pink lipstick worn by a middle-aged woman straining to peer over the cordon. A passerby, not official. Just someone out for an evening walk, drawn by the morbid allure of flashing lights.

The body was fresher than the others—two days old at most. George could feel it before he even saw it. The first cordon was already crowded a cluster of onlookers testing the patience of the high-visibility officers guarding the scene. The fading daylight added to the oppressive atmosphere, pressing on George's composure. His instincts, the wolf barely contained, threatened to break through. His vision flashed dark red, the primal urge scratching at the edges of control. He ducked behind Michael each time, hoping no one would notice.

The air was damp, clinging to his skin as they approached the slope leading beneath the bridge. He hadn't needed to ask if the body was there—it was inevitable. The pattern was holding, but something felt different this time. A shift in the air. A subtle, oppressive weight.

Then, the whispers began.

"Please don't forget us. Please, you must help."

The voices were faint but insistent, a haunting chorus that sent a chill rasping through George's chest. His muscles tensed, his jaw locking against the mounting pressure. The day was already teetering on the edge of chaos, and this new intrusion threatened to tip it over. He couldn't afford this now—not here.

The ghosts.

Rachel Darnley, Tracey Kent, Annabelle Kumar, Michelle Walters, Ross Walters, Mildred, and Mr. Kumar. They materialized near the shadowed side of the bridge, their decaying forms oozing blood and flickering like a half-formed nightmare. Their presence pushed George closer to the edge, tipping the already precarious scales of his sanity. He scanned their faces—familiar, haunting, and utterly wrong—morbidly counting their numbers, searching for anything new.

Who was it this time? Donna Armitage? Brian Thistle? Emily Blake?

He couldn't tell—not yet. And he couldn't tell Michael either. His partner was already rattled, barely holding himself together. Adding more to his plate wasn't an option. George forced himself to steady his breathing, raising his warrant card to push past the crowd of onlookers.

The officer at the cordon glanced up, his weary face cracking into a reluctant smile as he waved them through. But something was wrong. George sensed it immediately. It wasn't just the scene or the blood saturating the air with its metallic tang. There was an unsettling absence, a void that gnawed at the edges of his awareness.

Halfway down the slope, the realization struck.

"Elena's not here," he said abruptly, his voice edged with panic.

Michael frowned, his tension mirroring the damp, oppressive air. "What're you on about?"

"She's missing," George repeated, his instincts flaring like wildfire.

Michael sighed, irritation flaring. "Yeah, well, there's a fucking dead body. What else do you expect?"

"No, you don't get it," George snapped, his voice sharper now. "Walker's always here. Always."

At the base of the slope, Natasha stood near the edge of the cordon. Her usual brisk efficiency was conspicuously absent. She fumbled with a box of gloves, her trembling hands making no real effort to retrieve anything. Her lips moved, forming silent words, her panic as palpable as the tension in the air.

George's stomach twisted. "Michael, look at Natasha."

Michael followed his gaze. "What's with her?"

"She's mumbling. Stalling. Something's wrong."

As they approached, Natasha's voice became faintly audible. "What the hell is going on?" she muttered, dropping the glove box. Her hands shook violently as she crouched to retrieve it, her movements jerky and distracted.

George's unease deepened. His gaze shifted toward the bridge—a low, flat structure closer to the water than most in the area. He still couldn't see the body, but the air was suffocating, weighted with something more than rain and blood. Natasha wasn't acting like herself, and Elena's absence loomed large, a dark, foreboding shadow.

"Elena's missing," George said again, his voice low, his unease now full-blown dread.

Michael's irritation melted into concern, his face darkening. "If she's not here, where is she?"

Before George could respond, a chill swept through him. The fine hairs on his neck rose as a ripple of sulfur and death brushed past his cheek—too fleeting to pinpoint but potent enough to set his senses ablaze. The demons were nearby. They always were.

Then he saw her.

"Shit. That's Emily Fulton," George breathed, his voice barely audible above the growing din of the crowd. His stomach twisted violently as his eyes locked on the figure beneath the bridge.

Beside him, Michael froze, his mouth agape, his expression raw disbelief. The case had become one big, twisting nightmare. As they were getting sure of the Kanaima's master, this happened.

"But... she was having an affair with Jack," Michael stammered, his gravelly voice unsteady. "We were sure—she had to be the master."

George didn't respond. His focus was locked on Emily's body, the brutalized display before him far worse than anything they'd encountered before. This wasn't just murder—it was destruction. Her blonde hair was still tied back, starkly contrasting to the chaos inflicted on her. The rose tattoo on her forearm was a dreadful reminder of her identity.

Emily's naked body bore the marks of horrific violence. A deep incision ran from her collarbone, slicing cleanly between her breasts, and continued downward to the pale patch of hair at her groin. Two horizontal slashes crossed her torso—one from shoulder to shoulder, the other from hip to hip—forming a grotesque "T." Her hands and feet had been nailed in place like the first victim, but the depravity didn't stop there. Her flayed skin had been stretched and pinned open, exposing her insides in a chilling parody of an autopsy.

Her intestines hung like a twisted swing, swaying faintly in the damp evening breeze. Several organs were missing, likely washed into the water below. Blood, smeared across her exposed flesh, carried a message scrawled in jagged lines on a strip of intestine.

George's stomach churned. This wasn't just a crime scene—it was a declaration—a warning.

Michael pulled his radio from his belt, his voice strained as he barked into it. "Hotel Tango, dispatch. Has anyone reached our on-call pathologist?"

The reply came through a crackle of static. "So far, unreachable. She hasn't acknowledged the callout. We'll keep trying."

Michael's pacing quickened, his heels echoing off the pavement. Sweat beaded on his furrowed brow, frustration mounting with every passing second. George could sense his partner's unease but focused on the scene before him. The timing was deliberate and calculated. The killers were always one step ahead, and now they'd thrown another wrench into their investigation.

"Dispatch, this is DC Reynolds," George said, clicking his radio. "Requesting a unit to the home of our on-call pathologist. Treat as a threat to life."

"Received," came the response. "Is there cause for concern? Should we upgrade to immediate?"

George hesitated, the weight of the question pressing on him. His gaze returned to Emily's mutilated form, grotesque under the bridge's shadowed underbelly. Was this their way of taunting him? Of showing how far their reach extended? Elena's absence gnawed at him, her usual presence at these scenes an unspoken constant.

"Yes," he said, his voice steady despite the storm inside him. "Upgrade the call. This is linked to our current case. Life at risk."

The world around him blurred as the encroaching darkness pressed tighter. George clenched his fists, feeling the heat rise in his veins, his claws threatening to extend. The blood moon hung low, its pull stronger than ever, each passing second drawing him closer to the brink. But Elena's life was on the line, and the answers lay somewhere within Emily's brutalized remains.

He turned to Michael, his voice firm. "We need to widen the cordon. Push the crowd back and get Wainwright out of the way. I need to take the first look."

Michael hesitated, his jaw tight. "You sure that's a good idea? The moon's already screwing with you."

George met his gaze, his eyes hard, unwavering. "I'm the only one who can see what's here. Emily wouldn't be displayed like this without leaving a message. If there are clues, I'll find them."

Michael sighed, his shoulders sagging in reluctant agreement. "Alright. But make it quick. We can't afford to screw this up."

As the cordon widened, George stepped closer to the body, the sickly stench of death and sulfur thickening in the air. The blood moon cast a crimson hue over the crime scene, painting everything in shades of malice. Every instinct screamed at him to turn back, to let the wolf take over and run. But he forced himself to hold steady.

"You sure, mate?" Michael asked, his voice tinged with uncertainty.

George didn't take his eyes off Emily Fulton's mangled corpse. The moonlight shifted, casting eerie shadows that danced across the scene. His thoughts raced, a storm of fear and determination. "The way things are going, we can't be sure of anything," he replied, his voice low and measured. "But the fact that Elena isn't here? She never misses these. No, Michael, I'm not sure. But I feel it. Emily Fulton is going to tell us what we need to know."

Michael snorted, attempting to mask his unease with a flicker of humour. "You mean she'll spill her guts," he said, a grim chuckle escaping as he looked sideways at George, clearly pleased with his wit.

George turned away, his expression hardening into a grim mask. "Behave, Michael. Look at the body this time. It's different—more deliberate. And the scroll..." His eyes lingered on the bloodied intestines hanging grotesquely from Emily's mutilated form, the detail searing itself into his mind. "I need to reach it. Whatever message they've left, it's in that scroll."

Michael followed George's gaze, his brow furrowing as he caught sight of the hanging entrails. "What? Up there?" The discomfort in his voice was impossible to miss.

"Don't worry about that," George replied, his tone clipped and resolute. "You focus on keeping the coast clear. Natasha's barely holding it together—console her until the fire brigade arrives. She looks like she's about to crack."

Michael hesitated, his reluctance evident in the tense set of his shoulders. After a moment, he gave a small nod, shuffling toward Natasha, who furiously spoke into her radio. Her voice carried over the oppressive silence, high-pitched and strained, though

George couldn't make out her words. It wasn't the main channel—she was likely seeking updates on Elena. The knot in George's stomach tightened. Time was slipping away, and the impending failure weighed heavily on him. They were already too late. He could feel it.

Shaking off the thought, George turned back to Emily Fulton's grotesque display. He inhaled deeply, steadying himself against the sickening tableau. The blood moon's crimson light glinted off the viscera, casting them in a grotesque sheen, like some macabre parody of holiday decorations. His heightened senses sharpened every detail to an unbearable clarity: the dark streaks of drying blood, the gleaming wetness of exposed tissue, the faint metallic tang that clung to the air. It was a visceral assault designed to pull him under.

MORE TO NATASHA

28

Rusty grey nails, each at least three inches long, driven through flesh, bone, and deep into stone to support the weight of an adult woman. The first pierced Emily Fulton's left hand, a few centimetres left of her forefinger, with dried blood spattered across the metal. The second impaled the centre of her right palm, crushing through bone with brutal precision. Her left foot was nailed through the top ridge near the ankle joint, while the right was skewered just below the toes through bony ligaments. Her toes had curled and stiffened over time as though paralysed. Perhaps the toxin had worn off before the end. Emily had suffered.

Her chest skin had been pinned back like a grotesque exhibit, exposing breast tissue and a hollow cavity where her heart once was. George's eyes locked on the glistening pink and red flesh, and an unsettling hunger churned within him. The pull was growing stronger, an unrelenting desire gnawing at the edges of his thoughts. He forced himself to refocus. There was no room for weakness—not now, not with the risks of transforming under prying eyes.

The scene's brutality spoke volumes. Her abdomen had been savagely torn open. George noted the shocking cleanliness inside; there should have been blood painted across every inch of exposed skin, yet it was spotless except for a carved message:

corde volui quod non-poterat.

The heart wanted what it couldn't have.

The Latin words were sliced into her flesh with jagged precision, likely by claws—one or perhaps two. This wasn't the Kanaima's usual style of methodical hunting. This was personal. His thoughts lingered on the word "cheat," scrawled at a previous crime scene. Could this all circle back to Jack Sexton's wife? A motive of jealousy, betrayal, and revenge? George had never experienced that rage, but he imagined it would feel like cutting through butter—satisfying, yet terrifyingly smooth.

Every detail of Emily's body seemed to stand out under his heightened vision. Her anaemic skin displayed blue and white marbling beneath faint bruises on her thighs and forearms. Scratches, roughly three to four inches long, traced jagged paths across her body. They looked human—nail marks, he thought. Then his attention caught something else: a faint circular indent on her forearm, the surface of a ring. Its grooves were patterned, reminiscent of a coin's edge. The resemblance tugged at his thoughts, reminding him of the obsidian coins he carried.

Ring and coin, George thought. *How do they connect?*

His gaze drifted to Emily's hands. Her short, purple-painted nails were frayed and jagged, evidence of desperate clawing. He caught another detail: flecks of colour beneath her nails. At first, they seemed like dirt, but upon closer inspection, he realised they were painted flakes—blue and green.

She was on a blue-and-green surface before she died.

A boat. The thought crystallised in his mind. Blue and green, just like the paint he had seen on a canal boat at the beginning of the case. Thousands of boats shared those colours, but George had learned to trust his instincts long ago. Coincidences rarely remain coincidences in cases like this.

His mind raced as he pieced together the story her body told. The ring-shaped indent and the paint under her nails hinted at a violent, hasty encounter. It was almost sloppy compared to the calculated precision of previous murders. This wasn't the Kanaima's typical style. It felt desperate.

And then there was Jack's wife—her perfect motive. Allegations of an affair between Jack and Emily had driven her to leave, clearing out of their home without a trace. She was the perfect candidate for revenge. If she worked alongside the Kanaima, she had all the necessary tools to enact her vengeance.

George stepped back, his sharp eyes scanning the scene for more clues. The savagery of the murder weighed heavily on him. The killer hadn't just wanted Emily dead—they wanted her defiled, her body a statement of dominance and anger. But there was more to this. George could feel it, the truth lurking just out of reach.

The taunts, the escalating brutality—this was a game—a dangerous one—and George was running out of time to uncover its rules.

George hovered at the edge of the bridge; his boots balanced precariously on the tips of his toes as he reached for the scroll lodged in Emily's entrails. The stink of death hung thick in the air, a disgusting cocktail of decay and malevolence. His sharp senses picked up the faint traces of demons nearby—watching, waiting, their unseen presence gnawing at his nerves. The air seemed heavier beneath the bridge, shadows dancing wildly in the flickering glow of the overhead lamps. It felt like they were being drawn deeper into a web, one step closer to the killer's trap.

A sudden gust of wind swept through, forcing him to regain his balance as his fingertips brushed the scroll's edge. His claws extended instinctively—longer, thicker, deadlier than ever—and with a quick flick, he snagged the scroll. Tugging it free from the sticky entrails, he stumbled back, his heels skidding through the dust. The relief of not tumbling into the grim tableau behind him was short-lived.

George glanced at Michael, signalling it was time to stop stalling. Michael immediately straightened, chatting up Natasha to keep her grounded, sensing the shift in George's focus. Natasha, though, edged closer, the tension in her every movement betraying her unease. She hadn't stopped shaking since she'd arrived, and George didn't blame her. Elena's sudden absence had rattled everyone, but it was hitting Natasha the hardest. She looked as though she feared she might be next.

"You okay? See anything useful?" Michael asks, already fishing his ever-present notebook from his coat pocket. George half-expected the familiar rustle of a cigarette pack but was surprised when it didn't appear.

He unrolled the scroll, reading the smeared Latin words aloud. "*Corde volui quod non-poterat.* 'The heart wanted what it couldn't have.'" He paused, glancing back at the body. "That's also tattooed on the inside of her chest. And Emily's heart—it's missing."

He flexed his hands, relieved to see his claws had retracted. His bare fingers bore the sticky remnants of the scroll, but he didn't care. Gloves seemed pointless when every clue left behind felt deliberate, a taunt or a breadcrumb from the killer. It wouldn't be by accident if they were going to find anything.

George turned toward Natasha as she hesitated a few feet away, her gloved hands trembling under the weight of her flashlight. She looked pale, her usual composure cracking under the pressure of uncertainty.

"You alright?" George asks. She managed an awkward smile, but it didn't reach her eyes.

"I guess. Is there any news?" Her voice wavered, the fear beneath her words unmistakable. She shone her torch on Emily's body but avoided looking directly at it.

"I need you to scrape under her nails once the body's down," George says, gesturing to Emily's lifeless hands. "There's debris there—paint flakes, I think. We'll need them tested."

Natasha nodded, her face tightening with surprise at the detail. George wasn't sure why she still seemed startled by his observations. By now, she should have realised his instincts were rarely missed. But she wasn't here for his insights. She was here for reassurance.

"Do you think she's been taken?" Natasha asks, her voice dropping into a hoarse whisper. The weight of the question hung between them, and George hesitated. He couldn't bring himself to speak the worst aloud, not now—not with Natasha looking at him like he held all the answers.

"She's probably broken down somewhere," he says finally, forcing a calm he didn't feel. "Probably not near a phone."

The words felt hollow even as he said them. His body told a different story. The blood moon's pull wreaked havoc on his composure, anger boiling beneath his skin in volatile waves. His ears latched onto every sound—the mutter of the crowd, the distant hum of traffic, the rustle of leaves on the wind. It was maddening, a cacophony that refused to let him focus.

George shook his head sharply, trying to clear the noise. Both Michael and Natasha noticed their concerned stares cutting through the tension. He knew he had to keep it together—for them, for Elena, and for the victim whose death demanded justice. But the boundaries between the wolf and the man grew thinner with every passing minute. And the demons circling them in the shadows wouldn't wait for him to figure it out.

George's brow twitched as he muttered, "Sorry. Something flew into my ear." His voice was casual, but the tension in his posture betrayed him. Michael wasn't buying it. His sceptical stare lingered as he pulled George aside, his movements sharp, impatient. George's fingers danced over the scroll, turning it over and over as though it were a worry stone. He hadn't opened it yet, delaying the inevitable.

Michael's gaze dropped to George's hand, and his expression tightened. The faint lines on his forehead deepened as his Adam's apple bobbed nervously. Then, Michael's eyes locked onto the symbol for the first time, glowing faintly on George's skin. It wasn't a trick of the light; it was undeniably there. His face flickered between confusion and fear, a rare sight for someone so used to macabre scenes.

George noticed the shift in Michael's expression and let out a sharp exhale. The symbol had chosen now, of all times, to reveal itself again—on a day when everything seemed ready to spiral out of control.

"You think it's anything like the first one?" Michael asks, his voice steadying as he tries to regain his composure.

"I don't know," George admitted, his eyes flicking from the scroll to Emily Fulton's mutilated body. "This one feels rushed and forced, even. It's not as calculated as before, but there's still intent. Like... like they couldn't resist taking the opportunity."

Michael followed George's gaze to Emily's body. Her chest lay flayed open, the words *'corde volui quod non-poterat'* carved cruelly into the flesh. The smell of blood lingered in the air, sharper to George than anyone else. He fought against the primal urge bubbling within him, pushing the hunger down as he spoke. "That message, 'the heart wanted what it couldn't have'... It's love. That's what they're driving at, isn't it?"

Michael rubbed the back of his neck, pacing at the water's edge. "Love or obsession. It could've been a revenge kill. Emily's affair with Jack didn't exactly go unnoticed."

George nodded. The pieces were falling into place, but they still lacked clarity. "What if Lorraine wasn't part of the original expedition?" he suggests the idea forming as he spoke. "Let's say Jack stole the Kanaima relics from Kumar, planning to sell them. Teachers don't exactly rake it in, so maybe he thought he and Emily could use the cash to run away together."

Michael turned; his brow furrowed. George continued, the theory taking shape. "But Lorraine finds out about the affair. She gets her hands on the relics, realises what they can do, and,... revenge takes over. She doesn't care what the relic does to Jack as long as she gets her pound of flesh."

Michael let out a low whistle, pacing again. "It's twisted. Genius, even. But maybe it's too neat. If Lorraine were that deliberate, she wouldn't have let this slip so easily."

George glanced back at Emily's exposed body, the words carved into her chest echoing in his mind. "I think she understood what that relic could do and stopped caring about consequences. This kill was personal, though. Look at the brutality. It wasn't about making a statement. It was about making her suffer."

Michael stopped pacing and crossed his arms. "So, what do we do now?"

George hesitated, his eyes drawn upward. The moon hung heavy in the darkening sky, its crimson hue deepening with each passing moment. He could feel it tugging at his body, his senses sharper, his emotions heightened. The claws beneath his skin itched to emerge, but he fought them back. "We stay focused," he says finally, though the conviction in his voice wavered. "There's too much riding on this."

His attention shifted back to the scroll. The white ribbon slipped free as he unfurled the paper, his hands trembling slightly. The faint glow of his claws caught the edges of the scroll, a stark reminder of how close he was to losing control. He glanced at Michael, who was now on the radio, his voice tense as he requested updates. Georg realised he'd turned his radio down, muting the outside world without thinking.

The scroll felt heavier than it should, its weight pressing into his palm. Whatever was written on it held answers—or maybe more questions. Either way, George knew that time was running out for the case and himself.

George's mind was a whirlwind, spiralling between fury and a chilling clarity as the message scrawled on the scroll repeated in his head:

"Her heart wanted what it couldn't have, yet she took it anyway. Now I take hers. Your heart wants what you're too scared to have. She may even give you a little scratch behind the ears. I hear fleas are a bitch. That's if you can find her, that is. You have something we want and the information to find what's missing. Do that. The killing stops, and your heart can finally find happiness again. Until then, the hunter hunts. I know your history. So, quoting the past, let the games begin. Oh, I will know your every move."

He barely noticed Michael stepping toward him until the words broke his concentration.

"Are you okay, Georgie?" Michael's voice was unusually soft; concern laced through the words.

George didn't respond immediately. Instead, he shoved the note into Michael's hand, allowing him to read for himself. His partner's eyes scanned the paper, and George didn't miss the way Michael's lips tightened into a grim line. The faintest whisper escaped him: "Oh fuck."

George tuned out the rest of the world for a moment. His radio crackled back to life, dragging his attention.

"The front door has been smashed open; there's blood in the hallway and lounge. The place is a mess."

The words hit George like a freight train. His stomach plummeted. The rage simmering just beneath his skin turned volcanic. He barely registered Michael, mumbling under his breath as he stepped closer to him, trying to gauge how bad things had gotten.

"Elena's gone," George mutters, his voice tight with barely controlled anger. His eyes glistened with a crimson haze, a telltale sign of the beast within clawing to take over.

Michael was momentarily silent, digesting what he'd just heard. "Shit. This is all tied to the damn boat, isn't it?"

George nodded stiffly. His senses sharpened as his gaze scanned the surrounding chaos of flashing lights, murmuring crowds, and shifting shadows. Somewhere in the cacophony was the answer—or, at least, a clue. His nostrils flared as he caught the distinct, sulfuric stench of demons, faint but lingering. He tuned out the sound of Michael's pacing and the officers murmuring into their radios. He focused instead on the faint heartbeat fluttering just beyond the din.

His eyes caught her then: Natasha Wainwright. She wasn't panicked like the others. Her posture was stiff and deliberate, and her heart raced not with fear but with something else—excitement. George's heightened senses zeroed in on the glint of light reflecting off her hand. A ring. His stomach twisted.

What Happened?

29

'77 Wager Street Mile End.'

The walk to Elena's flat was fraught with an oppressive tension that clung to George like a second skin. Each step felt heavier than the last, burdened by the unrelenting weight of failure. The flickering blue of police lights reflected against the cracked walls, transforming the dim landing into a surreal, foreboding corridor. His blood churned beneath his skin, molten and alive, a feral tide warring against his fragile restraint. The moon hung high above, its silver face mocking him, whispering promises of release as if he'd only surrendered to the beast clawing within. Every instinct urged him to run, to relinquish control, and embrace what he dreaded most.

Michael's voice shattered the suffocating silence as they neared the flat. It sliced through George's haze like a jagged lifeline. "You all right there, matey? You're looking a bit... feral."

George's head snaps toward Michael, his jaw tightening. A shadow of irritation flickered across his face, but the anger underneath burned hotter. "Not really," he ground out, his voice low and sharp. "Since when has anything about this case been right? Dragging Elena into it—she didn't deserve this."

Michael's grim nod mirrored the frustration roiling inside George. "I don't know why or how, but we'll get her back. We always find a way."

The stench hit George long before they reached the police cordon. It crawled into his nose like an evil fog: the metallic tang of blood, the acrid bite of chemicals, and the sour, unmistakable scent of fear. It gripped his senses and refused to let go, sending a wave of nausea rolling through him. Beneath it all lingered Elena's scent—faint but distinct. She was alive but paralysed somewhere, her vulnerability a ghostly scream in his mind. His skin prickled with a helpless fury that begged for release.

The officer stationed by the battered brown door straightened as they approached, his face pallid and strained. Relief flickered in his eyes as he addressed them. "Detectives. The place is a mess... there's blood everywhere."

George didn't respond. The broken wood gaping like a wound, his attention tunnelled toward the open doorway. The chaos within felt suffocating, a claustrophobic weight pressing against his ribs. Papers and books littered the floor like fallen leaves, furniture lay shattered and askew, and blood streaked the walls in violent arcs—a silent chronicle of Elena's desperate fight.

A firm hand gripped George's arm, pulling him back from the brink. Michael's voice was steady, grounding. "Don't lose it here. We need to keep it together."

George inhaled deeply, the wolf beneath his skin clawing for dominance. "I'm trying," he says through gritted teeth, his voice raw with strain. "But it's building. My body's burning, Michael. It's like... like, I need to run. To let loose."

Michael's expression softened slightly, though his tone still carried its usual sharp edge. "You're allowed to feel, Georgie. You're not made of stone. And this—this has to twist the knife a bit, yeah? Seeing her dragged into this mess?"

George swallowed hard, the lump in his throat threatening to choke him. He had spent so much time burying his emotions, terrified they'd weaken him. But Michael's words hit like a hammer, cracking through his carefully constructed walls. For a fleeting moment, he let himself feel it all—the anger, the guilt, the fear. Elena was in his world now, paying the price for his cursed existence.

"Yeah," he mutters, his voice barely more than a growl. "She's in my head, and it's tearing me apart. If we don't find her soon..."

"We will," Michael interrupts, his tone firm. "And when we do, you can make those bastards regret they ever touched her. Just don't lose yourself, yeah? You've still got a heart somewhere under all that wolf crap."

George managed a bitter laugh, though it lacked any real humour. "Thanks for that. I'll try not to go full werewolf priest on you."

Michael smirked, the brief levity a flicker of light against the oppressive darkness. "Good, because I don't think the church is big on fangs."

George gave a faint nod, but the tightness in his chest didn't ease. The moon's slow ascent felt like a timer counting down, each passing moment threatening to unravel what little control he had left. Elena's life teetered on the brink, and he could feel the beast within clawing at his resolve, testing its cage. If they didn't move quickly, he wasn't sure how long he could hold it back—or if he even wanted to.

The hallway ahead stretched like a muted nightmare, its mundane features failing to mask the horrors lurking beneath. Light brown carpet and cream walls, a phone table perched to the right just before a narrow staircase. But the air was heavy with the stench of the toxin, more pungent now, acrid and invasive. A black handset hung off the hook, thick smears of the substance glistening on its surface like a vile signature. Nearby, a stack of papers rested unevenly, partially obscuring a set of keys.

George's eyes followed the telltale signs of violence. Blood marred the corner of the bannister post, a vivid crimson spray arcing up the steps before being smeared and dragged toward the front door. The story of Elena's struggle unfolded in his mind. She had gone to make a call, unaware of the toxin's effects. It had hit her fast, paralysing her. She must have stumbled to the left, her weakening body colliding with the fence before tumbling down the stairs.

The layout of the flat burned in George's memory: the kitchen to the left, the lounge straight ahead. But the evidence told him Elena hadn't made it far. Papers lay scattered, disturbed by her frantic movements. Among them was a bloodied sheet, its surface marred by a hastily scribbled message:

Does Melanie exist? Who is the third flaw in the photo?

George's breath hitched as he lifted the top paper, uncovering a familiar photograph. It was the one from Walter's house, the same eerie image that had refused to leave his mind. Beneath it, a list of addresses from the Museum lay neatly attached. His eyes caught a note scrawled beside Melanie's address: *Does not exist.*

His pulse quickened as he flipped through the papers. A checklist scribbled in Elena's handwriting jumped out: driver's license, voter registration, land registry—no trace. Beneath the stack was something more intriguing—a slim book, its cover bearing Elena's bold handwriting: *My Theory.*

George opened it with a mix of dread and determination. He expected disjointed notes, desperate scribbles that surfaced when connections refused to make sense. Instead, what he found made his hackles rise. The opening page contained a personnel file: SOCO Wainwright. Date of birth: December 2, 1960. Height: five foot one. A transferee from

Essex Police.

The details screamed at George. The Wainwright they worked with stood at least five foot six. Elena had seen it, too. Her notes ran alongside the official information:

"Natasha said she was born in Leytonstone, but this says Burnley. There is no evidence of higher education, despite what Natasha claimed. Are we being played?"

George's unease grew into a tangible thing, a clawing presence that gnawed at the back of his mind. His instincts screamed that Elena had uncovered something far more sinister than they'd realised.

"Michael, come look at this," he called, his voice tight as he sifted through the remaining papers. A map lay buried beneath the notes, its surface marked with a vivid red circle. *Limehouse Cut.*

Michael leaned over George's shoulder, his brow furrowing. "What is it?"

"Elena suspected something was off about Wainwright," George says, his voice a low growl. He jabbed a finger at the personnel file. "Does this description match her? Because it sure as hell doesn't sound right to me."

Michael's jaw tightened as he processed the information, the implications cutting deep. "You're saying we might've been screwed over by someone inside again?" His voice carried the weariness of someone too familiar with betrayal.

George didn't answer immediately, his mind racing through the possibilities. The blood, the toxin, the cryptic notes pointed to a setup. "It's looking that way. Elena saw it, too. If she's right... then this whole thing just got a hell of a lot worse."

"Not unless she's grown a few inches," Michael mutters, his voice low and edged with tension. Right on cue, Wainwright walked in. George hadn't expected her to arrive so soon. His movements were swift, shuffling the papers into a haphazard pile, concealing the damning notes. To the untrained eye, nothing seemed amiss with her. She carried herself with the same confidence as always—calculated, composed, and unnervingly precise. She was tall, easily matching the height Elena had described. But George was on guard now, every muscle coiled tight with the barely suppressed urge to lunge. To sink his claws into her throat and pin her against the wall until she screamed Elena's location.

His gaze locked onto her as she approached, and his senses sharpened, dissecting every detail. Her heartbeat thrummed faintly, just a fraction faster than normal. Her eyes lingered on the bloodstains too long, and the corner of her mouth twitched in what could only be described as a nervous smile. The stench hit George next. That peculiar, stale scent of old dust clung to her like an ancient shadow—different from the Kanaima or the death demons they'd encountered before, but still wrong.

He stepped closer to Michael, feigning interest in something Michael was holding, while the heat coursing through his body signalled an imminent shift. His vision swam, the world blurring as his wolf instincts clawed for dominance.

"Breathe, Georgie. Breathe," Michael murmurs, his voice a steady anchor. He'd noticed the shift in George's eyes, the glint of something otherworldly. Michael's heart raced, adrenaline spiking as he fought to remain calm.

"I'm trying," George growls through clenched teeth. "But it's Natasha. If she's involved in this, I want to rip her throat out."

"I get it," Michael says, his voice laced with suppressed frustration. "But what do we have so far? Scribbles on a document? It could be typos or outdated info. You know how H.R. screws things up."

"She has that old dust smell on her," George hisses, his nose wrinkling. "It's faint but distinct."

Michael's brow furrowed. "Like she's been around something? Could you pick it up at the crime scene?"

"No," George says, the single word heavy with implication.

"Right," Michael muttered. "If what Elena says is true, and she's doing—" George's hand shot up, cutting him off mid-sentence. His eyes darted toward Natasha, now moving closer. The realisation struck him like a thunderclap: she was the master. Her hearing might rival the Kanaima's, their supernatural bond amplifying her senses.

Grabbing his notebook, George scribbled hastily: *She might hear.* He passed it to Michael, whose face darkened as he read it. Michael scribbled a response: *Doing this with that thing. We need her followed.*

George nodded, writing back: *Surveillance aware?*

Michael's reply came quickly: *We need someone she won't recognise.*

She might not expect Locke. George suggested, his claws itching under the surface of his skin.

Michael's lips quirked into a grim smile as he wrote: *Andy?* He had read George's mind again. The idea was tempting, but George hesitated. Dragging Andy into this, especially on a night like this, felt reckless. As for Locke, convincing him would be an uphill battle.

Natasha's stealthy approach set George's nerves on edge. Her movements were too calculated, her presence suffocating. He quickly slipped the notebook into his pocket and tightened his grip on the stack of papers, hiding his hands behind Michael just in time as his claws slithered forward.

"Any news?" Natasha's voice cut through the air, sharp and probing. George tuned into every syllable, dissecting her accent and tone for any telltale slips. It was unmistakably London, but there was a chill to her cadence, a forced neutrality that set his teeth on edge.

"How come you've come here so soon?" Michael asks bluntly, his voice steady but carrying a faint reverb that betrays his irritation.

Natasha's response was curt, almost clinical. "The body was taken. The heart is missing. Nothing else."

George narrowed his eyes, scrutinising her every move. The debrief was too brief, too empty. She was hiding something. She wasn't here to report; she was here to assess. To see how close they were to the truth.

"Anything else?" George snaps, his tone harsher than intended. Michael's sharp glance warned him to steady himself. He flexed his hands behind his back, forcing his claws to retract.

Natasha's eyes flicked to him, then back to Michael. "The usual," she says coolly. "More toxins. Oh, and a unique message. It looked like the killer got up close and personal, wanted the victim to know who was pulling the strings."

George exchanged a dark look with Michael. The cryptic message was a warning, a taunt. They were running out of time to figure out whatever game Natasha- or whoever she was- was playing. And Elena's life hung in the balance.

"What makes you say that? The bit about controlling life?" George asks, his voice edged with scepticism. The phrasing struck him as strange, almost unnerving.

Natasha's expression didn't falter, and her tone was clinical. "The bruising on the thighs and arms suggests the killer manipulated the limbs, rendering the victim unable to escape. Then there's the phrase, 'the heart wants what it couldn't have.' It implies unrequited love or obsession. The killer likely thrived on the control they had, revelling in what they could take."

George's instincts roar to life, a relentless slap to the back of his mind. *Wake the fuck up.* There was something in her voice—a faint, almost imperceptible boast laced within her last comment.

"Something else, like what?" George pressed, his suspicion growing. "Were there any other bruising patterns?"

Natasha hesitated, a subtle pause that George didn't miss. "Not really. There was a faint pattern but nothing significant. Probably knuckles," she says, her voice even, almost too smooth.

George's ears pricked at the lie, his senses sharpening like blades. He remembered the glint—the black gloves Natasha wore, conveniently hiding any marks or traces. She was covering something, and the deliberate vagueness in her tone only deepened his mistrust.

"So," Michael interjected gruffly, his voice a low rumble. "Has Emily been taken?"

"Yeah, it's gone. That's why I'm here," Natasha replies, her tone shifting to something resembling concern. "Ellena was a friend. I want to help."

George's jaw tightened, the lie reverberating like a scream in his mind. *Ellena was a friend.* Past tense. His bullshit radar went haywire, but he forced himself to stay outwardly calm. Was he hearing what he wanted to hear to justify targeting Natasha? Or was she purposefully letting the truth slip through her carefully crafted facade?

The realisation burned through him. Natasha knew too much—everything they did, from the smallest details of the crime scene to the people handling the forensics. If she wasn't involved directly, she was still dangerous. Their unit was compromised, and the longer she stayed within their circle, the greater the risk.

Michael cast a sidelong glance at George, his unease barely masked. George met his eyes, unspoken understanding passing between them. Natasha's words, her behaviour, the timing of her arrival—it all pointed to a dangerous game, one they couldn't afford to lose.

CHILLING INTENT

30

'8 pm - 4 hours to go.'

In a world like this, only a handful of things move as fleetingly as a breeze—Time, Life, and Love if you're feeling sentimental. Time was out. Life? Brief and brutal. Love? Well, George had been unlucky so far, not had enough, not in a way that lasted.

Her words lingered in his mind, a mocking echo: *"Her heart wanted what it couldn't have, yet she took it anyway. Now I take hers. Your heart wants what you're too scared to have..."*

The statement twisted like a knife in his chest. Inaccuracy never stung so sharply. It wasn't fear in the ordinary sense. For George, it was the wolf. That part of him—unrelenting, primal, and cursed—cast a shadow over every connection. He wasn't scared; he was cautious. Ellena might never see past it, terrified of what lay beneath the surface, fearing she might get hurt. That was the real concern.

Who else had noticed the spark between them? Michael, certainly. Maybe Ellena had spilt her thoughts to Natasha before the stench of betrayal had tainted her.

While Michael kept Natasha busy with blood swabs and dusting for finger-prints—tasks they both knew would lead nowhere—George searched for something that might explain what Ellena had uncovered. Natasha needed to be kept at arm's length, and they needed time to strategize.

The lounge was almost a mirror of George's own space—neat, functional, lived-in, but without much warmth. A TV stood to the right, a long sofa stretched beneath the window, and stacks of books cluttered the corners. Ellena's taste in horror stood out, with her collection ranging from Mary Shelley's *Frankenstein* to Stephen King's *Cycle of the Werewolf.*

The coffee table was a makeshift workstation scattered with maps and notes. The map by the phone wasn't random; it was a systematic process of elimination. Ellena had been pulling extra hours to investigate on the side. George couldn't help but feel a mix of pride and frustration—she'd been helping them, but at what cost?

He allowed himself a moment to study the books. Horror. The irony wasn't lost on him. Ellena's fascination with the spooky, the supernatural, and the things that go bump in the night suddenly felt personal. He skimmed the shelves until his gaze landed on Stephen King, his thoughts distracted momentarily by admiration. King had a way of weaving stories within stories, painting the macabre with vibrant colours. But it wasn't the novels that caught George's eye—it was the notes tucked into them.

Curiosity won out. He flipped to a bookmarked page and read the hurried scrawl in Ellena's handwriting:

"Red eyes belong to an Alpha, yellow for a Beta, and blue for an Omega. From what I can gather—and it's fiction—other shapeshifters exist with different eye colours, especially green. Despite Georgie telling me otherwise, insisting he was just tired, I saw his eyes go red with black around the edges. Is he a wolf?"

George's stomach churned, a mix of unease and something he couldn't quite name. He turned the page, finding another note:

"Michael hasn't changed, but I overheard a conversation about green eyes and our murder suspect. I'm quite level-headed and would usually call it bullshit. A part of me, though, hopes it's true. Excited, even. Yet, that also means our murderer is dangerous, likely to kill again, and there's no normal way to stop it—or them."

Her words hung heavy in the air. Ellena had been closer to the truth than he realized. The growing danger tainted the excitement she'd written about—the thrill of uncovering something extraordinary. George's pulse quickened, the wolf stirring uneasily beneath his skin.

"What've you got there, matey? An autobiography?" Michael's voice cut through the tension like a knife. He shuffled over, his expression sceptical as he glanced at the notes in George's hands. It was clear they'd found little else of use here.

George folded the notes carefully, slipping them back into the book. He didn't answer

Michael right away, his thoughts racing. Ellena had been too close to the truth, and now she was missing. If her theories were right, their suspect wasn't just dangerous—they were something far worse.

"Funny fella. No, but look," George says, shoving the bookmark toward Michael. His eyes darted around him, scanning for Natasha, who was still busy swabbing surfaces and pretending to play detective. She was good—too good—at sneaking glances their way without breaking stride.

Michael smirked faintly, leaning closer to inspect the note. "See? There's hope for you yet. I told you she might surprise you. ClHas a hunch and wants to understand it all."

"Yeah, but she's also into the 'green eyes,'" George mutters darkly.

Michael raised an eyebrow. "Makes you wonder how Ellena caught wind of that. If—and it's a big *if*—we're right, do you think someone exploited her curiosity? Relationships, even friendship, can be weapons in the wrong hands."

The thought lingered in George's mind like a splinter. Ellena's fascination with the supernatural had led her to dig deeper than she should have. The implications were chilling if someone in their circle had used that against her. He glanced back at Natasha, who mindlessly swabbed at a bloodstain, holding up a sample bag like it actually mattered. The more George observed her mechanical movements, the harder it became to see how or why she would be involved. Yet something didn't sit right.

As he leaned forward to return the book, he accidentally flipped it upside down, causing a few pages to flutter open. A small, square object slipped out—a Polaroid.

"Georgie, quick," Michael whispers sharply, his eyes catching the object ju George did.

"Yeah, cover me," George replies, and Michael immediately steps into Natasha's line of sight, shuffling papers on the coffee table to distract her.

The back of the Polaroid was blank, but the faint, sharp scent of marker pens teased George's heightened senses. He flipped it over, his curiosity piqued. The image depicted a shipping yard—or perhaps the skeletal frame of a boat being constructed inside a cavernous warehouse.

"Do you see?"

The whisper scraped against George's nerves like ice shards, sending a shiver racing up his spine. He froze, hackles rising as he slowly looked up.

Emily's ghostly figure stood before him, her chest ripped open in a grotesque mockery of life. The crime scene flashed vividly in his mind. Surrounding her were other spectral figures, the victims of this case, their hollow eyes fixed on him.

"Do... you... see?" the whisper came again, louder and more grating, each word dripping with malice. George's body tensed, his instincts screaming as Emily lunged toward him, her shriek reverberating in the room. He stumbled backwards, nearly tripping over himself, his blood running cold as his vision swam.

"Gone," he gasps finally, the apparitions vanishing as quickly as they'd appeared. Michael gripped his elbow, steadying him.

"They were here, weren't they?" Michael asks in a hushed tone.

George nodded. "Emily kept asking... 'Do I see?'"

Michael frowned, glancing at the Polaroid still clutched in George's hand. "See what?"

George's gaze shifted to the window, the tension in his chest coiling tighter. The answer came with a surge of dread. He flipped the Polaroid, revealing more of Ellena's handwriting on the back:

Dear Georgie,

I'm playing a hunch and trusting you with my life. Natasha has been keeping tabs on me, and I fear we've been betrayed. If anything goes wrong and I disappear, I know you and Michael will do your best. The picture is Billingsgate Market near the Blackwall Basin. Berth 72. It's the last place I needed to check. It might be worth it.

"We have to go," George says, thrusting the Polaroid into Michael's hands.

Michael's lips tightened as he read it. "Ah, Billingsgate. Fill me in on the way."

Both men exchanged a brance at Natasha, who was packing her kit with unsettling precision.

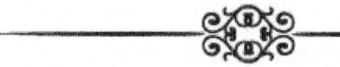

The large *Billingsgate Market* sign loomed overhead as they arrived at Trafalgar Way. The address matched perfectly, but so did George's growing unease. The moon hung low in the sky, ominously red, its light casting long, menacing shadows across the sprawling lot. His veins burned with the effort to suppress the shift clawing at him. Every breath stoked the fire within, anger threatening to overwhelm him.

A black iron fence surrounded the market's perimeter. Half-asleep at the gate, a heavy-set security guard barely acknowledged them. Michael flashed a warrant card, and the guard reluctantly pressed the oversized green button to let them through. It was too easy—another detail that set George on edge.

Inside, the lot was vast and quiet, save for the occasional shuffle of unseen creatures. A few red-brick warehouses stood near the water, their corrugated metal roofs reflecting the moonlight. George held up the Polaroid, matching the closest warehouse to the one in the image. Nearby, stacks of containers and lorry trailers were scattered across the lot, casting ominous shadows.

Their footsteps echoed across the cold tarmac, the chill of the night air forming white clouds with every exhale. The hairs on George's neck stood on end, just from the cold. Something was wrong. The silence felt oppressive, the vastness of the space a trap waiting to spring.

"Too quiet," Michael murmurs, echoing George's thoughts.

George tuned out the noise of rodents and the scurrying of unseen wildlife, straining to listen for anything human. His heightened senses caught nothing—no footsteps, no heartbeats other than their own. Still, the unease gnawed at him, and he couldn't shake the feeling that they were being watched.

"This place is wrong," George muttered. "Feels like a setup."

Michael nodded grimly, his hand brushing against the holster at his side. "Let's find berth 72 and get out of here. Fast."

"I don't like this," Michael mutters, exchanging one cloud for another as he lit a cigarette, the smoke curling around him like a restless spectre.

"Neither do I," George replies, his tone grim. "But Ellena's been circulated as missing, and her car's been flagged in case it shows up somewhere it shouldn't. Touch wood," he adds, tapping his head, "this is all one big misunderstanding, and she turns up safe and sound."

Michael exhaled a plume of smoke, watching it dissipate into the cold night air. "Her keys were inside, weren't they? Not that I checked to see if one belonged to a car." His voice tightened. "No, I think we're already staring down the worst-case scenario. All we can do now is pray to God she's still alive."

"May as well check the basin first," Michael says, trying to inject some practicality into their grim situation. "If her hunch was right, we might find the boat. If we do, the momentum swings back our way. At least a little." He flicked ash from his cigarette. "We'd have what they want. Use it to bargain, but never give it up."

George nodded, but his thoughts churned. Waist-high chain railings bordered the water's edge as they approached the basin. The bridge to the left separated a smaller area from the main expanse of water. The air reeked of pungent, slimy brine, each gust carrying the stench straight to his heightened senses. The swirling black waters churned restlessly, echoing faint, dripping sounds that rang between George's ears like a foreboding refrain.

He reached out, grabbing Michael's arm to stop him. His eyes scanned the surroundings, taking in every shadow, every flicker of movement. The unease in his gut coiled tighter. It might have been paranoia, the constant no-win scenarios they'd walked into before, but every sound—the creak of the chain railing, the faint ripple of water—felt amplified, oppressive.

The red moon looming above cast an ominous glow, painting the scene in shades of blood. George could feel his fear rising—not of the dripping water or the stink that clung to the air, but of what might happen next. Michael's pulse thudded steadily in George's ears, loud and rhythmic, a beacon that made his fangs itch and his claws twitch beneath his skin.

The hunger was thick and relentless. It clawed at his resolve, threatening to consume him. Michael, blissfully unaware, looked at him with faint concern etched into his features, the lines deepened by confusion. *Oh, to be that oblivious again,* George thought bitterly. Living in a simple world, one where monsters didn't lurk just out of sight. But their world wasn't like that—it was darker, twisted, and cruel.

"What's up?" Michael asks, taking another drag from his cigarette.

George snorted softly. "Other than the hunger building and your artery screaming Morse code for 'bite me'? Not much." He paused, his gaze drifting to the dark water ahead. "But the closer we get to the basin, the more I catch that familiar scent... and a feeling of unease."

Michael stiffened, his composure faltering for a moment. "I hope that's just a passing thought," he says with forced levity. "But I admit, this whole thing feels... off. Like a trap." His brow furrowed as doubt flickered across his face. "You don't think... I mean, could Ellena have set us up? It wouldn't be the first time we've been misdirected."

The suggestion hit George like a punch, and for a moment, he hesitated. The case had been one twist after another, and the thought of Ellena being part of a setup left a bitter taste in his mouth. But no—his gut told him this wasn't her doing. Still, the idea lingered, gnawing at the edges of his thoughts.

"Relax, old man," George says with a smirk that didn't reach his eyes. "If I wavering to tear your throat out, I'd have done it already." His tone softened, but the edge of tension remained. "It's difficult, though. It feels like being a hormonal teenager in the middle of a tantrum. Except I've got claws."

Michael shook his head with a wry chuckle. "What a way to reassure me." He glanced at George again, his expression growing serious. "You should be careful, though. No one might be around, but changing here? Not the best idea."

George tilted his head slightly, catching the concern in Michael's tone. "I thought it was just my eyes." He glanced at his hands. "Shit. Is it much different?"

Michael's jaw tightened. "Yeah. You're... shifting. Not all the way, but it's happening."

George clenched his fists, tending down the power thrumming through his veins. The wolf inside him was pushing harder than ever, strength rippling through his muscles, begging for release. The beast was ready, but he wasn't. Not yet.

"More demonic," Michael says, his voice low, though a nervous smile slipped onto his face. "Fierce as hell. Thank fuck you're on our side."

As they neared the basin's edge, George's lips twitched, not quite a smile. The scene ahead was a strange mix of eerie and mundane. A line of moored boats stretched along the water, their silhouettes faintly illuminated by the faint glow of a few string lights. Christmas colours twinkled here and there—cheery but misplaced this early in the season. Beyond that, the darkness was absolute.

George's nose caught it before anything else. Blood. The scent carried on the damp breeze, sharp and metallic. It wasn't easy to tell if it was old or fresh, but it was unmistakable. His instincts bristled. —the wolf within stirred at the scent, ready to hunt.

Michael's pace slowed, his caution outweighing his nerves. Years of experience had taught him when they were in over their heads, and this was one of those times. His movements became more deliberate, his breaths shorter. George noticed Michael's eyes darted to the shadows, his hand brushing his side where his weapon was holstered.

The path was silent, save for their footsteps and the faint lap of water against the boats. The radio controllers were the only ones who knew where they were, even though they had no specifics. Not even Locke was in the loop—and no one had been able to reach him. George's thoughts flickered briefly to their absent leader. Suspicious, maybe, but not surprising. Locke had a habit of disappearing at inconvenient times. It might have been harmless, a private affair or a personal errand. But with everything else happening, the absence felt heavier.

George shook the thought away. There was enough uncertainty without questioning Locke's whereabouts. The real threats were closer. If Natasha or Ellena were involved, they couldn't afford distractions if this was a trap.

"There it is. Number 72," Michael says, his voice barely above a whisper. He pointed to a canal boat halfway down the mooring platform.

The boat was dark, with no lights or movement. The silence around it pressed in like a physical weight. George's heightened senses strained to pick up heartbeats, but the sound was muddled, overwhelmed by the faint rattling of the environment—distant echoes of water, shifting boats, and the murmur of small creatures in the shadows.

Michael's heartbeat pounded loud and irregularly in George's ears, betraying his unease. His bottom lip curled inward, chewed raw as his hand fumbled in his jacket for a cigarette box. Empty.

Michael sighed, frustrated, his hand dropping back to his side. "The question is," he mutters, his voice thick with tension, "will it be the same for the boat?"

George's eyes locked on the vessel, his instincts screaming to be ready. His muscles tensed, the wolf clawing at the edges of his control. The stillness of the boat felt wrong, unnatural, as though it was holding its breath, waiting for them to draw closer.

"Stay behind me," George says, his voice low and firm. Michael didn't argue, falling into step just behind him as they moved toward the mooring platform.

The air grew colder as they approached, the scent of blood thicker now, almost suffocating. George's claws itched beneath his skin, and his pulse quickened, the primal side of him eager for release. But he forced it back, his focus razor-sharp.

BILLINGS GATE

31

As sick as it might sound, this felt like a grotesque reunion with Rachel Darnley, the case's starting point. Blood dripped lazily from the boat's edge into the dark water, forming ripples that seemed to whisper secrets beneath the surface. A puddle of crimson had gathered near the mooring rail, spilling over in slow, sinister trickles—human blood. There was no mistaking it. And it was driving George mad.

The red haze clouded his vision, revealing traces of old blood hurriedly wiped away—sloppy work. The puddles pooling on the boat's bow were a dead giveaway. Whose blood was it this time? His mind spun with possibilities when Michael's voice cut through the tension.

"Something's in the water," Michael says, his tone taut with unease.

George's gaze followed the mooring rope dangling into the murky depths. Michael was right. The water swirled unnaturally, and something breached the surface—a plastic-wrapped mass, the bunched-up end piercing through like a morbid buoy.

Without hesitation, George vaulted over the boat's rail inhumanly, landing on the bow in one fluid motion.

"What the hell?" Michael exclaims, his voice sharp behind him.

"Whatever it is, the rope's tied to it," George mutters, his claws twitching as he examines the situation. The rope is taut and pulled tightly into the water. Peering into the depths, his enhanced vision pierces through the murk, revealing the grotesque outline of a submerged form.

"Well?" Michael's voice carried a nervous urgency.

"It's a dead body," George says flatly, the words heavy in the cold air. The grim reality settled in, his stomach twisting as his thoughts leapt to Ellena. Could it be her?

"Shit. You okay?" Michael asks, his words distant against the pounding of George's pulse.

Anger surged through him, raw and feral. His grip on the rope tightened, black claws gleaming under the eerie red moonlight. He pulled the weight from the water with frightening ease with a single heave. The plastic-wrapped figure broke the surface, water cascading off the clear sheeting as the body revealed itself—a woman, her features obscured by the clinging film and mist forming from the temperature change.

Michael's sharp intake of breath echoed George's unspoken relief as the dimensions became clearer.

"Five feet to five one?" Michael asks, his breath visible in the frigid air.

George crouched beside the wrapped corpse, nodding grimly. "Yep, five foot one," he confirmed. Despite the relief that it wasn't Ellena, dread still settled deep in his chest. He couldn't smell blood from the body—something wasn't adding up.

"Will the real Miss Wainwright please stand up?" Michael quips bitterly. "You'd better open it. We need to see if there's anything useful. Forensics isn't much use on this one." His Cockney gravel carried a restrained fury, a frustration George shared.

George tore through the plastic with a single swipe of his claws, the airtight seal releasing a wave of death particles that made him gag. The body was preserved surprisingly well—submerged in water and sealed for at least a week, maybe two.

George caught sight of the woman's features as the plastic peeled away. Long black hair clung to her face, peachy cheeks marred by the faint indents of glasses. Bruises and small cuts below her eyelids suggested she'd taken a blow to the face—and her glasses were missing.

"Fake Natasha," George muttered. "She stole her glasses."

His gaze travelled down, noting the ligature marks around her neck. The killer had been taller, not by much, but enough to leave a pattern. This wasn't supernatural. For once, it was a straightforward case of human-on-human violence.

"Fake Natasha killed the real one," George says, his voice tight. "Took her place. And why not? She had to be confident—so sure of her ability to pass as someone else. That's why she made the scene at the first body, right? Showboating. Get everyone focused on her theatrics so no one asks too many questions."

Michael nodded, his jaw tight as the realisation sank in. "And she latched onto Ellena, used her expertise to cover her tracks. Guess that's what tipped Ellena off."

George exhaled, his breath misting in the cold night air. The pieces were falling into place, but with every answer, more questions loomed. What was the endgame? And how much danger was Ellena still in?

I had to credit the fake one; she knew enough about our techniques to stage the Mildred Thistle crime scene with surgical precision. She must've had Emily captive by then, smearing a faint print and stuffing that photo into Mildred's lifeless hand as if it were some kind of deathbed confession. A clue tailor-made to send us chasing shadows.

The real question now: Who is fake Natasha Wainwright?

"About one to two weeks," George mutters, his breath forming white clouds in the chill night air as he glances at Michael.

"So, she's played us all for fools. Rigged evidence staged the whole thing," Michael replies, his tone bitter.

"Yeah, at least with Mildred Thistle. Who knows how many others?" George's mind raced, trying to piece together the threads of this tangled web.

Michael fished a key out of his pocket and tossed it over. "Shall we see if it fits?"

George caught it easily, raising an eyebrow. "Keep watch, then, you super brave old man," he says, his sarcasm coming out sharper than intended.

Michael took it in stride, smirking. "Hey, you're the one with the claws. Besides, I'm not a fan of being *on* the water. Above it? Sure. Besides it? No problem. But the sway in motion? Turns my stomach. Don't worry—I'll shout if anything comes creeping."

George snorted, sliding the key into the cabin's lock. It turned smoothly, with no resistance, almost too easily. A new thought struck him, gnawing at the edges of his mind. At what point did Mr Kunar take this key? And did he know about Wainwright's body? Not that it would help him now.

His hand hovered over the handle, hesitating. The static buzz on the back of his neck returned, a familiar signal that something wasn't right. He looked around, scanning the darkened warehouses behind Michael.

"Michael, stay sharp," George says, his voice low and tense. "Something's off. I don't know what, but be ready."

Michael nodded, his shoulders squaring as his hand rested instinctively near his weapon.

George pushed the cabin door open, the hinges yawning with a low groan. A musty scent spilt out, wrapping around him like a shroud. It was the same old dust smell from the crime scenes, unmistakable. He shifted instinctively, his eyes lighting up the cabin's interior.

What he saw made him pause. The boat's interior was deceptively large, far more spacious than it looked outside. Long and wide enough to live in, it was crammed to the brim with what could only be described as ancient treasures. The floor was thick with dust, littered with footprints of various sizes, including a small set—size five, at a guess.

The contents of the cabin were staggering. Items seemed to predate modern history—artefacts that might've belonged to the Egyptians or Romans. Dusty tomes lined shelves, their spines brittle with age. If the museum had deemed a handful of these items priceless, then this collection was worth hundreds of millions to the right buyer—enough to kill for.

George's gaze swept over the hoard until it landed on something more personal—a photograph. It was a group photo, faded and yellowed with age but unmistakable. The faces in the image were all members of the travelling party.

George's pulse quickened. The real Natasha Wainwright was dead, her body pulled from the water. They had the key. They had the boat. Now, this photo might give them what they need.

"We're about to find out," George mutters under his breath, staring at the photo. "Who the hell is the fake one?"

George stepped outside to find Michael pacing near the boat, his boots scraping against the wooden platform. He looked like he either needed to piss or expected everything to go sideways any second. The way he moved, loose and fluid, ruled out the prune bladder theory. It had to be fear.

The cold air hit George like a slap, carrying with it the overwhelming rush of smells his heightened senses picked up now. The nearer they came to midnight, the more the little changes in him sharpened. He could smell everything pouring from Michael's pores—sweat, fear, nicotine, and a faint trace of last night's whiskey.

"Thank fuck you're back," Michael mutters, rubbing his hands together. "Something feels off. The hairs on my balls are tingling."

George raised an eyebrow. "You sure that's not the crabs talking?"

"Piss off," Michael shot back with a half-smirk. "That'd firmly put her on my shit list."

"Her? Oh, wait. Really?" George asks, catching the meaning behind the quip.

"This old dog's got plenty of life in him yet. Now I know why she was so keen," Michael replies, though his tone was brittle, like he was trying to convince himself as much as

George.

"Hey, sorry you're going through this," George offered, a rare flash of sincerity breaking through.

"Oh, shut up, for fuck's sake. It's a shag," Michael snaps, but the bitterness in his voice is unmistakable. The wounds from what his wife had done to him still bled, no matter how much he tried to cover them up.

George let the comment slide. "Well, shall we see who dear old Natasha is?" he asks, feeling the bounce of the water beneath his feet as he walks toward the boat.

The lighting was sparse, so Michael sparked his clipper and waved it around like he was at a concert. The small flame flickered, casting fleeting glimpses across the photo. He passed it over each face until it landed on the one dotted out.

"Wasn't it down there somewhere?" Michael asks, squinting.

"Melanie Blake," George says, his voice flat with realisation. "Not once did Kunar hint at her. So, what makes her do all this?"

They stood in silence for a moment, both stumped. They'd been so sure about Emily and Jack, and then Emily turned up dead. So naturally, they'd assumed the wife. Yet this—Melanie Blake—was a curveball.

"Beats me," Michael mutters, his frustration audible. "Would love to know what got her knickers twisted? Maybe it's just good old-fashioned greed."

George considered that for a moment, but then another memory surfaced. The way the "master" had spoken of *cheat and revenge*. What had Melanie Blake endured to screw her up so badly?

"Most people involved in stealing and selling the relics are dead," George muses aloud. "Maybe it was something that happened during an excursion. Or Melanie was being cheated out of her cut. So she engineered a way to take it all for herself."

Michael nodded, though his brow furrowed. "Right. We know who she is now. How do we prove she's controlling the Kanaima?"

The words had barely left his mouth when George glanced back at the real Natasha Wainwright's body. The dead woman lay still, pale and haunting in the dim light. They could only hope there was enough evidence to tie Melanie to her death. She'd been astute, fooling them all until Ellena connected some dots.

"We have to call this in now," Michael says, his voice firm. "Get the body secured and hope there's enough DNA to link."

George crouched beside the corpse again, letting the wind rush past him, carrying its scents. Blood. It was faint, different from the blood found elsewhere on the boat. There were no visible wounds on Natasha's body, but the scent lingered—coming from somewhere specific.

His gaze fixed on the downward curve of her left shoulder. He craned his neck, trying to peer into the gap without disturbing the body more than necessary. Moving her again might have been a mistake, but they needed answers.

"What is it, matey?" Michael asks, his voice laced with unease as he watches George crouch beside the body.

"A potential mistake," George mutters, his eyes narrowing on a faint, dry trail of blood.

"By who?"

"Melanie," George says, his voice heavy with the weight of realisation. The blood trail stood out against the preserved body, likely oxygenated by the trapped air in the plastic wrapping.

Michael leaned closer, his brow furrowing. "Really?"

George nodded. "I think we may have her blood. Natasha was strangled, but whatever Melanie used must have cut into her hand." He gestured toward the faint streak of blood. "The question is, how do we preserve this?"

Michael didn't hesitate. "Here, take this."

George blinked in surprise as Michael pulled a small swab kit from his pocket, holding it out like it was the most natural thing in the world.

"Seriously?" George asks, stunned.

"Absolutely," Michael says, a faint smirk tugging at the corners of his mouth. "Another teaching moment for you, Georgie. Detective work isn't just about chasing down suspects or shooting things that go bump in the night. It's about the details—the shit that matters. Anyone can run after a perp, but what happens if they slip away? Can you find the evidence that'll drag them into court later?"

"Good point," George admitted, grudgingly respecting the older detective.

"That wasn't a dig, by the way," Michael adds. "Not every suspect can vanish in a puff of black smoke. But the cases we deal with? They matter more than most. They're deeper and messier, and the ripples hit everyone left behind to grieve. You must be ready to spot what others might miss—like this." He gestured at the blood trail. "If you swab that, we might pin a DNA connection between Natasha, our suspect, and the scene. Sure, the case is tied up in supernatural shit we can't explain, but this? This is human. And it could be the only thread we can pull to get real justice."

George stared at him for a moment, absorbing the lesson. Michael had just dismantled his naïve approach to the case in under a minute, exposing the gaps in his thinking. And he was right. This murder—cold, calculated, and human—could be the only part of this nightmare they could prosecute.

"This feels like the calm before the storm," George mutters.

Michael nodded grimly. "Then be the good soldier and do the job. Swab it, bag it, and let's make this count."

George followed Michael's instructions, carefully swabbing the blood and sealing it in the provided bag. The plastic wrapping had miraculously preserved the evidence, another small victory in an otherwise chaotic investigation.

But one problem loomed large in George's mind as he worked: their SOCO, Natasha—the real one—was the victim. And the murderer was pretending to be her.

The irony was bitter and chilling. Even with the swab safely bagged, George couldn't shake the feeling that this was only the beginning of something far worse.

LET'S PLAY A GAME

32

George handed the evidence to Michael. It felt safer that way, considering what might be coming. The boat was locked, its contents—hundreds, perhaps thousands of priceless relics—etched into his mind. They had the grand prize, a bargaining chip, and maybe the means to save Ellena—if she was still alive.

He stood motionless, staring at the floating house of horrors and the restless black ripples lapping against it. His unease had grown into something monstrous, gnawing at his focus. His warm breath funnelled into the cold air, forming plumes of white that quickly dissipated. The night was too quiet. Save for the soft clap of water against the hull, the world seemed to have stopped.

Everything George was, and everything he feared becoming, screamed at him to pay attention. His heightened senses picked up on details that most would miss. The guard's cabin radio had gone silent, its faint hum replaced by a void. Then there were the steps—soft, deliberate, distant.

It could have been the guard stretching his legs or checking the grounds. But George knew better. The dread coiling in his gut told him this was something else. Something is wrong.

His gaze shifted to Michael, who was fidgeting with his radio, frustration etched into his face.

"I can't get out," Michael says, shaking the device toward the blood-red moon as if it might boost the signal.

George's attention flicked to the sky. The moon loomed impossibly large, its crimson light casting the world in an oppressive glow. It felt malevolent, like a predator watching from above, ready to strike. George's jaw tightened. Its presence wasn't just foreboding—it was a reminder of what was coming.

In a few hours, sins laid bare, control shattered. He could become something far worse than the beasts they hunted. Something far more dangerous.

"At all? Not even static feedback?" George asks, pulling his radio free and pressing the button. A sharp beep answered, but nothing else—just silence.

"Not a thing," Michael mutters, his face twisted into a scowl. "And I don't like it."

The look on Michael's face—part frustration, part dread—did little to calm George. His mind churned as he pieced together the clues. They'd been directed, step by step, manipulated into walking straight into this trap.

Ellena had led them with her breadcrumbs, but Melanie had already taken whatever information Ellena knew. George's thoughts darted back to the Polaroid. That strange scent, marker ink with a twist. He should've recognised it then. Words written in invisible ink meant for ultraviolet light or his "Alpha Eyes." He hadn't given it much thought. But now, it clicked.

The hairdryer plugged in by Ellena's sofa—heat had revealed the hidden message before they'd even arrived. Melanie, or "Natasha," hadn't just come to clean up the crime scene. She was watching them. To see what they found, confident her precautions would hold.

And now here they were, stuck in a fishmonger's market. The overwhelming stench of rotting fish, guts, and trash clung to the air, mingling with the damp chill of the nearby water. It wasn't just the smells—it was the noise. Rats, foxes, and seagulls filled the air with a cacophony of heartbeats, their chaotic rhythms making it impossible for George to focus.

"This is a setup," George says, the weight of the realisation sinking in.

Michael froze, spinning on his heels as his dread caught up. "We can't call for help," he says, his voice trembling with anger and fear.

"That may not be true," George says, his tone clipped. "Time to get your hands dirty and overcome your fear of boats before your next task." He glanced back at Natasha's body. Whatever played out tonight, they needed a backup plan. Improvised as it was, he had one.

Michael eyed him warily. "What are you planning?"

"Help me lift the body to that tarp by the barrels first," George replies, motioning to the stacks of waste barrels half-hidden in the shadows.

Michael groaned but reluctantly clambered onto the boat. His movements were hesitant, as though the boat itself might bite. George could've moved Natasha alone, but having Michael close allowed him to control the field of play.

Michael's expression was priceless, somewhere between disgust and disbelief. He'd probably never been in a position where he had to hide a corpse before—unless the stories of his Cockney swagger and "Kray's folklore" exploits had more truth than George assumed.

Lifting Natasha's body, they worked silently, placing her carefully on the tarp amidst the reeking barrels of discarded fish guts. The sight and smell were bad enough to churn anyone's stomach. Despite himself, George felt a pang of guilt. Natasha, or whoever she had been before this madness, deserved better than to end up discarded like trash.

"Thank you."

The words froze George mid-movement. A chill skated across the back of his neck, sharp and unnatural. He exhaled slowly, trying to suppress the instinct to jump out of his skin.

'Here we go again,' he thought grimly. The last time a ghost made itself known scared the living hell out of him.

Pausing, he glanced down at the tarp, half-expecting Michael to notice his unease. To Michael, this would probably look like a brief lapse in concentration. To George, it was anything but.

Natasha's ghostly form took centre stage this time, her figure shimmering faintly against the backdrop of night. Behind her, Emily stood, flanked by the other restless spirits that had taken to haunting George's steps. They hung there like a cheerleading squad for the dead.

Natasha moved closer, her translucent face illuminated by the faint light. George could see the ligature mark around her neck, the detail stark even in death. Despite the wound, she smiled—a faint, melancholic expression that spoke volumes about the person she might've been.

"Thank you," she says again, her voice soft but distinct.

George nodded slightly, though he wasn't sure they'd earned her gratitude. Not yet.

Back at the boat, the problem of what to do with it lingered. Neither of them had much experience with boats, and they couldn't just hand it over to anyone. George fiddled with the key, turning it in his fingers as he thought.

"Michael," he asks, breaking the silence. "What do you notice about this key?"

Michael turned, his face scrunched in confusion. "Nothing. It's just a small silver key."

"And?"

"It's on a keyring. Berth 72. What about it?"

"Anything else? Anything unusual?"

Michael squinted at the key again. "No. Why?"

"It's not just a locker key," George says, holding it up. "It's *my* locker key."

"What? Really?"

"Yes. Both are small and silver. I switched the tag. If we have to hand it over, it'll buy us time," George explains, hoping the ruse would hold if it came to that.

Time ticked on, and George's focus narrowed. Keeping busy helped distract him from the growing heat coursing through his body. The wolf inside clawed at his composure, threatening to break free. The hairs on his arms and neck bristled, every instinct screaming at him to be ready.

The heels echoed in the distance.

The sound sent a dry chill down George's throat. He froze, his attention snapping at the approaching noise. As much as he could use Michael's help, he couldn't let him be caught in whatever was coming. Michael wasn't built for this fight. If things went sideways, George would survive—or at least, he stood a chance. Michael would be torn to shreds.

He opened his mouth to suggest Michael head to the guard's hut to use the phone, but Michael stopped dead a few feet ahead, his arms flung wide to the sides.

"Michael?" George called, his voice low but urgent.

Michael didn't respond; his eyes locked on something in the darkness ahead. George's radar went wild, a sickening swirl twisting in the pit of his stomach. Something was wrong—wrong.

"Georgie, Georgie, Georgie. You're not one to disappoint, are you?" The voice echoed around George, chaotic and slippery, like oil on ice. It carried the same mocking edge he'd heard before—the one that had possessed the McDonald's drive-through worker. Only now, it was coming from Michael.

"Even with the slew of bodies chucked in your pathway, you still saw through it all. Perhaps you have dear old Ellena to thank... Oops, I meant had. Or did I? Suppose there's only one way to find out. Would you like to play a game?"

A biting winter breeze whipped around George, cutting through his jacket as the voice settled deep into his ears. It was a sickly blend of taunting and hostility that could burrow into your thoughts and rot them from the inside. The question lingered, circling his mind like a vulture. Which one was speaking? The Kanaima or Melanie Blake?

"You know what? I've gone off games," George says, forcing a smirk he didn't feel. "My brother saw to that. Makes family Christmas a little awkward."

The voice chuckled, low and grating. "Ah yes, yet so does having your brother explode in a ball of fire. How is he, by the way? Buried the hatchet yet?"

George's smirk vanished, his jaw tightening. They were toying with him, digging into old wounds, stoking the fire that was already dangerously close to raging out of control. The blood-red and overwhelming moonlight seemed to feed the anger coiling in his chest. He didn't need another psychopath to push him closer to the edge.

"Like you said, ball of fire. No way of surviving that. Stop the theatrics and tell me how to get Ellena back. We'll resolve this."

The voice hummed, feigning thought. "Oh, is he gone? Hmm. I wouldn't be so sure. Anyhow, that's a problem for another day. All I want is the key you recovered, and all you want is Ellena back. Nobody else?"

George froze, his mind racing. Nobody else? Who else could these bastards have? Unless they planned to keep Michael possessed—or worse, perhaps this would free up Jack.

"Who else and how?" he asks, his tone sharp.

"Ask not to reason, only to do or die," the voice taunted. "There's a little thing called insurance. I give you one to save, which would be easy with your unique talents and speed. I give you two, maybe three, and you'll be spoiled for choice. It's a little like Christmas. So don't say I never give you anything."

George clenched his fists, his claws itching beneath the surface. The games, the jokes—they weren't fooling anyone. All they were doing was pissing him off, feeding the urge to unleash the wolf and let the world feel his fury. The bastards were trying to keep him busy, to overwhelm him with impossible choices.

The truth settled heavily in his gut: there would be more death before the night was through. The only question was whether it would come before or after midnight.

"How about you get to the point and fuck off out of my friend?" George growls, his voice low and dangerous.

"Aww, missing the old git? I feel bad that he was only a means to an end. For an older man, he was quite the ride. Just not the happy one he would've liked."

George's glare deepened. "Why? What did you need from him?"

"Just his access to old case files," the voice replies smoothly. "This isn't so straightforward, you see. Jack and the others cheated me out of my share of the relics. But that wasn't the worst of it. Oh no. The worst part was what they did to my sister one year ago."

George's jaw tightened, his instincts screaming at him to brace himself.

"Jack groomed Charlotte," the voice continues, its tone dripping with venom. "Promised her he'd leave his wife, that they'd have a future. Then, one drunken night, the boys on a camp set upon her. They took turns and treated her like a piece of meat. When the museum caught wind of their thefts, suspicion fell on her. They used her name to sign the logs for the stolen crates. When the investigation opened, they left her to take the fall. She killed herself two weeks later."

The voice paused, letting the words settle like a sickness in the air. "We tried to persuade the police to look deeper, to see what they'd done to her. But they didn't listen. So now, they pay."

There it was—the motivation behind the madness—a brutal, twisted vengeance born of grief and betrayal. Jack had broken Charlotte, and now Melanie was using Jack.

But George's gut told him she didn't fully understand what she was wielding. The Kanaima wasn't just a tool for revenge. It was something far darker, something far more dangerous.

"So, murder is your answer to everything?" George asks, his voice edged with frustration but carefully controlled. "Let's end this. I sympathise with what happened, and I truly apologise for your loss. But don't you see what you've done? All you've created is more misery for innocent families caught in the crossfire. Is that fair?"

The voice responded with a mocking laugh, low and hollow. "What? The families who've reaped the benefits of their wrongdoing? You'll forgive me if I don't cry for them."

George clenched his fists, forcing himself to stay calm. "What's the game?"

"And just when we were getting on so well," the voice drawled. "Head to the warehouse in the Polaroid from that book, and you'll see. Make sure you bring the old git. It would be nice to see him again before it's over."

The presence left as abruptly as it had arrived, the oppressive weight lifting from the air. Michael stumbled backwards, his face pale and eyes wide, looking as though life had been drained from him. George lunged, catching him before he hit the ground.

Michael blinked up at him, dazed. "You okay, Bambi?" George asks, forcing some fun into his tone.

"Fuck off," Michael mutters, brushing himself off. "Stress must've made me light-headed."

George studied him, weighing whether to tell him the truth. Michael wouldn't remember if this possession was anything like the last. But George spared him no illusions.

"Not quite," George says, his voice lighter than the situation deserved. "A demon
possessed you."

Michael froze, his face twisting in disgust as he brushed at his shirt as though he could
shake the feeling off. "Seriously?"

"Yep. Made you its bitch for a good 90 seconds," George adds, grinning wryly. "Although, wait—no. That part was Melanie."

Michael's lips twitched into a wrinkled smile despite himself. "Piss off. It was a good
three minutes, at least. So, what's the plan?"

George glanced toward the darkened warehouse district, the weight of what was coming pressing heavily on his chest. His original plan was useless now. The game had shifted,
and they were herded toward the Polaroid warehouse. He hadn't told Michael yet, but
their destination was clear.

"We're heading to the warehouse," George says, his voice tight.

They started walking, the silence heavy with unspoken tension. George's heightened
senses churned with conflicting signals—dozens of heartbeats and faint signs of life.
Rats, foxes, and seagulls fluttered through his awareness, creating chaos in his mind. But
beneath it all, something darker lingered.

His hackles were firing on all cylinders, his every instinct screaming to turn back. Then
came the smell—a stinging mix of sulphur and rot. The stench of death itself, acrid and
cloying, rolled over him like a suffocating wave.

LURED

33

L ike flies to shit, this had drawn us in. The death demons were arriving, their intentions unknown but undoubtedly sinister. The numbers were already stacked
against George, and now he needed eyes in the back of his head just to survive.

As he and Michael approached the warehouse, the weight of it all bore down on
him—the lies, the death, the misdirection. It wasn't just this case; it was the last one,
the ghosts of which still haunted him. His soul felt tormented, every fibre of his being
dragged through the wringer. The wolf inside him clawed for release, its frustration and
rage mirroring his own.

It was fucking eating him alive.

His veins pulsed with adrenaline; his instincts heightened to a dangerous edge. The
ease with which the demon had possessed Michael earlier proved how unequipped they
were to handle what lay ahead.

"More guests," George mutters, the weight of the situation pressing harder.

"For fuck's sake," Michael groans, the exhaustion plain in his voice.

"Yep," George says, his tone dry but laced with anger. "Have you ever felt so pissed off
you just wanted to scream? Because that's me right now."

"All the time."

"Then let's do it," George says, a spark of recklessness creeping into his voice. He raised
his eyebrows at Michael, a challenge glinting in his eyes. "I'm not joking. They know we're
here. Let's make it official. It might even be cathartic."

Michael stared at him, incredulous. "Seriously?"

"Yes. Go on. You go first. I'll watch in case you keel over from a heart attack," George says, his smirk faint but present.

Michael hesitated, then shrugged. "Fuck it," he mutters.

He tilted his head back and let loose a scream, raw and full of pent-up anger and pain. It echoed off the surrounding buildings, reverberating through the night. When he stopped, his face was red, but there was a faint smile there, too, as though he'd shed a layer of the weight he carried.

"Wow," Michael says, his breath catching. "You're right. I feel lighter. Your turn."

George stepped back, giving Michael space and readying himself. He could feel the beast stirring deep inside, coiling with the anger, pain, and frustration bottled up for far too long. This wasn't just a scream; it was a purge.

He leaned forward as if pulling the rage from the depths of hell, drawing it up through his lungs and throat. When he threw his head back, what emerged wasn't a scream—a *roar.*

There was a deep, guttural, primal roar that shook the very ground beneath them. Michael staggered, rocking on his heels as the force rippled outward, the sheer power of it momentarily smoothing his wrinkles.

The sound seemed to carry for miles, a warning that something dangerous and unstoppable was coming. Windows rattled in their frames, and for a moment, the world felt like it was holding its breath.

George straightened, panting, the raw power of the roar still echoing in his chest. He felt lighter like he'd shed the chains holding him down. But as the euphoria faded, a question lingered in his mind: *How the hell did I do that?*

It didn't feel like a skill he'd learned. It felt like instinct—something buried deep within him, clawing to the surface when needed.

Michael was quiet beside him, his hand trembling slightly at his side. The two of them stood before a rusty red door, ajar by a few inches, the darkness beyond beckoning.

The stench of death circled them, pungent and oppressive, but George couldn't pinpoint its source. It was everywhere and nowhere.

He hesitated. He couldn't enter as a werewolf—not with Ellena or whoever else might be inside. She might have written about her excitement for the supernatural, but George couldn't be sure how much of that was genuine or how much Melanie had exploited. He had to assume everything was compromised.

"You, okay?" George asks, glancing at Michael. When the older man didn't respond,

George reached over and dabbed two fingers to his wrist. "Checking your pulse," he says with a smirk, trying to break the tension.

"I'm getting on a bit, but I'm not dead, you cheeky twat," Michael mutters, his voice tinged with mock annoyance.

"Just checking," George says, his tone light, though the tension lingered beneath it. "Hard to tell if you're having a stroke." Humour was always his defence mechanism, a thin shield against the chaos around them.

"Keep it up, sunshine, and you'll be bypassing the 'stroke' and heading straight to a coffin," Michael shot back, finally cracking a smile. His sigh of relief drifted into the cold night air, a cloudy exhalation that eased the moment's weight.

"It'll take more than you to put this dog down!" George replies with a smirk. If these were his last normal moments before hell broke loose, he'd take them—laughing with a friend amidst the madness.

But the laughter couldn't mask what he sensed. Pain. It bled through the air, sharp and raw from the warehouse. Whether the bodies inside were feeling or radiating it was another question, but it riled him up, making his pulse thrum faster.

"There's one... two... three... four... Wait, no, six... then four again," George says, his voice tight as he counts the presence inside. The death demons were moving their positions and throwing off his heightened senses.

"Breathe, Georgie," Michael says, his voice steady. He gestured exaggeratedly, miming a deep inhale. "Calm down. Try to focus—figure out who they are."

George closed his eyes, inhaling deeply and letting the scents and signals filter through the noise. He concentrated, sifting through the chaos.

"Melanie. The Kanaima—Jack. Ellena and... Fuck, it's ADI Locke," he says, his stomach sinking at the realisation. Locke was here, tangled in this mess.

"That explains why nobody could reach him," Michael says grimly, his face darkening.

Did George have a plan? Not really. The moon hung low and blood-red, tormenting him, gnawing at his control. The wolf inside clawed for release, eager for a fight, and George's doubt grew. His hand rested on the rusty door, but a heavy hesitation held him back.

"Michael," George says, glancing at his companion. "You don't have to do this. You know that, right?"

Michael's smirk was faint but unwavering. "No way. I'm in this for the long haul. Come what may, and however the cards fall. Besides," he adds, his eyes narrowing, "you need someone to corroborate your story at the end of this, you bloody idiot."

Before George could respond, a voice sliced through the stillness like a razor.

"Well, look what the cat dragged in." Melanie's mocking tone glanced around the warehouse, bouncing off the walls with evil glee.

The space was dark, but George's sharp eyes picked out the outlines of two up-side-down crosses in the centre of the open floor. He stepped forward cautiously, his boots scuffing against what felt like sawdust. The air was thick with old dust, the sharp stench of sulphur, and the coppery tang of blood.

George's hackles rose, a visceral warning vibrating through his body. Every second in this no-man's-land ratcheted up the change within him, the wolf stirring dangerously close to the surface.

"'Will you walk into my parlour?' said the Spider to the Fly..." Melanie's voice came again, lilting and singsong, the nursery rhyme dripping with malice. "'Tis the prettiest little parlour that ever you spy.'"

The eerie cadence of her words tightened the knot in George's gut. It was like hearing the ghost of his brother—the same theatrical, taunting delivery that had haunted his past.

"Why don't you cut the shit?" George snaps, stepping closer and holding up the key. "I have what you want."

Melanie didn't miss a beat, her voice oozing mockery. "'I'm sure you must be weary, dear, with soaring up so high. Will you rest upon my little bed?'"

"Oh no, no," says the little Fly, her voice trembling with defiance. "'For I've often heard it said, they never, never wake again, who sleep upon your bed!'"

Melanie's tone shifted, taking on a mockingly sweet cadence. "Said the cunning Spider to the Fly; dear friend, what can I do to prove the warm affection I've always felt for you? I have a good store within my pantry; that's nice. I'm sure you're very welcome. Will you please take a slice?"

The darkness seemed to tighten its grip as Melanie continued her twisted recital, her voice bouncing off the walls like an eerie echo.

"Oh no, no," says the little Fly, "'Kind sir, that cannot be; I've heard what's in your pantry, and I do not wish to see!'"

The air around George shifted abruptly, cold and sharp, as rushes of wind whipped past him. It twisted him left and right, disorienting and pulling at his senses. The pitch-black surroundings spun in his mind, leaving him reeling and blind.

"Michael!" he shouts, his voice sharp and urgent. "You okay? Stay close!"

The silence that followed punched George in the chest. He reached out with his arms, searching for his friend in the suffocating darkness, but all he found was emptiness.

Panic surged like an electric jolt. His instincts screamed at him, a storm of anger and fear that made his wolf stir dangerously close to the surface.

"He's a little tied up right now," Melanie's voice rang out, followed by a burst of laughter—high-pitched and manic, like a cackling witch.

"Let them go!" George demands, his voice hardening. "There's no need for this."

"I said two, maybe more," Melanie replies, her voice dripping with evil amusement. "Now, the thing is... I'm not a fan of witnesses. I've read books and watched crime shows. People get caught because there's always someone left to tell the tale."

George took a slow, deliberate breath, forcing himself to think clearly. "Did you think we wouldn't expect this? That we wouldn't have a plan to get out of here? Did you think I wouldn't leave a paper trail?"

Melanie's laughter quieted, her tone sharpening. "What trail? You have nothing."

"Do you want to roll the dice?" George counters, his mind racing. "You were right about Ellena—she connected some dots. But we finished the picture. You couldn't explain the bruising on Emily's body, but that ring print? It matches the sovereign on your left hand. The gleam under the bridge played on my mind, and just before we left, I called the station to seal the CCTV tapes for the last week. Those tapes show you wearing that ring."

Melanie didn't respond immediately, but George pressed on. "Then there's your H.R. file. You don't match Natasha's height. For someone who's played at forensics, you've been sloppy. And if we don't turn up, I've told someone to investigate you immediately."

A silence fell, the kind that stretched thin and taut, ready to snap. Then Melanie's voice came again, light and mocking.

"Oh, Georgie. I give up. Come, take me away. I confess... You're not the only one who can read body expressions."

She started again, her voice a sickly sing-song: "'Sweet creature!' says the Spider, 'you're witty, and you're wise; how handsome are your gauzy wings! How brilliant are your eyes! I've a little looking glass on my parlour shelf. If you'll step in one moment, dear, you shall behold yourself.'"

George's teeth clenched as he forced himself to stay calm. "Why don't you cut the shit, Melanie? I have what you want." He held up the key, letting it catch what little light the darkness allowed.

But Melanie wasn't done playing her game. "'I thank you, gentle sir,'" she says, her voice adopting the Fly's character, "'for what you're pleased to say, and bidding you good morning now. I'll call another day.'"

Her laughter came again, grating and triumphant. The shadows seemed to close tighter as George took another step forward, his boots crunching through sawdust. The air grew heavier, the stench of death and sulphur thickening.

He could feel her presence, lingering just out of reach, weaving her web. The nursery rhyme continued in his mind, Melanie's voice blending with the creeping sense of doom.

"The Spider turned him roundabout and went into his den. For well, he knew the silly Fly would soon come back again..."

"So, he wove a subtle web in a little corner and set his table ready to dine upon the Fly," Melanie recited, her voice dripping with venom.

"Then he came out to his door again and merrily did sing: Come hither, hither, pretty Fly, with the pearl and silver wing; Your robes are green and purple—there's a crest upon your head; Your eyes are like the diamond bright, but mine are dull as lead!'

Her voice rose, lilting with cruel glee as she reached the climax.

"Alas, alas! How soon this silly little Fly, hearing his wily, flattering words, came slowly flitting by. With buzzing wings, she hung aloft, then near and nearer drew, thinking only of her brilliant eyes and green and purple hue—thinking only of her crested head—poor foolish thing! At last, up jumped the cunning spider and fiercely held her fast. He dragged her up his winding stair into his dismal den, within his little parlour—but she never came out again!"

Her twisted nursery rhyme ended, and the lights bolted on, flooding the warehouse in a stark, sterile glow. George blinked against the brightness, his heightened senses snapping to attention as the scene unfolded before him.

Two gurney tables were overturned in the centre of the room, each holding a captive. Locke and Ellena were strapped down, their heads tossing side to side, unable to move or scream. Each was attached to drips holding bags of misty-coloured fluid. The sharp chemical tang in the air told George all he needed to know—some toxin variation was fed directly into their bodies.

Then he saw Michael.

The Kanaima—Jack—had him. Jack's claws pierced Michael's throat, holding him in a precarious, deadly grip. They stood on a raised platform behind the gurneys, their figures silhouetted against the glaring lights. And there, standing next to them, was Melanie

Blake, her presence commanding and lethal.

George's stomach sank. He was fucked.

Ten to fifteen feet. That was the space he had to cross to reach any of them. His mind raced, calculating the impossible. Who first? Michael—before his throat was ripped out? Or Locke and Ellena—before the toxin reached their hearts?

The sickly sweet stench of death demons lingered in the air, always shifting, always close. George's heightened senses caught their movements, shadows circling the room's edges like predators waiting for the kill.

Could the Kanaima feel them, too?

George gritted his teeth, pushing back against the pain tearing through his body. The wolf inside was straining to break free, his insides twisting and burning as he fought the shift. He couldn't let go now—not in front of them. Not yet.

He needed a moment. A chance to disrupt the connection between Jack and the Kanaima, to create a rift that would allow him to separate Michael from those claws. But time was slipping through his fingers like sand, bringing them closer to death every second.

Melanie's voice broke through his thoughts, sharp and mocking. "What's the matter, Georgie? Weighing up who to save first?"

George's jaw tightened, his eyes locking on hers.

"Why don't you come clean?" she continues, her tone almost playful. "Show everyone your true self as you flail and fail them. Little by little, watered-down toxins are feeding into their organs. First, the paralysis. Then, one by one, their organs will shut down until..." She paused, smiling cruelly. "They die."

George's chest tightened, the knot of rage and fear coiling tighter.

"It's been going for the last minute," Melanie adds, her grin widening. "I reckon you've got about as much time left to try saving them. Tick-tock, Georgie."

The clock was ticking, and every fibre of George's being screamed at him to move. But with every step he planned, every angle he considered, the wolf inside him threatened to break free.

If he lost control, he'd lose them all.

"Maybe just my little *bedfellow* here," Melanie purrs, her voice slithering like venom. She glanced at Michael, her lips curling into a cruel smirk. "A quick flick and his throat will be gushing. Which reminds me... Michael, I'll cherish those thirty seconds for the rest of my life. A shame you won't get the chance to go again."

"Fuck off," Michael croaked, his voice strained but defiant. His glare burned with fire despite the claws at his throat. "You should feel privileged. I wasted three minutes of my time on you."

Melanie's laughter echoed through the warehouse, sharp and grating. "Agree to disagree," she says with a mocking shrug. "Now, who first? Oh, and George," she adds, her eyes gleaming with malice, "I feel bad you and Ellena didn't get the chance to... knock boots."

George's fists clenched, his breath ragged as he tried to focus through the haze of fury building inside him. Every word she spoke was to needle him, to unbalance him. But Melanie wasn't done.

"Jack," George called out, his voice steady despite the storm. "I know you're in there. How did it feel, huh? Killing Emily? Especially after your wife fucked you off and left you crawling back to your miserable existence. How did it feel to gut her like a fish because your *master* demanded it? Revenge wasn't enough—you had to carve up the one person you loved. That's fucking sick."

The room fell into a charged silence, the thick tension suffocating. George's words hung in the air like a challenge directed at the Kanaima and the man beneath the monster.

Jack's body twitched, his claws flexing slightly against Michael's throat. For the briefest moment, his expression faltered, a flicker of humanity piercing through the darkness. It wasn't much, but it was enough for George to know his words had landed.

Melanie's laughter cut through the moment, brittle and sharp. "Oh, Georgie, that's cute," she sneers. "Trying to appeal to a conscience that no longer exists? Let me save you some time. Jack's mine. And he does what I want when I want. Isn't that right, Jack?"

But George ignored Melanie's taunts and didn't take his eyes off Jack. He leaned forward, his voice low and sharp. "You didn't just lose her, Jack. You betrayed her. You *let her die*. All because Melanie whispered the right poison in your ear."

The demon stirred, its presence flickering in Jack's eyes like a dying flame. For a moment, it seemed to waver. George could only hope it was enough to buy him a chance.

BLOOD MOON PEAK

34

A twitch. Jack's eyes flickered between their human hue and the sickly green of the Kanaima. His claws extended and retracted, a telltale sign of the internal war raging within him. George's words had hit their mark. Jack's gaze turned toward Melanie, his expression twisting into a grimace. George felt a spark of hope—if he had used everything, he could get to Michael in time.

"Don't think about it," Melanie snaps her tone sharper now, cracking with tension. She held up a remote, her thumb hovering menacingly over a button. "I control every-thing. If I press this, the toxins are released immediately. And you, Georgie," she hisses, "won't control *anything* in a minute—thanks to the blood."

George clenched his jaw, hiding his hands as he felt the shift creeping through him. His gaze met Ellena's across the room. Her tear-streaked face gave away her fear, but she held his eyes, silently urging him forward. She was right. He could feel it, t too.

Locke was watching from his gurney, his expression taut with helplessness. George wanted to move, to act, but the pain hit like a thunderbolt, sending him crumpling to his knees. His breath came in sharp gasps as his body betrayed him, shifting faster than he could control. His hands dug into the sawdust, claws extending beyond his will.

"It's okay, Georgie," Ellena whispers through her tears. "Let it happen."

"I... I can't," George rasped, the words dragging through gritted teeth as his bones cracked and reformed with horrifying intensity.

"It's okay. I know. I *trust* you," she whispers. Locke nodded in silent agreement. *Did he know?* George wondered.

The pain built to a crescendo, threatening to consume him entirely. His lips curled back, and a roar tore from his throat, shaking the warehouse and rattling the gurneys. His fangs grew, and his vision painted red as the wolf surged to the forefront. When his sight finally cleared, Melanie stepped back, beads of sweat glistening on her forehead.

Jack stared down at his trembling claws or what was left of him. The Kanaima's eyes were streaked with black against the green, a sign of conflict. For the first time, George saw fear in Melanie's face. Her pupils darted toward the exits as her throat vibrated with suppressed panic.

"Don't be stupid, Georgie," Melanie says, her voice quivering despite her attempt to sound commanding.

Jack's claws flickered again, his human side barely clinging to control. Now was the moment. George pushed through the lingering haze of the shift, his body a surging mass of raw power. The lights cut out, plunging the room into darkness.

George moved.

In a blur, he yanked the drips from Ellena and Locke, their fragile bodies slumping but still breathing. The platform loomed before him, and with one final leap, he crashed into Jack and Michael, separating them with sheer force.

The lights snapped back on, revealing the chaos left in his wake. Jack—Kanaima—staggered, claws embedded in its abdomen. The toxin flowed into the demon's body, and George only hoped the old lore was true.

He rose from the dust, panting, but his victory was short-lived. His gaze snapped to Melanie, who now stood over Michael's body. Blood poured from Michael's throat, pooling in the sawdust as his body writhed weakly.

"Aww," Melanie cooed, tilting her head mockingly. "You killed the thirty-second man. Tut-tut. Another lesson I learned from the books— is always to have a Plan B."

She held the remote high, her finger hovering over the button. "Don't do it, Melanie," George growls, his voice low and guttural, the wolf still surging beneath his words. "The game's over."

"Not yet, it isn't," Melanie smirked, her thumb pressing down. "While you decide who to save, I'll take that key and go."

A blast of wind surged through the warehouse. The Kanaima staggered but remained stricken by its toxin. Melanie's smirk faltered momentarily, and George tensed, ready to act.

Then, four words echoed through the room, bringing an unexpected flicker of hope.

"Hey-up, Georgie, lad."

George turned toward the booming voice, his jaw-dropping in stunned disbelief.

Standing in the doorway were his old Skipper and Beta, Andy Morris, his grin wide and confident

"What the hell? How?" George asks, his voice shaky but filled with relief.

Andy beamed, stepping forward as if he hadn't a care in the world. "I heard you call, so I came. Now save them."

George's gaze fell on Michael, his skin pale as death, lying limp in a growing pool of blood. The tables behind him loomed like grim sentinels; and the rigged toxin drips swaying slightly as if mocking George's helplessness. Without hesitation, he ripped the needles free and slammed the tables flat, tearing through the straps that bound Ellena and Locke.

Returning to Michael's side, George froze. He was dying, slipping away with every second, and there wasn't enough time to get him to a hospital.

"What can I do?" George whispers, his voice breaking as he knelt beside his friend. His hands trembled, hovering uselessly over Michael's bleeding body. "Skip, please... tell me how," he pleads, his voice cracking under the weight of failure. They had stopped Melanie, but the cost had been too great. Michael was slipping away, and George was drowning in his helplessness.

"Bite him, lad," Skip says firmly, gripping Melanie's struggling form tighter. "There's no other way."

George looked up sharply, his eyes blazing with conflict. His gaze locked on Melanie's face, her smugness replaced with something almost fearful. His rage swirled, begging him to let Skip do whatever he wanted to her.

"I can't," George choked, the words clawing tut. "What will everyone see of me?"

"They'll see a man who saved his friend," Skip says, his tone resolute.

"It's okay, Georgie," Ellena whispers, her voice like a balm against his fraying nerves.

George turned to her, finding reassurance in her tear-streaked face. And then Locke—silent, unreadable—spoke, his voice steady despite everything.

"Do it, George. Save him. We don't have long."

The command shocked George, but there was no time to argue. His hands gripped Michael's arm, slick with blood, as the slowing beat of his heart thudded weakly in George's ears.

Fuck it.

He leaned down, sinking his fangs into Michael's flesh. The skin gave way, his teeth piercing deep, nicking a vein. Blood spurted in a warm spray, splattering George's face as he held on, his instincts surging uncontrollably. The taste sent a shudder through him, primal and all-consuming.

His eyes blazed red, brighter than they had ever been. Bloodlust surged through him, alive and ravenous, flooding him with raw power. The urge to rip Michael's arm apart, to feast, consumed him.

"That's enough, Georgie!" Skip barks, but the words barely reach him.

George's jaw tightened, his grip growing harder as Michael squirmed beneath him.

A soft breeze grazed his skin, and then Ellena was beside him. Her hand rested gently on his neck, her scent intoxicating and grounding all at once. She leaned close, her lips brushing his ear.

"That's enough, Georgie," she murmurs, her voice lilting, soothing. "Let go now. I'm here for you."

The words echoed in his mind, charming and irresistible. His jaw loosened, the blood-lust dimming as he drew back. His chest heaved as he staggered backwards, shame crashing over him like a wave.

"I'm here for you," Ellena whispers again, her eyes holding his with quiet strength. George tried to hide his face, but she wouldn't let him. Her hands gripped his claws, firm and reassuring.

"You don't need to hide anymore," she whispers, her words a lifeline.

A groan pulled George's attention to Michael. Colour was returning to his skin, his wounds knitting themselves together. George stared, relief flooding his chest as Michael stirred.

"What the hell happened?" Michael croaked, his voice hoarse but alive.

"You were all but dead," Skip says, his voice booming with authority. "Now stop lying around and come arrest this bitch, will you?"

Michael blinked, confused but gathering himself. "What? Really?"

"Yeah," Locke says, his voice heavy as he pulls himself up. "Georgie saved you. He saved us all."

Michael sat up slowly, wincing. "So, you bit me, huh? Does that mean I have to be flea and wormed every month now?" he mutters, his smirk faint but present.

George managed a weak laugh, but the fun was short-lived. Midnight was fast approaching, and the air was thick with tension. The Kanaima stirred again, dragging out its claws.

The smell of death lingered heavily, suffocating. The Kanaima moved, readying itself, and George prepared to spring. But before he could, a surge of electricity rippled through the lights, casting the warehouse in flickering shadows. Black smoke billowed in, carrying an unnatural chill.

Panic gripped the room as the smoke swirled, and from its depths, two figures emerged. The death demons had returned.

"Don't fear," one of them says, his voice calm and eerily human. He stepped forward, dressed simply in khaki trousers, his expression unreadable. "We mean no harm."

"What do you want?" George asks, his voice was heavy with exhaustion and suspicion.

"To take the Kanaima back to where it belongs," one demon replies calmly.

George's gaze sharpened as the demon stepped forward, holding up a relic—the one Melanie had stolen.

"We are its guardians," the demon continued. "We ensure it remains imprisoned. The Kanaima cannot be killed, but it can be trapped within this."

"How?" George demands confusion and caution when lacing his words.

"That's for us to know," the demon says in their tone, leaving no room for debate. "These people disturbed a sacred crypt with their greed, bringing death upon themselves and others. The last time this happened, it cost thousands of lives. Consider yourselves lucky."

George's jaw tightened, but his resolve wavered. "How will you do it?"

"Like this."

Before George could react, the demon in jeans moved with swift precision, driving a dagger into Jack's stomach. Jack's eyes widened, his body stiffening as black smoke poured from him, writhing like a living thing. The smoke spiralled into the gem at the heart of the relic, captured and contained instantly.

The demon slotted the gem into the relic's base with practised efficiency.

The Kanaima was gone.

As the black clouds of the demons' departure filled the room, George could only stare, speechless. His legs buckled, and he dropped backwards, the adrenaline crash hitting like a freight train. The room spun in a haze of exhaustion and pain.

It was over.

Except for him.

The shrill beep of an alarm broke the silence, signalling midnight—*the witching hour.*

George's body convulsed, a searing heat surging through his veins. He collapsed onto all fours, his bones cracking and reshaping with unbearable agony. His blood felt like it was boiling, and a feral hunger clawed its way up from the depths, making everyone around him feel like prey.

"Georgie!" Skip shouts, but his voice is distant, a muffled echo in George's mind.

Before the wolf could fully take over, George felt a sharp sting in his neck. His body became heavy, his movements sluggish. He tried to roar, but the sound came out as a garbled growl.

Ellena's voice broke through the haze, soft but persistent. "Sorry, Georgie," she whispered, clutching the paralytic syringe she'd driven into him.

George collapsed, the world fading into darkness as his body shut down.

When George came to, the Kanaima Demon was no more, and he was still alive. He could finally rest, at least for now. The case was solved—at great cost—but solved either way.

This was their first case as a new team, pushing them to their limits. Betrayed by someone they least expected, for reasons as horrific as they were personal, they emerged battered, bruised, and bloodied. Michael—more than anyone—had paid dearly.

George owed Skip a debt for his last-minute intervention. Without him, the Kanaima might still be free, and Michael would die.

Now came the fallout.

George had beaten the clock, but the future loomed uncertain. Something within him had changed, something that wouldn't be ignored. Michael, too, would have his battles to endure. But George believed they could face anything—together, as a team.

Jack lay in a coma, his body ravaged by the Kanaima's possession. Melanie, though, would be held accountable for as much as the law could throw at her—starting with the murder of Natasha Wainwright, a crime that had been far too personal.

There was still the matter of the canal boat crime scene, its priceless relics waiting for proper caretakers. But those were tasks for another day. For now, the darkness that had claimed their world remained their home—a new reality none would deny.

Ellena, George reflected, had proven herself in ways he hadn't expected. She had trusted him and grounded him when he was on the brink. And perhaps, like all good things, waiting to know her had been worth it truly.

As for Locke, he remained an enigma. He had stood by their side, but there was something about him—a glimmer beneath the surface—that George couldn't shake.

Locke's facade of normalcy didn't quite fit. There was more to him. George was certain of that, though, what remained to be seen.

The case of the Kanaima Demon was officially closed.

For now, they could breathe. But George knew the darkness was far from done with them.

The road ahead was shrouded in shadows, but he welcomed it. Whatever came next, they would face it together.

Printed in Great Britain
by Amazon

61907052R00157